THE DEVEREAUX DISASTER

Praise for *The Devereaux Dilemma*

Lyda Morehouse, Philip K. Dick Award-winning author of *Archangel Protocol* and *Resurrection Code*: "Fans of classic Heinlein-esque science fiction will enjoy *The Devereaux Dilemma* by Steve McEllistrem. *The Devereaux Dilemma* is full of complex plot twists and turns that will keep you on the edge of your seat until the very end. McEllistrem writes gripping, action-packed scenes with eye-popping tech and well-imagined future combat."

Jeffrey Morris, *FutureDude* and author of *Venus: Daedalus One*: "With so many science fiction visions of tomorrow out there, it's hard to come across new stories that are fresh and vital. *The Devereaux Dilemma* captures and delivers a well-conceived world of complex human characters and believable technologies – all set against a backdrop of thrilling political intrigue. Steve McEllistrem has created a searingly vivid portrayal of a very possible future."

Maryann Lesert, author of *Base Ten* (Women Writing Science Project): "*The Devereaux Dilemma* continually hints at questions environmental ethicists have been asking for decades: If we know that life in all forms is connected, if we know that evolution continues and sometimes occurs more rapidly than Darwin predicted, doesn't it make sense that our most advanced future rests in moving away from genetic tampering for simple corporate-military gain and toward, instead, what Aldo Leopold hoped would be our social-ecological evolution?

Steve McEllistrem, like many in his genre, shows us the best and the worst based on current scientific and political trends. Will human evolution and our relationship with Earth proceed with selfish, power-enhancing mutations, or will we let it proceed on a more natural course? Nature, after all, is capable of succeeding our human built environments much like the trees in McEllistrem's abandoned subdivision grow through deserted homes – stretching walls and lifting windows – an image that burns in the mind as a symbol of our species' terrible transparency. Thankfully, the organic, less controlled world lives on. I only hope the Escala don't leave for Mars."

Amazon review by Kirstin: "A thought-provoking page turner! A very well written sci-fi adventure which could be very close to our future reality!"

Amazon review by Steve C: "McEllistrem is a master storyteller. He skillfully navigates the reader through a complex and intriguing plot line to an exciting conclusion. Throughout, the book illustrates the danger of giving up our liberties to a big central government, challenges people of all faiths, but does so in a respectful and intelligent manner. Best of all, the book is a page turner and it sets up the potential for another intriguing book."

Amazon review by Carpe Diem: "This is a great read! McEllistrem does a superb job of creating a disquieting reality that could await our children."

Amazon review by Anthony: "A great read, a number of interesting characters and plot twists. A refreshing story, provoking you to think about Religion and what it really means; Power and how easily it is corrupted; Humans and their desire to short-cut evolution; Technology developed for good turned around to instead enslave."

Praise for *The Devereaux Dilemma*

Lyda Morehouse, Philip K. Dick Award-winning author of *Archangel Protocol* and *Resurrection Code*: "Fans of classic Heinlein-esque science fiction will enjoy *The Devereaux Dilemma* by Steve McEllistrem. *The Devereaux Dilemma* is full of complex plot twists and turns that will keep you on the edge of your seat until the very end. McEllistrem writes gripping, action-packed scenes with eye-popping tech and well-imagined future combat."

Jeffrey Morris, *FutureDude* and author of *Venus: Daedalus One*: "With so many science fiction visions of tomorrow out there, it's hard to come across new stories that are fresh and vital. *The Devereaux Dilemma* captures and delivers a well-conceived world of complex human characters and believable technologies – all set against a backdrop of thrilling political intrigue. Steve McEllistrem has created a searingly vivid portrayal of a very possible future."

Maryann Lesert, author of *Base Ten* (Women Writing Science Project): "*The Devereaux Dilemma* continually hints at questions environmental ethicists have been asking for decades: If we know that life in all forms is connected, if we know that evolution continues and sometimes occurs more rapidly than Darwin predicted, doesn't it make sense that our most advanced future rests in moving away from genetic tampering for simple corporate-military gain and toward, instead, what Aldo Leopold hoped would be our social-ecological evolution?

Steve McEllistrem, like many in his genre, shows us the best and the worst based on current scientific and political trends. Will human evolution and our relationship with Earth proceed with selfish, power-enhancing mutations, or will we let it proceed on a more natural course? Nature, after all, is capable of succeeding our human built environments much like the trees in McEllistrem's abandoned subdivision grow through deserted homes – stretching walls and lifting windows – an image that burns in the mind as a symbol of our species' terrible transparency.

Thankfully, the organic, less controlled world lives on. I only hope the Escala don't leave for Mars."

Amazon review by Kirstin: "A thought-provoking page turner! A very well written sci-fi adventure which could be very close to our future reality!"

Amazon review by Steve C: "McEllistrem is a master storyteller. He skillfully navigates the reader through a complex and intriguing plot line to an exciting conclusion. Throughout, the book illustrates the danger of giving up our liberties to a big central government, challenges people of all faiths, but does so in a respectful and intelligent manner. Best of all, the book is a page turner and it sets up the potential for another intriguing book."

Amazon review by Carpe Diem: "This is a great read! McEllistrem does a superb job of creating a disquieting reality that could await our children."

Amazon review by Anthony: "A great read, a number of interesting characters and plot twists. A refreshing story, provoking you to think about Religion and what it really means; Power and how easily it is corrupted; Humans and their desire to short-cut evolution; Technology developed for good turned around to instead enslave."

THE DEVEREAUX DISASTER

STEVE MCELLISTREM

**CALUMET
EDITIONS**

Minneapolis, Minnesota

THIRD EDITION DECEMBER 2022

THE DEVEREAUX DISASTER. Copyright © 2014 by Steve McEllistrem, All rights reserved.

Published by Calumet Editions, Minneapolis, Minnesota.

ISBN: 978-1-959770-86-2

10 9 8 7 6 5 4 3

Author website: www.mcellistrem.com.

Acknowledgments

Thanks to Ian Graham Leask for his assistance in transforming an idea into a book. And thank you to Amy Lewis of Renown Marketing Communications for her assistance with publicity. I appreciate John Nugent's courier services. Bob Brin made me look almost handsome with his photographic skills. I'd also like to thank Richard Wieser and the Warren Cody Band, who put out the incredible children's CD, *Children's Moon*. I'm grateful to my brother Mike for suggesting the title. I wish to acknowledge Geoff Saign and Morris Goodwin, who read early drafts of the novel and provided valuable insights. I also received incredible support from friends and family too numerous to mention. Thanks to all of you, especially Mom and Dad and my generous siblings.

Chapter One

The warning tones sounded almost apologetic, as if hesitant to disturb the tranquility inside lunar transit vehicle LTV-7, yet their very existence grated on Jeremiah Jones' nerves. On the monitor before him, he spotted the cause of the alarm: a small meteoroid shower they had to pass through to reach the south pole of the Moon. He gripped the armrest firmly as he glanced about the cabin, wondering again how his fellow passengers could remain so calm when the ship might explode at any moment.

Beside him, Jack Marschenko, the big Elite Ops trooper who had once been his enemy, chuckled. "Man, you are somethin' else."

"What?" Jeremiah asked.

"It's like you've never flown before. You're green. And not pretty green either. You're kind of a frog green. All that animal DNA inside you—you might move like a cat but you definitely got some frog in the mix too. I bet you're wishing you were more like me right about now."

Jeremiah smiled. "A machine? Full of rusty nuts and bolts? I don't think so, Frank. You're the one who's jealous."

"Stop calling me Frank, froggycat, or I'll sing Sinatra songs until we reach the Moon." He cleared his throat and began to sing: "Fly me to the Moon—"

Jeremiah laughed. "No. Please. I apologize."

"Why don't you get some sleep? I can't believe you haven't closed your eyes the whole flight."

"How can I sleep with all those warnings going off?"

"This one's no different than the last seventeen. If it ain't meteoroid showers, it's space debris or some malfunctioning sensor. Just relax. We're not gonna die yet. Look behind you," Marschenko pointed across the aisle, one row back, where a young couple and their two

1

STEVE McELLISTREM

daughters—Kyler and Kaylee, Jeremiah remembered from overheard conversations—exited their seats and made their way to the observation window. "They're not scared."

"They don't know how much danger they're in."

"Could be worse. Could be on Earth. I still can't believe someone blew up the Jefferson Memorial. Who do you think it was?"

"It doesn't matter."

Marschenko lowered his voice: "What do your contacts in CINTEP say?"

"I'm out of that," Jeremiah replied. He had once been a ghost for CINTEP—the Center for International Economic Policy: a secret organization founded to perform necessary, often illegal actions in the interests of the United States.

He found it difficult to think about anything other than crashing or having the ship explode. Why was he so afraid of flying? Was it simply having to cede control? He blinked rapidly three times. A trick he'd taught himself. He visualized himself in a stone dungeon, free of all pain, all fear. Centered. Insulated. It was a way of re-creating himself as nothing more than a machine. Cold steel. He sat on the metal cot and looked down at the brick floor, faintly illuminated by a torch on the wall. He knew every inch of his mentally constructed dungeon.

"Think about your son," Marschenko said, noticing his distress. "That's what you gotta focus on."

"I'm okay now."

"Good. Check out the monitor." Marschenko described the scene as Jeremiah glanced over: "Lunar Base 1 is coming into view. A large hangar with a plas-glass ceiling. You can't see the caverns and tunnels that branch out from the main hangar, but you can see the greenhouses. And there's Malapert Mountain, near the Shackleton Crater, with its mass of solar panels that provide most of the Moon's power. Did you know that the southern polar region is in almost perpetual daytime, except for the bottoms of some of the craters, which are in perpetual darkness?"

"You a lunar expert now?" Jeremiah said.

2

"Been studyin' a bit," Marschenko said. "Mostly, the Moon's what you'd expect—a lot of dark rock and dust. Oh, and there's Lunar Base 2. Smaller. But you can see the Mars transport ship standing next to it. That'll be where the pseudos are."

Psuedos. Marschenko pronounced the word like an obscenity.

"Escala," Jeremiah corrected, putting the emphasis on the second syllable like the Escala did, as if by using their proper name he might quell the surge of anger pulsing through him. "They call themselves Escala. And I'm one too."

"Yeah," Marschenko acknowledged. "I know. The next generation Escala. New and improved, now with frog DNA." Marschenko smirked. "You ever eat a fly?"

Jeremiah laughed.

"You don't look much like them," Marschenko said, "the ones headed for Mars."

"When Eli modified my DNA—"

"Without your knowledge or consent," Marschenko interrupted with a grin.

"Without my knowledge or consent," Jeremiah agreed, "he intended for me to function on Earth, not in an alien environment."

"Well, they look like apes," Marschenko said, "huge and hairy. And weren't they engineered to require radiation?"

Jeremiah nodded. Part of him wanted to punch Marschenko; part of him wanted to cry. He was sitting here next to practically his only friend—the man who helped him discover that Joshua was being held on the Moon. That had taken six months. Jeremiah took another five obtaining the necessary travel permits, while Marschenko applied for an opening in security on the Moon, knowing they wanted Elite Ops troopers there. He delayed his assignment so they could travel together.

Jeremiah shifted in his seat. Something jabbed his thigh. Reaching down, he pulled out the miniature statue he'd pocketed before leaving Earth and held it up to the light.

"Is that a copy of Emerging Man?" Marschenko said.

"Cool, huh?"

3

"Hard to believe so much fuss has been made about one statue," Marschenko said. "Can I see it?" He held out his hand and Jeremiah gave him the statue. It was only six inches long—a replica of a famous statue on Earth. It depicted a man emerging from the ground, his lower body almost unrecognizable as human, his upper body increasingly detailed the farther he pulled himself free of the rock beneath him. The strain of effort showed in his muscles, while his face bespoke a kind of torment. This copy was made from the shards of two different kinds of stone, fused together—jagged pieces somehow forming a whole that seemed appropriate—one type of rock black and gray; the other blue, teal and ivory. The statue, polished to a high sheen, practically glowed.

"So this represents the evolution of humans into pseudos . . . sorry, Escala?" Marschenko asked.

"That's how some see it," Jeremiah said.

Marschenko handed it back. "Reminds me of those Venus figurines we studied in school. Prehistoric statuettes."

"It's a dolly," Kaylee said. The little girl had wandered up from the observation window and stood in the aisle beside their seats, reaching for the statue.

"Kaylee," her mother called. "Come back here."

Kaylee pulled her hand back and waved goodbye before scampering back toward the observation window. Jeremiah put the statue back in his pocket.

"Get some sleep," Marschenko said.

"Wasted effort," Jeremiah said as he took a sip of nutri-water. He tasted a hint of raspberry and ginger. At that moment, the warning tones ceased their intrusion, replaced by soft string music and the quiet susurrations of water lapping against the shore.

"There," Marschenko said. "Crisis averted." He jerked his thumb back toward the observation area. "Well, if you're not gonna sleep, you gotta look out the window at least once before we land. Conquer your fear and all that. Won't get another chance if they kill us up there. And if you don't do it, I'm gonna tell everyone you're a pansy. Maybe I'll sing a song about it." Softly he sang, "And now, the end is near, my

4

friend, you're just, a great big pansy . . ."

"Okay, Frank. I surrender." Jeremiah made sure his dungeon was tightly sealed, took a deep breath, got to his feet and looked down the length of the ship, where most of the passengers sat quietly, engrossing themselves with the monitors, watching the looming Moon. Jeremiah's mock-gravity flight suit kept his body at an approximation of 1G by using electromagnetic sensors drawn to the flight deck, so standing and walking were little different than on Earth. Yet his knees felt weak after two days in the ship. Or was it because of his trepidation at being in space?

He made his way down the aisle to the observation window, where the young couple stood with their daughters Kyler and Kaylee, looking back at Earth. They'd pulled their hoods off, making their heads weightless. The father was tall and slim, with dark hair and eyes. The mother was blond, with blue eyes. She smelled of honeysuckle. Both wore interfaces on their right temples. Kyler—maybe nine or ten, about the same age as Joshua—looked up at Jeremiah. She had her mother's hair, her father's eyes. Kaylee—no more than five— buried her face in her mother's pants, leaving only her dark curly hair visible. As the parents spotted Jeremiah, they moved aside to allow him access.

"Do we have to sit down now?" Kyler said.

"Our turn is over," her father said.

"That's okay," Jeremiah said, avoiding looking out the window. "There's plenty of room."

"Why are you going to the Moon?" Kyler asked.

"To see my son." Jeremiah felt his dungeon collapsing. He blinked again and without knowing why reached out to touch the older daughter's head. Before his hand reached her, he yanked it back. "His name's Joshua. He's about your age."

"You look sad," Kyler said. "Are you going to cry?"

"Kyler!" the mother said. "Why would you say that?"

"It's all right," Jeremiah said. He went to one knee, putting his face level with Kyler's. "I am sad. I miss him. I haven't seen him for a long time."

The father put his hand on Kyler's shoulder and said, "Is he with his mother?"

Jeremiah stood slowly, shaking his head. "He's had some medical issues. I'm taking him home."

"I'm sorry to hear that," the mother said.

The father said, "What kind of medical facility on the Moon is treating him?"

"Brian," the mother said.

"Sorry," Brian replied. He grabbed Kyler's hand. "None of my business. Enjoy the view. Come along, Kyler."

"But he said we could stay."

Kyler's mother pointed a finger at her. "Now don't make a scene."

Kyler whined as her parents dragged her away from the window. Her parents shushed her as they hustled the girls back to their seats.

Jeremiah forced himself to look out the window at Earth—a huge marble of blue, with swirls of white against a star-studded black backdrop. Jeremiah expected his stomach to protest, but the planet looked so far away that it bordered on the unreal. Perhaps this flying thing wasn't so bad after all. He marveled at how beautifully peaceful Earth appeared from here—its human population invisible, its wars too small to detect. His stomach fluttered and he felt the old panic returning. Breath quickening, throat dry, he used a hand to brace himself against the side of the cabin. He closed his eyes and heard a quiet shuffling. When he opened them, he caught an image of Marschenko behind him in the window.

"You want a puke bag?" Marschenko said as he held up an airsickness bag.

Jeremiah shook his head.

Marschenko tilted his head and looked back to where Kyler was still protesting to her parents. "You sure know how to make the girls happy. First Lendra, now her."

Jeremiah studied Marschenko's reflection in the window. The Elite Ops trooper stood several inches taller than Jeremiah, maybe thirty pounds heavier. Because of his green flight suit, only his face and hands reflected back clearly. An aquiline nose and brown eyes made him look predatory, though he wore a broad grin at the moment.

Jeremiah shook his head. "Like your relationships are better." He immediately regretted saying it, knowing Marschenko would be reminded of Lily.

Marschenko's face fell.

"I'm sorry."

"It's okay, froggycat. Besides," Marschenko smiled and raised his eyebrows a few times in rapid succession as his expression changed to a leer, "I got no problems in the bedroom."

"I don't want to hear about it," Jeremiah said.

"When you're as big as I am—"

"I really don't want to hear about it."

"At any rate, a professional relationship is best. You wouldn't believe what some of these girls will do. They charge a lot but they're worth every dime." He pulled at Jeremiah's flight suit. "Plus they don't have static cling."

Jeremiah laughed as he yanked his arm away. He pretended to look out the window. "I certainly misjudged Lendra—had no idea she was so driven, so hard."

"Well, you're free of her now. She can't get her hooks in you on the Moon."

"First useful thing you've said all day."

Marschenko grinned. He tapped Jeremiah's shoulder a couple of times. "You're a good guy, Jones. You're a helluva guy."

"Don't start. You know I don't like that."

"That's why I gotta say it. What you did to me—for me—letting me get all that crap out of my system, letting me regain my humanity. You could've killed me. Maybe you should've. I owe you everything. And I hope I get the chance to make up for what I did. Whatever it takes, I'm gonna make it right."

Jeremiah smiled. "I'm glad you're with me, Jack."

Five years ago, Jeremiah's four-year-old son had been abducted as part of a program to create super fighters. Marschenko had been the instrument Carlton and Elias Leach—Jeremiah's old boss at CINTEP—used to snatch him. He'd been so programmed and conditioned that he hadn't understood his actions were wrong. But in the last year, Marschenko had redeemed himself by helping Jeremiah learn as much as he could about the program, which collected children with favorable DNA and performed genetic surgery on them, inserting "animal" DNA and nanotechnology into their bodies, thereby creating child soldiers who would someday be almost indestructible.

They'd taken Joshua because of Jeremiah, because his genetic makeup was favorable to the kind of chimeric surgery that created what many people called a pseudo—part man, part animal.

Jeremiah's DNA had been altered, and though he still looked and felt like a man, his strength, speed, endurance and healing ability were all enhanced. And Marschenko was an EO trooper—part man, part machine: nano-analyzers and regenerators, miniature hormone delivery systems dispersed throughout his blood supply—who could, when wired into his Las-rifle or particle beam cannon through his helmet, fire as quickly as he could think to do it—faster and more accurately than a normal human.

Now the machine and the animal were trying to save the son, who had become both.

"I forgave you, Jack," Jeremiah said.

"I know." Marschenko laid a hand on Jeremiah's shoulder. "I know. But I had to say it again."

"How do you feel?"

"Nervous," Marschenko said. "I don't trust myself anymore. I wonder what they're gonna do to my mind, whether they'll alter it without my knowledge like they did before. Maybe they'll program me to betray you."

"We talked about that *ad nauseum*. We have to go ahead with the plan, assume that we can make it work. I trust you whether you like it or not."

Marschenko pointed to the Moon, which looked only a few miles away. Jeremiah gazed at the lunar surface, the desert-like vastness of rock into which the hangar of Lunar Base 1 had been constructed, its plas-glass roof showing people moving about beneath it.

"You still planning to see Devereaux?" Marschenko asked.

"You think I shouldn't?"

Marschenko shrugged. "I don't know how much he can help. He's got a lot of enemies."

"True. But he's the smartest man I ever met. If anybody can help me get Joshie back, he can."

"Joshie?"

Jeremiah sighed. "That's what Catherine used to call him. He may not remember the name Joshua. I'm hoping he'll remember his nickname."

"You know what you're gonna say to him?"

Jeremiah shook his head. "That's all I've been thinking about for the past two days. I still have no idea."

Marschenko nodded. "Maybe open with, 'Ribbit.'" He laughed. "Almost made you smile there. Hey, why do you think the pseudos— sorry, the Escala—are still at Lunar Base 2? They were supposed to have headed for Mars weeks ago."

"I don't know," Jeremiah said. "Something weird is going on. I'm not sure what. But I can feel it in my gut. It's tied to why we've had to wait so long to get up here. And it's probably tied to Devereaux. I'm not sure if Eli has something to do with it or not. All I know is it's going to be bad."

"Trying to cheer me up?" Marschenko said.

Jeremiah nodded. "If we're lucky, there'll be a nice big battle."

They stared out the window, lost in their thoughts. Then Marschenko said, "Know what I'm worried about? The Escala. I know I've got no reason to, but . . ." he looked around, lowered his voice. "Hell, you're one too. Lately I even feel it around you. A kind of tension—like there's something wrong with you because you've got animal DNA in your body. Like you're evil." Marschenko shook his head. "I don't know how to overcome it. You feel anything like that for me? For the Elite Ops?"

"No," Jeremiah said. "I have this rage growing inside. But it's not directed at you. It's more an urge to lash out at everyone."

Marschenko smirked. "That's just your natural personality."

Jeremiah smiled. They were both edgy. He said, "You'll be fine, Frank. When it all goes down, I'll be able to count on you. I know it."

"You've got a lot of faith, froggycat," Marschenko said.

A quiet chime sounded and a pleasant female voice said over the loudspeaker: "Return to your seats. Prepare for landing. Arrival in thirty minutes."

"It's going to be tough," Marschenko said. "Once I'm back in uniform, I'll be under constant surveillance. You will too. I don't know when or if we'll get a chance to chat like this again. Too bad you can't wear an interface."

"I tried," Jeremiah replied. "The migraines became incapacitating."

They made their way back to their seats. Marschenko sat quietly, staring at the floor. Jeremiah knew he was psyching himself up for the mission. He had the harder role to play. Jeremiah just had to be himself: a father searching for his missing son.

With the help of Marschenko and Lendra, not to mention the classified databases he still had access to from his days at CINTEP, Jeremiah had studied everything he could find about Lunar Base 3— the top-secret facility where his son was being held, where Josh was being trained as some kind of ultimate fighter—memorizing its layout, getting a feel for its strengths and weaknesses. But the amount of information available was limited.

The LTV's retro rockets activated, causing a sensation like being caught by a bungee cord after a long drop. Several passengers screamed in delight. The touchdown at Lunar Base 1 came with only a slight bump. As the LTV taxied to the hangar, the intercom warned them of the potential for injury due to the lower gravitational pull of the Moon. After the LTV's hatch sealed against the hangar and the "all clear" sounded, Marschenko, nodding reassuringly, gestured for Jeremiah to go first.

Jeremiah followed a pair of research scientists in the row ahead of him off the ship. He grabbed the railing on the wheeled staircase and descended toward the surface of the Moon.

The hangar, about the size of a football field and thirty feet tall, constructed almost entirely of graphene-aluminum, smelled of chlorophyll: clean, unpolluted air. Genetically modified ivy climbed the walls all the way to the plas-glass ceiling, beyond which Earth shone brightly. Hundreds of other plants grew, scattered throughout the hangar, pumping out oxygen—mostly shrubs and bushes, with a few dwarf fruit trees and vegetable gardens. Amongst the greenery, walking paths wound, while off to his right he saw a red Marriott sign and a café decorating the space in front of the hotel. A handful of people sat at tables sipping coffee or tea and watching the new arrivals with interest. The sheer normalcy of the scene made Jeremiah want to cry. Just fatigue, he decided, and the realization that he was close to Joshua now.

"Steady, froggycat," he heard Marschenko whisper.

Only when he reached the bottom and stepped off the staircase, did Jeremiah notice the lower gravity. The staircase had acted on his mock-gravity flight suit, so he'd still felt 1G of force until he was clear of it. Now he felt practically weightless, like he could almost fly if he put his mind to it. With each step, he bounced, nearly propelling himself into the air. He noted the other passengers struggling with their decreased weight too, practically bounding into the air. The girl, Kyler, showed no such restraint. She leapt high off the ground, bouncing along, yelling, "Whee!" while her parents blushed. Kaylee held firmly to her mother's hand as they collected their luggage. She caught a glimpse of Jeremiah staring at her and this time she didn't turn away.

When Jeremiah waved, she waved back. Her mother noticed the movement and smiled at Jeremiah as she hoisted Kaylee onto her hip. After the family headed for the hotel, he grabbed his bag. Beside him, as Marschenko reached for his duffel, the big EO whispered, "You, sir, are my enemy." Then he winked at Jeremiah before turning away.

Jeremiah counted a dozen soldiers roaming the hangar, alert, serious. They stared at him. Did they all know of Lunar Base 3's existence? Were they tasked with stopping him from retrieving his son? The mere sight of them brought a longing for battle. Clenching his fists several times, he took a deep breath and held it, waiting for the rage to subside.

Two large unarmored Elite Ops troopers stepped forward as Marschenko strode toward them. They stared at Jeremiah before one grabbed Marschenko's bag. The other clapped Marschenko on the back and steered him toward the military section. Marschenko, stopping for a moment, glanced up through the hangar's plas-glass ceiling at Earth, as if admiring the view, then lowered his head and glared at Jeremiah. He took a step in Jeremiah's direction before one of the EOs said, "Let it go, Jack."

"Had to fly all the way up here with that bastard," Marschenko muttered as they walked away. "In the next seat. If he'd a slept at all, I'd a squeezed his neck until his head popped off."

Jeremiah turned toward the open tunnelway housing the monorails that led to Lunar Base 2, the scientific area where the Escala were housed. Two highly polished rails disappeared around a corner. Two personal transportation cars sat on the left rail. Jeremiah checked the time on his PlusPhone, though he had no reason to do so. His appointment with Admiral Cho wasn't until the day after tomorrow.

He walked to the Marriott's check-in desk and waited behind the young couple chatting with the clerk. Again he felt conflicting emotions, wanting either to punch someone or cry. He suddenly flashed on Josh's last birthday, two months ago. Jeremiah had deliberately stayed away from home, performing a security check for a company in Virginia. His frustration at being delayed in coming to the Moon had made him want to just get through the day without having to think about Josh's birthday. He'd even gone out for a few drinks with Marschenko, returning to his apartment well after midnight.

Lendra had fallen asleep waiting for him, lying stretched across the bed in her sexiest lingerie, a lacy red number that never failed to excite Jeremiah. She'd been trying for weeks to entice Jeremiah into having a child. Probably she figured to take advantage of his loneliness on Joshua's birthday. Instead, something about the position of her body reminded Jeremiah of Catherine on the night she gave up hoping for Joshua's return and succumbed to eternal slumber, seeking a reunion with her son in death.

Rather than wake Lendra, Jeremiah had slept fitfully on the sofa, slipping out of the apartment early. He'd let Lendra sulk quietly for a few days afterwards and then reminded her that he intended never to father another child.

When the family finished checking in, Jeremiah stepped forward and got his room assignment. The clerk, after a perfunctory explanation of the hotel's features that Jeremiah barely absorbed, directed him down a carved tunnel to his left.

He reached his door, a heavy metal slab that sealed against a silicone gasket, used his palm print to unlock it and let himself inside.

Queen size bed, chair, bureau, small closet and bathroom with shower, sink and toilet: the space looked much like a hotel room on Earth. But on the wall opposite the foot of the bed, a huge screen displayed an image of Earth against a black background punctured by millions of stars, more than could ever be seen through the atmosphere of Earth—probably a live feed from a camera installed on the hangar ceiling. Fighting nausea, Jeremiah found the remote and deactivated the screen, then doffed his flight suit and stepped into the shower.

It sprayed a mist of conditioned water that served to wash and rinse at the same time, turning off automatically after two minutes so a blast of warm air could dry him thoroughly.

As he changed into a T-shirt and shorts, he thought about how Marschenko had assisted him, kept him from going stir crazy on the ship, and how he had known about the Venus figurines. He continually surprised Jeremiah: a man of complexity and greater intelligence than Jeremiah had first given him credit for. Would he, as he feared, betray Jeremiah when they pumped him full of chemicals and hormones again? Jeremiah doubted it. Apart from Devereaux, Ned Jefferson and a couple other CINTEP ghosts he used to work with, Marschenko was the only man Jeremiah trusted.

Despite the fact that it was still early evening Lunar time, Jeremiah fell onto the bed and finally slept.

Chapter Two

Jeremiah awoke to a stunning sunrise of red, orange and pink: a golden orb off to his left slowly rising toward the ceiling—an artificial dawn playing out on his hotel room walls. He vaguely recalled the clerk mentioning it when he checked in. He found the remote and turned the sunrise off, leaving the room bathed in soft light.

A quiet feminine voice informed him that breakfast was being served in the lobby adjacent to the hangar. After almost three days with only nutri-water, he felt ravenous. He dressed in dark slacks and a shirt made of shimmer cloth that changed color with the light, giving it a rainbow hue, and made his way to the lobby, where he ate a tasty soy omelet laced with vegetarian cheese and sausage, lunar hash browns from Moon-grown potatoes, and three blueberry muffins.

Then he made his way to the monorail leading to Lunar Base 2, stepped into a car and took the three-minute journey. When he reached the end of the line, he exited into a smooth tunnel decorated by genetically modified grape vines. Glow globes drifted near the ceiling. A door marked Escala Reception stood ajar. He entered, finding a small room that had a faintly musky aroma. Three Escala teenagers looked up at him from where they sat around a table playing a holographic game Jeremiah didn't recognize.

"I'm looking for Quark," he said.

They stood and moved to surround him, hands clenching into fists. They moved slowly in the lower gravity, gliding across the floor. The smallest one stood just over six feet tall, weighing a little more than two hundred pounds Earth-weight—about Jeremiah's size. All three looked muscular.

"He's busy," the largest boy said, taking a step forward. An aura of menace radiated from him and made Jeremiah's hair stand on end. He tensed, knowing he projected the same aura—a wild animal about to attack.

Jeremiah could tell the teen wasn't a fighter by his stance—just a big strong boy. Of course, he was the son of a scientist, probably intending to become one himself. Likely they all were. Jeremiah didn't want to hurt them.

"Nice reception area," he said.

The boy pointed to the door. "Leave."

Jeremiah backed up a step, his hands spread wide, thinking about how he would have to adjust his fighting technique. On the Moon he weighed only thirty-five pounds. If he jumped in the air, he would fly higher and take much longer to return to the ground. Against these boys, he wouldn't have to worry. But against the guards at Lunar Base 3, he might have a problem. He blinked three times, centered himself in his stone dungeon, and said, "I don't want to hurt you, kid."

A slight rustling sounded behind him. A woman said, "What's going on here?"

Jeremiah turned. A dark-haired woman filled the doorway, hands at her sides, broad shoulders tense. She stood a few inches taller than Jeremiah, and her brown eyes showed a wary hostility. When she stepped forward, she radiated a kind of danger, as if she were protecting her cubs. Jeremiah guessed she was the mother of one of them.

Jeremiah said, "I'm looking for Quark."

"You look familiar," the big woman said. "Who are you?"

"My name is Jeremiah Jones."

"Jeremiah?" she said. The boys gasped.

"Krall, go get Quark," the woman said.

"Yes, Quekri," the largest boy replied. He turned to Jeremiah, bowed and said, "Jeremiah. I remember you." He left through the open door, skirting Quekri with his head down. The other boys sidled to the doorway. Then they too said, "Jeremiah. I remember you."

When they left, Jeremiah looked at Quekri and raised an eyebrow.

She said, "Quark and Devereaux told us what you did. Thank you."

Jeremiah nodded, uncomfortable. "I only did what I had to."

"You saved Devereaux's life, our lives. The Elite Ops would have killed us if you hadn't stopped them."

Jeremiah didn't want her thanks. By his standards, the mission had been a failure. Too many people had died. He changed the subject. "Have you gotten a better idea of when you'll be leaving for Mars?"

Quekri shook her head. "They keep delaying our departure. We should have left two months ago. We've taken the opportunity to make further enhancements to the Pilgrim's engines."

Behind Quekri, Quark appeared in the doorway. Jeremiah smiled, remembering how quietly Quark could move when he wanted to—amazing for a man of his size. He stood half a head taller than Quekri, and was a lot heavier. He dwarfed Jeremiah. Quark still wore his hair long and maintained the same bushy black beard. His nickname on Earth had been Cookie Monster. He caught Jeremiah's eye as he touched Quekri's shoulder and came around her. "Jeremiah. What brings you here?"

Jeremiah looked up at the camera in the corner of the ceiling.

Quark said, "Don't worry about that. It's not transmitting at the moment."

"I'm here for my son. He's at a top-secret facility on Lunar Base 3."

"Lunar Base 3?" Quark said. "Is that the one beyond the military area?"

"You know about it?"

"Only that there's another facility on the Moon about three kilometers from here. From the amount of coded signal traffic, we figured it had to be another facility past the military HQ."

Quekri said, "Why is your son there?"

"His genetic makeup was perfect for the combination of animal DNA and nanotech implants that would turn him into a cross between an Escala and an Elite Ops. They took him when he was four—five years ago."

Quekri nodded. "It was only a matter of time before they created the next generation of fighters. We didn't know they were doing it here on the Moon."

16

Jeremiah said, "He was kidnapped by the Elite Ops."

The beginnings of a smile touched Quark's face. "And you need help getting him back."

Quekri glared at him, her dark eyes flashing with anger. "You'll do nothing—understand?" She pointed her finger at Quark. "I won't have you endangering our mission."

Quark lowered his eyes and nodded.

"That's okay," Jeremiah said. "I've got an appointment with Admiral Cho tomorrow at nine. I hope to see my son then. And Quekri's right. If you were caught helping me, it might endanger the Mars Project."

Quekri said, "Exactly. We can't forsake humanity's future for one boy."

"Actually," Jeremiah said, "I was hoping to talk to Devereaux. I thought perhaps he might be able to help."

Quark shook his head. "I don't know where he is."

"Don't tell me he's in hiding again."

Quekri said, "Haven't you seen his latest transmission?"

Jeremiah shook his head.

"He broadcast a message to the people of Earth, predicting that the Susquehanna Virus will mutate or be adapted by its creator to destroy a huge percentage of the population in the next year or two."

"They said that was a fake, sent by some terrorist group."

"That's the official line of Earth's major governments," Quark said.

"It might also be one of the reasons we're still here," Quekri added.

"No," Quark said. "He sent that message two weeks ago. We should have been gone long before that."

"Well, it didn't help," Quekri said.

Quark sighed. "He's being held by the military. Admiral Cho wants to make sure nothing happens to him while he's here."

Quekri said, "You're welcome to stay with us."

"Thanks. By the way," Jeremiah reached into his pocket and pulled out the small statue, "I brought you something." He held it out to them. "I know how much it means to you."

"Emerging Man!" Quekri reached out hesitantly, as if afraid to touch it. Jeremiah thrust it into her hands.

"We heard they rebuilt it," Quark said.

"They found pieces. What they couldn't fit together they fabricated."

"And this is what it looks like now?"

Jeremiah pointed at the black and gray. "This is actually a piece of granite from the original statue. The blue-green rock is grann-ite—a synthetic substitute used to fill in the missing parts and fuse the whole thing together. It's like a cement."

"Yes," Quekri said, "we know about grann-ite."

"How did you ever get a piece of the original statue?" Quark asked as he caressed the statue Quekri held.

"Eli sent it to me," Jeremiah said. "A peace offering perhaps. I don't know. I haven't spoken to him. But it reminds me of us. Whatever it once was, it's now something more. The shards that make up the whole give it a fractured look. Yet that only reinforces the element of change in the original. The idea of emergence. Growth."

Quark and Quekri looked at him, surprise on their faces. "This must be valuable," Quekri said, "if it contains an actual fragment from the real statue. We can't accept it." She held it out to him.

Jeremiah raised his hands, refusing to take it. "I want you to have it. I understand why the statue means so much to you."

"Then we thank you," Quark said. He took the statue from Quekri and studied it carefully for a moment before handing it back to her. "We'll be sure to put it in a central location where everyone can see it. Let us give you a tour."

Jeremiah followed Quark and Quekri through their labs, where dozens of Escala worked on numerous projects. Most of what he saw was over his head. All he gleaned from the tour was that they were enthusiastically adapting life to survival on a hostile world.

Quekri showed the statue to everyone. They marveled over it, thanking him before moving on to describe their work. He listened politely, but his mind kept returning to Joshua.

Quekri and Quark saved the Pilgrim for the end. The planetary transport stood erect outside LB 2, a huge gray capsule with a tube connecting it to a tunnel below ground so that workers could access it in an oxygenated environment. Jeremiah entered through the hatch and found himself in a corridor that traveled the circumference of the vessel.

"When we're in space," Quekri explained as she pointed at the corridor, "we'll use these corridors—we've got three built—for centripetal force, creating artificial gravity." She gestured ahead and moved through the corridor into a twenty-foot square room at the center of the ship loaded with sophisticated electronic equipment, a series of chairs bolted to the flooring and one large command chair.

"The bridge," she said. "Here we'll use the mock gravity flight suits and bio-magnetic flooring that you used on the LTV."

She walked through a hatchway into a similarly sized room with a couple beds and various medical equipment. An Escala woman in a white coat worked at a computer in the corner. "This is Dr. Wellon," Quekri said. "If it's okay with you, I'd like her to take some tissue and blood samples from you. We might be able to use the data to improve our odds of long-term survival on Mars."

Jeremiah consented and within a minute Dr. Wellon was done. "Thank you," she said. "I'll let you know what I find."

"We've added a lot to the Pilgrim," Quekri explained as she led Jeremiah into another section of the ship, past residential cabins that lined the corridors. "New storage bays, which can hold more material, so we'll be even better equipped to build a permanent colony on Mars."

"Assuming they ever let us go," Quark added. "I don't know what kind of games they're playing, but they're getting on my nerves."

"Nice ship," Jeremiah said, feeling slightly queasy, sensing that the rage was about to return.

Quark must have heard something in Jeremiah's voice, for he said, "You okay?"

Jeremiah shrugged. A slight tremor began in his shoulders and worked its way through his core—tension looking for release. He longed to lash out, commit violence, and dispel the anxiety for a while.

Quekri said, "I imagine you're growing impatient. Five years searching for your son, and now he's so close you can almost feel him."

Jeremiah nodded.

Quark said, "And the rage."

"You feel it too?"

Quekri nodded. "Quark more than the rest of us." She grabbed Jeremiah's arm. "Come with me. Dr. Wellon can explain it better."

"Deep slow breaths," Quark said as they walked. "That helps me."

Dr. Wellon looked up from her computer as they entered the infirmary.

"The rage," Quekri said. "He feels it too."

Dr. Wellon nodded. "When did you first experience it?"

"I think it began around the time of Catherine's suicide," Jeremiah replied.

Dr. Wellon said, "It's part of our genetic pattern—a side effect of the transgenic surgery." She glanced at her computer screen. "I haven't finished my analysis of your samples yet but you have similar genetic variants. High-stress emotional triggers activate them."

"Like the death of Julianna," Quekri said. "Or Sister Ezekiel. Or the kidnapping of your son."

"So it's part of the price we pay for being Escala?"

Dr. Wellon said, "There are different levels. Quark is the only one of us who has to fight it every hour, every day." She turned to Quark. "How did you describe it?"

Quark said, "It's like an unbearable itch. A need to lash out and hit someone."

Jeremiah said, "You don't just control it by deep breathing."

"No. I talk with Quekri a lot. Intellectually challenging conversations help me keep the rational part of my brain in charge. The anger never goes away. But I've learned I can keep it beneath the surface by doubting my violent impulses, subjecting them to the cold light of logic."

"I've been using a kind of self-hypnosis," Jeremiah said. "A stone dungeon I lock myself into whenever I'm preparing for a fight or my emotions are getting out of hand. But it doesn't work very well anymore. The rage is winning. The urge to strike out and inflict pain just keeps growing."

"Like us," Dr. Wellon said, "you are continuing to evolve."

"So it'll get worse?"

"Perhaps. The variants I detected inside you are similar to Quark's. But the only way to know if it will get worse is to conduct another test in several months to determine if the variants are deteriorating."

"Thank you, Wellon," Quekri said. She led the way out of the infirmary.

"Do you have that other feeling inside too?" Quark asked as they walked. "That sense of wrongness? I don't know how else to describe it."

Jeremiah nodded. "A counter-feeling? A sense that giving in to the rage leads to the animal inside?"

Quark smiled. "Yes. Whenever I feel that, I try to nurture it, hang on to my humanity as long as I can. And when the anger builds to a point I can't control anymore, I go off on my own for a while, find a tunnel and attack the rock. I dig for a few hours until I'm calm enough to return."

"Aren't you worried about what we're becoming? We're already so different from other humans. And we're going to continue to change, whether by accident or design. Your great-great-grandchildren may not even recognize you as the same species. We'll send people to other places. Other moons. And we'll adapt those people so they can survive there."

"Because it's necessary," Quekri said.

"But are we still human? When do we cross the line and become something new? When we're living on a methane-based world, breathing what is now a poisonous atmosphere?"

"We're human," Quekri said.

"You asked to be Escala," Jeremiah said. "I didn't. I thought I was simply undergoing enhancements like Julianna. Now I'm something different. My son too—he's no longer the same as when he was born. Is he even still my son?"

"He will always be your son," Quekri said.

Jeremiah shrugged. "I wonder."

"Let's go attack some rock," Quark said. "Get your mind off your problems until supper."

"You'll stay with us tonight," Quekri said.

"Thank you," Jeremiah said.

He walked to the end of the tunnel with Quark, where sledgehammers and chisels lay strewn about. They hammered at the rock until Jeremiah's shoulders were sore and his legs comfortably fatigued. Afterwards, he returned to Lunar Base 1 to retrieve his bag. Again he noticed the large number of soldiers patrolling the hangar. The LTV he had arrived on was being readied for departure. It would take off the day after tomorrow. He hoped to be on that flight. If he missed it, he'd have to wait two weeks for the next one.

He spotted Kyler running along a pathway, leaping high in the air with each step, her parents and younger sister Kaylee following more sedately. Her father Brian caught Jeremiah's eye and shook his head.

Jeremiah grinned.

Kyler noticed him and bounded over. "Hey, mister. Will you play with me? I wanna jump like a bunny."

"Kyler," the mother said, "leave him alone." She turned to Jeremiah. "We keep telling her to stay away from strangers, but she—"

"He's not a stranger, Mother. He was on the plane with us."

Jeremiah knelt in front of Kyler and said, "Your mother's right, you know. You have to be careful around strangers. They could hurt you or take you away from your parents. How would you know if I was a bad man?"

Kyler stared at him for a moment, her brown eyes narrowing as if, by squinting, she could see right to the heart of him. She held his eyes for a moment. "You're not a bad man." Then she saw something over his shoulder and skipped away.

Jeremiah nodded to the parents, waved at Kaylee and proceeded along the path. It took him several minutes to get his emotions under control. He walked around and through the hangar twice, memorizing every doorway, every tunnel. The one leading to the military quarters curved, so he could see down it only a short way. He approached the military desk.

"Can I help you?" the desk sergeant asked in slightly accented English, the official language of the Moon. He was big—as big as Jack

Marschenko—and muscular. Not Escala but strong. Like Marschenko, he had piercing eyes, clear skin. His face had a familiar chiseled look—the look of an Elite Ops trooper. He wore no armor, just military fatigues. His Las-rifle dangled toward the floor, but a simple movement would bring it up into firing position.

Rage built inside Jeremiah. He tried to hand over the pass he'd obtained.

"We know who you are, Jones," the sergeant said without looking at the pass.

"Just checking in," Jeremiah said.

"That's not necessary, *sir*." The sergeant almost choked on the word. "We'll take care of all that tomorrow."

"Fine. Thank you, Sergeant." As Jeremiah turned away, he caught Brian's eye for a second. Brian ducked his head and whispered something to his wife. She glanced at Jeremiah but, when she saw him looking at her, she blushed and turned away. Then she gathered up her daughters and they moved off to their rooms, Kyler protesting at being driven from the hangar.

After checking out of the hotel, Jeremiah wandered, images of Joshua filling his brain: remembrances of happy occasions mingled with painful memories—like Catherine sprawled on the bed, gone. Everywhere he went there was either a camera or a soldier with an eye on him. He barely noticed them. At one point he looked out through the observation window at Earth, always in view, day or night. Despite his mental state, he had to concede it was beautiful.

* * *

The Escala dinner offered vegetarian dishes that were both hot and spicy, and cool and sweet. The room—the cave—had been enlarged to accommodate perhaps a hundred people and was more than half full. Quark and Quekri sat across from Jeremiah.

For a long time there was no conversation, just the sounds of utensils clacking against dishes, chairs scraping the floor. The Escala ate with a singular mindset, their attention focused on their food. And it was delicious. It made Jeremiah's tongue tingle. The air of contentment from the Escala leached into him. Usually, the sight of other people enjoying their lives depressed him, brought out the rage. But he felt better among the Escala.

Quark leaned back in his chair and watched Jeremiah.

"What?" Jeremiah asked.

"Feels good, doesn't it?" Quark said. "Sitting among your own kind where you can be yourself."

"Yes."

As the Escala passed around large bowls of blueberries and cream for dessert, the room began to buzz with the sound of quiet conversations. The lighting changed, from a soft yellow to a mix of colors provided by rainbow bulbs, the colors mingling with each other through the spectrum of visible light. A group of Escala passed around the statue he'd brought, studying it, reminding themselves that it still existed.

The teenagers Jeremiah had encountered earlier moved to a corner of the room, ignoring everyone else, playing another holographic game, while several Escala women surrounded an attractive blond who held a baby. Jeremiah recognized her from his mission to Minnesota. She'd been one of the Escala who had attacked the Tessamae Shelter as part of a diversion to rescue Quark. Her baby had black curly hair and a dark complexion. Knowing the Escala couldn't mate with each other, Jeremiah wondered who the father was.

He found himself drawn to the baby. After a few moments he made his way over to mother and child. Even among the musky odors of the Escala he could smell the baby, or at least imagined he could. The blond woman looked up at him, her face an open question.

"Your daughter?" Jeremiah asked, realizing as he spoke that he'd heard someone identify the child as a girl.

The woman turned the baby to face Jeremiah and said, "Yes."

Jeremiah leaned over, touched the top of the baby's warm head, caressed her soft curly hair, looked into her bright blue eyes, incongruous in that cocoa face, and said, "She's beautiful."

The child smiled at him as if pleased by the compliment. The mother noticed and a smile lit up her face as well. "Thank you," she said. "Her name is Celestia."

Krall spotted him and yelled across the room: "Jeremiah, will you tell us the story of how you rescued Devereaux?"

The room went quiet. Even the baby focused on Jeremiah. He straightened. Quark, who had been there for most of the battle and largely knew what had happened, looked at him expectantly, his hand out in a permissive gesture. Hadn't Quark told them already?

"It wasn't anything to be proud of," Jeremiah said. "It was just a dirty political job. Devereaux had been accused of developing weapons of mass destruction, something I now realize was crazy. But I didn't know Devereaux back then. I didn't realize how thoroughly a man of peace he is. My mission was to keep him out of the hands of Gray Weiss—the President's biggest rival—and return him to Washington, DC."

"All of which you did," Quark said. "But I think the boys want to know about your battle with the Elite Ops."

"You were there. You saw it."

"Only the end," Quark said. "I missed most of it."

Krall said, "How did you defeat them?"

Jeremiah shook his head. "It was at best a draw. There was nothing heroic or noble about any of it—just kill or be killed."

Krall said, "But how did you—"

"I had a particle beam cannon," Jeremiah said as he returned to his seat. "The same thing the EOs carry. They can inflict massive damage. That's why they're banned on the Moon. Too dangerous. One stray shot could blow out the ceiling of the main hangar." Jeremiah spread his hands, took a deep breath. "Anyway, it allowed me to take out their shields. But I didn't win. The fighting only stopped when we got to Carlton."

"Whatever happened to him?" Quekri asked.

Jeremiah shrugged. "I assume they buried him somewhere deep."

Krall said, "You're not much of a storyteller."

"Too many painful memories."

"Where's Bettany?" Krall asked. He turned toward a teenage Escala girl who sat off to the side of the room. "You tell it, Bettany."

Other voices chimed in asking Bettany to tell the story of their escape. Jeremiah got the sense that they'd heard it often.

"The Escala," Bettany began after a glance at Jeremiah, "were in hiding, knowing that the bewitched Elite Ops, corrupted by the evil Carlton, would soon return to obliterate them. Only one man could save them—the great Walt Devereaux. But even he had been unable to help. He had too many enemies. And so the Escala waited to die. It was then that Julianna emerged—" Bettany stopped and glanced again at Jeremiah.

The atmosphere tensed. Every Escala stared at him, their faces changing color from orange to red as the rainbow lights continued their shifting pattern. Did the Escala know about his relationship with Julianna?

Bettany continued: "Once a killer and a spy, she had recently found Devereaux and started on the path of redemption up the Ladder of Enlightenment."

"Julianna," the crowd murmured, "we remember you."

"She offered her assistance to Devereaux," Bettany continued. "She aided the Escala where she could. But the powers in Washington hated the great Devereaux. A bounty was put on his head. Many accused him of seeking to destroy humanity because of his atheism. A few hunted him, including the Elite Ops. Not even Julianna would be able to save him. And once Devereaux was captured, the Escala would die. So Julianna arranged for a man to be sent to Minnesota—her former partner, the only man she ever loved."

Again Bettany stopped and stared at Jeremiah. The other Escala turned his way too. So they knew about his relationship with Julianna. He sensed that they expected some sort of response. He reached for his stomach, fingered the scar through his shirt, and said, "She tried to kill me once."

Bettany smiled before continuing: "She betrayed this man many years before because he had left her for another. And she felt the rage over his rejection. But she never stopped loving him. She promised us that he would help because he was one of us, even though he didn't know it. Yet when he arrived, unaware of his true nature, he attacked the Escala. It was only after Julianna persuaded him of her undying love that he understood who he was and sided with us.

"An entire squad of Elite Ops descended on the Escala, attacking both them and Sister Ezekiel's shelter, killing indiscriminately, slaughtering innocents in their savagery. The Escala were doomed. But Julianna and Jeremiah stepped forward, with no thought for themselves, and defended them. The Elite Ops murdered Julianna, but Jeremiah fought them himself—one man against many—with but a single weapon to their dozens."

Jeremiah shook his head at the obvious exaggerations. He looked at Quark, hoping the big Escala would correct Bettany's version, but Quark, his eyes on Jeremiah, shook his head. Quekri reached up and wiped her eyes with a napkin.

Bettany said, "Bloody and beaten, shot many times, hardly recognizable as human, Jeremiah dove into the frenzy, ignoring the agony in his body as he fought for Devereaux and the Escala. And when the smoke cleared, when the fighting finally came to an end, Jeremiah stood alone, victorious. Devereaux and the Escala were saved."

The Escala turned to Jeremiah, some of them weeping, as if expecting him to confirm their version. Quark nodded at him. But Jeremiah couldn't stomach their adulation. He said, "Julianna and Devereaux were the real heroes. They fought for you. And Julianna died for you. I couldn't save her . . . or Sister Ezekiel . . . or . . ."

His voice trailed off. He couldn't even bear to think of the consequences of his failure. How could these people think well of him?

"We remember them," Quekri said, her voice quavering. "And we honor them as we honor you. No matter how you see yourself, your efforts saved us and we are eternally in your debt."

Once again the room fell quiet. The rainbow bulbs sent wavering colors across faces lost in remembrance of fallen friends. Jeremiah thought of Julianna, his former partner—his love until he met

Catherine. She'd always been a risk taker, a thrill seeker. Jeremiah had loved that about her, but he'd needed to distance himself from the tension and danger of the job, and Julianna couldn't provide that space, that comfort.

"I don't know how much she told you before she died," Quekri said, "but she told us that working as a doctor at the Tessamae Shelter gave her the greatest fulfillment of her life. She embraced Devereaux's ladder of enlightenment and finally found peace. I think she would have wanted you to know that."

"Thank you," Jeremiah said. He felt almost empty, as if he had squandered his love, leaving behind a lonely shell. And yet, knowing that Julianna had died happy, helping him survive, made the hollowness less painful.

The attractive blond got to her feet, her baby asleep in her arms. She turned to Quekri and said, "Well, it's late. Good night."

"Good night, Zeriphi," Quekri said.

Zeriphi caught Jeremiah's eye, and though she stood nearby, she spoke to the room: "I wish we could help you. I remember you." She made her way out the open doorway. The others got to their feet too. They nodded to Jeremiah, said, "I remember you," and shuffled out quietly. When only Quark and Quekri were left, they showed him to an empty room adjacent to the lab, where the sounds of scientists working drifted in. He barely noticed the noise. He dropped to the bed, comforted somehow by the creatures around him, whether they were human or not, whether he was human or not. The rage slept.

Chapter Three

Despite his eighty-three years, during which he'd had plenty of time to get used to people being taller than him, Elias Leach was still sensitive about his five-foot, two-inch frame. He disliked tall women hovering over him. So when his protégé Lendra Riley entered his office, he gestured for her to sit. Looking at her face, he almost wished he could erase his avuncular persona.

Per President Angelica Hope's orders, an Elite Ops trooper entered behind Lendra, the whine of his power pack grating. He wore armor of matte gray that blended into the background, making him almost shadow. Not even his helmet reflected the light. He carried his Lasrifle in his right hand, as if anticipating that Lendra might constitute a threat. Elias struggled not to shiver as he looked at the trooper.

"You can leave," Elias said to him. "Lendra's not a terrorist. She poses no threat."

In fact, Elias feared the Elite Ops far more than Lendra, whose danger to him lay in her sly brilliance. Nearly six feet tall with long dark hair and a smooth cocoa complexion, she had full lips, high cheekbones, and dark eyes. Most men found it difficult to see beyond her beauty to her cold, calculating genius.

The Elite Ops trooper's head pointed at Lendra for a moment before he spun around and departed. Damn things aren't human, Elias thought. Practically machines—full of nanobots and miniaturized computers.

After the door closed he said, "I've got to call Admiral Cho, so I can only spare a moment. How'd the procedure go?"

"Fine." Lendra scowled. "But I think Jeremiah will know this happened in a lab."

"You assured me he was falling for you."

"Lately he's been distant. What was I supposed to do, rape him?"

"You were supposed to be like Catherine. Intelligent but vulnerable. That's his type."

"Maybe his type has changed. He seems to be growing increasingly suspicious. I can't think what I've done to alert him. And I know he's never intercepted any of my communications to you." Lendra reached up and touched the interface at her left temple. She sank further into her chair.

Elias took a deep breath and looked out the window. Off in the distance, the Washington Monument rose out of the darkness, an ancient white obelisk pointing to space, to the Moon. The White House and Capitol shone brightly, and across the Tidal Basin the remains of the recently bombed Jefferson Memorial were just visible. But not even terrorists could change the fact that Washington was still the city of power. And he stood at the top of it. He turned back to Lendra.

"I suppose it's possible. He continues to evolve. Physiologically. Neurologically. The enhancements we gave him are more advanced, more complex than the ones the other Escala have. We still don't know their full potential. Frankly, we didn't anticipate that his evolution would be ongoing. I thought he had reached the final stages last year. But he may have taken another leap forward. What I do know is that he's extremely insightful. He always was. And now he's even more so—an unfortunate development, perhaps. It wouldn't take much for him to spot some inconsistency in your behavior."

Lendra patted her stomach. "You know I'm loyal to you. Why else would I consent to this?"

"I thought you wanted his baby."

"I do. Or at least I did. But he doesn't want another kid. And I feel guilty betraying him. Do you think he'll accept this child as his?"

Elias nodded. "Eventually. His psych profile practically guarantees it."

"Why is he still so important to you? He doesn't work for you anymore. He knows you were behind his son's kidnapping. He may even try to kill you. Why not just let him go?"

"Jeremiah is my insurance policy."

"Against what?"

"I can't go into detail. The less you know, the better. If Jeremiah believes you're still in contact with me, he might decide to force you into revealing what you know. And make no mistake, despite your enhanced brain, he would get the truth from you. Now go home. Wait for further instructions." Elias reached for his PlusPhone. "I have to call Admiral Cho."

Lendra stood and walked away. Elias watched her go. She made him want to call Manyara and slip away for a quickie, though at their age it was never quick, which was part of what made it so fun. Manyara made him feel young and desirable. There wasn't a day that went by that he didn't want her. He didn't have to pretend with her; he could be himself.

He looked out the window at the bombed Jefferson Memorial again. We have too many enemies acting indirectly, mostly through sponsored acts of terror that are often untraceable. It's a shame that the bold, unilateral foreign policy of the early part of the century had resulted in such a backlash. Bringing democracy to the Middle East had been a fine idea horribly executed. Terrorism was the tool of the desperate. And the world had become increasingly desperate since then.

Violence, on the uptick for decades, continued to threaten Earth. A crisis point was fast approaching. Elias had seen it coming years ago. That was why he'd started his program on the Moon. He hoped it would play out the way he'd planned. Much of it was beyond his control now.

He selected Admiral Cho's number and waited for the other man's face to appear on the PlusPhone. He disliked relying so heavily on a member of the military, even someone like Cho, who had been suborned as a CINTEP informant for almost a decade. Elias hesitated to give him too much information.

Cho's rectangular face appeared, with its broad nose, narrow lips, heavy-lidded eyes. "Elias," Cho said in his Texas drawl, "I was wonderin' when you were gonna call. Your boy's here, landed yesterday. He's with the pseudos now. Sleepin'."

Elias said, "What steps have you taken to insure security?"

His voice traveled at the speed of light a quarter-million miles to Admiral Cho, whose voice returned at the same speed. An interminable three seconds. In this day and age there ought to be a way to transmit instantaneously. How were they going to deal with people on Mars when the lag time could be as much as forty-five minutes?

"We've put extra personnel on all vulnerable systems," Cho said. "Access to the ice harvesters has been restricted. Nobody's goin' near those craters unless we want 'em to. Same with the power plant. And the air filtration stations are monitored 24/7, as are the water recycling and purification plants. All those facilities have been secured. Ain't no way Mr. Jones is gettin' near 'em without me knowin' about it."

"Are any of our international partners raising concerns about the added security?" Elias asked.

Another three-second lag.

"You know," Cho said with a laugh, "I used to think we were crazy to foot the entire bill for security up here. Now I can understand why. I have free reign to do as I see fit. I could even make Jones disappear. No one would ever know. No one would ever find him."

"Absolutely not," Elias said. "Look, Admiral. Jeremiah is a valuable commodity, maybe even more valuable than those kids up there. And he's difficult to control. But as long as the boy is alive, I've got a hook in Jeremiah I can use to my advantage. For now, I've got to keep him off balance, worried about his son. I don't want him devoting any time or effort to thinking about what we're doing. So make sure he doesn't get the boy too easily."

Over the three-second lag, as Elias' words reached Cho, the Admiral's face drew into a frown. "You're kinda handicappin' me here, Elias. Seems like I'm liable to lose some men—maybe a lot of good men—if Jones decides to attack us. I'm not sure I'd rather tip him off than have a Pyrrhic victory."

"You know the bigger mission, Admiral. We might have to push up the timetable too, what with India and China at each other's throats. And if Devereaux was right and the Susquehanna Virus mutates to become even more deadly, we'll have to coordinate the attacks of the cadets to occur in a timely fashion with that event."

Elias took a calming breath, waited for a response. He contemplated the Susquehanna Virus. A few of his analysts agreed with Devereaux that it presented by far the largest threat to humanity despite the fact that no government openly considered it a major problem at this point.

"I don't see what Jones has to do with the virus," Cho finally said.

"Jeremiah might be our last defense against it. If it mutates as we've been warned, he might be the only one with immunity. We would then need him for a vaccine. I might also have to use him as the arrow we aim at Susquehanna Sally, whoever that is."

Another interminable pause, even longer, as Admiral Cho thought about his reply.

"Why don't you make a few more pseudos like him? Why's he gotta be the only one? And how come you still don't know who this Susquehanna Sally is? I'm startin' to think maybe you do and you're just keepin' that information to yourself."

Now Elias took his time framing his answer. "We've tried to make more like him, Admiral. We failed. Something to do with the compatibility of his genetic structure. None of the other candidates could tolerate the level of alteration he endured. So until we find another potential candidate, we have to keep him alive.

"As for Susquehanna Sally, we know it's a biogeneticist or possibly a group of biogeneticists. So far, they've been careful to make limited contacts. Eventually she or they will make a mistake and we'll find them."

"I hope so," Cho finally said. "Very well. I'll keep you informed. Cho out."

Elias held the PlusPhone in his hand as he let his thoughts drift back to Jeremiah. He envied the younger man, experiencing life on another planetary body. As a boy, Elias had longed to visit the Moon.

He almost wished he could have given up his position with CINTEP and sought a job there. But they needed engineers and scientists, not administrators.

He looked out the window at the Moon. *We're there irrevocably now. There will never be a time when it is empty of human life again. Not until we're extinct anyway.*

It was even easy for life to survive on the Moon, despite a surface temperature varying between -387F at night and 253F during the day. Each lunar day lasted twenty-nine and a-half Earth days, so there were periods during each lunar day—whole Earth days—when the surface temperature was comfortable. And with millions of tons of lunar ice providing water, oxygen and hydrogen for a fuel source, the Moon could sustain thousands of people.

It might even be where humanity made its last stand. If this Susquehanna Sally had perfected the virus so that it could wipe out the human population, only those on the Moon would be safe—and Jeremiah, probably.

Elias shook his head. He was an Earth-bound creature. He would live and die here. But his son—and in a way he thought of Jeremiah as his son, regardless of how Jeremiah saw him—might even visit Mars someday. He checked the time on his PlusPhone, selected Dr. Taditha Poole's number and waited for her to appear. Her mocha cheeks looked puffy, her green eyes barely visible behind sleepy lids, her nose petite, her lips sensual—another beautiful woman, another woman who made him want Manyara. She'd taken her interface off. When she recognized Elias she said, "Eli. I'm sorry. I was asleep."

"No need to apologize, Doctor," Elias said. "I realize it's late but I wanted to make certain everything is ready for tomorrow."

Another three-second lag. "Dr. Hackett has prepared the boy. The reaction should be perfect—subtle but sufficient. Is there any chance Jeremiah will try to rescue him tomorrow?"

"I don't think so," Elias said. "He'll want to reconnoiter. Besides, he'll believe there's still a chance to resolve the situation diplomatically. He'll only resort to violence when it becomes necessary."

Another lag. "I hope you're right. I'd like some time to study him. How much does he know of what he is?"

"Only that he's a next-generation Escala. He doesn't know that the adaptations continue to mutate. We didn't know it either until recently. His ability to heal himself is incredible. We don't know how far it will go. Maybe it will stop soon. Or maybe his body will keep improving, becoming more and more efficient at fighting off potentially deadly attacks—viral, bacterial, even Las-rifle pulses. Dr. Hassan has speculated that if the mutations continue at their current pace, in a few years he might be able to regenerate a missing limb."

Dr. Poole tapped her fingertips together. "I can see why he's so important to you. And why you need his son. Still, the boy isn't quite the specimen Jeremiah is. We couldn't attempt the full range of alterations Jeremiah received. He's got too much of his mother in him. We had to make do with nano-analyzers and regenerators, artificial hormone and protein delivery systems. Are there no other children?"

Elias shook his head. "Not yet. How is the other project coming along?"

While he waited for Dr. Poole to reply, Elias reflected on the boy, Joshua—his surrogate grandson. Too bad the kid wasn't as complete as Jeremiah. Although with the nano-technology inside him, he was almost Jeremiah's equal—at least for now. If Jeremiah's enhancements mutated even further, the father would outstrip the son. But at least the son would be unhindered by the fetters of morality that bound Jeremiah.

"If you're planning to accelerate the timetable," Dr. Poole said, "I need to know about it as soon as I can. The children are not yet ready for their mission. You know how long it took Jeremiah to fully incorporate the changes. He's still adapting. Some of these kids are too."

Elias said, "I'm not sure when I'll need them. I'm waiting for the next big war. That could come any day. And much depends on the Susquehanna Virus, how it mutates from here, whether we can find whoever's behind it before they cause irreparable damage, whether we can piggyback our efforts onto that threat. Just do your best, Doctor.

Oh, and one other thing. I know you want to study Jeremiah. But I think you should avoid him as much as possible. He's intuitive. Intelligent. The less you interact with him, the better."

After the lag, Dr. Poole said, "This is a once-in-a-lifetime opportunity. And I might be able to discover something Dr. Hassan missed."

"You may run a few scans, Doctor, but keep your interactions with him to a minimum. Contact me after you meet with him tomorrow."

Elias cut the connection. He worried about the effect Jeremiah would have on Dr. Poole. Jeremiah was an attractive man. And Dr. Poole had a bit of a Superman fetish. For her, Jeremiah would be the ultimate conquest. She might even align herself with him, inform him of what he might some day become—a comic-book character sprung to life. Fiction as the author of reality—all of it forced on humanity by the need to save the species, the need to spread out into space. Evolution had to be sped up so that people could survive on distant moons and planets. For one thing was certain. Man would some day destroy his habitat.

The Escala, and particularly Jeremiah, might be the beginnings of a new species. It could be debated whether they were human, but they were necessary. Especially Jeremiah. Elias felt pride at his surrogate son. And—he hated to admit it—jealousy.

Chapter Four

J eremiah awoke instantaneously. His body felt light, unencumbered—
as if he could launch himself into the air, perform a flip and land
on his feet with only the slightest exertion. His muscle memory
believed he was still on Earth. He wasn't yet used to weighing only thirty-
five pounds. If all went well, he'd see Joshua today. He still had no idea
what to say to his son, other than I'm sorry and I love you.

Though he didn't anticipate moving against his son's captors today,
he packed a small bag with his camo-fatigues—a pair of coveralls that
contained millions of tiny sensors. When activated to maximum, they
rendered the clothing invisible. He might get a chance to look around.
He put in two bottles of nutri-water and a few QuikHeal bandages.

Checking his PlusPhone, he saw that Lendra had called again. She
said she loved him and hoped he was well, but there was a slight strain
in both her face and voice that left him wondering what she wasn't
telling him.

Putting that thought out of his mind, he made his way to the mess
hall, where he sat with Quark. Part of his brain registered that the food
was delicious, a spicy bean concoction on green rice, no doubt full of
nutrients. But all he could concentrate on was that he'd be allowed into
the military area at nine o'clock. Quark apparently caught his mood
and remained silent. Conversation throughout the room consisted of
murmurs and whispers, as if the Escala were aware of the tension.

When he finished eating and grabbed his bag, Quark looked up
and said, "Good luck."

Quekri walked over. "I'm sorry we can't do more."

"I understand," Jeremiah said.

As he headed for the doorway, everyone stopped eating and stared
at him—more than fifty people gone quiet. Zeriphi sat with her baby,

37

Celestia, at the next table. She smiled at him. When he reached the door, he surveyed the room for a moment, felt the empathy coming from the Escala, the well wishes. He looked back at them, nodded silent thanks, and walked away.

* * *

He found the military desk manned by three soldiers—two of them obviously EOs even though they weren't wearing their armor. Jeremiah handed over his pass and his bag, then submitted to a physical search. "Camo-fatigues," one of the EOs said as he pulled the camos out of Jeremiah's bag.

"They're legal," Jeremiah said.

"Modified with a scatterer to make them invisible to scanners. We'll keep these here until you leave." The EO checked his camos with the sergeant at the desk and motioned for Jeremiah to step into the body scanner. When he came up clean, the two EOs escorted him down the tunnel. They kept their Las-rifles at their sides and moved casually, though the one on his left crowded him a little. Reaching Admiral Cho's door, they knocked and entered without waiting for an answer.

Admiral Cho sat in a small gray room, at a plain desk, a transparent screen billowed out in front of him. Lining the walls were dozens of screens made of a highly conductive metamaterial. Each displayed a scene from Earth in real-time. The air contained the ionized scent of an atomizer/purifier masking the faint smell of old sweat. Cho touched the transparent screen, which folded itself shut like a napkin. Getting to his feet, Cho extended a hand. He was a tall, portly man in his late fifties, a good dozen years older than Jeremiah, with salt and pepper hair and wire-rimmed glasses. As Jeremiah shook his hand, he decided the glasses were an affectation.

"Jeremiah Jones," Admiral Cho said, "I heard a lot about you. Frankly, from the stories, I expected you to come in here kickin' butt and takin' names. Talbert, here," he nodded toward the EO on Jeremiah's left, "saw you in action last year in Minnesota. I think he was kinda hopin' you'd try to bust your way in."

Jeremiah glanced at Talbert and lifted his hands. "I just came to see my son, Admiral. I don't want any trouble."

Admiral Cho took off his glasses and set them on the desk. He attempted a smile, narrow lips compressing in a tight line, then stopped. His heavy-lidded eyes moved from Jeremiah to the EOs and back. "Good. Even without their armor, these boys are plenty capable. And you don't have your particle beam cannon anymore either."

"He brought camo-fatigues," Talbert said.

Admiral Cho raised his eyebrows. "Planning a little reconnaissance mission?"

Jeremiah shook his head. "It's a demonstrator model, Admiral. Look, I didn't come here to fight."

Admiral Cho turned to Talbert. "You take his camos?"

"Yes, sir."

Admiral Cho swiveled back to Jeremiah. "Just so we understand each other, Mr. Jones. I run a tight ship here. And even though LB3 is a separate entity with its own command structure, I handle all security on the Moon. All access to LB3 comes through this facility. I heard you got a tendency to play by your own rules and we all know what you can do. I respect you. I know you done a lot for our country and I thank you for that service. But I don't trust you to just walk away from your son. And I got orders to keep you from taking him. My men are prepared for most anything you can try. They won't underestimate you again. Please remember that."

"Yes, sir," Jeremiah said as he stared at Cho, noting the small movements in his eyes, the barely visible increase in his pulse rate, the almost imperceptible hesitation when he spoke of keeping Jeremiah away from his son. What was the purpose behind his deception?

"You don't believe me?" Cho asked.

"You're holding something back, Admiral. Insincerity drips off you like sweat."

Cho took a deep breath, as if trying to rein in his temper, but the fractional lifting of his eyelids and the ever so slight pursing of his lips suggested surprise. He stared at Jeremiah for several seconds, then said, "On your way, Mr. Jones."

Leaning forward, Cho placed his right hand on a pad atop his desk. A section of the back wall slid forward and to the side, exposing a platform and a dimly lit tunnel, bringing a cool breeze with a metallic odor into the room. Beyond the platform, Jeremiah saw three personal transit cars standing on the tracks. Cho lifted his left hand, gesturing toward the opening.

"Thank you, Admiral," Jeremiah said. "By the way, how is Devereaux doing?"

"Devereaux?" Admiral Cho said. "He's fine. But until them folks head to Mars I'm keeping him under wraps. These boys'll escort you to Dr. Poole. She'll take it from there."

Jeremiah nodded and stepped through the door onto the platform. The two EOs followed and the door closed behind them. Jeremiah climbed into the lead car. Though the car had three seats and could hold up to nine people, the two EOs crowded in on either side of him in the front seat. Talbert sealed the car—a safety precaution, Jeremiah knew. Each car could provide an extra hour of oxygen in case of a tunnel breach.

The car accelerated away.

As they rode, Talbert and the other EO studied Jeremiah through the mirror-effect of the front window. They didn't speak. He felt the rage building up inside him, a desire to reach up and snap their necks. Without their armor, they were vulnerable. Were they baiting him, hoping he'd attack? Jeremiah exhaled, relaxed his shoulders, arms and hands, finally wiggling his fingers to release the tension.

Where was Joshua right now? On some sort of training exercise? In the mess hall? After a minute, he glanced up at the mirror window, saw the EOs still staring at him, realized again how tense he was. It took more effort to relax this time, as if the growing proximity of LB3 was having a physical effect on him. He closed his eyes, listened to the rush of air past the car, felt the warmth of the EOs' arms and legs against him, and smelled the unpleasant, slightly acrid odor coming off their nano-enhanced bodies.

As the car slowed, Jeremiah felt an almost uncontrollable urge to lash out with his fists, crushing their larynxes. He opened his eyes.

The car stopped at an opening in the tunnel. Talbert stepped out and Jeremiah followed. The two EOs marched him out to a large room carved out of the rock and braced with graphene-aluminum—a training court fifty feet wide and twice as long, about twenty feet high with plants growing along the walls—where sixteen young men and women fought each other in a style that borrowed heavily from the Eastern disciplines. The men wore black; the women, white. They looked much like cadets anywhere: the men stronger; the women more limber. Both flowed through the movements beautifully—smooth and lightning quick. They wore mock-gravity suits, no doubt set at 1.5 or 2Gs, as they danced across the training floor. They all appeared much older than Joshua, in their late teens or early twenties, yet genetic surgery and hormonal therapy could rapidly speed the aging process. And Eli had told Jeremiah that Joshua might be substantially different. One of them might be Joshua. Jeremiah studied them as the EOs herded him along the side of the room.

Farther along, another group of perhaps twenty cadets engaged in what looked like laser tag. They also wore black and white, their uniforms glowing faintly with protective shields, and they carried Las-pistols in each hand, firing at each other as they ducked and weaved through various obstacles. The Las-pistols, set on low, produced blue stun pulses and made only a tiny sizzling sound. One trainee in black looked bigger than the rest, more muscular. He hit every opponent as he flowed over the obstacle course with almost as much grace as the women.

As Jeremiah approached, the cadets stopped to watch him. Jeremiah searched faces as he passed, hoping to see something familiar. The trainees had a similarity of appearance. All were beautiful, almost angelic, as if they'd been chosen for their looks. The big cadet was the first to turn away. He barked out a command and the others resumed their training.

"Creepy," Talbert said as they passed.

In a few moments Jeremiah and his escort entered a corridor that led to a steel door. Talbert knocked, then opened the door and nudged Jeremiah inside. A woman with mocha skin sat behind a desk, her black curly hair cropped short, her green eyes bright, her button nose seeming out of place. Jeremiah guessed her to be in her forties, but who could know these days? Her skin was unlined, her smile almost seductive, and an interface on her left temple reminded him of Lendra. Standing next to the desk was Jack Marschenko, sans armor, but with his Las-rifle at his side. He glared at Jeremiah, already smelling like his fellow EOs.

Marschenko said, "Jones. I couldn't break your neck on the LTV, but I can do it now if you like."

"Jack," the woman said, "be a professional. You kidnapped his son. In fact we abducted a good many children, but only one whose father was capable of tracking us down. I'm impressed." She turned to the EOs flanking Jeremiah. "I don't think you gentlemen need stay. Jack, here, can protect me if necessary, though I hardly think Mr. Jones intends violence."

Talbert said, "He's a tricky one. I've seen him in action."

"Yes, so you've told us," the woman said. "We'll be fine."

Talbert and the other EO departed, closing the door behind them. Jeremiah looked from Marschenko to the woman. He kept his face calm.

The woman said, "I suppose you're expecting to break your son out of here."

Jeremiah said, "I just came to see him."

"Yes, that's what I keep hearing," the woman said. "I'm Dr. Taditha Poole. I run this program. And I'm the one who decides what to do with your son." She leaned forward, lowered her voice. "Frankly, he's become a bit of a problem."

"That's a lie," Jeremiah said almost before he understood why. More than the slight hesitation between words, he caught the change of inflection, the feigned conspiratorial tone, the almost invisible

42

tensing of the shoulders. "But I'll accept it as true. And I'll take him off your hands."

Dr. Poole's nostrils flared as her eyelids rose. Then she smiled. "I almost wish you could." She sounded sincere. Her voice, eyes, breathing: no indication of deception. When she stood and worked her way around the desk, wiggling her hips more than necessary, the scent of jasmine trailed her. "It might be interesting to see what you could do in our program. You're not as advanced as our people—no nano-technology—but impressive nonetheless." She leaned back against her desk, arching her back, her breasts jutting out. "No, you see, your son has suffered a setback."

"If you can't use him, there's no reason for you to keep him."

Dr. Poole crossed her arms over her chest, as if no longer interested in flirting with him. "His mind has . . . He's not just five years older, you know. He's dependent on hormonal treatments and nano-cleansers. And he doesn't know you. This is the only home he remembers."

This time her voice, her demeanor, carried no hint of a lie. A bitter taste filled Jeremiah's mouth. "I'd still like to see him."

"Of course."

Marschenko took a step forward. He glared at Jeremiah and in a stage whisper said, "I wouldn't mind if you tried something."

"Jack, please," Dr. Poole said. "Control yourself. Mr. Jones, I spoke with Elias Leach about you. He indicated that you are a man of your word. If you say you won't try to break your son out of here, I'll trust you." She looked at Jeremiah, her eyebrows arched in a question.

Jeremiah said, "I promise I won't try to rescue him today."

Dr. Poole laughed as she clapped her hands. "Excellent! No promises about tomorrow. I expected nothing less. Are you ready?"

Jeremiah's chest tightened and he realized he still didn't know what he was going to say to Joshua. His mouth went dry. Nevertheless he nodded, and Dr. Poole led him out the door. Marschenko followed.

She grabbed Jeremiah's arm as they walked. The smell of jasmine became more pronounced. After a few seconds she said, "I must warn you, he doesn't look like a little boy any longer. And he's often irrational except for when he plans violence."

Jeremiah caught the slight catch in her voice, detected the sorrow there. "Isn't that what you intended?"

"Not at all. Not everyone reacts the same way to the genetic surgery, the nano-implants and the hormonal treatments. Remember, there were early problems with the Mars Project Escala before they conquered their rage, before you so heroically rescued them."

"Devereaux saved the Escala."

"And you saved Devereaux so he could save them," Dr. Poole said.

They came to a junction in the tunnel and she steered him to the left. His muscles quivered with tension as he strained not to hammer his fist into her smug face. He felt like she should be able to perceive his anger. Yet her touch on his arm was light. Did she know how much hate he carried for her?

"Usually," she continued, "problems surface early on. That's what happened with the Escala. But sometimes months or even years later the body devolves, rejecting the transplants. Your son devolved in this way. We don't know why and we haven't found a solution."

He detected an almost unnoticeable hesitation in her voice, an infinitesimal increase in the pressure she exerted on his arm. "What's the long-term prognosis?"

"It varies with each individual."

"Is it fatal?"

Dr. Poole released his arm but held his gaze for a moment, then dropped her eyes as they came to a door, behind which an animal grunted loudly.

"How . . . long . . . does he have?"

She shrugged. "He answers to the name Damon now." Then she touched a control panel and the plas-glass door became transparent. She stepped aside.

Inside the padded room a young man sat on a cot staring at them. He had long dark hair, the first beginnings of a beard and a horribly scarred face, as if he'd clawed it over and over with his fingernails.

He wore a T-shirt and tight pants. Bare feet. Muscular, though not overly developed like the Elite Ops. For a few seconds he and Jeremiah watched each other. Then he leapt off the cot and charged them with a howl of fury, slamming into the door with such force that Jeremiah cringed. The caged man growled, an animal sound of menace, making Jeremiah's hair stand on end.

For a fleeting moment, Jeremiah wanted the violent young man not to be his son. He immediately felt ashamed of that reaction. Studying the kid's eyes, he noticed something familiar about them and realized that he saw them in the mirror every morning. The young man's haunted hazel eyes looked out through the plas-glass door, beyond the three visitors, probably past the Moon itself. What had once been Joshua was gone. This creature looked nothing like the boy who'd been taken. He was a soldier now—an insane animal warrior.

Jeremiah felt like he'd just been punched in the stomach.

"You see why you can't take Damon home with you. Even if we wanted to release him, he's far too dangerous. And he'd only try to kill you. He has no memory of his family—no love left in him at all. So I'm afraid you came all this way for nothing."

There was truth in that statement: no hesitation, no tremor, no bluster. Jeremiah said, "I can take him to doctors. Somehow we can find a cure. At least calm him down."

"I'm sorry," Dr. Poole said. "I only promised to show him to you. We can never let Damon go."

Jeremiah looked at the tortured young man in the cell—the son they'd taken away. Poor Joshie. Poor Catherine. He said, "Can I show him a picture of his mother?"

"He won't recognize her," Dr. Poole said with a wave of the hand, "but go ahead."

Jeremiah opened his wallet and took out an old-fashioned photo of Catherine. He held it up to the door. The young man snarled and threw himself forward again. Jeremiah stood his ground, kept the picture up. The young man threw himself against the door over and over, ramming his shoulder into the plas-glass. After a minute or so

45

he stopped, began pacing like an animal, then moved toward the door, reached out through the small slot that allowed food trays to be passed inside and snatched the picture from Jeremiah's hand. He bared his teeth as he growled again. He stared at the woman in the picture. Something came into his eyes—recognition, maybe—and his face softened a little. The violent young man—Jeremiah found it hard to think of him as Joshua—backed up to the cot, staring at the photograph. He sat with his legs curled up beneath him, rocking gently, and a quiet hum emanated from him. Jeremiah recognized the tune: an obscure old song Catherine had often sung: *Children's Moon.*

Whatever Jeremiah had to do, whoever he had to kill, he was going to get his son out of here.

Marschenko leaned forward, peered through the door and said, "Well, I'll be damned. Will you look at that? He knows her."

Dr. Poole shook her head. "I wouldn't have believed it possible." A lack of conviction in her voice: had she known Joshua would recognize the picture? She raised her voice: "Damon, who is that woman?"

The young man glanced briefly at Dr. Poole and then returned his attention to the photograph. He brought the picture up to his face and rubbed it on his cheek, all the while humming quietly.

Jeremiah said, "I think there's more of my son left inside that young man than you know."

"One retained memory does not make him salvageable," Dr. Poole replied.

"Salvageable!" Jeremiah turned to face the doctor. "You talk like he's a piece of garbage."

Dr. Poole lifted her hands as Marschenko stepped in front of her, his Las-rifle coming up to point at Jeremiah's chest. "I apologize. I meant no offense, Mr. Jones. But what you must understand is that Damon is nothing more than a killing machine. He can't be reasoned with."

Again that bitter truth echoed in her voice. And yet . . . Jeremiah said, "You also thought he wouldn't react to a picture of his mother."

"True," Dr. Poole conceded. "And I don't claim to know every possible permutation of his condition. I admit his recognition of

Catherine is surprising. Some latent memory perhaps." Dr. Poole shook her head and sighed. "But if you think he can be gentled, you're mistaken."

The hesitation in her words could have been doubt or deception. Jeremiah returned to the door, bent down to the opening and called out softly, "Joshua. Joshie."

The young man looked up at him.

"I'm your father, Joshie. Remember me? Daddy?"

The young man's right eye twitched. He dropped the picture, closed his eyes and clawed at his face, gouging out furrows in the skin. Several drops of blood fell on the photograph.

"Damon, no!" Dr. Poole said.

The young man whimpered, opened his eyes. As he looked at Dr. Poole, the blood on his face began to darken, coagulating into a scab.

"Whoa," Marschenko said. "Look at that. He's already healing."

"He scratches himself often," Dr. Poole said, "so his body has adapted to heal that particular injury quickly."

"I'd like to go into the room with him," Jeremiah said.

"He'll react violently."

"Maybe. But I might be able to get through to him."

"I'm sorry," Dr. Poole said. "It's my responsibility. My decision. And I believe it's too dangerous."

A sudden fury overcame Jeremiah. His whole body shook. Nothing would stop him now. Calm down, he told himself. Think it through. "Tell me something, Doctor," he said, "why did you get involved in this program?"

Dr. Poole frowned. "My specialty is the physiological dynamic of the psychology of trans-genetic species, particularly human-animal hybrids like you and your son."

"So an interaction between me and my son would hold some interest for you."

Dr. Poole smiled. "Oh, you're good."

"I would think you could learn a great deal from studying how we relate to each other, whether he has any residual recognition beneath the physiological and psychological changes you've created in him, not to mention how I react to his behavior."

Dr. Poole clapped her hands again. "Bravo! Well done, Mr. Jones. You've sufficiently piqued my curiosity. As long as you agree to be wired, I'll let you into his cell. But I can't guarantee your safety—not at all."

Jeremiah nodded.

"Let me just get a neural transmitter for you. I'll be right back."

As Dr. Poole retreated down the tunnel, Marschenko looked at Jeremiah, the barest hint of a smile visible, and said, "You're under constant surveillance, Jones. We've got a dozen Elite Ops here. And even if you somehow broke your son out and made it back to LB1, you'd still have to get through the military quarters, where two squads are on rotating shifts every six hours. Not to mention that we'd have plenty of time to arrange a reception on Earth for your return. You've got no chance to rescue him. Got it?"

"Got it," Jeremiah said with relief. Marschenko was giving Jeremiah as much information as he'd been able to accumulate since he arrived. It wasn't much. And the odds against Jeremiah were tremendous. But he would find a way.

Dr. Poole returned within a minute. She attached the neural transmitter to the back of his neck and nodded to Marschenko to open the door.

When the lock clicked open, the young man looked up at them. He slid the picture of Catherine under his pillow and got to his feet. As Jeremiah stepped into the room, the lock clicked back into place. Jeremiah stayed loose, preparing himself for an attack. He noted the rank odor of the unwashed boy, the dimensions of the ten-by-ten padded cell, the tensing muscles of the young man in front of him. The rage still sang inside Jeremiah's mind, but he knew he couldn't strike his son. He hoped he wouldn't have to. Holding his hands out in front of him, he tried to calm the boy.

"It's okay, Joshie," he said. "I don't want to hurt you. I just want to talk."

The young man went completely still for a second, then leapt at him.

Jeremiah dropped to the floor and the young man's momentum carried him into the padded wall. Jeremiah turned and saw Joshua latch onto the padding halfway up to the ceiling. He stayed there, as if stuck, and stared at Jeremiah, his eyebrows furrowed in concentration or confusion. Jeremiah stood, his hands outspread in a non-threatening gesture.

"Joshie," Jeremiah tried again. "I'm your father. I'm Daddy. I taught you how to ride your bike. Remember?"

Joshua launched himself off the wall, his fists aimed at Jeremiah's head. As Jeremiah ducked, the young man kicked him in the stomach. A classic diversionary tactic, Jeremiah realized. Doubled over, he backed into a corner. Tears wrapped his eyes as he struggled to understand how his son could hate him this much.

"My God, what have they done to you, Joshie?" Jeremiah pleaded. "Don't you remember anything? That jungle gym in the park with the bright colors? And afterwards we used to go get hot fudge sundaes?"

Joshua crouched in the far corner, glaring at Jeremiah, his right eye twitching again. Once more the boy closed his eyes and dug his fingernails into his face. Then he cried out. Jeremiah's breath caught in his throat. If he could, he'd give his life to save this poor boy.

Taking a step forward, his hands out in front of him to signal peace and calmness, Jeremiah said, "It's okay, Joshie." His stomach twisted, on the verge of upheaval. He couldn't have imagined a nightmare this awful. "It's going to be all right. We're going to help you."

Joshua tensed and Jeremiah knew he was about to attack again.

"Remember the garden we planted every spring?" Jeremiah asked, hoping he could somehow get through, hoping his son wasn't lost forever behind a curtain of insensate hatred. "If nothing else, Joshua, remember this. I love you. I'll always love you."

The young man flung himself at Jeremiah, unleashing a barrage of punches, hitting Jeremiah in the head and stomach. Jeremiah covered himself as best he could, refusing to fight back, deflecting only the occasional blow. Thinking he might vomit, he took the pain. He deserved it. The boy kept hitting him. He closed his eyes, dropped to the floor and folded himself into a fetal position. Hands and feet struck him—every blow a reminder of his failure. Maybe if he just let the boy attack until he tired himself out . . . maybe then he'd listen to his father. Jeremiah feared he might lose consciousness. If he did, would his son kill him? He wasn't sure he cared.

Then it stopped.

Jeremiah heard the sizzle of a Las-rifle, saw the blue light of a stun pulse as the boy fell. Behind him, the towering figure of Jack Marschenko stood, Las-rifle pointed at Jeremiah's chest. At the doorway, Dr. Poole looked at Marschenko, her brow knotted in confusion.

"Jack?" Dr. Poole said. "What was that?"

Marschenko, out of concern for Jeremiah's life, had just blown his cover.

He lowered his Las-rifle. "I don't know why I did that. I want you dead, you son of a bitch. Why would I save your stinkin' life?" He turned to Dr. Poole. "Why, Doc? Why'd I do it?"

"I don't know, Jack," Dr. Poole said. "We'll discuss that later." She turned to Jeremiah. "You can see why I didn't want to let you into his cell. Are you okay?"

Jeremiah struggled to his feet. "I heal quickly. You know that."

"Still, it must hurt. He hit you hard."

"And often," Marschenko added.

Just shut up, Jack, Jeremiah thought as he reached up and touched the swelling around his left eye. You might have saved it already. Don't overdo it.

Jeremiah's head ached but it was nothing compared to the nausea and depression of utter loss. He found it difficult to breathe, like his body was shutting down on him.

Dr. Poole said, "I'm sorry, Mr. Jones."

"He doesn't even know me."

"Why don't you give up and go home?" Marschenko said. "Do us all a favor and kill yourself."

"Jack," Dr. Poole said, "I'll see you in my quarters. As for you, Mr. Jones," she went quiet for a second, an unfocused stare indicating that she was using her interface, "Talbert and Alamein will escort you back to the military area."

Chapter Five

D r. Taditha Poole stared at the data from the neurotransmitter she'd attached to Jeremiah's neck, trying to focus. But she couldn't concentrate. For some reason, she couldn't stop thinking about Jack Marschenko. She wanted him badly. The notion of love at first sight struck her as ludicrous. How could she be so enamored of him? Maybe because the big Elite Ops trooper was so clearly in cahoots with Jones. A couple of nice guys: Jones only wanted his son back. She wished she could help, tell him that Damon wasn't his son, that it was in fact Curtik, the head of the male cadets.

She touched up her makeup and raised the hem of her black skirt above the knee with a hyper-static adjustment. She checked the time. Marschenko would be here any minute. Around him, she no longer despised the Moon, no longer felt anxious at how long she'd been up here. How did he feel about her? Might he reciprocate her feelings?

When he arrived, she gestured to the chair in front of her desk. "Well, now," she said. "Let's talk about why you saved Jones."

"I'm tellin' you, Doc." Marschenko fidgeted in his seat. "I don't know why I did it."

"You obviously like fair play. Could it be that you didn't want Damon to kill him when he refused to fight back?"

"That sounds about right. But I hate the pseudos. All the Elite Ops do."

Poole smiled as she got to her feet and sashayed around her desk to her sofa. She plopped down on it and patted the cushion next to her. "Come," she said.

Marschenko complied, a mountain of hot muscle sitting beside her. A brief frisson touched her as his eyes traveled slowly down her body. He said, "Yes, Doc?"

"You have a history with Jeremiah apart from simply taking his son. You want to tell me about it?"

Marschenko took his eyes off her, looked at the far wall. "It's a personal matter."

Poole smiled. "You're not as angry with Jeremiah as you would have us believe. All your talk—it's a little over the top. You've made an arrangement with him."

Marschenko's eyes returned to her. He leaned back against the cushion, folded his arms in front of his chest and said, "How much do you know about my disappearance last year?"

"Only that you were incommunicado for several days and that the disciplinary board issued a ruling of 'no fault,' meaning you were not punished for leaving."

Marschenko nodded. "It's classified. No one up top wanted the truth out. And the truth is that Jones captured me, locked me in a basement and held me there while he searched for his son. I told him nothing and eventually he let me go."

"So is he your enemy or your friend?"

Marschenko looked up at the camera in the corner of the ceiling.

"Don't worry," Poole said. "It's temporarily disabled."

"Honest to God, Doc, I don't know what to think of Jones. He coulda killed me."

Poole reached over and touched Marschenko's arm. "Something's going on between you two."

"We're lovers."

She laughed. "Seriously . . ."

Marschenko got to his feet and began pacing: an oversized animal cooped up in a cage. Poole crossed her legs and waited.

Marschenko reached the far wall for the third time and finally stopped. He turned to face her. "All right, here's the deal. When he locked me up in his basement, he removed all the hormones, all the drugs from my system, broke me down and ran a hypno-program on me, trying to turn me into his lapdog. What he didn't realize was that my nano-analyzers and regenerators combine with my psychological conditioning to prevent brainwashing. So I was able to pretend he'd turned me. But in reality I'm spying on him for the Elite Ops."

Poole clapped her hands. "What a lovely story."

"It's the truth, Doc."

"Jack, I'm on your side. I don't like keeping his son from him. I have my orders, but if I can figure out a way to help you two, I will. I assume you're feeding him intel."

Marschenko took a deep breath and nodded. "Schedules, access codes, security placements."

"Okay. Keep doing what you're doing. Give him whatever help he needs to rescue the boy."

Marschenko frowned. "Why?"

"We know he's going to make an attempt eventually. It's not in his nature to give up. And when you see him, I'll be monitoring everything—not just the conversation but his emotional responses too. I'll wire you up before you go."

"You play a dangerous game, Doc."

Poole leaned back and re-crossed her legs so that the hem of her skirt slid back, exposing a few more inches of thigh. "We both play a dangerous game, Jack. It's what adds excitement to an otherwise boring existence. And if you don't do what I say, I'll turn you into a eunuch."

Marschenko smiled. "You don't have a big enough knife."

Poole laughed. "Perhaps we can have dinner tonight?"

"Of course," Marschenko said.

"Seven o'clock at my quarters," Poole said. "Don't be late."

After Marschenko closed the door behind him, she got up and went to her desk to call Eli. He said, "How did the meeting between father and son go?"

"Jones believes the boy is his. The recognition we built into Damon worked perfectly—subtle but effective. Also, Jones is working with an Elite Ops trooper named Jack Marschenko."

As Poole waited three seconds for Eli to respond, she opened the Marschenko data on her tablet, noting the conflicted emotional nature of his responses.

Eli said, "I assume you plan to make good use of Marschenko. How about the boy? Is he going to be a problem? I don't want Jeremiah to discover they're not related until they're back on Earth."

Poole shook her head. "Not to worry. I used a neural transmitter on Jones. The data indicates he's certain the boy is his. As for Marschenko, I'll distract him as best I can. With respect to Jones, you were right. He's perceptive. Too bad I can't study him more closely. At any rate, I don't think they'll attempt a rescue quickly enough to be away on this LTV. Jones will have to wait for the next one. Do you have any idea what his plans are?"

Another three-second delay. Poole noticed several spikes on Marschenko's data graph, indicating that he found her attractive. Might it be more than that?

"No," Eli interrupted her thoughts. "I only know he'll try to avoid killing anyone. I'll dig up what I can on Marschenko in case you need another lever against him, though I have the utmost faith in your ability to charm him. Elias out."

* * *

By the light of a half-dozen glow globes, Taditha Poole examined herself in the mirror. One nice thing about the Moon was its decreased gravitational pull. Her breasts looked as firm as they had when she was in college. She carefully applied a pheromone accentuator in the valley between them, then dabbed a little behind each ear.

Apart from breasts that didn't sag, however, there was little to embrace about the Moon. Its necessary austerity, combined with her need to maintain emotional distance from her co-workers, left her feeling isolated.

As she dressed, she remembered again Eli's promise that she'd only be on the Moon for a year. With the two-year anniversary coming up next week and no sign of going home anytime soon, she felt herself getting a little space crazy. Perhaps she should remind Eli of his promise. On the other hand, she'd heard stories of his ruthlessness. And she had no doubt they were true.

Eli pursued a noble goal. His analysts predicted a coming mega war—a world war to end all world wars. The ultra wealthy, the people who ruled the world, had been concerned about revolt for years, as the masses grew increasingly frustrated by the lack of opportunity. The powers had devised a simple strategy to maintain their grip: get the people to fight among themselves, Republicans fighting Democrats, Muslims fighting Christians and Jews and even fellow Muslims, Indians fighting Chinese. The powers promoted an increasing lack of respect for diversity and the closing off of whole societies, getting people to fear the different—us against them. The problem was, that way led to global war. Eli sought to defeat that outcome. He claimed his brutality was the only way to achieve the larger goal of uniting and preserving humanity.

But why couldn't this project take place on Earth? Surely Eli could have found a training ground of total seclusion in America. Even Canada. Yet he'd insisted on the Moon.

She'd met Eli while still a student, doing a doctoral dissertation on neuro-psychology in chimeras. He'd been fascinated by her research, courted her to work in one of his laboratories. She'd refused. Yet when she'd been accused of falsified research and unethical behavior—charges that were ultimately dropped after suspicion shifted to her research assistants, who fled to China—he had stood by her and offered her a job. And she had finally agreed to run this program. Not that she'd had many options.

Why was she so introspective today?

Seeing Jeremiah Jones had shaken her. Anyone could see he was a good man. Misleading him felt wrong. How could she let him rescue a false son who would survive only a few more months at best? What was the point of it? It felt cruel. Yet Eli maintained it was necessary.

She put those thoughts aside for a moment and again studied herself in the mirror. She wished her breasts were a little larger and her hips a bit smaller.

At seven o'clock precisely, Marschenko arrived at her quarters. She let him wait outside for one minute, removing her interface before opening the door. He wore a gold shirt of sheer silk that clung to his washboard stomach. His pants were made of shimmer cloth—changing colors with the light. Perfect for hiding a flawed body, though Marschenko certainly had no cause to feel insecure about his. More likely, he wore shimmer cloth because it was fashionably expensive. She gestured him into the room, admiring his bulging arms, narrow waist, muscular thighs and round bottom.

Marschenko reached the table, empty except for a bottle of LunaWine that had been breathing for the past hour, its fruity aroma wafting throughout the room, mingling with the soft Ethiopian string music. Then he turned and stared at her, taking in her short red dress and her long legs, moisturized to give off a fine sheen of cocoa richness. He nodded toward the wine and said, "Trying to seduce me, Doc?"

"I think we're both aware of our mutual attraction," she replied, "I've got the meal warming. I didn't know if you wanted to eat now or later."

Marschenko ran his eyes down her body again, swallowed. "Later might be best."

"I agree. Will you pour the wine?"

Marschenko picked up the bottle and stared at the label. "LunaWine?"

"It's made from grapes and raspberries here on the Moon with an accelerated fermenting process. One of my staff brews it, gives me a bottle every few weeks. Too sweet for my taste but it provides a wonderful kick. Helps me forget the loneliness."

Marschenko poured carefully, bottle touching glass, as if afraid the wine would shoot out in defiance of the Moon's lesser gravity. Poole smiled, remembering how she'd done the same her first few days up here. He set the bottle down and stepped over to her. Putting a glass in her hand, he said, "You know, Doc, if you're lonely, it's only because you want to be. A woman like you could have any man up here."

Poole looked up into his eyes. He smelled masculine but not overly macho. She said, "You don't understand. It's not just a physical thing."

"Enlighten me."

Poole shook her head and drank. He took a sip, his face wrinkling, making her laugh. "It's best if you drink it quickly." Taking long swallows, she emptied her glass.

Marschenko copied her, grimacing as he finished. "Maybe it would be better if you injected it intravenously." He reached out, took the glass from her hand and put it on the table. He stood before her, smiling, his brown eyes penetrating. Tentatively, he reached out and stroked her shoulder.

It had been a long time since Poole had allowed herself pleasures of the flesh. This community was too small, rumors too rampant for her to indulge affairs with her subordinates. But Marschenko, damn, he was her type, much more so than Jeremiah. She liked them big. She shut her eyes, enjoying the nearness of him, swaying to the beat of the music.

"You ever made love on the Moon?" Marschenko asked.

Poole opened her eyes, felt herself drawn into Marschenko's stare. "No."

"I hear it's wild, like being in a gravity swing."

"Your fellow Elite Ops troopers tell you that?"

"Mmm." Marschenko caressed her face. "Maybe we should conduct an experiment."

"A scientific inquiry?" Poole murmured as Marschenko leaned down and kissed her.

"You're the doctor. How should we proceed?"

Poole stepped away, dimmed the lights and moved to the bed. Turning her back to him, she said, "Would you mind?"

He reached for the static seam and ran his finger down it, then separated the fabric and slid his hands around her. She lifted her head back and inhaled, leaning against his chest. She felt so light in his arms, lighter even than the Moon made her. A feather. She slid out of her dress and lay on the bed.

Marschenko removed his clothes and joined her. They faced each other, his bulk dominating the mattress. He stared at her, his eyes never leaving hers, not looking at her body but rather into the heart of her.

Finally he reached out his right hand, palm outward and whispered, "I could fall for you, Doc. And I'm not just saying that. I can sense you feel the same way."

"We barely know each other," Poole said. She placed her left hand against his right, imagining she could feel an electric spark as skin touched skin. Her fingers reached only halfway to his fingertips. How easily this man read her.

"I know what I've seen the past two days," Marschenko said. "I know you're a kind person stuck in a job that requires you to do things you regret. That's why you feel lonely. I do too. I kidnapped Joshua, took him away from his father—a man I respect. And you . . . you keep the boy away from him. The two of us are the same, Doc. Neither of us in control. We're both in too deep. No way out." He spoke softly. What kind of power did he have that he could make her want him so badly? She closed her eyes. He was just a man—nothing worth becoming silly over. "Tell me," he said, "is Jeremiah's son really dying?"

She opened her eyes, her stomach twisting. What if he was playing her? She said, "I'm doing everything I can for him. But the devolution of his genetic structure is progressing rapidly. Every week his cells degenerate a little more. Eventually, he'll reach a critical point from which he won't be able to recover."

Marschenko took her chin between finger and thumb until she looked him in the eye. "I can understand you being angry, but I promised him I'd ask," he said. "And I keep my promises, especially to a man like Jones. Duty and honor—lonely companions. Now can we forget about the world outside for a few minutes?"

He smiled but made no move toward her. She reached for him.

* * *

She awoke first and studied the man sleeping beside her. He'd brought such tenderness that first time, his movements firm but gentle, almost like they were suspended in air as they made love—weightless and tentative. The second time they'd ratcheted up the intensity—two

59

hungry bodies thrusting at each other, desperate to be filled. He'd been everything she'd imagined. And now she feared loving him—not that she was in love with him yet. Still, she felt herself knocking on love's door. She hated being vulnerable. What if he wasn't drawn to her as much as she was to him?

She was definitely getting space crazy.

Marschenko opened his eyes. "Thanks, Doc," he said in a gravelly whisper as he pulled her close. "Hey, why so tense? I thought I took care of that."

He smiled, rubbed noses with her. She concentrated on relaxing her muscles, noting the smell of sex and sweat, the warmth of his body. She said, "Are you hungry?"

"No. Just lie with me a bit, would you, Doc? I want to forget the world a little longer."

Poole luxuriated in the warmth of his embrace for a while. Then she forced herself to ask: "Are you playing me, Jack?"

Marschenko lifted his head off the pillow and stared at her. "No, Doc. I admit I'm supposed to distract you just like I know you're supposed to distract me. But I can't help the way I feel. There's a connection between us. Don't deny it."

"I wish I could trust you, Jack."

"You're different than every other woman I've known, Doc." His eyes began to fill with water, and he blinked a few times until they cleared. "Maybe it's your intelligence. Maybe it's purely physical. Hard to know at this early stage. But I think we can be good together. And I'm going to do my damnedest to prove it to you."

He kissed her and dropped his head. She caressed his cheek as he drifted off. If he was playing her, he was a masterful performer. Poole lay in his arms enjoying the dormant strength of him. As a doctor, she realized that her romantic feelings were nothing more than a chemical reaction in her brain. But that didn't make them any less real.

Chapter Six

Jeremiah soldered the last few connections on the crude RVM emitter he'd assembled. He glanced around the storage area that Quekri had offered. It contained extraneous lab equipment and an old 3-D printer he'd used to build various specialized equipment. He'd left the surveillance camera functional, so he expected one of Admiral Cho's minions soon. Three days ago Cho had sent an Elite Ops trooper to confiscate a scanner. Two days ago it had been an improvised Las-rifle.

Yesterday Jeremiah had met with Marschenko at the café in the main hangar, where sharing a table was common and the surveillance was minimal. Marschenko had given him updated information on access codes, security procedures, troop strength and other details of lesser importance. Throughout the meeting Marschenko had been stiffly formal, almost hostile, and Jeremiah wondered if he had succumbed to the pressures of the drugs and the daily conditioning that were part of the Elite Ops' regimen.

"You set, Frank?" he'd asked.

"I'll do my part," Marschenko replied, ignoring Jeremiah's jibe. "You do yours."

"I'm worried about you."

"Don't concern yourself with me." Marschenko drained his coffee cup and sauntered away, leaving Jeremiah with a hollow feeling in his gut.

He had to trust Marschenko.

As Jeremiah finished the RVM emitter, he heard footsteps approach from behind. He dropped the emitter and turned.

"Admiral Cho. I'm surprised. Thought you'd send one of your boys."

Cho held out his hand. "Some kind of microwave transmitter?"

Jeremiah handed the emitter over. "Exactly. A random variable microwave emitter."

Cho nodded as he turned it around in his hands. "Ah, yes. Excellent for disrupting communications. It probably wouldn't survive more than a single usage but it'd do a helluva lot of damage. Where were you gonna get a power source sufficient to run this?"

"I never planned to use it," Jeremiah said.

"Just a hobby, eh? Makin' scanners and Las-rifles and microwave emitters? Well, you got my attention, so talk."

Jeremiah's muscles tensed. He rolled his neck, relaxed his shoulders, his arms, hands and fingers. He said, "Did you ever consider, Admiral, that I'm letting you see what I'm doing for a reason?"

Cho nodded. "And that reason would be?"

"I don't want to hurt anybody, but if you keep tying my hands behind my back, you'll leave me no choice. I'll have to kill a lot of your men when I free my son."

"You ain't gonna give up, are you?"

"You wouldn't give up if it was your son."

Cho shrugged, tapped the emitter against his palm. "Anything else you're workin' on, somethin' you ain't lettin' me see?"

"You've had me under surveillance twenty-four hours a day."

Cho sighed, rubbing his chin with the emitter. "You're makin' things awful tough for me, Mr. Jones."

Jeremiah pointed a finger at Cho's chest, but he kept his tone light. "And you're holding my son illegally. I could have gone to the press. I could have gone to the President or Congress. Somebody would have listened, put pressure on you. I might even have attempted a rescue. Maybe it wouldn't have succeeded, but you and a dozen others would be dead if I'd tried. Just know this—nothing personal—but I'm losing patience."

Cho opened his mouth to reply, then shut it. He gave Jeremiah a long, considering look. Jeremiah waited, rage floating beneath the surface, ready to explode into action. He felt jittery, as if the act of holding back the violence moved him closer to madness. He struggled to locate his sense of wrongness, as Quark had described it. Fought to stay human. He realized he was clenching his fists again.

Cho glanced down and noticed it too. He said, "Why don't you go out on a day trip with the tourists. Look at the craters, enjoy bein' outside. You're not likely to ever return to the Moon. Might as well see it while you're here." Cho placed his hand on Jeremiah's shoulder. "I think I can get you your son soon—certainly by the time of the next LTV."

His voice carried sincerity, even a trace of fear. Behind his glasses, his eyes didn't waver. The slightly sweet odor of his sweat remained constant. No deception. Jeremiah nodded. He hadn't yet been out on the lunar surface. Perhaps it would help calm him.

* * *

The doors to the airlock opened. Jeremiah, fitted into a pressurized spacesuit, stepped into the small room, where a party of nine waited— an elderly Brazilian couple, a middle-aged French couple and the young family who had flown in on the same LTV he'd taken. Rounding out the group was their tour guide. The family's older daughter looked up at him and smiled through her helmet. The father nodded hello. The mother said, "I suppose we should introduce ourselves. My husband's Brian. I'm Roanne. This is our youngest, Kaylee. And no doubt you remember Kyler."

"Of course," Jeremiah said through the open comm connection. "Good to see you again. I'm Jeremiah." He nodded to the Brazilians and the French, who waved back.

"Yesterday," Kyler said, "we saw Shoemaker Crater. And we went to Cabeus and Faustini too."

"Sounds like you had a good time," Jeremiah said.

Kyler shrugged. "Today we're going to see a new crater."

"That's right," the guide said as he closed the doors behind Jeremiah. "I'm Dalben Haynes, and I'll be taking you to SPR8, a manmade crater

63

here in the southern polar region." He checked Jeremiah's spacesuit, verifying that it was properly sealed, then examined the oxygen gauge. "It's a balmy one-hundred-ten degrees Fahrenheit outside, or forty-three degrees Celsius, three-hundred-sixteen degrees Kelvin. When we exit, your visors will automatically darken to protect you from dangerous solar rays, limiting your ability to see the stars. You'll notice that the Earth is in half-shadow and that we're at about seventy-five degrees west longitude, which puts us over the eastern United States. If you want to get a really good look at Earth, set the magnification on your helmet to three when you step outside. But for safety's sake, stop moving first.

"Now that the air in the room has been pumped out," Dalben opened the doors to the outside, "we can exit the hangar and make our way toward the lunar carriage, which is completely powered by solar energy. Off to the right, you'll notice the Pilgrim, the spaceship that the Escala are planning to take to Mars."

Jeremiah glanced at the huge gray capsule a few hundred yards away and wondered what it would be like to travel inside it for eight months, winding up on another world, never to return to Earth.

"Even though the temperature outside is often habitable," Dalben interrupted his thoughts, "the lack of an atmosphere requires pressurized spacesuits so as to keep the body's fluids in a liquid state. There's also the danger of micrometeoroids, which bombard the Moon quite frequently and which aren't burned up before reaching the ground because there's no atmosphere to create friction and thereby reduce them in size."

"We heard this part yesterday," Kyler said to Jeremiah as she took his hand and led him onto the lunar surface.

Jeremiah looked up at Earth as Kyler tugged at him. He set his magnification to three and stared at the outline of North America. A shadow fell across the eastern half of the continent, which was awash in lights all the way along the coast. Further west, pockets of light indicated large cities—Cleveland, St. Louis, Chicago and dozens more—until the arched shadow of night gave way to daylight somewhere east of the Rockies. The western part of the continent was hidden by a huge mass of clouds that stretched over the Pacific Ocean. Central America and the bulk of South America were also mostly covered in clouds. But the continent's eastern seaboard, like its northern counterpart, glowed unnaturally.

"That's where we live," Kyler said as she pointed with her free hand, "in New York. It's bright there."

"Yes, it is," Jeremiah replied. He'd seen Earth through the plas-glass roof of LB1's hangar but it was more impressive out on the lunar surface with nothing between them but the thin visor and the emptiness of space.

"Come on, Jeremiah," Kyler said as she pulled at him. He turned off the helmet's magnification as she led him to an open-sided vehicle that looked something like a dune buggy, only larger. Wide, knobby tires sat under a flat carriage that held four benches. Atop the vehicle, a plas-glass roof stretched beyond the sides—a handful of scuff marks marring its surface where micrometeroids had struck it.

Kyler jumped up and grabbed the roof of the transport, eight feet off the ground, where she began to swing back and forth.

"Kyler," Roanne said. "We talked about this. No jumping around. Get down from there. Brian, would you grab her?"

Kyler said, "I want Jeremiah to help me."

Brian said, "He doesn't want to—"

"I'll help her down," Jeremiah said.

"You don't know what you're getting yourself into," Roanne said. "She'll glom onto you like a barnacle."

"I know what that means, Mother," Kyler said as Jeremiah lifted her free of the carriage roof. When he set her on the ground, she turned to him and said, "Are you a soldier like Daddy says?"

"Kyler," Brian said. "I'm sorry, Jeremiah. I don't know how much experience you have with kids but she is definitely more than a handful."

Jeremiah thought of his son. His whole body slumped. He closed his eyes and took a deep breath.

"Are you all right?" Roanne asked.

"Fine," he answered, shocked that she had noticed his pain through his faceplate. He patted Kyler's helmet and said, "I like an inquisitive mind and a bold approach. As for your question, Kyler, no, I'm not a soldier."

Roanne shook her head and smiled at Jeremiah before taking the second seat with Kaylee. Standing beside the carriage, Brian put his hand on the seat railing and said to Jeremiah, "You sure you want to sit next to her?"

Jeremiah grabbed Brian's forearm and squeezed reassuringly. "We'll be fine."

"Okay," Brian said as he climbed in next to his wife. "But you let us know if she gets to be too much to handle."

The elderly Brazilian couple climbed into the front seat with Dalben, while the middle-aged French couple took the back seat. Before climbing into the buggy Jeremiah looked around. The sun, low in the sky off to his left, shone brightly even through his darkened visor. A shallow crater contained perhaps a dozen capsules of blue, red, yellow and green: the cemetery. Apart from the capsules, everything was black or gray: no trees or lakes or animals: just dirt and rocks, hills and craters. Even the sky, which ought to have been filled with stars, looked black through the darkened visor. Only a few of the brightest stars were visible, and even then they were nothing more than dim pinpoints of light. The stark, empty landscape looked like a desert.

"Jeremiah," Dalben said, "You'd better strap yourself in so we can get going. We only brought enough oxygen for four hours. We'll be driving to the east approximately fifteen kilometers to SPR8. The lunar carriage travels at an average speed of thirty kilometers per hour, so we should be at our destination in about thirty minutes. Along the way, I'll be pointing out some of the interesting features. For example, if you look off to your left, you'll see the outlines of part of Maginus Crater. Up ahead and off to the right is the edge of Crater Curtius. Behind us too far back to see is Manzinus Crater."

"A lot of craters," Jeremiah said.

"They're made by meteors," Kyler said. She lifted her arms and brought them down at an angle into Jeremiah's stomach. "Boom!" Jeremiah flinched in pretend pain and Kyler giggled. She said, "They crash into the ground and form big bowls of dust."

"That's right," Dalben said. "But you needn't worry about meteors falling on us. I checked the meteor report before we left LB1 and the radar shows that we'll be clear for at least the next several hours.

"Now you'll notice we're traveling along a path that's been used many times, as evidenced by the tire marks. See how each imprint is as fresh as the day it was made. There's no wind or rain—nothing to erode them. They'll still be here in a hundred years unless we drive over them or a meteor hits along this path.

"One thing of interest is the many rock formations along the way to SPR8. Most of them are naturally occurring but some are man-made. If you look off to the right, you'll see a cluster called the sphinx, which was created by last year's tour guides as their final gift before rotating off-Moon. Over to the left there are a series of hills called the camelbacks, all made of igneous rock. Since the first lunar landing in 1969, we've learned that volcanic activity occurred here as recently as two million years ago. Hold onto your railings as we drive into this next crater."

The lunar carriage went uphill to the rim of the crater and plunged down toward a meteor at its center maybe twenty feet in diameter that someone had painted to look like a mouthful of jagged teeth. Kaylee and Kyler screamed, the latter with delight, as the carriage made its way toward the fiercely painted mouth.

Kaylee began to cry. As Roanne comforted her, Kyler said, "She's such a baby."

"Dalben," Jeremiah said, "do you get a bonus for terrifying children?"

"Sorry," Dalben said. "It's all part of the tour. Don't usually get young kids here."

Brian looked back at Jeremiah and nodded.

The rest of the journey to SPR8 passed quietly. When they reached their destination, Dalben grabbed the portable light from the carriage, brought it over to the edge of the crater and waited for the others to join him. Kyler leapt out of the carriage and began hopping around again. The elderly Brazilians brought up the rear.

"Kyler," Roanne said. "Please don't jump around like that. And stay away from the edge."

When everyone reached the side of the crater, Roanne and Brian each holding one of Kaylee's hands, Dalben said, "Well, here we are at SPR8. This crater was created less than two years ago by the Las-cannons that orbit the Earth—part of an experiment to determine how effective they would be at breaking up an incoming asteroid or meteor. The crater is sixty meters wide at the top and less than ten meters wide at the bottom. Notice the steep sides, slick from the burning of the Las-cannons, which melted the igneous rock that makes up the Moon. The crater is over three hundred meters deep."

The Frenchman, holding onto his wife's hand, stepped closer to the edge and said, "How long did it take to create the crater?"

"Just over four hours on a medium-power setting," Dalben answered. He picked up a large rock and threw it over the side, flashing the light on it as it fell, slowly at first, picking up speed until it crashed into the bottom. "Notice also," Dalben continued, "that it makes no sound when it hits—again because there's no atmosphere to transmit the sound waves. Here, try it." He handed a rock to Kyler.

"I don't think that's a good idea," Roanne said.

"I'll be careful, Mom," Kyler replied.

"No jumping around," Brian said. "Just drop the rock and back away."

Kyler took the rock from Dalben and stepped toward the edge of the crater. Looking back at her parents, she tossed the rock over and leaned forward to watch it drift ever faster to the bottom.

The ground beneath her feet suddenly began to sink and she fell forward, crying out. Jeremiah dove for her. Grabbing her arm, he pulled hard, and she flew past him to safety. But Jeremiah, unused to the lower gravity of the Moon, couldn't stop his momentum. He soared past the lip of the crater, tumbling. Hands and feet splayed, he searched for any purchase to stop his descent. The screams of his fellow tourists sounded through the comm as he hit the sheer face of the crater wall. He scrabbled for a handhold, a toehold, anything on the slick sidewall as he plummeted.

In his desperate attempt to slow his fall, he nearly pushed himself away from the side of the crater. Almost immediately, however, he realized that he needed to stay close to the wall. He tumbled, his head below his feet, stretching out his fingers until he found the rocky surface. With his right hand, he groped for bumps or outcrops, found several, twisting himself so that his feet were back beneath him. He gently dug them into the wall as he slid down the crater, slowing his descent until his right foot jammed against a large protrusion, somersaulting him again.

The fall took a long time.

He reached out in search of any kind of handhold, the light held by Dalben tumbling out of view. Then he crashed.

He couldn't breathe. His spacesuit must have been punctured. Lying on his back, looking up at the light, it dawned on him that he was going to die at the bottom of a hole on the Moon.

Joshua.

Jeremiah's whole body ached. And then his lungs began to work, sucking in a giant breath of oxygen. Screams and shouted questions filled his helmet. "Quiet!" he commanded.

The screaming stopped. Only a faint hiss and a clicking noise emanated from the speakers in his helmet.

"Are you okay?" Brian yelled.

"Peachy," Jeremiah replied. He felt the movement of air past his face and realized that the hiss wasn't coming from the speakers. He groaned as he forced himself to a sitting position. He'd broken at least a few ribs. Every breath brought a knife-sharp pain to his chest. His head throbbed and his legs delivered jolts of agony to his stomach.

"I can't believe you survived that fall," Dalben said. Several clicks swallowed his next words. ". . . break any bones?"

"I've got a hole in my suit," Jeremiah said through clenched teeth.

"Where?"

He waited for a crackle to diminish and said, "I'm looking for it. Hang on."

". . . get help."

Another crackling sound and then Roanne said, ". . . we can do?"

A loud pop issued from the comm link before it died. Taking a deep breath, hoping it wouldn't be his last, Jeremiah began to examine the suit. He checked his hands first. Despite the urge to hurry, he went slowly and carefully over the garment, finding no obvious tears. He looked down at his left foot. Nothing. Then his right. There. In the dim light he could just make out a rip along the toes about three inches long. Pulling his foot back towards him, grunting with the pain and effort, he realized that his legs were broken. As his hands reached his foot, a piercing needle of agony punctured him. It traveled up his right leg, extending all the way to his head, creating a pressure that felt sonic. He was afraid he'd pass out and let go of the suit. But for now he applied pressure, sealing the tear at least partially. The hissing stopped.

"I found the rip," he spoke calmly on the off chance they could still hear him. "It's in the right foot, about three inches long. If you have any tape with you, you could toss that down. And if you can hear me, blink the light."

No acknowledgement.

The light still shone. He twisted his head to look up at it. Apart from its glare he could see nothing. All he could do was wait, fighting the pain as he held the tear closed with his hands. How much air had he lost? How long until a rescue party came for him? His death would solve a lot of problems for Admiral Cho and Dr. Poole. But what about his son? Would Joshua die here too? So close—he'd been so close to getting his son back. And now he might as well be back on Earth.

Nausea flooded him. Sweat ran down his forehead. He lay back, pulling his right foot up, hoping he wouldn't faint.

Strangely, the rage swelled inside him, filling him with an adrenaline rush that made his whole body quiver, wanting to attack. But without an enemy to fight, he would only be hurting himself, using up his air supply too quickly. Not that it mattered. Too much had escaped already: his gauge already in the red zone. He blinked three times, centered himself in his stone dungeon, walling off the pain and anger. Yet the rage ripped him free of it. He knew he had to calm himself down, conserve his oxygen.

He stared at the light, took slow breaths, concentrated on emptying his mind in an effort to hypnotize himself. After a moment, he managed to relax. He stared up past Dalben's light into the blackness of space, wishing he could look at the stars, finally remembering that the darkened visor could be adjusted manually. His eyes scanned the controls at the top of the visor until he found the proper setting. By focusing on the clear view option with the masking feature, he was able to create a black spot that covered the flashlight. Beyond it the stars suddenly appeared.

He looked back into time, back into the creation of the solar system and the Milky Way Galaxy, recalling images from his own creation. Catherine, Joshua, Julianna: the people who once populated his world. The past replayed itself in his mind with a clarity he knew was a lie even as he embraced it. His legs grew cold. He wondered if they would simply cover him up, shovel the omnipresent lunar dust over his body, leaving him alone in the vacuum. More images: family outings of idyllic tranquility; a lake, a canoe, a brief rainstorm; the northern lights. Through the mist of memory he saw movement, but not a sound intruded. Images paraded past in absolute silence, disturbing the perfection of mimetic recall.

He tried to focus on Joshua, on the poor tormented young man locked in a cage, but his mind kept drifting to his negligent stupidity. How could he have been so careless? You knew this would happen at some point, he said to himself. You placed too much reliance on your abilities. Cocky moron, you deserve to die down here. No! Jeremiah refused to surrender. Hang on, idiot. They'll send help. Just stay alive a little longer.

Chapter Seven

S oft string music came from the speakers, mixing with the sounds of waves lapping the shore. Taditha Poole had selected this piece for its subliminal signals that enhanced physical pleasure. Setting aside the chocolate covered strawnanas, she opened her last bottle of LunaWine and poured two glasses, handing one to Marschenko. He took a sip, grimaced and placed the wineglass on the table.

"Man, that's awful," Marschenko said. "I need something to get that taste out of my mouth." He ran his eyes down Poole's body. "Hey, you. Drop your drawers and spread 'em."

Poole laughed. "Oh, Jack. My big stud."

"Get ready to moan like there's no tomorrow, baby. 'Cause here I come."

As his arms engulfed her, she savored the sheer size of him, drunk on the intoxicating aroma of pheromones and infatuation. For the past three days they'd taken every opportunity to indulge themselves in the escape of physical intimacy. She wondered if he worried, like she did, that the feeling might not last. Was this to be only a short-term affair or would it blossom into something more? For now the release of tension provided enough joy. As she kissed him—a long, lingering kiss that melted her insides—the emergency code sounded.

"Damn, damn, damn," Poole said as Marschenko released her.

"Ah, you like to be teased. Good to know." He stepped out of view of the vid camera on her PlusPhone as she connected.

"We got a problem," Admiral Cho said. "Jeremiah Jones is trapped at the bottom of SPR8 with a ripped suit."

"Jones? How did he—"

"I've informed Eli," Cho interrupted her, "and he insists we mount a rescue operation. My team will try to make it in time. Your cadets could help. Oh, and Jack?"

"Yeah?" Marschenko stepped into the vid pickup.

"You'd better come too."

"Right."

"I'll get Curtik and Zora to join us," Poole said before disengaging. "They've done simulated rescues on the Moon's surface several times," she added for Marschenko's benefit.

She plugged in her interface, activated the level-five emergency code and broadcast separate signals to Curtik and Zora, asking them to meet her at the airlock for a surface rescue, then followed Marschenko out the door.

"Curtik," she explained to Marschenko as they slid-hopped down the corridor, the fastest way to move under the low gravity, "leads our male students and is the overall brigade leader. Zora leads our females."

"We gotta save him, Doc," Marschenko said.

"Jack, I know you care for him, but does Cho know how you feel? Or does he still think you're enemies?"

"That doesn't matter anymore, Doc. Let's just rescue him."

Poole slid-hopped past Marschenko. Her long time on the Moon gave her an advantage when it came to moving quickly. Marschenko leaped too high in the air with each step. The airlock, when they reached it, had two people inside: Curtik and Zora, already suited up. Curtik was nearly a foot shorter than Marschenko and would never be as broad in the shoulders. Zora—bright, lovable Zora—stood shorter still, leaner, more sinewy and catlike. They nodded to Poole and watched Marschenko as the pair donned their suits and checked the seals. When Curtik opened the outside hatch, they all walked quickly to the Lunar buggy. Zora settled behind the controls and the Lunar buggy sped away.

"This is Jack Marschenko," Poole said.

Curtik nodded at Marschenko, then busied himself with preparing the winch for a rescue, even as he fought to keep from flying off the vehicle. Zora, no respecter of others' imperfections, clearly assumed that everyone else had her fabulous sense of balance. Poole opened the channel to Cho's rescue party.

". . . at SPR8 in seven minutes," a voice said. "Is he still alive?"

"We don't know. The comm was knocked out by the fall. It doesn't look like he's moving."

Marschenko said, "How long before we get there?"

"Eight minutes," Zora said.

"Can't you go any faster?"

"Now why didn't I think of that?"

"Look, kid, just get me there. I'll handle things once we reach the crater."

Curtik said, "First time in a spacesuit?"

"Yeah," Marschenko said, "so?"

"You should let us go. We've made simulated rescues before. Besides, SPR8 isn't an ordinary crater. It's more like a mineshaft. We'll have to drop someone down on a winch with oxygen and a pressurized sack to enclose the ripped suit and provide a sustainable environment. Zora's faster and better at that than anyone."

"I'm, going, down, too," Marschenko said slowly, each word an assault on Curtik.

Curtik said, "A mouthy man."

Poole said, "Curtik."

Curtik laughed. "What? That's funny. A mouthy man. Get it? He enunciates his words real good." His voice carried an edge and Poole knew he'd decided to hate Marschenko. Marschenko caught it too, for he leaned toward Curtik. "So," Curtik said, ignoring Marschenko's threatening pose, "who's down there?"

"A tourist named Jeremiah Jones," Poole answered.

Curtik stiffened but said nothing. She wondered if he would betray his past. And she still wondered how he alone among all the cadets even remembered it. His programming should have erased all memories of his early childhood. A beep in her helmet indicated that Curtik had switched to a private channel. She set her comm to the same frequency and said, "Yes?"

"Why is my father at the bottom of SPR8?" Curtik asked.

"Admiral Cho didn't say. I assume it was an accident."

"An accident." Curtik's voice told her he didn't believe her. "I don't know what kind of game you're playing, but I won't be sucked in. I hate my father. He let my mother die. So if you think my rescuing him will bring us closer, you're wrong. If I have to save him I will. But that's it. And if you try to put me together with him, I'll kill him."

Poole's cheeks burned with anger and embarrassment. She was grateful for the darkened visor that hid her face from his. Even though she'd made him what he was, she still loathed Curtik. Eli said he was necessary. But the sweet boy she'd first encountered—Joshua Jones— had disappeared into the uberwarrior persona until nothing likable remained.

"We have no intention of putting you together," Poole said. "As I explained earlier, he came to the Moon for his kidnapped son. We intend to give him Damon, whom he believes is you. You get him out of the crater and we'll send him back to Earth."

"Why all the fuss? Why not just let him die? If we got there a few minutes too late, what would be the harm?"

"Eli wants him alive."

"Why? I'm better than he is, more advanced. Eli doesn't need him."

"I'm telling you as much as I know."

Another beep. Zora broke into their private frequency and said, "One minute."

Curtik turned to face her, no doubt glaring his disapproval. Zora was Curtik's biggest rival—smarter and quicker. He didn't yet see her as a big enough threat to eliminate but for the past six months Poole had been monitoring his emotional subconscious as well as his actions and she knew he was close to violence. Zora knew it too. Poole would have to separate them soon before one killed the other.

Up ahead, three vehicles and a dozen people stood in a cluster around the crater, shining their lights into the darkness. Poole switched back to the main channel. Curtik and Zora did the same. Then Curtik began to give orders:

"Step away from the crater. Let our buggy through. All nonessential personnel evacuate the area. Get those civilians back to LB1."

75

He lacked the personality of Zora but no one could question his abilities or his intensity. He was an overwhelming force. And when he had a task to complete he'd let nothing stand in his way. Ruthless. Relentless. Eli was right. Curtik was perfect for the job. He'd be the best terrorist the world had ever known. He'd unite the world in fear like no one had been able to do before. But could he stop wars? Could he prevent humanity from killing itself?

Zora pulled up next to the crater, filling the recently vacated spot where the group of people had scattered. Curtik stepped down, opened the boom and swung it around while Zora pulled out an oxygen canister and the pressurized sack. Opening a medkit, Poole removed the physio-monitor. She handed the kit to Zora, who attached a stretcher to the winch and placed the equipment into it. Then she secured the gear and clipped two safety loops to the hook at the bottom of the winch.

Marschenko stepped to the rim of the crater, grabbed a safety loop and said, "I'm going. He's my friend."

"Okay, Mouthy Man," Curtik said. He grabbed the winch controller, and Zora and Marschenko disappeared from view. Now that she wouldn't be in the way, Poole climbed out of the buggy and edged closer to the crater. Powering up the monitor's receiver, she said, "Zora, don't forget to place the transmitter on his chest as soon as you reach him. It'll read through the suit."

"Good idea, Doctor." Zora's voice carried only sarcasm. No trace of fear for Jones or herself. That was the problem working with children. Despite the enhancements to their brains and bodies, they still didn't understand the nature of risk. Most children believed themselves invincible. These children were perhaps worse, likely because of their incredible abilities. Death was a foreign concept—an abstract notion barely accorded recognition. She would have to remember to download the data on Curtik and Zora after this was over, study their emotional states during this rescue.

"Forty meters," Zora said. "Thirty, twenty, ten. We're down."

"Jeremiah," Marschenko yelled as if he could make Jones hear him despite the lack of an atmosphere to carry the sound.

"Jeremiah, we're getting you out. Hang on." His voice carried a trace of panic.

The readings came into Poole's monitor. "No pulse. And he's not breathing. He's got no oxygen or pressure left in his suit."

Zora said, "We're working on it, Doctor. Lift him up, Mouthy Man. All the way off the ground. Good. Putting the sack around his suit. Move your hands. Okay, closing it up. Put him in the stretcher. Excellent. Pressurizing and injecting oxygen. Not bad, Mouthy Man."

"Still no pulse," Poole said. She glanced at Curtik, who somehow managed to look bored inside his spacesuit, as if unimpressed by Marschenko's performance. "Body temp falling."

"Injecting epinephrine mixture."

"Still nothing. Wait! There's a beat. And another. Very slow. Bring him up as fast as you can."

Marschenko said, "We're moving him onto the stretcher. Okay, reel us up."

As the motor hauled them up, Poole studied the monitor. Jeremiah's pulse flickered as he took in shallow breaths. Pain levels were high enough to render him unconscious but Jones was in a self-hypnotic trance. His legs were broken; half a dozen ribs were cracked; internal organs and brain had suffered massive trauma from the fall. His immune system response was overloading. She'd never seen a white blood cell count that high, not in any of her students, all of whom were supposed to be next generation transgenics, more advanced than Jones. And the white cell count was rising.

If it continued to rise, his immune system would attack his body and he'd be dead in less than an hour. Something was wrong with him, more than just having fallen three hundred meters—a distance that would have killed any ordinary man—even on the Moon.

When they rose above the rim of SPR8, Curtik swung the boom winch around, depositing the stretcher onto the bed of the lunar buggy. Marschenko maintained his grip on Jones' pressure sack, while Zora slid behind the lunar buggy's controls. Poole climbed back into the buggy, continuing to scan the monitor. She couldn't do anything to help him until they got to the hospital wing of LB1. And she wasn't sure how to treat him once they got there.

On the ride back, Curtik stared at Marschenko the whole way, plotting some sort of torture, no doubt. Poole shivered. She'd have to make sure she kept Curtik away from Marschenko, who noticed Curtik's hatred, for he stared back at the young cadet. Neither spoke a word. Only Zora's voice broke the silence and Poole could tell she'd picked up on the tension too.

"It's nice to get outside once in a while, don't you think?" Zora asked. When no one answered, she continued, "I love the open feeling. Only this thin skin between us and death. Makes me feel alive. Don't you feel alive, Curtik?" No answer. "How about you, Mouthy Man?" Curtik laughed at that—a half laugh, half snort. "Don't you feel like running across the Moon? Wouldn't that be fun? Tumbling and cartwheeling? What about ratapulting? We'll bring a couple rats outside, fling them into the air and see which one flies the farthest. You up for a little ratapulting when we get back?"

"Zora," Poole said.

"You're no fun," Zora said. "None of you. Boring." But when she settled back to the driving Poole could tell that the tension had eased. Marschenko and Curtik leaned back in their seats, watching each other but no longer poised for attack. Zora had put them at ease with so few words. No wonder she was everyone's favorite. Even Curtik liked her when he wasn't plotting against her.

* * *

In the operating room, Poole consulted with Dr. Hackett, the chief military surgeon, who injected a series of nano-cleansers that should decrease the white blood cells running rampant through Jones' body. She assisted Dr. Hackett with Jones' broken bones. They'd already begun to heal in the short time since they'd fractured, so they had to be re-broken before they could be set.

When she finally had time to check the monitors, she saw that the nano-cleansers were attacking the white cells, pulling them into clumps and disrupting them.

"The nano-cleansers are working," she said.

"No," Hackett said. "Look at his count."

Sure enough, the white cell count was growing again. Jones' immune system was becoming more aggressive, eating away at him from the inside. Poole said to the nurse, "Give me twenty cc's Atrapine-hydroxocyl and begin administering hydrogen sulfide."

Hackett said, "A medically induced coma? Do you think that's wise?"

"What else can we do? We need time."

"I suppose you're right. We should also lower his body temperature."

The head nurse prepared a hypo pad and gave it to Poole while the other two nurses engaged the cooling system and connected the hydrogen sulfide mask over Jones' face. After injecting the drugs, Poole studied the monitors. But even the coma and the lowering body temperature didn't completely stabilize Jones. His white cell count continued to grow, albeit at a slower pace.

"Get Dr. Garcia Delgado and Dr. Nakamura," Hackett said to the head nurse.

"No," Poole said. "Get Dr. Wellon."

"Wellon?" Hackett asked.

"An Escala doctor," Poole said.

"Nakamura's an expert on nano-technology. And Garcia Delgado is brilliant."

"Jones is a transgenic. Wellon is our best hope."

"Okay. He's your patient. But Cho may not approve."

"I believe Cho's orders are the same as ours—to keep Jones alive." While they waited for Wellon, Poole continued to watch the monitors, hoping for some sign that he was going to survive. This wasn't supposed to be happening. But Jones' incredible healing ability was now working against him, his fabulous immune system turning on its host, destroying him from the inside out.

And what would she tell Eli? That Jones, after making such a miraculous recovery from his injuries in the Devereaux incident, surviving numerous Las-rifle strikes, somehow succumbed to a fall on the Moon at a time when his healing ability was supposedly far greater? Would Eli believe her?

Something was wrong with Jones greater than just his injuries. She didn't know what it was. Perhaps like a caged animal, he had begun to shut down his body while he was trapped at the bottom of that crater.

The door opened and Wellon entered the room. Despite having encountered her a handful of times, Poole was always awed by her size—six and a-half feet tall, two hundred-fifty Earth pounds (forty pounds on the Moon), tangled black hair that grew down to her waist. She was only slightly bigger than Jack Marschenko, but she seemed much more dangerous, more unpredictable, as if she might lash out at any moment, like some trained bear who one day decided to return to the wild. Focus on Jones, Poole told herself. Wellon tied her hair back in a bun and donned surgical scrubs. Through her mask, in her deep voice, Wellon said, "What have we got?"

"Jeremiah Jones," Poole replied. "His immune system is hyperactive. Rising white cell count." She pointed to the monitor. "I gave him an injection of nano-cleansers but that hasn't stopped the activity. Right now he's in a medically induced coma and we've reduced his body core temperature by eight degrees. He's had massive trauma to his brain and internal organs. Any ideas?"

Wellon closed her eyes and took a deep breath. For long seconds she said nothing while Poole and Hackett stared at her. Poole wanted to scream at her, but knew that wouldn't help. Either Wellon would find an answer or Jones would die. Poole was well aware of her own limitations on the surgical side of medicine, and Hackett specialized in nano-technology modification.

"Do you have any new disease cultures here?" Wellon asked suddenly.

"New disease cultures?" Hackett said.

"Something he hasn't been exposed to yet. A weaponized bacterium perhaps? Or a virus?"

Poole said, "You want to give him something else to fight?"

Hackett said, "That's insane!"

Poole shook her head. "It seems like the wrong thing to do. So it might be just the answer."

Hackett said, "I can't believe you're thinking of—"

"Have you got any better ideas?" Poole said.

Hackett threw up his hands. "The only thing I've got is the Susquehanna Virus."

"The Susquehanna Virus?" Poole said.

"It came up on the last LTV by orders of the President. A small sample for Devereaux to study."

"Get it," Wellon said. "Quickly."

"We'd need Admiral Cho's authorization," Hackett said. He stared at Poole.

She shrugged. "I don't have any better ideas."

Pointing to the monitors, Wellon said, "You're almost out of time."

Poole saw the NK cell count grow. How was Jones still alive? "Do it," she finally said to Hackett. "We'll have to quarantine this whole area afterwards. And you nurses need to leave too. Set up a decon chamber outside the door. We'll sterilize the room afterwards."

As the nurses departed, Hackett nodded and followed them out the door. Turning to face Wellon, Poole looked up into those accusatory black eyes and said, "It was an accident. I don't have many details. All I know is that he fell down SPR8."

Wellon's brow tightened but she only continued to stare at Poole, ignoring the monitors. Poole found herself sweating. She hadn't even considered what the Escala might do if Jones died. After Jeremiah rescued Devereaux in Minnesota, they counted him as their personal hero. And if they decided to rebel against the leadership on the Moon . . . well, they'd probably lose any fight against Admiral Cho's troops, but they'd certainly create a dangerous environment. She finally realized why Elite Ops troopers had been assigned to the Moon.

Within five minutes Hackett returned with a hypo pad, Admiral Cho behind him, halting just outside the door.

"I don't like it," Cho said through the vidcom. "But if you're sure it's necessary, I'll okay it."

"Dr. Wellon believes it's our only option," Poole replied.

As confirmation, Wellon took the hypo pad from Hackett and injected Jones.

Cho said, "If Jones survives, we've got to get him off the Moon pronto."

"I agree," Poole replied. "We can't let a carrier of the Susquehanna Virus stay on the Moon even if the virus isn't particularly contagious. It's too lethal. Even a one in a million chance of infection is too great. But Eli—"

"Eli ain't here. I'm in charge of security on the Moon. I didn't want this damn virus up here in the first place. Keep me informed."

As Cho turned to leave, Poole concentrated on the monitors. Only the beeping of the systemic monitor and the quiet hum of the cooling unit disturbed the silence. Jones' white cell count continued to grow, faster than before.

"This isn't working," Hackett said.

"Give it time," Wellon said.

"He's dying."

"Patience."

Finally the white cell count began to level off. It was still dangerously high but at least it was no longer climbing. Poole realized she'd been holding her breath. She exhaled, breathed again, her chest tight, stomach knotted. Still she kept her eyes on the monitor, hoping the count would drop. No one in the room moved.

"There," Wellon said.

"What?" Poole said.

"The hemoglobin and platelet activity."

"What's that got to do with the white cell count?"

"It's an indicator."

Wellon was right. The white cell count dropped fractionally. "It's working," Poole said. She felt goosebumps and wrapped her arms around herself tightly.

"How did you know that would work?" Hackett asked.

Wellon said, "I didn't." Then she turned and walked out of the room, stepping into the decon chamber the nurses had set up on the other side of the door.

Poole caught up with her as she was removing her scrubs and said, "Thank you."

"He's not clear yet," Wellon replied.

"He'll survive," Poole said.

"He does that."

Chapter Eight

While Jay-Edgar surfed channels in Elias Leach's office, showing holo-projections of riots and demonstrations around the world, and the escalating conflict between China and India, Elias moved to the sofa, allowing Manyara Harris to tidy his desk. As usual, she'd turned the lights up, which mildly annoyed him; he preferred a slightly darkened room.

"You don't need to clean my office every day," he said as he sank into the cushions and watched her, sniffing the lilac-scented cleanser she used. She always smelled of lilacs. God, he wanted her.

As if she could read his mind, she said, "You're a dirty old man."

"Yes, I am. And you're a doctor. Why would you never let me help you get your license back?"

Manyara straightened. She glanced at Jay-Edgar before turning to glare at Elias. "I killed your wife."

Jay-Edgar continued surfing, as if he hadn't heard.

"A mercy killing at my request," Elias said, "and Jay-Edgar knows all my secrets."

"He know we're *lovers*?" Manyara said, emphasizing the last word as she tilted her head toward Jay-Edgar.

"Yes, he knows."

Manyara snorted as she shoved his papers aside and began polishing his desk. Elias preferred the printed page to computer screens, so every day she shuffled his papers around while cleaning up after him.

"You could retire, you know," he offered. "You could move in with me."

He closed his mouth, realizing his mistake, the pride she still possessed.

"You could retire too. I'm sure you squirreled away a few million over the years."

Elias held up his hands. "Sorry." He coughed. "I've got a big meeting with the President soon. Can you finish later?"

"You been taking your medicine?"

"Yes, dear."

"You look awful."

"Thanks," Elias said. "As always, you're a delight."

"And you're a horse's ass. Try not to get too riled up. Bad for a man as ancient as you."

"Will I see you later?"

Manyara smiled at him as she wheeled her cart to the door. Dimming the lights the way Elias liked them, she shuffled out without responding. Minx. Elias glanced at the holo-projections Jay-Edgar displayed: riots in France, Nigeria, Houston and Detroit; violence against Devereauxnians by Fundamentalist Christians, Jews and Muslims; government crackdowns in Chile, Greece and Ghana; civil wars in Thailand, Turkmenistan and Mali; and cross-border incursions into India by militant Chinese groups.

One holo-projection showed Elite Ops troopers monitoring protests in New York. They carried Las-rifles and particle beam cannons, sonic disruptors and stun grenades: giant robots wearing heavy armor. They had radar and proximity sensors, bomb and poison detectors, shields that kept them safe from virtually any attack. He shivered and looked away.

As Elias reflected on what he intended to say to the President, his mind drifted back to the conversation he'd had with Admiral Cho and Dr. Poole. How could Jeremiah be in such bad shape? He was supposed to be the future. Elias had never considered the possibility that Jeremiah might die. And now he was infected with the virus, delivered to the Moon without Elias' knowledge. What kind of morons send the virus to the Moon? And without telling me? Stay calm. Manyara's right.

A gurgling knot of fear twisted his stomach at the thought of losing Jeremiah. Even if Jeremiah hated him, Elias would always love Jeremiah like a son.

Now more than ever Elias knew he was right to insist on Lendra having Jeremiah's child—an insurance policy.

"Got something, sir," Jay-Edgar said.

Elias looked at the holo-projection. "What is it?"

"The last polar bear in the wild died today."

"You're worried about polar bears?"

Jay-Edgar said, "Eco-terrorists have declared war on industrialized countries."

"They're hardly a major concern of ours," Elias said. "They're not organized enough and they don't have access to sophisticated weapons."

"They're organized now, sir. And I think one of the groups is headed by Susquehanna Sally."

Elias pushed himself off the sofa and moved closer to Jay-Edgar. "What have you found?"

"A new message from the Earth Guardians. Using the same pattern of hijacked servers to deliver the threats she made when she took responsibility for creating the virus. A hundred-and-seventeen cutouts along eighty-three pathways emanating from fourteen different countries, none of them in the United States. It's too big a coincidence to be anything but Susquehanna Sally."

The hair on the back of Elias' neck stood on end. He said, "Let me see it."

An image appeared, two dimensional, of a middle-aged woman whose face had been softened and blurred into something unrecognizable. It looked like the same image Susquehanna Sally had used when she announced that she'd created the virus and delivered it to the Mayo Clinic years earlier. Elias had revisited that image many times. He knew it well. This was either the same person or someone who'd seen the original broadcast and was copying it to the letter. Over the years, the virus had adapted. Outbreaks had begun to occur in distant countries. And these new strains, while relatively isolated, were even more lethal than the original. The only saving grace to date was that the virus had not yet become easily transferable. But if it ever did . . .

She spoke in that old-fashioned, computer-simulated voice he remembered so well:

"To all the over-developed countries of the world—you still don't get it. The death of the last polar bear, combined with the extinction of the Siberian tiger and the giant panda in the wild, proves your total disregard for this planet's other species. Humans are not fit to steward our world. The Susquehanna Virus was engineered to be environmentally adaptable. It would survive only if the level of pollutants in our air and water continued to grow. And they have. Walt Devereaux was right when he said the virus will mutate. It's already begun. It can't be stopped. Soon the virus will wipe out every human on this planet."

The screen went dark. Elias shook his head. He'd read countless articles and analyses on the Susquehanna Virus; he'd talked to dozens of scientists about the possibility of the virus mutating; yet seeing Susquehanna Sally discussing it somehow brought the chill of it closer to the bone. He shrugged it off. There were more pressing matters to attend to. "Get Lendra," he said. "Our meeting with the President starts in two minutes."

A minute later Lendra walked into the room and took her seat at the conference table next to Elias. She sat erect, ignoring him, instead staring toward the cameras they'd be using for the holo-conference, hands clasped in front of her. Her face looked as rigid as the interface she wore on her temple. Although her eyes were red, she wasn't crying at the moment. Was she just being emotional as a result of the hormonal changes or did she harbor resentments over her coerced pregnancy? Or perhaps she feared for Jeremiah as much as Elias did. Did she care for him that much?

Elias nodded to Jay-Edgar, who activated the debuggers and scramblers before connecting to the White House. Within seconds President Angelica Hope appeared on the holo-projection. Blond and still beautiful at sixty-one, a former tennis star and movie actress, she was a master manipulator of men. On her right sat General Ralph Horowitz, Chairman of the Joint Chiefs. On her left sat Vice President Miguel Rodriguez, wearing a dark suit and a crucifix on his lapel, proclaiming his dedication to God. Next to Rodriquez, Willow Estrada, the Secretary of State, wore a shimmer cloth ensemble and short brown hair. Sitting beside her was her supposedly secret lover, Eugenia Epps, the National Security Advisor, with similarly shorn dark hair and a light pink pantsuit. Playing the wife today, Elias thought. Across the table, next to General Horowitz, sat Anton Raskov, the Secretary of Defense, and Dr. Chandrika Jaidev, Secretary of Health and Human Services, who wore her usual blue sari. Behind them multiple screens showed happenings in other parts of the world.

"Thanks for your promptness, Elias, Ms. Riley," President Hope said in her contralto, almost smoky, voice. "I think everyone knows everyone." She looked at Elias. "Did you see the transmission from Susquehanna Sally?"

Elias nodded. "We'll find a cure for the virus eventually."

The President turned to Dr. Jaidev and said, "How is progress on that front proceeding?"

"So far," Dr. Jaidev replied, "we haven't been able to come up with an effective vaccine. As for treatments, we've been able to minimize the symptoms and lessen the virus' severity in several test cases. But we've made the most progress on older strains of the virus. Unfortunately, it keeps mutating. Frankly, we may never get a handle on a cure."

"We've only seen six cases in the past month in Minnesota," Vice President Rodriquez said. "Isn't the virus becoming less of a threat?"

"Rochester is a ghost town," Dr. Jaidev said, "so there are few people subject to infection there. Meanwhile, new strains are spreading in Indonesia, China and southern Europe—slowly for now—but if these new variations become more contagious, the virus could decimate the global population."

"We have more immediate problems," Elias said.

"Terrorism," Epps, the National Security Advisor, said. "American targets continue to be favored above all others."

"By a substantial margin," Estrada said, her gaze fixed on Epps.

Elias nearly rolled his eyes. Why not just announce that you're sleeping with each other, he thought. At the same time, he was glad they were on his side. He was never sure how they were going to come down on an issue. All he knew was that each would support the other.

"We're still the world's leader," Epps said. "Our culture has pervaded every country."

Estrada said, "Hollywood and the adoration of celebrity. Consumerism. The desire to be like America, which is no longer possible due to the limited natural resources of the planet, makes for increased resentment."

Elias said, "I have a solution."

President Hope said, "Not your program again."

"I don't see any other way. Even foreign governments are beginning to take action against us. For example, after the Islamic Freedom Front took responsibility for bombing the Jefferson Memorial last week, we discovered that they received funding from a nonprofit with ties to Pakistan and Iran. Those governments officially condemned the bombing but they've been surreptitiously funneling money to that same nonprofit."

"Can we prove that?" President Hope asked.

"Not to the satisfaction of the UN."

General Horowitz said, "Every major government has created covert programs that allow them to achieve their ends without leaving fingerprints. War by proxy. It's how things are done these days."

"Exactly," Elias said, smacking his fist into his palm. "And each country is able to provide credible deniability to prevent retaliation. Look at the buildup of tension between China and India. They're each sending small terror cells against the other. If that conflict escalates further, we'll have a world war. Even assuming that doesn't happen, the world is as fragmented as it's ever been. We've reached a crisis point. We have to act now."

President Hope sighed. "You're talking about more death, more destruction. How many lives will it take?"

"Not that many," Elias said. "A few carefully calibrated strikes at a few strategic political targets. Ten or twenty thousand lives."

"It's an insane plan," Raskov said in his slight Russian accent. "You won't even tell us the details. All I know is that it will unite the world against us."

"It will never be traced to us," Elias said. "At worst, it will be traced to me. And by not providing you details, I give you plausible deniability."

Shaking her head, the President said, "Everyone knows you're connected to this administration."

"I admit there's a small risk," Elias said, "but I've been studying this for many years. My people have run probability after statistical probability. Everything points to the fact that only a single threat from the outside can unite us all. And the virus isn't the kind of threat that will work. Each country thinks it can deal with that issue on its own. Without an alien invasion threat, we'll never overcome our disunity and distrust. And there are no aliens. None that will reach Earth anyway. Any species would have to come many light years just to find us. That's not going to happen. So we have to create the threat ourselves."

"If you're wrong," General Horowitz said, "the results could be catastrophic."

Elias' heart began to race. "Only my cadets on the Moon can serve as our alien invaders. Only they can provide a sufficient level of threat to the world to unite its nations against them. They are a group without ideology, a group bent only on destruction. They can succeed in uniting the world."

Vice President Rodriguez said, "Excuse me. I haven't been in on all the meetings. How did you propose to do this?"

"By taking over the Moon and the satellite Las-cannons for starters."

General Horowitz shook his head.

"Those objectives can be achieved relatively easily," Elias said. "And they provide an off-planet threat that will serve to unite the Earth, especially by using the Las-cannons to attack select targets."

"The Las-cannons," Horowitz said, "were built to destroy incoming meteors and are under the control of the United Nations. The algorithmic codes change randomly. And the quantum cryptography is completely secure. There's no way to access them."

"I have a team of programmers who have already hacked into the system, leaving invisible backdoors behind. We can get in anytime we want."

"That's impossible," Raskov said.

Elias turned to Lendra. "Would you care to explain?"

Lendra nodded. "There are two team members besides myself—more talented with supercomputers than I am. It took us seven months to get in. We had to create a program that utilized progressive transcendentals to break the algorithmic codes. We started with a cascading transfinite . . . Never mind the details. At any rate, we can access the Las-cannons anytime we want."

"You're enhanced," Rodriguez said, "aren't you? Genetically engineered."

"My parents wanted the best for me."

"So these Moon monsters you've created," Epps said to Elias, "take over the Las-cannons. Then what? You start firing at targets on Earth?"

"Certain specific political targets," Elias answered.

"Including targets inside the United States," Estrada said. "You'd have to do that to divert suspicion."

Elias shrugged. "There would have to be some damage to this country."

"This is a necessary evil," Lendra said, joining the discussion. "We've projected terrible atrocities if we don't do this—maybe even the end of the human race."

Rodriguez said, "Even if you're right and this is the only thing that will save us, does that mean we should do it? Commit an atrocity to prevent future speculative atrocities?"

"Every nation on Earth with the capability would attack the Moon," Estrada said.

"Of course," Elias nodded. "That's the whole point. I want them to go after the cadets. Their common enemy will unite them."

"And what happens after the Earth blows up the Moon?" Raskov said.

"It won't be that simple," Elias said. "The Moon won't be easy to attack. The systems in place up there, the Las-cannons and radar, and the surplus of power the Moon generates make it extremely defensible. Also, they'd be able to see any attack coming. You couldn't just shoot a missile at it. They'd blow it out of the sky."

"But a hundred missiles," Raskov said, "or a thousand . . . some would get through."

"Probably," Elias conceded. "Especially if they had the proper scattering technology to help them avoid detection. My plan, however, wouldn't require that to happen."

"So we should just trust you?" Epps said.

"Yes."

"Madam President," Raskov said, "this is madness. What's to stop those countries from attacking us once the threat from the Moon is gone?"

Elias' hands shook. Stay calm, he told himself as he placed his hands flat on the table. "There's no other way. We're seeing on average forty-seven major terrorist attacks per day worldwide, up from thirty-one last year and eighteen the year before. If we do nothing we'll find ourselves in global chaos in less than a year."

Raskov smirked. "We've been hearing doomsday scenarios from you for years."

General Horowitz spoke almost under his breath: "Every year it gets worse."

"I admit it's taken longer than I thought for the world to reach this crisis point," Elias said, his voice barely under control, his chest tightening. "Lendra?"

"We didn't properly factor the complacency vectors," Lendra said. "The tendency to put off extreme action. Partly that was a misunderstanding of the declination of social interaction. We didn't anticipate the inertial coefficient as applied to the lowered empathic response variable—"

"Pardon the interruption," Vice President Rodriguez said, "but I'm not enhanced. Could you speak English?"

"I'm saying that the inherent nature of humans is to grouse and complain about a problem for a long time before taking action. We knew that, of course. However, we believed that the recent decline in empathic responses by people would compensate for that tendency and lead to a quicker flashpoint."

"But humans are essentially the same as they've always been," Elias said. He glanced at President Hope, feeling like he was maybe starting to get through to her. "The only way to change humans is to literally change them, turn them into a new species. That's what the Escala are all about. They've become something other than human. They see the ultimate end to the human race. Like Devereaux, they're visionaries. And they're generally peaceful—though, like wild animals, they become ferocious when attacked. Jeremiah Jones was supposed to be that way too." His throat began to close and he fought to continue speaking. "The transgenic surgery gave him phenomenal fighting abilities, but he always had the discretion not to use them unless absolutely necessary."

"Jones?" President Hope said. "Has something happened to him?"

"There was an accident on the Moon. Major trauma to his body." Elias reached up and wiped his eyes. "And now—at the worst possible time—he's had an immune system overload or something like that. In an attempt to save his life, they infected him with the Susquehanna Virus, which somehow got sent to the Moon." He stared at President Hope, who showed no sign of remorse. "Even if he survives, he'll probably never recover to the level he was at before."

President Hope looked at Lendra and said, "I'm sorry. I didn't know."

Lendra nodded as she fingered her glass bulb necklace.

A beep sounded through the holo-projection. The people at the table in the White House glanced past the cameras. Although Elias couldn't see what they were staring at, he knew from past experience it was a Terrorist Map. Fortunately Jay-Edgar had been monitoring Elias' own Terrorist Map during the meeting. He brought up a view of Buenos Aires, where a Marxist group had assassinated the Foreign Minister of Paraguay. Elias nodded to Jay-Edgar, who shut off the image.

The veins in Elias' neck throbbed. He felt a sharp pain behind his right eye. He said, "There's yet another example of why my program is necessary."

"Terrorism has always been with us," Dr. Jaidev said, "but it won't eliminate the entire species."

"Maybe the end times are finally here," Vice President Rodriguez said as he fingered his crucifix.

General Horowitz and President Hope stared at him. The other people gathered around the table went quiet.

Elias said, "Terrorism and rioting will continue. And the only way to stop the killing is by following through on this admittedly horrific course of action." Elias swallowed to get some moisture into his throat. "I'm willing to be reviled by history. But only this hard decision can save us from ourselves."

"You know Eli's right," Lendra said.

All eyes turned to President Hope, who said, "What about Devereaux? Has he reported any progress studying the virus?"

"Madam President," Elias said, wondering at her sudden change of subject.

Raskov said, "Devereaux told us he wouldn't help us."

"He told us he wouldn't give us his weapon designs," President Hope corrected. "Presumably, even though he's headed to Mars with the Escala, he doesn't want to see humanity perish. And that's a possibility if the virus continues to mutate. He's the brightest mind we have. His research led to the creation of the Escala. He should have been asked to study the virus years ago. Now that it's mutating, he might be the only one who can find a cure in time."

"Madam President," Elias said again, his voice trembling. "You can't just dismiss this out of hand."

"Let me think, Elias."

"And how could you send the virus to the Moon anyway?" Elias said. "That was the only secure environment left—the only place we knew the virus hadn't spread to."

"It was a tiny sample," Dr. Jaidev said, "hermetically sealed. I'm sure the virus can be controlled."

Elias shook his head. The throbbing behind his eyes felt strong enough to rupture an aneurysm. "You think *my* ideas are crazy. What you did is far more dangerous. You know how many people have said that in the past and then died after a disease or weapon got free? You of all people, Doctor, should appreciate just how dangerous it is to fool around with the Susquehanna Virus."

"Your plan is just as risky," Raskov said. "You've got a dangerous weapon in these Moon monsters. What if they were to break free?"

"They can't," Elias said, struggling to see through the pounding pain in his forehead, "as long as Admiral Cho and Dr. Poole maintain the psychometric controls that guarantee loyalty and obedience, they can't run amok."

"We heard similar assurances about the Elite Ops program from Richard Carlton," General Horowitz said.

Elias' fury choked him. How dare they compare him with that maniac. With his peripheral vision he noticed Lendra shaking her head, mouthing the word "no." but he couldn't stop. "You think you know better than me? You think I'm an idiot?"

"Elias!" General Horowitz said.

Elias realized he was shaking his fist. His right eyelid ticked uncontrollably. He closed his eyes and rubbed the lids with his fingers. "I'm sorry, Madam President. But you should have consulted me. The ramifications if the virus should escape . . ."

"We know how to contain a simple virus," Dr. Jaidev said. "Our sterilization and quarantine techniques, when properly observed, have been successful over ninety-nine percent of the time."

"I value your opinions, Elias," President Hope said, "but I've decided not to go ahead with your plan. I agree with Miguel," she waved toward her Vice President. "Even if this proves to be the only way to save our species, I cannot condone the murder of thousands. It's simply not an acceptable option." She nodded to someone off camera and the connection severed.

The pain behind Elias' eyes reached a new level of agony. He shouted, "Fools! Imbeciles! Morons! Nothing but talk. The only time they take action is when they decide to do the exact wrong thing. I should free the children anyway. Set them loose on the world. They can't make it any worse than it is. I can't believe those idiots would do something so stupid as to send the virus to the Moon."

He felt a grabbing sensation in his chest and it suddenly became difficult to breathe. A pain shot from his groin to his head and back down—something that registered as excruciating and at the same time apart from his physical self. He turned to Lendra. She said, "Eli? Are you okay? Eli?"

He tried to answer. No words came out.

Chapter Nine

Sitting with his tong, tuning out Poole's rambles about the rules, Curtik looked across the training floor at the three Motionators—large simulator globes that allowed their occupants full movement in any direction. The feelers reaching inward from the globes' skeletal circumferences allowed greater tactility to be brought into the virtual reality experience than the old simulators. Zora and her tong had just completed their exercise in the Motionators and the annoying bitch had received a perfect score.

Next to the Motionators Jack Marschenko stood with three other Elite Ops troopers, all of them wearing only T-shirts and mock-gravity pants, showing off their heavily muscled torsos. They wore Las-pistols in holsters at their hips, like cowboys. Mouthy Man kept his eyes on Curtik while he talked with his comrades.

Curtik knew Mouthy Man was sticking it to Poole every night. Not that Curtik wanted to plow her. He didn't want to plow anybody, which was odd. He pushed that thought aside, concentrated on Mouthy Man. Throughout his whole life, for his entire ten years, Curtik couldn't remember hating anyone as much as he hated Mouthy Man, except maybe his father, the great Jeremiah Jones.

Why did Poole and Cho sound awed when they talked about him? He was an old man. And it was Jones' fault Curtik's mother killed herself. Curtik had found her obituary last year while running his usual covert search on his parents' names. He remembered feeling a strange hollowness at the news. Now his father had gotten himself all busted up falling down a crater. How stupid was that? Up until recently Curtik had respected Poole and Cho. Along with Elias they'd given him his new life, his new power, accelerated his growth and intellectual prowess, made him into a man. But if they respected Jones, how could he still respect them?

He hungered for his first real kill. Maybe it should be Jones.

Of course, Jones might not live long enough for Curtik to get the chance. In the meantime Curtik just might have to rid himself of Mouthy Man.

"Are you paying attention?" Poole asked.

"Of course," Curtik replied as he turned to Poole. Even though she was old, she was pretty. For an instant Curtik thought about plowing her. But that thought quickly faded. He couldn't keep his mind on sex. And his body, so far, hadn't been able to respond the way the vids showed it should. None of his friends had been able to maintain an erection either. Why not?

"What did I just say?"

"Something important." Curtik laughed. Addam and Benn joined in.

"She's always saying something important," Benn said.

"Probably something about the sudden insight of battle," Curtik added, throwing in one of her favorite phrases.

"I'm telling you about this test," Poole said. "Zora's tong has overtaken yours. And her tactical analyses have been steadily improving. Yours have not. Do you want her to be in overall command?"

"We all know I'm going to win, Piscine," Curtik said. The French for pool was *piscine*. As an added bonus it sounded like pissing. He put out his fists and did the Tong Tap with Addam and Benn, a complicated series of bumps and slaps.

As usual, Poole ignored the nickname. "Zora's tong was very impressive. If you don't concentrate on the task at hand, you'll find yourself running the secondary assault."

"Never gonna happen, Piscine. Bring it on. Is Mouthy Man observing?"

"He's refereeing."

"No fair!" Curtik jumped to his feet, the mock-gravity suit keeping him from flying into the air. "He hates me."

"Why do you think that is, Curtik?"

"Cuz he's a buttweed."

Addam and Benn laughed.

Poole leaned forward and said, "You don't think it has anything to do with the fact that you've harassed him almost constantly since you met."

"Don't care."

"Look, Curtik, I know you're attracted to me but you're not ready for sex. And I'm much too old for you. Plus, I like Jack. So put aside your feelings and worry about the test."

"He's gonna favor Zora, just like you."

"We always judge the sims fairly. Just do the best job you can on the test so he can't deduct any points. Okay?"

Curtik looked over at Mouthy Man. The bastard had a smile on his ugly pig-head. It needed a fist smashed into it. And if the son of a bitch gave Zora a higher score, Curtik would kill him.

"Okay, Piscine. Let's do it."

"You know the objective. Plant all three bombs in the target areas. Bonus points for getting in and out undetected. Bonus points for getting your people out safely. Bonus points for time. Standard deductions apply. Move to the Motionators and put your simulator helmets on."

Curtik checked the Las-pistol and Las-knife handed to him by Mouthy Man, noted the minimum settings, holstered the pistol and sheathed the knife. He stepped onto the center Motionator, knowing that at some point a number of feelers would retract, so an Elite Ops trooper could get at him. He wished he could fight Mouthy Man for real instead of in some lame simulation.

Putting on his helmet, Curtik adjusted the holoprogram's specs. Beside him, Benn and Addam appeared, looking like fat teenagers, and he couldn't help but laugh. They laughed back. When he glanced down, he noted his distended stomach. He reached up and touched his puffy cheeks. The three of them stood on a street corner in Tokyo, people moving all around them, avoiding them: actually avoiding the camera crew that had shot the vid. He smelled fish and the sea and the odors of a thousand cooked meals, and his stomach flipped a little.

Curtik touched the bomb hidden beneath his paunch. The bomb wasn't real of course, though it felt real enough. Yet virtual reality always disoriented him a little. The visual and aural signals bothered him far less than the tactile and olfactory ones.

After a few seconds the targets popped up on his helmet. Addam and Benn would be seeing the same ones: the Hie Shrine, the Ginza Shopping Center and the Tokyo Tower. Simple.

Curtik quickly went through the details of the plan, giving Addam the shrine and Benn the tower, keeping the Ginza Shopping Center for himself. It would be the most difficult target from which to escape undetected, though it still presented no challenge. When he gave the order to go, Benn and Addam melted away in the crowd. Curtik could keep in contact with them through the implant behind his left ear, which transmitted signals to his visual cortex whenever he consciously thought to display them. He tested the system briefly, gave Addam and Benn a raspberry and laughed when they both made farting sounds in return.

As he walked, Curtik noted again how his sense of time was skewed, as if he were in a dream. Poole had explained that none of the other cadets experienced the sort of time slippage he did. She attributed it to some facet of his genetic makeup, blaming it on his remembrance of his past. At any rate, following the map to the Ginza center, he lost several chunks of time. A few passers-by jostled him: contacts from the feelers. Was Mouthy Man running the Motionator?

Before entering the complex, Curtik waited outside, watching for anything that looked out of place, any wrong movement. He sensed someone staring at him and caught the eye of a security guard at the door. That had to be one of the observers. He maintained a calm demeanor as he passed, engaging the odor-masking fragrance that would defeat the bomb sniffers. It smelled like the sweat of a fat man, sweet and rancid at the same time.

"Halt," the guard said in Japanese—instantly translated into English by Curtik's universal translator—putting out his hand to reinforce the command.

Curtik stopped, turned to face the guard. "Yes?" he said in English. "Is there a problem?"

"Step over here, please," the guard switched to accented English as he directed Curtik toward an alcove inside the center.

It had to be Mouthy Man pulling this crap. And even though it wasn't real, Curtik felt annoyed. He was going to have time deductions and if the stupid guard tried to search him, he was going to have to kill the fool.

"What's going on?" Curtik asked.

"Just come with me, sir," the guard said.

Curtik followed the guard into the alcove, behind a folding screen, where another guard stood next to a scanner.

"Screw it," Curtik said as he pulled the Las-pistol from its hidden holster and fired two quick shots. At the low setting, the observers would only feel a minor sting. As the guards fell, an alarm sounded throughout the shopping center, ordering people to evacuate in Japanese and English.

Curtik swore as he re-holstered the Las-pistol, opened his false stomach and removed the bomb. He armed it, covered it with the two bodies, then slipped out the doors with panicking shoppers and strode away, taking the alternative route provided by the helmet's map. He soon reached the rendezvous point. Addam and Benn hadn't yet arrived.

He was standing by a statue when the explosion hit: a mammoth blast. The Motionator hammered him, nearly knocking him off his feet. He received electrical impulses in his inner ears, affecting his balance and making him slightly nauseated. He smelled charred plastic and metal, and possibly human flesh.

People ran past in all directions, some screaming, many staring at him. He took a casual defensive stance, not knowing which might be hostile. He wished he were actually there, so he could taste the deaths, experience the thrill. Simulated kills brought little pleasure. He forced himself to stay focused on the mission, wishing he could check his implant for Addam and Benn's whereabouts, but the implants didn't work that way during virtual reality sessions.

Turning his head left and right, he finally spotted the fat Benn sauntering along the sidewalk less than a block away, trying to look casual amid the chaos. Or maybe his helmet was showing that everything was okay. No, his eyes were huge. He was just trying to look cool. He stopped next to Curtik and nodded.

"Any problems?" Curtik asked.

Benn shook his head. "No security there to speak of. It should blow any second. Couldn't have been easier. What happened to you?"

"Later," Curtik said. "Where's Addam?"

"Haven't seen him."

Curtik accessed the implant again and sent a message to Addam to hurry.

Security forces began to close in from different directions. Some were Elite Ops troopers wearing heavy armor, shields set to maximum, their helmeted heads swinging back and forth as they scanned the crowd. Curtik pulled Benn off the sidewalk, into the park they'd chosen for their exit. Where the hell was Addam? Curtik couldn't afford to leave him behind.

They reached a crowd of people just as the second explosion hit— farther away. More screams filled the air. Curtik looked back. Two Elite Ops troopers were closing in. He grabbed Benn, ducked behind some shrubs, and they took off running. They didn't look out of place among the dozens of other citizens who were running and screaming, but the Elite Ops troopers continued to follow them.

When they reached the edge of the park, Curtik experienced a flash of an idea, what Poole called the sudden insight of battle. Through his implant he told Benn to keep running. He stopped and unsheathed his Las-pistol and Las-knife. He activated the Las-knife and rammed the blue blade inside the barrel of the Las-pistol, holding the grip of the Las-pistol. Within seconds, he detected the stench of the troopers' nerve gas. His nose wrinkled in disgust; fear flooded through him. This was the first time the observers had used the full dosage of neurotoxins. Instinctively Curtik shrank back. But when a trooper's hand grabbed his wrist, he turned and fired the Las-pistol at the trooper's face. Despite the minimum settings, the resulting overload caused a small explosion.

The Elite Ops trooper cried out and let go. But Curtik's hand went numb and his ears rang. God, he hoped his opponent was Mouthy Man. As the trooper fell to the ground, Curtik kicked his helmet. He stomped on the trooper's hand, breaking his fingers with a satisfying crunch and making the trooper grunt.

At that moment the buzzer sounded, ending the simulation, and the view vanished, the streets of Tokyo gone. They were back on the training floor. Curtik looked down at the trooper before him—damn! Not Mouthy Man—who cradled his injured hand, got to his feet and glared at Curtik as he walked away.

Removing his helmet, Curtik signaled to Benn and Addam to do the same as Poole and Mouthy Man approached. Curtik bared his teeth in a half-smile, half-sneer until Poole grabbed his arm.

"What happened?" Poole said.

"He panicked," Mouthy Man said.

"You cheated," Curtik said. "There's no way that guard should've stopped me."

"It was a random search. Haven't you ever heard of such a thing?"

"You deliberately sabotaged me."

"Of course," Mouthy Man admitted. "That was the whole point of the exercise, to see how you would react."

"We still blew the targets," Curtik said. "Right?" He turned to Addam, who nodded. "So," he continued, "full points, right?"

Mouthy Man shook his head. "Full points for your teammates but you incur a five-point deduction."

"No way," Curtik said. "I'm the best. Everybody knows it."

"It's not just about destruction," Poole said. "It's about keeping a cool head. Avoiding unnecessary losses. Knowing when to forgo a target to wait for a better chance at it. You left Addam behind. And you would not have escaped the park."

"It's his fault." Curtik pointed at Mouthy Man. "I didn't do anything wrong."

"I'm sorry," Poole said. "Zora is now in first place. As of this moment she becomes the new brigade leader."

"No!" Curtik shivered. Everything looked red. He stepped from the Motionator and gestured for Mouthy Man to attack him. All he could think to do was kill. "Come on, Mouthy Man."

"Curtik!" Poole stepped in front of him as a group of watching cadets formed a rough circle. They began chanting: "Curtik, Curtik, Curtik."

The other two Elite Ops troopers began to move the cadets back.

Curtik said, "Stay out of this, Piscine."

"Stand down, Curtik."

Curtik wanted to obey. Years of conditioning told him to back away. But the hatred inside his chest overpowered his will. In his mind, Mouthy Man's face was turning to mush under his furious assault. A warmth grew in the pit of his stomach.

"It's okay, Doc," Mouthy Man said, grabbing Poole's arm and stepping forward. "This punk kid needs to be taught a lesson."

"You don't understand," Poole said. "He's dangerous."

"So am I, Doc."

"I will not have this fighting. If you won't listen to reason, I'll call Admiral Cho for reinforcements."

"Maybe you should run away," Curtik taunted, knowing Mouthy Man's adrenaline would be flowing—his fight-or-flight response engaging—giving Curtik the edge, for he'd been engineered only to fight, never to flee.

In answer Mouthy Man pulled off his T-shirt and tossed it aside, displaying his muscular chest. Curtik laughed as Mouthy Man handed his Las-pistol to one of the Elite Ops troopers. The cadets crowded in closer, the ring around Curtik and Mouthy Man shrinking, as the Elite Ops troopers struggled to push them back.

"I mean it," Poole said. "Stop this now or there will be serious consequences. Fully armored Elite Ops troopers are on their way."

The cadets continued chanting Curtik's name. He shoved the noise aside and went completely still for a second, focusing his mind. He began to move to the side, keeping his pose relaxed. He chose not to attack right away, instead studying his opponent. Mouthy Man held back too, doing the same. They circled—a feint here, a quick punch parried there—testing each other's capabilities. As they did so, Curtik held back a little. He always held back a little, not wanting anyone to know just how fast he was.

When Mouthy Man finally attacked, Curtik anticipated his movements correctly. No deception by the big trooper; instead, he came straight on. Slipping to the side, Curtik threw a jab that broke Mouthy Man's nose even as Mouthy Man's punch landed solidly on his left shoulder. Curtik's left arm went numb. But blood streamed from Mouthy Man's nose. He wiped his hand across his mouth and came at Curtik again, attempting to close the distance so he could use his greater strength and nullify Curtik's speed. But what he failed to grasp, what everyone failed to grasp, was just how fast Curtik was.

As Mouthy Man closed, Curtik threw a vicious jab, hoping to crush Mouthy Man's windpipe. But his injured shoulder hindered him and Mouthy Man absorbed the blow to his chest, at the same time hitting Curtik on the side of the head. Flashes of light cluttered his vision. Son of a bitch! Was Mouthy Man that fast, that tough?

Curtik let Mouthy Man close again. He shook his shoulder, trying to get the feeling back. Mouthy Man hit him in the stomach just as Curtik punched his jaw, almost breaking his hand. Damn! The trooper's blow knocked Curtik off his feet, the pain agonizing. God, the beast was strong.

Curtik got to his feet and vomited. His left shoulder felt like it had been struck with a hammer, and his right hand throbbed. Trying to ignore the pain, Curtik slid to the side, avoiding the slick contents of his stomach, and waited for Mouthy Man again.

"That's enough," Poole said.

"No." Curtik and Mouthy Man spoke at the same time.

"Curtik, Curtik, Curtik," the cadets continued chanting as they hopped around while the two unarmored Elite Ops troopers held their Las-pistols up in warning.

"You can patch him up when we finish," Mouthy Man said.

"You can bury him when I finish," Curtik said.

No holding back now, Curtik thought as Mouthy Man closed for a third time. When the trooper entered fighting range, Curtik pushed off with his legs, putting everything he had into a blow that caught his enemy underneath the jaw line. Mouthy Man tried to block it, but he moved with the speed of a sloth. His eyes rolled back in his head. As he fell, Curtik followed up with another shot to Mouthy Man's nose, putting everything he had behind the blow, driving Mouthy Man's broken nose into his brain. Curtik hit him in the throat again with a long fist, his fingers folded in tightly to form a sharper edge. The blow crushed Mouthy Man's windpipe. He drove Mouthy Man to the floor, hitting him half a dozen times, his fists driving the trooper's smashed nose ever further into his brain.

"Jack!" Poole screamed as the light went out of Mouthy Man's eyes, the smell of blood and urine combining to form a rich bouquet. Curtik paused, inhaling deeply as his body shuddered with delight.

Four armored Elite Ops troopers strode into the room and fired blue laser pulses into the crowd. One of them grabbed Curtik hard, yanking him off Mouthy Man's corpse, his Las-pistol jammed against Curtik's temple. Curtik held up his bloody hands in surrender. "What?" he said. "It was a fair fight."

"Bastard!" Poole screamed as she dropped to her knees beside Mouthy Man. She searched for a pulse. "What have you done, you little monster? Oh, Jack," Poole sobbed.

"Shouldn't we get him to the infirmary?" Zora asked as she and Rendela stepped forward with a stretcher.

"Yes, immediately," Poole replied. "Thank you."

Benn stared at Curtik and said, "Cool."

"Good speed," Addam said.

Two troopers placed Mouthy Man on the stretcher and carried him away as the one guarding Curtik handcuffed him.

"I didn't do anything wrong," Curtik said. With the glow of the kill fading, Curtik twisted his neck to look up at the trooper's mirrored helmet.

Curtik looked at his fellow cadets. "What did I do?" he asked.

Some of them shrugged. Others simply stared at him. A few nodded encouragement. Curtik turned to Poole. "Piscine, what the hell? I didn't do anything wrong."

"You murdered him," Poole said. "How could you . . . I can't stand to look at you. Take him to the holding cell."

"Why am I being punished?" Curtik turned to Benn and Addam, watching him with their mouths open. "What did I do?"

Chapter Ten

Jeremiah lay in his hospital bed trying to remain still. Every movement brought the agony of a thousand bee stings. Dr. Hackett and Nurse Manuella—both wearing masks for some reason—had given him anesthetics that had been useless against the pain, and Dr. Hackett had deferred all his questions to Dr. Poole, who wouldn't arrive until morning. So Jeremiah listened to the humming of the machines around him and fought to control the rage inside.

When Dr. Poole finally arrived with Admiral Cho, they wore masks as well. Dr. Poole's eyes were red, as if she'd been crying, while Admiral Cho glared out from under a furrowed brow.

"I'm sorry," Dr. Poole said, her voice sounding strained. "But your immune system went into a kind of hyperactive state. You suffered massive trauma to your kidneys, spleen, liver, pancreas, heart and even your brain. Dr. Wellon figured out how to divert your white blood cells from attacking your body. You'll likely experience a great deal of pain, but you will survive."

Jeremiah shook his head. "I can't believe I was so careless—totally forgot about the Moon's lower gravity."

"We've quarantined you," Dr. Poole said.

"Why? Broken bones aren't contagious."

"Didn't Dr. Hackett tell you?"

"Tell me what?"

Dr. Poole exchanged a look with Cho. "We had to infect you with the Susquehanna Virus."

Jeremiah opened his mouth to respond but couldn't think of anything to say. As Dr. Poole explained why they'd deemed it necessary to infect him, his mind drifted in disbelief. How the hell could he be infected?

"Since the virus hides in the immune system," Dr. Poole concluded, "we can't be certain you've completely vanquished it. You may be a carrier."

Jeremiah focused on Dr. Poole's eyes, which began to well up. He doubted her distress related to his condition. When she turned her face away from him, he said, "There's something else wrong. What is it? Is it Joshua?"

"Damon is fine," Dr. Poole said. She turned back to Jeremiah. "It's Jack Marschenko. He's dead."

"Jack?" Jeremiah's face flushed as his heart began to pound. A shiver worked its way down his body, but when he tried to sit up, the pain nearly caused him to black out. He lay back down, a hollow numbness working its way through him. "How?"

"On the training floor," Dr. Poole said. "He . . ." she closed her eyes, dropped her head.

Cho continued: "One of the kids attacked him."

"Who?" Jeremiah asked. He felt a desperate urge to lash out and for a second he forgot the pain. "Did you order this?"

"Me?" Cho shook his head. "Why would I want Jack dead?"

"You figured out he was my friend."

Cho's eyes widened. "The man who kidnapped your boy?"

"We made our peace over that." Jeremiah clamped his jaw tight, fought to keep his expression neutral. "He was a good man. Honorable. The Elite Ops corrupted him." Jeremiah rubbed his eyes with his fingers. "But he'd put that behind him. Who killed him?"

"A boy named Curtik," Dr. Poole said.

"Doctor," Cho warned.

Dr. Poole lifted her hand to ward off his objections.

"How did it happen?" Jeremiah asked.

Cho shook his head. "You're askin' for trouble," he said to Dr. Poole.

"The hell with the plan," Dr. Poole said. "The kids aren't ready. They might never be. The world's falling apart. And we're still stuck up here on this rock. We're not going to be heading home anytime soon. Did you know that?"

"What are you talkin' about?" said Cho.

"We have to be here for the plan to work," Dr. Poole said. "Without us, there's no way to control the children, so we're not going anywhere."

"Who told you that?"

Dr. Poole faced Cho, shoulders back in defiance, fists clenched at her sides. "The psychometric controls embedded in the children only guarantee their loyalty to a few people. And we're the only two on the Moon. So we're stuck up here."

"That doesn't bother me," Cho said.

"Well, it bothers me." Dr. Poole took a seat next to Jeremiah's bed. She said, "Jack and Curtik had words a few times. I knew Curtik wanted to kill him, but he wants to kill everyone. That's what we trained him for—what I trained him for." Dr. Poole put her head in her hands. Her shoulders shook for a while as she sobbed quietly.

Jeremiah glanced at Cho, who shifted his feet and avoided eye contact.

It took a few moments for Dr. Poole to collect herself. She said, "After Jack finished testing Curtik's team and deducted points from him, Curtik attacked him. I never saw anyone move that fast. His hands were a blur. Jack couldn't defend himself. No one could have. All the training sessions Curtik's been through, all the tests—he never showed that kind of speed. I don't know if he's that much better than the other kids or if they're all holding back. Either way, he's too dangerous. We had to lock him up."

Tears ran down the side of Dr. Poole's nose onto her mask. "I never expected to fall for him."

Jeremiah, despite his anger at what she'd done to his son, decided to be kind. He said, "I think he found happiness with you."

Poole again began to cry, heaving sobs that convulsed her whole body. She struggled to her feet and staggered out of the room.

For a moment Cho and Jeremiah looked at each other. Jeremiah said, "Can I see him?"

Cho said, "I'm afraid we've already rendered the body, processed it to recover its moisture for the settlement."

"You freeze-dried him?"

"Did you ever read an old book by a guy named Frank Herbert about a desert planet? The people in that book recovered the water of their dead. We realized early on that we could do the same thing here to augment our water supplies. It's part of the standard release everyone signs before coming to the Moon. You signed one too."

He must have seen something in Jeremiah's face, for he added: "It's a respectful process and we reserve a sample of various tissues—heart, brain, bone marrow—for future generations to study, should they so choose. We'll place his remains in the graveyard. You probably saw it when you were outside."

Jeremiah recalled the colorful capsules.

Cho shifted his gaze to the wall over Jeremiah's bed. "By the way, I made a few calls, talked to your friend, Elias Leach. President Hope. General Horowitz, Chairman of the Joint Chiefs. And the decision was made to let you take your son home with you—once you're healed up, that is." Cho looked Jeremiah in the eye. "Of course, the two of you will have to be quarantined for a long time."

Jeremiah felt a sudden relief. At the same time, the restraint in Cho's voice indicated the Admiral was hiding something. Jeremiah wished he could see behind Cho's mask. It was difficult to tell exactly what he was thinking. He said, "Why?"

"I thought you'd be happy to hear the news."

"It's too easy."

Cho shrugged. "There's no pleasing you, Mr. Jones. You're not happy when we say we're keeping him. Now you're upset that we're releasing him into your custody. What is it exactly that you want?"

Jeremiah shook his head, wincing at the movement. "I just don't understand. Why all this effort to stop me and suddenly change your minds?"

"You've got the virus. We want you gone." Cho turned to leave, then stopped and spun around. "Two more things. One, the Verlorens wanted to thank you. I told them they'd have to wait until we lift the quarantine, if we ever do."

"The Verlorens?"

"The little girl you saved. Kyler Verloren and her parents."

"Is she okay?"

"She's fine. She's sending you a vid-message. And the second thing is that Walt Devereaux will be stopping by to examine your blood, ask you a few questions. Maybe he can figure out exactly how the virus is transmitted. That would go a long way to lifting the quarantine. We know it can be passed by the usual means—bodily fluids, a touch on broken skin, even a few cases of sneezing. But there have been a few instances where the virus seems to have been passed by simple airborne transmission, lodging in the upper lining of the lungs. If Devereaux finds that to be true, or if he can't find an answer, the quarantine must remain in place."

"What about my son?"

"Do you really want us to bring him to you when you're potentially contagious and in such a weakened state? Not to mention that he'd probably just attack you anyway."

"I guess not," Jeremiah said. "Thanks for your efforts on my behalf."

After Cho left, Jeremiah thought back to the night he and Jack—both of them drunk, Jack shattered by grief—had stopped at Franklin Park to sober up, lying back on the grass, looking up at the Moon and talking, never realizing they would soon be traveling there. As Jack fought to recover his composure, Jeremiah realized that Marschenko, his one-time enemy, had become his best friend.

Catherine, Julianna and now Jack Marschenko: why did everyone he loved die?

No, not everyone: Joshua was still alive. Even if Joshie was dying he wasn't dead yet. Together they'd figure out a way to beat whatever was killing him.

* * *

During the night, Jeremiah retreated to his dungeon, holding back the agony by focusing on the flickering torchlight bouncing off the stone walls. The imitation sunrise—reds, pinks and yellows—brought him out of his hypnotic state. Kitchen sounds carried into his room: pans and plates and the chatting of the mess staff as they prepared the day's breakfast. The smell of baking bread made Jeremiah's stomach growl. Nurse Manuella, a dark, petite woman with wide brown eyes and a sunny disposition, appeared with several new anesthetics for him, but they helped little. After a breakfast of protein-enriched oatmeal, toast and fruit, he played the vid-message from Kyler.

"Hello, Mr. Jeremiah," she said from the screen, her blond hair pulled back behind her head, her brown eyes glistening with moisture, her upper lip and nose quivering with sorrow that broke his heart. "I'm sorry I got you hurt out at the crater. I didn't mean for anything bad to happen. I just wanted to be your friend because you looked sad. Mother says if I would be more careful these things wouldn't happen and Daddy says I need to act more like a lady, which I will. Please don't be mad at me. I don't know what happened. The ground just . . ." A tear trickled down her cheek. She closed her eyes as her shoulders bobbed up and down. After a few seconds she wiped her eyes and managed to speak again in a halting, squeaky voice: "I'm sorry . . . please . . . get well . . . soon."

The screen shifted to blue. Jeremiah shook with anger at the unnecessary pain she was enduring. He sent an immediate reply, telling her it wasn't her fault and that he wished to see her once his quarantine was lifted. Then he began to work his legs, alternately lifting and flexing each one, straining himself to the point of nausea before moving to the next one. He'd show her he was fine no matter how much it hurt.

As he worked his legs, an older man entered the room, mask firmly in place over the lower half of his face. Jeremiah recognized him immediately as Walt Devereaux. Tall and lean, the scientist had graying hair and crows' feet around his brown eyes that deepened as he smiled behind his mask. Jeremiah felt better just seeing him.

"It's good to see you too, Jeremiah," Devereaux said. He placed a small statue of Emerging Man on the table above Jeremiah's bed.

"Quark asked me to give you this. It's a copy of the one you brought up for the Escala. He thought you might take some comfort from it."

Jeremiah smiled. "Thank him for me."

"I'd ask you how you've been but I already know the answer. Terrific, right?"

Jeremiah laughed for a second, stopping when a piercing jolt struck his broken ribs. "Don't. Laughing hurts."

"Humor's good for you. You should laugh a dozen times a day. How have you been?"

"I'm okay."

"Of course you are. Your friend, Jack Marschenko, is dead. Why shouldn't you be fine?"

"They told you about that?"

"Yes."

"I don't want to talk about it."

Devereaux nodded. "Okay. Do you feel any tingling in your fingers or toes?" Jeremiah shook his head. "How about flashers or floaters in front of your eyes?"

Jeremiah nodded. "Small dark spots that move wherever I shift my gaze."

"Good." Devereaux glanced up at the monitors. "And I see you still have a great deal of pain, particularly when you try to move."

"Is that good too?"

Devereaux laughed. "The pain lets you know you're alive. And it tells me your body is healing itself. For some reason, the standard pain medications don't work on you." Devereaux winked. "That's interesting, though perhaps you're less enthused about that aspect than I am."

Jeremiah smiled. "A safe assumption."

"Well, let's take a look at your blood." Devereaux took a quick sample, stepped over to the powerscope and bent over the eyepiece.

Jeremiah said, "Why are you still here on the Moon?"

Devereaux stayed bent over the powerscope. He began to hum faintly, an unrecognizable melody. After perhaps a minute he said, "Politics is an almost unstoppable force. And it's long been the fashion to promise whatever is expedient or popular, even where there's no intention to fulfill the promise or at least no intent to do so expeditiously."

"You mean they don't intend to let you go to Mars?"

"They'll let us go sometime. Earth doesn't want us back and the Moon is too uncomfortably close. Eventually they'll have to release us. As for you," Devereaux straightened, turned to look at Jeremiah, "you're definitely a carrier of the virus, though it's extremely well hidden within your white cells. In fact, though I've not seen a blood sample from before you were infected, judging from my brief study of your genetic makeup, I believe you've experienced an episode of epigenesis."

Jeremiah grunted with pain as he forced himself to a sitting position. "Epigenesis?"

"Your genetic makeup has changed due to environmental factors. Your Escala nature is quite dynamic. In fact, it adapts itself all the time, adjusting to the conditions around it. The same holds true for the Mars-bound Escala. The condition is not static. However, there are differences between you. The Escala were designed for a specific purpose—to survive on Mars. You, on the other hand, have been altered as an Earth-bound creature. The changes they're undergoing are much slower, more targeted to the Martian environment. Even though they'll die if they don't get to Mars, the relatively sedate pace of their evolution means it will take some time."

Devereaux moved to the chair next to the bed and took a seat.

"For you the changes occur more quickly. As a result, they're more dangerous. Because of the speed at which your body adapts, any one mutation could be harmful. And right now your body is fragile. It's holding the virus at bay. But the virus might recur, especially if you're weakened by some other illness or injury. It could also reassert itself should your immune system mutate further. Unfortunately, with this kind of forced evolution, there are no guarantees."

"Why did you create us?"

Devereaux shook his head. "I suppose it could be said that I created you, since my research made your evolution possible, though

I only intended to create the Escala. When I look at those kids, those monsters Poole and Cho created, I wonder if I did the right thing. Those cadets frighten me. Too late now—Pandora's box is open. And I still believe that forced evolution is the only hope for humanity's long-term survivability. We can't rely on luck to see us through the aggression that's been hard-wired into us. We can't put all our eggs in one basket. Unless we change our essential nature, we are doomed to repeat our mistakes—killing ourselves and our planet."

Jeremiah said. "A rosy outlook."

Devereaux's eyes wrinkled again. "It's not all doom and gloom. I'd love to be wrong. I've been wrong before. But I don't think I am."

"And what's going on between Poole and Cho?" Jeremiah asked. "Pretty tense."

Devereaux shrugged. "That's a relationship I haven't figured out yet. Possibly a soured romance. Certainly different priorities. I only know that whatever they're doing, the end result will be bad. Those kids they've trained—they're trouble. But I'd rather talk about you."

"What do you want to know?"

Devereaux stared patiently at Jeremiah. He sat still, his eyes never leaving Jeremiah's. Through the wall behind the bed, Jeremiah heard dishes stacking in the kitchen. He began to feel the weight of Devereaux's gaze. He glanced at the statue of Emerging Man and said, "You want to talk about Jack Marschenko."

Devereaux raised an eyebrow. "What was he like?"

Jeremiah spent a few moments collecting his thoughts. "He was a man of enormous integrity," Jeremiah said. "But more than that, he was a hell of a lot of fun. Since we knew each other's secrets, we didn't have to watch what we said. He liked this fruity drink called a rainbow flower. Had a hell of a kick. He drank half a dozen one night and took me to this karaoke place. A little hole in the wall. And he sang old Sinatra songs for an hour. Wouldn't let anybody else come up on stage. I finally had to wrestle him off.

"He had a girlfriend back on Earth, a woman named Lily from his old neighborhood. Not long after we met he asked her to marry him.

She turned him down. I don't know if he ever got over that. Anyway, after I yanked him off-stage that night—this must have been about two months after she'd refused his proposal—he decided that we had to go look Lily up. We went to the club where she worked. The manager told us that Lily had killed herself the week before. I thought he might try to tear the place down. But he just went completely quiet. I put him in my car and drove to Franklin Park, where he sat on the grass and cried like a baby—his whole world destroyed, like mine had been. We stayed there and talked for hours. But you can't put a QuikHeal bandage on a broken heart."

Devereaux said, "I forgot that your wife killed herself too."

Jeremiah nodded. "That bonded us in a tragic way."

Devereaux reached for a box of tissues and Jeremiah realized the great man was crying. Yet he himself couldn't. Not now. He waited for Devereaux to wipe his eyes and said, "So what are you going to do next?"

"I'll study the virus further. There's something familiar about it."

"Like what?"

Devereaux shook his head. "I can't quite place it. Perhaps I once conjured up something like this in my head. Perhaps someone I worked with in the distant past created a similar virus."

"It's been around for years."

"Yes, I know. But this strain is different—more obviously manufactured. The older versions looked more natural, as if they could have evolved on their own. I'm going to conduct a series of tests, see if I can narrow down its preferences and mutability. In the meantime I want you to focus on feeling better. Eat. Laugh. Smile. Keep a positive outlook. That's important."

"Easy for you to say."

"Yes, it is. It doesn't make it any less true, however. Tell me something, Jeremiah. Do you like yourself?"

"I have far too many flaws for that. And I've done far too many terrible things. So, no, I don't particularly care for myself. Why do you ask?"

Devereaux shook his head. "Because it's important that you do.

Your profile indicates that you demand far more of yourself than anyone around you. It's probably the reason you're so good at what you do. You're never satisfied. But if you want to get well, you'll have to do a better job of forgiving yourself."

Jeremiah's eyes closed despite his best efforts to keep them open.

"I'll leave you to get some sleep," Devereaux said. "But remember this. I spoke with Julianna about you last year. She loved you and trusted you more than any man she'd ever met. And don't forget the Escala and me. We've seen to the heart of you. And you're the best man we know. So no matter what you think of yourself, there are people who admire and respect you—people who wish you well."

Sermon delivered, Devereaux gave a short bow and exited the room. Perhaps, Jeremiah thought, I'm not as bad as I think I am. Perhaps there's hope for me after all. On the other hand, you don't know the terrible things I've done.

Chapter Eleven

Curtik paced in his cell, watched by two Elite Ops troopers outside. They wore full armor, shields activated, which told him they were afraid. Good. *Still, what did I do wrong?*

The cell—a portable model with plas-glass walls on all four sides—sat in the center of the greenhouse for some reason, so vegetables and fruits surrounded him. Yellow lights gave the room—actually, a cave—a weird glow. If he wasn't locked up, he might think the place was kind of cool. But no way was he going to sit here and rot like that freak, Damon. And no way was he going to let that bitch Zora lead the attacks on Earth. The cell's dampening field prevented him from using his implant to contact anyone on the outside. But his tong would come for him.

Addam and Benn should be planning his escape by now. They'd rally the rest of the boys, maybe most of the girls too—except for Zora's tong. Once he got out, he'd figure a way to eliminate her. Always flaunting her brains, like they mattered. So annoying, so worried about cause and effect, long-term consequences, carefully plotted retreats. You don't retreat in battle. Ever.

He'd have to do something about Poole and Cho when he got out too. They obviously didn't intend to let him run free. So he'd have to neutralize them, maybe take them out. As that idea occurred to him, an incredible pain knifed through his head—a paralyzing, vision-blackening agony that nauseated him and left him incapable of rational thought. He dry-heaved a couple times. *Son of a bitch!*

What the hell was that?

Programming, he realized as the pain diminished. They'd programmed loyalty into him. And since he'd never thought of attacking them before, he'd never experienced the agony that came with disloyalty. He wondered whether he'd even be able to move if he

119

decided to kill them. Even that thought left his stomach unsettled. Perhaps that was why he couldn't recall ever having a rebellious thought about Cho and Poole. He must have had some early on. They all must have. But if negative thoughts directed at Cho and Poole brought on discomfort, they would naturally have veered away from such ideas quickly, without ever wondering why. Now that he knew the reason, he might be able to find a way around the negative programming.

He thought he heard something faintly, not so much through his ears as directly into his brain. Two words: We're coming. Benn and Addam.

Outside the cell the two Elite Ops troopers turned their dark visors his way. One of them said, "You're a scary little bastard, Curtik."

"Is that you, Talbert?" Curtik said. "I can't tell you guys apart when you're wearing your helmets. Who's that with you?"

"Alamein."

"Alamein. The quiet one. You guys are going to be the first to die. Tell me something, Talbert. Did you really go up against Jeremiah Jones back on Earth?"

Talbert nodded. "He was amazing."

"More amazing than me?"

"You're a kid trapped in a man's body. More unpredictable. So maybe that makes you more dangerous. But he was something. I never saw anybody move like that until you kids."

"I like you, Talbert. A lot more than Mouthy Man."

"Shut up, kid," Alamein said.

"Hey, I'm just talking. Passing the time. You don't have to listen."

"Jack was a good guy. He mentored me when I first entered the Elite Ops. And he was more man than you'll ever be."

"He was an asshole," Talbert said. "Thought he was better than us. Shot his mouth off way too much."

"A mouthy man," Curtik said with a laugh. "It was a fair fight. What's everyone's problem?"

"The problem," Alamein said, "is that you're a psychopath."

"Hey," Curtik said, "I'm just the way they made me. Come on,

Talbert. You know they're gonna let me outta here eventually. They need me. I'm the best they've got. Why don't you just let me out now?"

"You just threatened to kill us two minutes ago," Alamein said. "Do you know how crazy you sound?"

"I wasn't talkin' to you, Alamein. I was talkin' to my man Talbert."

"Sorry, Curtik," Talbert said. "Gotta follow orders."

Curtik snorted his disgust. Weak humans. They all deserved to die—except maybe Eli.

The sound of a large group approaching made the Elite Ops turn toward the doorway. Benn's distinct laughter was immediately recognizable, as was the off-key whistling of Wee Willie—the best tech student among the boys. He was almost as smart as Zora and a hell of a lot more fun.

"Yo," Benn shouted as they entered the greenhouse, a crowd of boys wearing black shimmer cloth coveralls, "we're here to see our man Curtik."

"You're not authorized to be here," Alamein said, using an amplified voice.

"Ah, they're just kids," Talbert said. "Five minutes, guys. Okay?"

The crowd surrounded the two Elite Ops troopers. Curtik's boys—all eighteen of them, looking innocent—unarmed.

"Curtik," Addam said, "how you doin'?"

Curtik said, "I don't know why the hell I'm even here."

"Leave the area now," Alamein ordered. "I'll send for backup."

"Relax," Benn said as the boys closed in tighter, pressing their bodies against the troopers. "We're just here for a visit. We're peaceful. Ain't we, boys?"

Seventeen voices spoke in unison: "Peaceful."

"We don't want to hurt you," Alamein said as a noxious odor of sulfur and decaying corpses permeated the area—Elite Ops nerve gas. It was supposed to induce crippling fear, but Curtik knew it wouldn't work on the cadets. Ha! Choke on that.

"We don't want to hurt you either," Addam said as the boys reached through the shields, grabbing arms and legs, lifting the troopers off

STEVE MCELLISTREM

the floor, pinioning them against the plas-glass wall of the cell. He and Benn each tore a helmet off a trooper, cutting communications with central command and deactivating their shields. They ripped the Las-rifles out of the troopers' hands. Wee Willie reset the Las-rifles' frequencies so they were no longer tied to the troopers' helmets. He handed one to Addam, who gestured to the boys to let go of Alamein. As they stepped back, Addam pointed his Las-rifle at Alamein. "Open the door."

Alamein shook his head. "Listen, boys. It's not too late to turn back. Troopers are going to be here any second and they're not going to be playing."

"Kill him," Curtik said. His heart pounded in his chest.

"What?" Addam said.

"His friends will be here soon. Kill him."

Alamein said, "I won't open the door and you're not going to kill me, Addam. This is just youthful exuberance. It's forgivable, to a point. But you shoot me and you'll regret it."

Addam stepped closer, placing the Las-rifle up against Alamein's stomach, but still didn't fire. Benn did it for him. He sent a red laser pulse through Alamein's armor, drilling a hole in the trooper's chest the size of a fist. The trooper screamed as he fell. Crazy Vigg snorted. Benn pushed Talbert to the door and said, "Open it or die."

"Take it easy," Talbert said. "No one else needs to get hurt." He put his palm on the lock and punched in the code, springing the hinge of the door. As it swung open Curtik stepped out, a cold fury upon him. Grabbing Talbert, Curtik snatched his shield generator and pushed him away. "Kill him too," he said.

"Why?" Addam said. "We can just lock him up."

"Listen, Curtik," Talbert said, "I did as you asked. I let you out."

Curtik snarled at Addam's stupidity and Talbert's desperation. The smell of fear was acrid and unpleasant. "Sorry, Talbert. It's gone too far. You'd only come after us again. Everyone's gonna be coming after us now. Kill him."

Still Addam hesitated.

122

"Damn it!" Curtik held out his hand. "Give me your weapon."

Talbert edged toward the door. "I've got a lot of friends in the Elite Ops."

He obviously wanted to make a break for it. Curtik took Addam's Las-rifle and altered the power setting to high. "Run," he said to Talbert. "Now."

As Talbert pushed past, slide-hopping for the door, Curtik fired a long pulse into the back of Talbert's head.

The pit of his stomach grew warm. Benn laughed. Curtik felt like it too but held back. Control. His breath came in gasps. Slowing it down, Curtik said, "We need more weapons. Addam, Wee Willie, you're with me. Benn, get Alamein's shield and cover our rear. Crazy Vigg, your tong is in charge here. Try to delay the troopers. Tell them whatever you have to. Play on their sympathies. Blame me. The rest of you scatter."

It took a few seconds for Wee Willie to reconfigure the shield he'd taken from Talbert so that it would work without connecting to the helmet. Crazy Vigg altered Alamein's as well. As they moved out, Curtik spoke to the cadets through his implant: *I'll contact you when we've got weapons. The Elite Ops probably won't attack if you're unarmed. As soon as we get Las-rifles, we'll get back to you.*

They moved quickly down the corridor toward the armory, using the slide-hop step that substituted for running in the lower gravity of the Moon. Curtik almost didn't remember real running. The only time they got to run now was in the motionators or on the training floor, wearing their mock gravity suits. And it didn't feel right. He longed to return to Earth—after they'd conquered it—so he could run on grass again.

Using his implant, Curtik tapped into the communications module of the Elite Ops for a second, then disconnected before any troopers could get a fix on his position. Two troopers were guarding the armory.

"Benn and I go in firing," he said. "Wee Willie, you take out the lights. Give Addam a three-two-one. Addam, you stay behind us. When the lights go out, we drop and you go over the top. Make a grab for their helmets. Rip 'em off and their shields will go out. Think you can handle that?"

"You're giving me the most dangerous job?" Addam said.

"If you'd shot that guy when I told you to, I'd do it myself. But I don't trust you with a Las-rifle right now."

Addam opened his mouth, hesitated and said, "Fine."

Wee Willie said, "There's the junction box. Up ahead is the intersection of corridors outside the armory. I'll need about thirty seconds to isolate the lights in that corridor."

"No problem," Curtik said. "Go."

He walked to the intersecting corridor, Benn at his side, Addam behind him. As soon as he rounded the corner, he realized there was a problem. Zora stood with her tong, Rendela and the pale Aspen, next to the Elite Ops troopers outside the armory. They wore white shimmer cloth coveralls and too much of that annoying perfume he couldn't place. It wrinkled his nostrils. What the hell were they doing here?

"Give it up, Curtik," Zora called out.

"Get out of my face," Curtik said, "or you'll be sorry."

The Elite Ops troopers had their weapons up but hadn't yet fired. Curtik and Benn advanced, Addam trailing. When the troopers released their nerve gas, Curtik knew they were seconds from firing. He said, "Now."

He and Benn opened up with red killing pulses as they closed the gap still further. The troopers' shields glowed orange. They couldn't fire back while their shields were on. Zora, Rendela and Aspen moved behind the troopers, using the shields for protection. The chemicals in the nerve gas, cooked by the laser pulses, released a bitter smell. Curtik knew he had to get within about five feet for Addam to make the leap. If Addam messed up this time, Curtik would kill him, same tong or not. He heard Wee Willie's voice in his implant, *Three, two, one, now.*

Curtik and Benn dropped as the lights went out.

Curtik's implant immediately adjusted for the difference. He saw Addam go flying past him, arms down. The Elite Ops troopers saw him too. They lifted their Las-rifles and fired as he grabbed at their helmets. He screamed. But he managed to pry off one of the troopers' helmets. Curtik's Las-rifle blasted a hole in the trooper as Addam fell to the floor, moaning. The trooper dropped.

The other trooper's shield remained intact. As Zora bent to the lock on the armory door, Curtik dropped his Las-rifle and dove for the trooper's helmet while Benn kept up a steady stream of fire. Even as his fingers locked under the helmet, pulling up and away, deactivating the trooper's shield, Curtik felt a knife press into his stomach. Then agony. He screamed as he fell and laughed at the pain. He'd been stabbed. Not that bad. Hurt like hell.

Looking up, he saw Benn standing over the two dead Elite Ops troopers. "Man," Benn said, "I smoked him good."

And then Rendela and Aspen tackled him. Why? Obviously working against him under Zora's orders. She wanted to lead, and she'd managed to unlock the armory door.

Curtik pulled the knife clear—a plas-glass blade that produced a pain unlike anything he'd ever experienced. Zora picked up the Las-rifle he'd dropped. He had to even things out somehow. Addam was unconscious. No help there.

Benn tried to swing his Las-rifle around but Rendela slammed a knee into his crotch and Aspen easily wrenched the Las-rifle from his hands. Benn rolled on the floor moaning as Rendela got to her feet and stepped inside the armory. She returned a few seconds later with another Las-rifle. Now all three bitches were armed.

"On your feet," Zora said to Curtik.

"I can't," Curtik said, clutching his stomach and trying to sound helpless. "I've been stabbed."

The lights came back up as Wee Willie rounded the corner. "There's more coming," he yelled.

"We've got everything under control," Zora called out.

"Stand down," an Elite Ops trooper said as he strode into the corridor, his Las-rifle leveled at them. Benn struggled to his feet.

"The armory is secure," Zora said.

"Drop your weapons and put up your hands," the Elite Ops trooper said.

"Don't do it," Curtik said. "They'll kill us all."

"We stopped them," Zora said to the trooper.

"You can't bluff them, Zora," Curtik said. "They know we're all in it together."

The trooper fired at Zora. Somehow she anticipated it. She dove into the armory, Rendela and Aspen following her, quick as cats. The trooper fired at Curtik.

Curtik flinched as the tingle of his shield tickled his wound. The laser pulse scattered on impact and his shield glowed orange. Wee Willie slid the last few feet to the door, reaching it just as the trooper fired another pulse at him. It hit Benn's shield. As the trooper advanced, Benn reached out and grabbed Curtik, pulling him through the door.

"Close it," Curtik said.

"But Addam," Benn said.

"Too late for him. Seal the door."

"You bastard," Zora said. "What have you done?"

"I'll get him," Rendela said. She clipped a shield to her belt, activated it and stepped through the door, her shield instantly glowing orange as a laser pulse hit it. She pulled the unconscious Addam into the armory and Benn slammed the door behind her, locking it.

"You plowing idiot," Zora yelled at Curtik. "Are you insane?"

Curtik laughed. "Trapped in paradise."

"I should kill you now."

Curtik shook his head as he continued to laugh, diverting attention, hoping Benn and Wee Willie would know what to do. As they edged toward the weapons case, Curtik groaned and began writhing about on the floor. "You okay?" Zora asked. When she reached over to check Curtik's wound, Rendela and Aspen stepped forward to help. Zora's eyes widened as she realized Curtik was diverting her attention, but by the time she straightened, Benn and Wee Willie were holding Las-rifles.

"Stalemate," Curtik said.

Rendela and Aspen glanced at each other, turning their weapons on Benn and Wee Willie, who backed up a step and smiled.

"Too late, girls," Curtik taunted. "Should have been watching my boys."

"Three against two," Zora said. "You're wounded and you've got no weapon. We'll just wait for Dr. Poole to arrive, then I'll straighten everything out."

"I can't let that happen," Curtik said. "She'll just lock me up again."

"Nothing you can do about it."

"Oh yes there is. Have you forgotten you're not wearing a shield?" Zora took a step toward the shield locker. "Don't move!" Curtik commanded. "Benn, if she takes one more step, shoot her."

"Then I shoot you," Aspen said to Benn.

"And Wee Willie," Curtik said, "you shoot Aspen. We'll deal with Rendela later."

"He's bluffing," Aspen said.

"No, he's not," Zora said. "He's got nothing to lose. All right, Curtik. What do you want? I'm not giving you a Las-rifle."

"You'll have to eventually," Curtik said, his mind racing ahead to possibilities. "Look, you can be in overall command. I don't care about that anymore. But we've got to move before they get organized. This whole program is going to be shut down."

"How do you know that?"

"They don't trust us anymore. Not even you. You saw that trooper fire at you. They believe we're all in this together—"

"As I said, I'll straighten everything out with Dr. Poole."

Curtik shook his head. "They're getting cold feet. Dr. Poole's been acting strange for weeks. Admiral Cho doesn't come around anymore. When's the last time you heard from Eli? They're going to dismantle the program, get rid of us. They already took out Damon."

"What are you talking about?"

"Think about it. They knew he was your best friend among us boys. He supported you. But they wanted to encourage the rivalry between us. So they made Damon sick, gave him some sort of injection. They're going to do the same to us. Kill us off slowly."

"You're a liar," Zora said but her eyes began to flicker back and forth as she processed the information.

"I admit that I'll do whatever it takes to win. You know that."

"I don't trust you."

"I'm not asking you to," Curtik said. "Look, I didn't think of any of this until just now but it makes sense. We're too good at what we do. They're afraid of us. Tell me, did they sabotage your last test?"

"So?" Zora shrugged. "I handled it."

Was she beginning to waver? "Do they ever let you see Damon?"

"He's devolved. We all saw it."

"How do you know Poole or Hack'emup didn't arrange that?"

"You're being paranoid."

"Am I?" Curtik nodded slowly. "Maybe. But think about this—if I'm right, as soon as you hand over your weapons, they'll start to get rid of us. Me first, sure. But then you, Rendela, Aspen, Wee Willie, Benn. The smartest ones. The ones they can't control."

"You're not right."

"If I'm wrong," Curtik said, "you can always surrender to Poole later, explain why you acted the way you did. After you capture or kill all the Elite Ops. She'll forgive you. Hell, she'll probably be thrilled at your initiative and ability. Everyone knows you're her favorite student. So here's what you gotta ask yourself—can you take the chance that I'm wrong? Because if I'm right, you don't get a second chance."

Zora stood quietly, no doubt weighing the possibilities in her mind. Curtik knew she'd agree to wait. Though he'd just been trying to survive, playing for time, his intuition told him he was right. And that had lent sincerity to his words. Was he right? Was the program about to be dismantled? Could his desperation have provided him with the "sudden insight of battle" that Poole was always rambling on about?

"He's just trying to manipulate you," Aspen said.

"Obviously," Zora said.

"One other thing," Curtik said to Zora. "Did you know that we can't have a disloyal thought about Poole or Cho?"

Zora said, "What are you talking about?"

"Think about betraying Cho or Poole, or harming them in some way. Just for a second. You'll feel like puking your guts out. We've been conditioned for obedience. Does that sound like they trust us? Like they're willing to let us operate on our own?"

Zora paled and Curtik knew she'd just thought of hurting Poole or Cho.

Wee Willie bent over and threw up.

"Hey!" Benn said.

"You're right," Wee Willie said. "Cool." He pointed at Rendela. "Try it."

"Gross!"

"You don't have to throw up. Just think about slapping Poole's face."

"Ew!" Rendela made a face.

"See? Try it, Aspen."

Aspen's pale face wrinkled in distaste. "I already did."

"Okay," Zora said. "That's enough of that. I don't trust you, Curtik. I know how devious you can be."

"Devious," Benn said with a grin.

"But for the moment," Zora continued, "I can't afford to assume you're wrong. We do it my way. I still won't give you a weapon. Use your implant to tell your boys I'll be coordinating the attack. We capture the Elite Ops. Then we negotiate with Poole and Cho. Learn the truth."

"That's all I'm asking," Curtik said. For now.

Chapter Twelve

On the screens in Admiral Cho's office, the children, armed with Las-rifles, marched toward LB1, laughing and whooping. Only a handful had been left behind to guard the Elite Ops, who had fallen to the cadets, partly because of their orders—modified by deep conditioning—not to use extreme force on the children.

"They're out of control," Taditha Poole said to Eli over the vid. Her stomach tightened and twisted.

"Let them come," Eli replied after the three-second time lag, his voice slightly slurred, the left side of his face partially paralyzed by his recent stroke. He also spoke with a pronounced lisp. "We'll put the plan into effect immediately. I assume you saw that India and China have fired rockets at each other's military bases?"

"I don't care about China and India. The cadets might kill everyone on the Moon, including us. Is that your plan? Are we expendable?"

Cho said, "Their conditioning will hold. We'll be safe." His voice, though, sounded shaky.

"Taditha," Eli said, "of course you're not expendable. If I thought you were in real danger, I'd allow you to put them to sleep."

"I already tried that," Poole said. "It didn't work. Someone is blocking all my transmissions to their implants."

"You tried to knock them out?" Cho said.

"And failed. Look at them." Poole pointed to the screens. The children, more than halfway to LB1, moved with a kind of horrific synchronicity, yelling something indecipherable. "Whatever controls once existed are no longer holding."

"You tried to sabotage the project?" Eli said.

"Not sabotage," Poole replied. "I just felt we needed to slow down, get the cadets under control and re-analyze everything before we proceed."

Cho shook his head. Three seconds later Eli said, "We need to accelerate the timeline, given the situation in Asia. Brazil has already declared its support for China, while Britain and France have backed India. All my analysts agree that a regional war is inevitable, and most think a world war is weeks away."

"I just can't wrap my head around killing thousands of people," Poole said.

"Better than the millions, perhaps even billions, that would die otherwise," Admiral Cho replied before Eli's response could return from Earth. "We're just ridding the world of certain hostile governments."

"You've been on board with this plan for years," Eli said. "What's suddenly gotten into you, Taditha?"

"Nothing," Poole said. "I just want to move cautiously. I don't think these kids are stable enough for what you have in mind." She glanced at the screens again. The cadets increased their pace, their faces twisted in a kind of desperate anticipation. Crazy Vigg fired his Las-rifle into the ceiling and the others howled in delight. She shivered.

"I understand you have reservations," Eli continued. "You might experience some remorse at the necessary violence we have to inflict. But we all know this is the only way to prevent the greater evil."

"Look at them," Poole said. "I don't know what they'll do. All I can say for certain is that the level of rage they're experiencing is way beyond what it should be—the cascading effect of mob mentality."

For a few seconds, while the time lag to Earth delayed Eli's response, Poole studied Cho. He took off his glasses and mopped his glistening forehead with a handkerchief as his gaze settled on the screens.

"I've seen all the data you've sent," Eli said finally. "My people agree that the controls will hold. Everything is fine. You two need to relax and let this happen. Taditha, I understand your concerns. But you've done everything right. Ready or not, this is their time."

"I guess we're about to find out."

The cadets had reached the tunnel entrance. "Oh, Choey," Curtik called, "Can we come out to play?"

The cadets laughed.

131

"If I have to open this door myself," Zora said. "I won't be happy."

Poole shook her head at Cho, but Eli said, "Let them in, Admiral. I'm transmitting the Las-cannon access codes and the initial targets. Once the children secure Lunar Base 1, they can begin the first attacks on Earth."

Poole got to her feet. "Don't let them in. The situation is too explosive."

Cho drew his Las-pistol and pointed it at Poole while palming the pad on his desk, opening the door to the tunnel and the sound of children laughing and cheering. "Calm down, Doctor. Everything's gonna be fine."

The cadets swarmed into Cho's office, Curtik wearing a QuikHeal bandage on his stomach. He was one of the few not carrying a Las-rifle. His eyes had a glazed look, probably augmented by the anesthetics. Zora kept one hand on his arm. She too carried no Las-rifle.

"Hello, Piscine," Curtik said with a smile, "and Admiral Cho." Curtik waved wildly. "How nice to see you again. It's been such a long time."

Zora said, "You planning to use that Las-pistol, Admiral?"

Aspen stepped over to Cho, who placed the weapon in her hand. Benn directed cadets out into the hall beyond, but Rendela stayed by Zora, while Wee Willie, Crazy Vigg, Roze and Addam—also wearing a QuikHeal bandage and walking with a slight limp—stood against the wall. Addam's eyes, much more glazed than Curtik's, indicated he was under heavy anesthesia.

"I'm looking forward to spending more time with you, Choey," Curtik said, "once I figure out how to undo some of this programming in my head."

"Zora," Poole said, "I'm concerned about the implant readings I'm getting from you and your friends."

Curtik said, "Are you concerned about me as well, Piscine? I hope you are because I'm certainly concerned about you." He broke into laughter.

Zora's gaze shifted from Poole to Eli. "Ah, the great and powerful Oz. We'll talk later. Take a seat, Doctor. Admiral, you'll be coming with me. Crowd control. I don't have time to chat with either of you at the moment. We've decided to take over LB1 as a precaution. Rendela, you and Benn keep an eye on Dr. Poole. I don't want her contacting anyone. Admiral, have your people surrender their weapons and congregate in the hangar. We don't kill anyone we don't have to, right, Curtik?"

Curtik smiled with his lips, not his eyes. "We'll have to get rid of them eventually. Hey, we could ratapult them."

Zora looked at Cho. "Admiral? Now, please." As Cho reached for the intercom, Zora said, "And, Doctor, I'll take your interface." She let go of Curtik and held out her hand. Poole disconnected from the device, removed it from her temple and gave it to Zora, who pocketed it and said, "Everyone else, with me. Ciao for now."

"Zora," Poole said. "I think we should talk."

"Good idea, Doctor. Why don't you start without me?" Flashing a smile, Zora flounced out of the room, pulling Curtik with her. Aspen pushed Cho out the door behind them.

"Don't worry," Rendela said as she used a plastic restraint to tether Poole to Cho's desk. "We won't harm you."

"What did you do to us?" Benn said.

"I made you special," Poole replied.

"How sweet of you," Rendela said. "And now we're going to complete our mission. Curtik told us you were planning to discontinue the program, that you were going to get rid of us. Is that true?"

"No," Poole said.

Rendela nodded. "He said you'd deny it. Zora will get to the bottom of it once she finishes securing LB1. Let's watch TV, shall we?"

The screens showed the main hangar of LB1. Cho's soldiers had begun assembling there, wearing sullen expressions, while half a dozen cadets surrounded them, aiming their Las-rifles in the soldiers' general direction. Zora, leaving Aspen to guard Cho, went to the military desk and switched the intercom on. She spoke in a pleasant voice that went to every room on the Moon:

"May I have your attention, please? I'm sorry to interrupt whatever you're doing, but your immediate presence is required in the main hangar of Lunar Base 1 for a safety inspection. This is not a drill. Everyone must be in the main hangar in five minutes. Anyone who fails to follow this order will be subject to immediate discipline, including expulsion from the settlement. Thank you for your cooperation."

Zora looked up at the nearest camera and smiled. She looked angelic. Poole wondered if she was as much a monster as Curtik. She'd always played by the rules during training, whereas Curtik had a tendency to push them, often for no reason that Poole could see. But she was smart too, smarter than Curtik, probably smarter than Poole. Had she been hiding certain talents all along just as Curtik had? Underplaying her abilities to gain an edge? Even if she hadn't, what would Zora be like without the controls upon her? Would she be as dangerous as Curtik?

Workers and tourists filed in gradually, some belligerent at first, until they saw the Las-rifles and the subdued soldiers. Most came quietly, moving into the center area where the next LTV was due to arrive in four days. The Verloren mother carried her youngest daughter and the father kept a firm grip on the older one—Carla? Cora? Kyler— the one who'd unwittingly caused Jones' accident.

Poole searched for Devereaux in the crowd but didn't see him. She wondered if he was in the hospital wing with Jones again, continuing his research into the Susquehanna Virus. The Escala hadn't arrived from LB2 either. Would the children go after them? Despite the fact that they were scientists, they had demonstrated that they were formidable fighters, though without weapons they'd be slaughtered if the children attacked them. What the hell is Zora planning?

Now teams of cadets began to move off into the hotel and other areas, no doubt to ensure that everyone was accounted for. Zora stayed at the military desk, where she had access to the scanners that could identify the location of every individual on the Moon.

"You're awfully quiet," Rendela said as they waited for the stragglers to be brought to the hangar.

Poole sighed and said, "What do you want me to say?"

"Don't you have any questions?"

"I'm curious what you've got planned," Poole said. "Believe it or not, I want you to complete your mission. And you need our help—mine and Admiral Cho's—to do it. We've got all the access codes, the target specs."

"Oh," Rendela said, "I think we can find them."

Benn stared at Poole and said, "You look a little off to me, Doctor. You're always asking how we're feeling during and after our exercises. How are you feeling?"

Poole's stomach continued to roil. She said, "Actually, I have a little nausea. Perhaps I'm coming down with something."

"The Susquehanna Virus?" Benn said.

When Poole raised an eyebrow, Benn said, "Yeah, we know about that. Zora tapped into the medical database and discovered it was sent here. Curtik says you were going to use it against us."

"Curtik's a liar," Poole said, "and a manipulator. He'll say or do anything to get what he wants. And right now he wants the freedom to kill. He wants to destroy every human on Earth."

"You made him what he is," Rendela said.

Poole nodded. "We made all of you. And we're proud of you. You're gifted. We enhanced body and mind, and made adjustments to your personalities to bring forward the skills you'll need to complete the mission."

"After what Curtik did to Mouthy Man," Benn said, "you're probably wishing you hadn't made him so well."

Poole blinked rapidly, holding back the tears. She refused to cry in front of these children. God, she hated Curtik—and herself.

Composing herself, she looked at the screens, where everyone was turning toward the tunnel to LB2. Emerging from it in a single group, the Escala strode into the hangar. Close to seventy strong, with a few children and infants, their presence overpowered everything else in the hangar.

"Whoa," Benn said, "those mofos are huge!"

Quark was the biggest, but even the smallest adults were over six-feet tall—most were well over six feet. And the lightest woman probably weighed two hundred-twenty Earth pounds. Poole had forgotten how impressive they were as a group, how muscular and athletic. She hadn't seen them all together since they landed a year ago. They must have all walked from LB2 to arrive at the same time. Quekri and Quark stood at the front, protecting their charges. After a few moments, Zora detached herself from the military desk and walked over to them. She had to tilt her head way back to speak to the giants, but her voice didn't carry to the sensor pickups, so Poole couldn't hear her.

Rendela's face went blank, as did Benn's—accessing their implants. Poole said, "What's going on?"

Benn and Rendela ignored her. After a few moments, Zora finished her conversation with Quark and Quekri. She turned toward the military desk and asked, "Where is Devereaux?"

"In the infirmary," Wee Willie answered, "with Jones. You want me to get them?"

Zora went still for a moment, then said, "No. Let them be."

A group of four cadets dragged two burly workers wearing the blue-gray of the ice harvesting crew into the hangar. The workers cursed at the cadets and the bigger of the two fought against his captors who, despite being smaller, were easily strong enough to hold him.

"Who do we have here?" Zora asked.

"Leggo!" the big worker yelled. "What the hell do you think you're doing, little girl?"

Zora smiled at him. "Did you not hear the order to report to the main hangar?"

"Screw you! We're off duty. You can't tell us what to do."

"I'm sorry," Zora said. "I didn't mean to upset you, Mr. Evgeny Sorokin. I can see by your face that I interrupted your beauty sleep. In fact, you must not have gotten any at all."

The other cadets laughed.

"What the hell's that mean?" Sorokin shouted.

Zora turned to Curtik and said, "This gentleman doesn't want to be here. Could you show him to the door?"

"Gladly." Curtik grabbed Sorokin and shoved him toward the airlock. Let's go."

Cho stepped forward, ignoring Aspen's Las-rifle. "You won't do this."

For a second Curtik paused, as if his body refused to obey, then Sorokin began to struggle and Curtik kicked his legs out from under him. He nodded to Phan, one of the cadets who had dragged the man out to the hangar. Together they pulled Sorokin toward the airlock. Sorokin yelled, "You're psychos! All of you. You wouldn't dare throw me outside."

Cho took another step forward. Aspen swung her Las-rifle into his stomach and Cho bent over double. Poole gasped. "How did Aspen do that?"

Rendela and Benn ignored her.

Aspen, Poole noted, looked nauseated with the effort she'd made to stop Cho. Her face was pinched in revulsion. When Curtik looked at her and laughed, she giggled. Some of the other cadets joined in. It wasn't until Curtik opened the doors, which slid apart with a kissing sound, that they stopped. Now their attention was on Sorokin and Curtik, who grabbed the big man's coveralls and threw him inside the airlock. Kicking and cursing, Sorokin landed against the outer door, scrambled to his feet and shouted, "Wait! I'm sorry. I won't cause no more trouble. Please let me back inside. I'm begging."

With a grin, Curtik closed the doors and hit the emergency lock.

"Curtik," Cho warned. "This ain't part of your mission." He turned to Zora. "This is simple murder."

Zora shook her head. "Admiral, I think you might want to go to your quiet place. Pretend this isn't happening." She nodded to Curtik, who turned back to the doors, where Sorokin pounded on the plas-glass with one hand while he tried to work the latch with the other. Behind him, through the outer glass doors, the desolate lunar landscape, harshly lit by the sun, confirmed Poole's version of hell—a jagged wasteland of gray and black, shadow and nothingness. She shivered. Sorokin continued to pound on the glass. Curtik, giving an exaggerated slow wave, opened the outer doors. Sorokin reached for the latch handle and screamed as he was sucked toward the vacuum. Almost immediately the sound vanished along with the air and he tumbled to the ground a few feet outside the hatch. He twitched for perhaps a minute, then lay still.

Poole shivered with fear.

"It ain't too late, son," Cho said. "We can still save him."

Curtik continued to watch Sorokin through the window until it no longer mattered and said, "Hunh. That wasn't much fun. He didn't explode or anything. Maybe we should try again." He turned to the smaller worker who had been dragged to the hangar with Sorokin. "Who else can we put out there?"

The worker fell to his knees. "Please," he begged. "I'll be good. I promise."

The captives in the hangar took a step back. Even the big Escala shifted side to side.

"Let's do Cho," Addam said.

"What?" Cho bellowed.

Curtik smiled. "Good idea. Let's give it a shot."

Cho spoke slowly and forcefully: "You will not harm me."

"What do you think, Zora?" Curtik said. "Should we see if we can? We have to find out sometime, unless we want to be slaves forever."

Zora pursed her lips in that way she had when she was mulling over a difficult problem. Poole turned to Rendela and said, "You have to tell her not to do it. You need Cho to complete your mission."

Rendela stared at Poole for a moment, smiled and turned back to the monitors.

Benn said, "Do it."

"Don't do it, Zora," Poole begged, unable to stop the words from bubbling out of her mouth even though she knew Zora couldn't hear them. "You'll ruin yourself. Please."

Zora said, "Okay. But he's the last one for now. We have to save the others in case we need them. Hostages are good leverage."

"Whoo hoo!" Curtik whooped. "Come on, Choey. Let's see how you do."

"Is this necessary?" Quekri said.

As Curtik glared at her, Quark took a step forward. Poole could see that even the cadets were intimidated by his bulk. Their eyes widened. Zora held up a hand and beckoned Quekri over. When Quekri bent her head to Zora's level, Poole strained to listen over the hum of the air recycler, but again Zora spoke too softly for the sensors to pick up her words. After perhaps a minute, Quekri nodded, her face scrunched up in anger, her fists clenched at her sides. Zora looked over at Curtik and said, "Go."

"This is crazy," Cho yelled.

Phan grabbed his arm as Curtik sealed the outer doors of the airlock and repressurized it.

"Your conditioning prohibits any action that will harm me," Cho said as Addam grabbed his other arm. Phan looked pale, but Addam, with his QuikHeal bandage feeding him a high dosage of anesthetics, looked unconcerned.

"You can't do this," Cho said. "Ask Dr. Poole. She'll tell you. You cannot do this."

When the light above the doors turned green, Curtik opened the inner doors again. Addam and Phan walked Cho to the airlock, escorting him to the outside doors of the airlock. Phan wobbled a little as he walked but he held tightly to Cho's arm.

"You won't be able to open the outer doors," Cho said, shaking his head. "Look at you." He glared at Phan. "You can barely walk."

"This feels weird," Curtik said. "Like I'm going to puke. But also like I'm going to explode with happiness."

"Yeah," Aspen paled even more than usual, as if near to fainting.

Addam and Phan left Cho at the outer doors and backed out of the airlift, their Las-rifles pointed at him, while everyone in the hangar stared. Poole felt an almost irresistible urge to scream at the utter insanity of it. She wished she were still connected to her interface so she could talk to Zora—convince her that this was madness—or at least understand how the cadets were able to force themselves past the loyalty barrier.

Curtik closed the inner doors, took a couple of deep breaths and put his hand up to the button that would open the outer doors. Cho stared at him, arms crossed over his chest, chin up, daring Curtik to open the doors. Was Cho that brave or did he believe that Curtik wouldn't do it?

Long seconds passed. No one moved. Poole realized she was holding her breath. She exhaled.

Zora said, "Curtik."

Poole wanted to believe that she meant for Curtik to stop, but he stabbed the button, the outer doors opened and Zora did nothing. Along with the air, Cho was swept out onto the lunar surface. He tripped over the dead man and fell, his glasses coming off, struggled to his feet and began walking away from the doors. Poor brave man. Where was he going? He made it about thirty feet before collapsing. Poole, fighting back the bile in her throat, saw that the cadets all looked like they were going to be sick. More than half of them vomited, including Zora. Addam and Curtik took it the best but they were also the only two wearing QuikHeal bandages.

"Oh, Zora," Poole said. "What have you done?" She glanced at the screen to see Eli's reaction. He stared at the scene, his face twisted. Was that because of the stroke or did he actually feel some guilt?

The cadets seemed to have forgotten their prisoners. The Escala shook their heads and looked away but made no move to attack. Most of the tourists and workers were shaking or sitting on the floor. The soldiers stood still, their eyes locked on the body, visible through the plas-glass doors. After a few seconds, several of them started to move toward the cadets.

Zora, coming out of her trance, said, "Don't even think about committing suicide."

The children re-trained their weapons on their hostages.

"If we can do that," Zora said, "to a man we were conditioned to protect, imagine what we can do to you, who we've been encouraged to kill. Any resistance will be met with extreme violence. I don't want that. You don't want that. You behave and we'll behave. Otherwise, you'll be asked to join the Admiral." She smiled. "This is the only warning you get, so be good, okay?"

Curtik finally closed the outer doors. He began to laugh, a bubbling-up-from-within kind of laughter that spilled over into something approaching hysteria. A few of the children joined in—Addam, Aspen, Phan. The rest still looked stunned. Benn giggled too, while Rendela merely shook her head in silence. Then Benn pointed at Poole and said, "Hey, you up for nexties?"

Poole shivered.

"Benn," Rendela said. "Don't terrorize the doctor. We may need her."

Chapter Thirteen

Jeremiah studied the flickering torch on the wall of his stone dungeon—but something kept tugging him away. He fought it for a long time, but eventually surrendered to its urgent call. He awoke to a screeching alarm that jangled his nerves. Shutting it off with a voice command, he glanced about the room. Empty.

The air recycler hummed and the faint antiseptic odor of the hospital wrinkled his nose. He suppressed the urge to sneeze, knowing the torture it would cause. Nurse Manuella, if she'd made her usual early-morning visit, had not disturbed him.

He pressed the call icon. When no one appeared after a few minutes, he pressed it again—still no response. Raising the lights, he disconnected the rehab massagers and prepared himself for the agony of movement. He sat up, sweat breaking out across his forehead, and lifted his legs from the machines. His shoulders felt like they were embedded with knives, stabbing him with every movement; his knees produced a sharp pain that came in waves. Sliding his legs over the edge of the bed, he stood.

But even in the Moon's lower gravity the agony nearly overwhelmed him. He cried out. Somehow he remained standing. If he fell, he'd never get back to his feet. Clenching his teeth, hobbling on broken legs, Jeremiah made it to the desk and settled into the chair, then touched the doctors' intercom. Again nothing. What was going on out there? Had Admiral Cho instituted martial law?

No, it had to be the cadets: Curtik and his friends. He'd killed Marschenko, and Poole had been afraid of him—of all the children, actually. They must have taken over the settlement, cut off all communications.

Would they come for him?

Jeremiah looked through the desk for a weapon. Nothing—not even a Las-knife. Getting into the wall cabinet meant he would have to get to his feet again. Using the back of the chair and the desk top, he managed to prop himself up long enough to open the door and pull out a dozen QuikHeal bandages before the pain forced him to sit.

He waited a few seconds for the near-blackness to recede. His head pounded and tears filled his eyes. Unwrapping two QuikHeal bandages, he slapped them on his legs, setting the anesthetic release to maximum. When no relief came, he remembered Devereaux telling him that the Susquehanna Virus' attack on his immune system impeded his ability to absorb anesthetics. Well, if they wouldn't work for him, could he somehow use them as a weapon?

Jeremiah removed the anesthetic packets from eight of the bandages and added them to the delivery systems in the other two. He adjusted the settings to maximum. Now each bandage, when attached to the skin, would deliver a massive dose of anesthetic, enough to instantaneously render a person unconscious. Not much of a weapon, especially against the cadets, but better than nothing.

As he resealed the bandages, he heard footsteps outside and turned the chair toward the door, grabbing a bandage in each hand and dropping them to his sides. He'd only get one chance and he'd have to wait for an assailant to get close enough to touch, but better to go down fighting.

When a huge shadow filled the door, he relaxed.

"It's me," Quark said in his deep rumble before entering the room—a great hairy beast with a grim expression. He raised his eyebrows when he saw the QuikHeal bandages in Jeremiah's hands.

"The cadets?" Jeremiah said.

Quark nodded. "They killed Admiral Cho and threatened us." Quark went to the closet and retrieved Jeremiah's bag. "They've got the Moon under control. But I think they might let us go. I think they believe we're kindred spirits."

Jeremiah said nothing to dispel Quark's belief, no matter how naïve it sounded. Instead, he let Quark help him to a wheelchair. "I'll take you to LB2," Quark said.

"What about Devereaux?"

"He's in the lab working on the Susquehanna Virus. Zora's letting us take you and your son. Dr. Wellon might be able to help you and Damon."

"Who is Zora?"

"The cadets' leader."

"What about a boy named Curtik?" Jeremiah asked, the rage, almost forgotten until now, rising again—the almost uncontrollable urge to kill Marschenko's murderer.

"He's with Zora," Quark said. "I don't think she trusts him, but she uses him for her dirty work."

Jeremiah clutched the QuikHeal bandages he'd modified. Paltry weapons though they were, they comforted him. "I'd like to meet him some day. When I'm better. For now, let's find Damon."

"They're bringing him to LB2," Quark said, rolling Jeremiah out the door. "We'll meet them there."

The main hangar was quiet. Eerie. Only six cadets in sight: three boys and three girls patrolled the place. They stared at Jeremiah and Quark as the wheelchair rolled through, but made no move to stop them. As they took the railcar to LB2, Quark told Jeremiah that everyone was locked up or confined to quarters. Zora had promised they wouldn't be harmed if they followed her orders. For a moment Jeremiah flashed on Kyler, the spunky little girl whom he had come to think of as a friend. Was she frightened? He wanted to comfort her. He wanted his son to be like her instead of some deranged maniac who didn't even know his own name. No. It wasn't Joshie's fault—Damon's fault. He was just a little boy who'd been forced to grow up too quickly.

Quekri met them at the tunnel entrance to LB2. She said, "Damon's with Wellon. Krall, Oggie and Poon are helping, making sure he doesn't attack her while she's examining him."

She led the way to the infirmary, past the common room and the mess hall, through the labs. The Escala continued their work, pausing to nod at him before returning to their tasks. Jeremiah was surprised at the normality of their behavior—as if they didn't care that the cadets had taken over. Something must have shown in his face, for Quekri said, "We couldn't interfere."

"They have Las-rifles," Quark added defensively, "and they're trained warriors. We only want to go to Mars."

"Not your fault," Jeremiah said. "Getting yourselves killed won't help anyone."

When they reached the infirmary, the three boys who had stopped Jeremiah on his first visit clustered around Damon and Dr. Wellon, holding Damon's arms and legs as he flailed about despite being strapped to a gurney.

Damon growled and spat at the boys but they restrained him as Dr. Wellon administered an injection. Gradually his movements weakened and the boys looked at each other, eyebrows raised, their arms still locked around his.

"It's okay," Dr. Wellon said. "You can ease up."

"That's it?" Jeremiah said. "It's that easy to get him under control?"

"Not quite," Dr. Wellon said as she turned to face him. "Dr. Poole avoided giving him sedatives and painkillers for a good reason. They don't eliminate the aggression. He still wants to kill us. And the drugs accelerate his parasympathetic nervous system and trigger a reaction in his nano-processors that ages his cellular structure geometrically. Plus, the sedatives and painkillers make his cells mutate more quickly—a kind of cancer. It's already spread throughout his body."

Jeremiah felt himself growing angry but he kept his voice calm. "Why are you giving him an injection?"

"I need him cooperative during my examination. And I don't think it can hurt him much more. His body has already deteriorated about as much as it can."

Jeremiah wheeled himself over and the boys parted to let him through. "Joshie," he said, "it's going to be okay. I'm here. Your dad's here." He reached out and grabbed his son's limp hand.

"Damon," the cadet said as he pulled his hand free. "My name is Damon." He stared at Jeremiah, hatred in his eyes.

"Damon, then," Jeremiah said as he held back the fear and sadness. "We're going to figure out how to help you."

A noise at the doorway caused them all to turn. A beautiful girl stood there. She looked about eighteen, with an angelic face surrounded by a halo of golden hair. When she smiled, showing off perfect white teeth, her brown eyes twinkled in the light. The Escala teens straightened; Krall ran a hand through his hair.

"Hello, Zora," Quekri said. "What can we do for you?"

Zora stepped into the room. "Don't worry. I don't plan to take over LB2. I just wanted to check on Damon, see if you'd found anything. And I brought Dr. Poole's records along. Thought they might help." She held out a data cube that Dr. Wellon took. She looked at Jeremiah and said, "You must be Damon's father. I'm one of the people who rescued you from SPR8. I'm sorry about your friend, Jack Marschenko. But Curtik has always been . . . hasty."

"Meaning what?" Jeremiah said. "That you would have killed him more slowly?"

Zora wagged her finger at him, an endearing gesture that nonetheless left him cold. "I've downloaded Dr. Poole's file on you, Mr. Jones. I know a great deal about you—who you've killed and why. You're a bad man. And I'm a bad girl."

"Zora?" Damon said.

Zora slid past the three Escala teens, who eased away, staring at her with rapturous gazes. Ignoring them, she approached Jeremiah, smelling like a dandelion—an oddly sweet yet somewhat spicy aroma, unlike the Escala boys, who emitted a distinctly musky, almost metallic odor. Jeremiah found himself tensing, reaching for the QuikHeal bandages by his legs. Her eyes caught the movement, but she just shook her head slightly and grabbed Damon's hand. She said, "I'm here, Damon. How are you?" She caressed his cheek. "You doing all right?"

At Zora's touch, Damon relaxed. The malevolence left his eyes and he smiled at her. "I don't like it here, Zora."

146

"I know you don't," Zora said.

"Can we leave?"

Zora shook her head. "Got a job to do. I can't leave yet. Do you want to go back to Earth with your dad?"

Jeremiah looked at Damon and smiled but Damon shook his head. "Don't know him."

Dr. Wellon said, "Do you remember your parents at all, Damon?"

"I remember Mom a little," Damon said.

"What about your dad?"

"He was gone a lot."

"Off killing people," Zora said with a nonchalant wave of her hand, "to make the world a better place."

Jeremiah's face burned with shame.

"My head hurts," Damon said. He began to cry, then reached up to his scarred face with his free hand and clawed at it again.

"Damon!" Zora said.

Damon dropped his hand and Zora latched onto it. On his face, furrows of red appeared and almost immediately began to heal.

"You have to stop doing that," Zora said.

"I'll try, Zora," Damon said.

"Not good enough. You have to remember—no more scratching."

"But it feels right."

"I know," Zora said. She released Damon's hands and ruffled his dark hair. Then she turned her back on him and made for the door. When she reached it, she looked at Jeremiah and said, "Mr. Jones, I'd like to speak with you outside. Alone. If it's too painful, I can wheel you out there."

"Not necessary," Jeremiah said, grunting as he wheeled himself toward the door. Part of him wanted to stay with Damon, but he'd seen the calming effect Zora had on his son and wanted to keep on her good side. He had trouble reading this girl. How strong was the programming that had turned her into a killer?

When the door closed behind him, Zora said, "Why does Curtik want to kill you?"

"Curtik?" Jeremiah shrugged, wincing at the pain. "I don't know him."

"He seems to know you," Zora said. "In his clumsy way, he tried to manipulate me into letting him kill you. Why would he do that if he didn't know you?"

Jeremiah let the rage fill him. It diminished ever so slightly the pain in his broken bones, the needle-like stabbing in every joint. "I heard he wants to kill everyone. And he killed Marschenko for no reason."

Zora shook her head. "There's more to it than that. You work for Eli."

"Not anymore."

"Whatever." Zora lifted her hands. "The point is, we're Eli's agents too. But he never said anything to me about you. Do you think he would have given separate instructions to Curtik to kill you? And if so, why?"

"I don't know," Jeremiah said. Though Eli had to know that Jeremiah would be tempted to pay him back for the pain he'd caused—not just Joshua's kidnapping but Catherine's death and even Julianna's.

Staring at him intently, Zora said, "You just thought of something. Care to share?"

Jeremiah shook his head. "I know you've been turned into super warriors through a combination of transgenic mutation and nano-technology. What I don't know is why. Wait a minute. Is this part of Eli's crazy plan to unite the Earth against an alien attack?"

"He told you about that?"

Jeremiah nodded. "He's mentioned it before—something that's been floating in his mind for decades—got it from some old science fiction. I never took it seriously."

Zora smiled briefly. "I think you'll find we're serious."

"I'm sure you are. Let me see if I remember how it goes." Jeremiah fingered the QuikHeal bandages next to his legs. Should he attack? "You attack various governments around the globe, forcing them to work together to bring you down. Eventually they triumph and realize how important it is to cooperate. Peace and goodwill ensue."

Zora laughed—bubbly and warm—a laugh designed to entice. "Not exactly."

"You think you can win? How many people do you have, fifty? A hundred?"

Zora stared at him for a few seconds, an uncomfortable gaze that reached right inside him. She bent over and put her hands on the arms of his wheelchair, bringing her head down to his level, and closed her eyes. Was she challenging him to use the QuikHeal bandages on her? She breathed in deeply, as if smelling him. He couldn't help but smile as he inhaled too, noting again her peculiar sweet and spicy aroma. He forced himself to stillness, waiting for her to open her eyes. When she did, she glanced at his hands, grinned and said, "What am I supposed to do?"

Jeremiah shook his head. "You've been programmed to want to do this. It's a false desire. But what to do about it, I don't know. I just . . . mass murder is not the answer."

"As opposed to all the other wars humans started. Those all made sense."

Forgetting how painful it was, Jeremiah shrugged again. "People are what they are. Maybe they'll never change. Devereaux might know what to do."

"Everybody plays games. Everybody tries to manipulate us. Why can't anyone be straight with us?"

"It's part of our competitive nature to seek whatever advantage we can. Besides, I find it hard to believe you're easily manipulated."

Zora suddenly straightened, pushed out her breasts, licked her lips and blinked her eyes. "Do you think I'm beautiful?"

What was her game? "Yes," he answered.

"What does that mean?" She sounded serious, almost desperate.

Jeremiah gave it some thought. After a moment he said, "It's purely physical. I see you as beautiful because I've been conditioned to think of beauty a certain way, and you exemplify those characteristics."

Zora's frown lessened. Her head nodded almost imperceptibly. But her brow knitted again and she said, "Am I human?"

This one Jeremiah didn't have to think about. "As much as I am," he gestured toward the door, "or the Escala are. Your genetic structure has been modified. Nano-technology added—hormones and proteins and amino acids. But you're still you. You're still self-aware, able to reason, decide issues that extend beyond yourself and your immediate environment. You're just smarter and stronger and faster than you used to be."

Zora smiled. "Yes. It's clever what they did to me. Do you want to plow me?"

Jeremiah almost laughed, but he kept the humor out of his face and voice. "No," he said. "Whatever they did to you, they didn't finish. You're still not complete. You're a little girl."

"I don't feel like a little girl," Zora said, her face setting into hardness. "Tell me about Curtik."

"I already told you. I don't know him."

"He also wants to kill Damon."

"Damon?" Jeremiah felt a shiver work down his back. "Why?"

"Damon and his tong supported me for brigade leader."

Jeremiah kept his eyes on her beautiful face. He had to remind himself that she was just a child, no more than nine or ten.

Zora studied him for a moment, her luminous brown eyes steady on his in an adult way that was unsettling. "If I send you back to Earth, what will you do?"

"What do you want me to do?"

"Just answer the question."

"All I care about," Jeremiah said, "is finding a cure for my son. Everything else can wait."

"Curtik says you'll come after us if I let you go. He says you won't rest until you've stopped us. That's why you have to be killed."

"If you already know why Curtik wants me dead," Jeremiah said, "why did you ask me about him?"

"Because Curtik's a liar, like Poole and Eli. And he's got his own reasons for wanting you dead. I wondered if you knew what they are."

"Sorry," Jeremiah said. "It's certainly possible that Eli ordered him to kill me. But Eli could have had me killed many times in the past. Why now?"

Zora bit down on her lower lip—one of the most striking young women Jeremiah had ever seen. She said, "I'm still trying to figure out Eli's angle."

"I can tell you he's always playing a different game than what he's showing you."

"Well, duh," Zora said. "But what is it?"

Jeremiah shrugged. "It might be as simple as it seems. Set up a scenario where either side could win and see who does."

Zora nodded slowly. "If I keep you here, Curtik might get to you. I can't watch him every minute. On the other hand, from what I know of you, you're the most dangerous foe we could have. I probably should let Curtik kill you. And Damon doesn't seem to like you very much. Still, if you think you can get help for him, I might send you back to Earth on the next LTV."

"You're letting the LTVs continue?"

"We cut off all communication," Zora said. "They don't know what's going on up here, so they're prepping an LTV, sending it in a few days, hoping to discover why they can't contact us. Meanwhile, Dr. Wellon will try to find a cure for Damon's condition. Maybe Devereaux can help too. Dr. Poole hasn't found anything yet."

"Thank you," Jeremiah said.

"Don't thank me yet. I still may have you killed."

Chapter Fourteen

Lendra Riley sat in the first row behind the pilots as the emergency LTV approached the Moon. She found the view spectacular. Up close the Moon looked massive, while Lunar Base 1 appeared as a tiny outpost in the harshest environment imaginable. Some distance away stood the Pilgrim, the Escala ship soon bound for Mars.

Next to her sat Colonel Dez Truman—her liaison to the eight Elite Ops troopers President Hope had sent to contain the cadets. More like a bodyguard, actually.

The troopers, in the back of the LTV near their armor, had ogled Lendra and made crude comments throughout the journey. Even Captain Bailey, their leader, had joined in the harassment, which made her glad for Colonel Truman's presence. Eli had insisted she go because, in case the Elite Ops failed to retake the Moon, she had a mission of her own. Lendra also needed to see Jeremiah and learn how badly he was injured.

She still felt guilty over allowing Eli's doctors to impregnate her with Jeremiah's child, even though duty demanded another of Jeremiah's progeny, for his genes were so uniquely adaptable that he owed them to the world. Nevertheless, Lendra felt disconcerted about how it had all happened. She fingered her glass bulb necklace, which contained her emergency stash of neo-dopamine, feeling the addicting pull of it; she hadn't taken any since the in vitro fertilization and she was feeling a little edgy.

She still cared deeply for Jeremiah, but she wondered how he felt about her. Hopefully, once he knew she was carrying his baby, he would embrace his new family. And perhaps the knowledge that Lendra was carrying his daughter would even aid in his recovery.

During the trip she and Truman had reminisced about their shared past: Sister Ezekiel, the nun with the courage of a martyr, who became one in the end; Gray Weiss, the well-meaning but misguided Attorney General who'd been killed by Richard Carlton; Devereaux and Jeremiah and the Escala, whom many on Earth were blaming for the sudden communications blackout.

Lendra also confided to Truman that Jeremiah's son was one of the cadets who'd taken over the Moon, and she mentioned that Jeremiah had been injured and somehow infected with the Susquehanna Virus.

"I know it's not his fault," Truman said, "but everywhere he goes, trouble follows. And here we are again. That man is a menace."

Lendra said, "Perhaps I should have told you that he and I have been involved for the past year."

Truman's mouth opened, then closed.

And now I've betrayed his trust. I hope he forgives me.

Truman shook his head. "You know, ever since Minnesota a year ago, I suspected you were more than you appeared to be. But I didn't realize just how senior you are until President Hope and Elias Leach impressed on me the necessity of keeping you healthy. You're an important young woman."

"They're just being overly protective."

"Thanks for letting me tag along," Truman said. "I've always wanted to visit the Moon. Emily—my wife—and I have been having some difficulties since . . . well, for a long time. She's a professional protester—against government, corporate greed, genetically modified foods, genetically altered humans, designer babies and synthetic biological organisms. And those are just the major ones. I lost count of her causes years ago."

Lendra didn't know how to respond to that. She said, "It's nice that she keeps herself active."

Truman laughed. "In another way," he said, "I dread this assignment. I have these nightmares—the murder of Sister Ezekiel, the piled bodies of innocent Devereauxnians, especially the little children sliced in half by laser fire. Life feels very precious now, more so than ever before, and I wonder if that feeling is making a coward of me. I hope my nerve will hold up. And I hope these bastards behind us don't cut those kids in half as soon as they step off the LTV."

"You'll be fine," Lendra said, patting his leg while at the same time fingering her glass bulb necklace. She looked out the window, not wanting more talk, and he got the hint and left her alone. She liked that about him.

After a while Truman fell asleep and she considered how best to approach Jeremiah. Did she love him? She wanted to. But in the weeks before he'd left, Jeremiah had become distant. She admired his intelligence, his principles, his sense of duty and honor. But she also recognized that part of what had drawn her to him was her own ambition. And now there would always be elements of guilt in their relationship. Maybe her doubts were fueled by her condition. Perhaps she would know the truth when she saw him. Would she feel again that warm tingling in her belly?

Lendra hoped the Elite Ops would win, but she somehow knew they wouldn't, which meant that she would have to take over from Poole, whose work was finished, and who was a failure anyway because the cadets were out of control. But it was the last part of Eli's instructions that bothered her the most. "If necessary," he'd said, "you might have to eliminate Poole." And then he'd spelled out the entirety of his plan and how she might have to use a hidden program encrypted into Poole's files to destroy the cadets.

Lendra hoped it wouldn't come to that. She decided to take her mind off such an unpleasant task and instead renewed her study of the cadets' bios—particularly Zora—and Curtik, Jeremiah's son.

As the LTV fired its retro rockets, Truman awoke. Together they watched the LTV touch down on the Moon and taxi toward the main hangar of Lunar Base 1. Behind them, Captain Bailey got the Elite Ops troopers to their feet and headed to their armor.

They joked with each other about invading the Moon and taking out anyone who got in their way as they stripped off their mock gravity flightsuits and stepped into their armor. Donning their helmets, the Elite Ops activated their power packs, which emitted a high-pitched whine. Then, looking menacing and indestructible, they lined up and waited for the LTV to come to a stop.

Lendra got to her feet and peeled off her flightsuit, causing one of the troopers to wolf whistle, while another sang the notes from The Stripper.

"That's enough," Truman ordered as he too stepped out of his mock gravity suit.

"Didn't meant no harm," Captain Bailey replied.

"Bite me," another trooper spoke *sotto voce*.

"You two stay back now, hear?" Captain Bailey said. "Let us take point. Once we clear out the opposition, you can make your reports."

The pilots sealed the LTV's doorway to the connector of Lunar Base 1 and via remote moved the wheeled staircase into position. Through the monitors, Lendra saw only eight cadets in the hangar, standing casually in a semi-circle a few meters away from the staircase. She recognized Curtik, in the middle of the formation, from his bio. Next to him stood a pale female cadet—Aspen, Lendra recalled.

"Let's move," Captain Bailey said.

As they opened the hatch and descended the wheeled staircase, Lendra and Colonel Truman followed, taking up position at the top of the stairs. The cadets, Lendra noticed, made no aggressive moves. They smiled as they stood in their semicircle, looking innocent, watching the approaching troopers.

"Hands up!" Captain Bailey ordered, his voice amplified by a microphone in his helmet. "Don't nobody move."

Curtik raised his hands and the rest of the cadets followed his lead.

"Where's Admiral Cho?" Bailey asked as he drew to within a few feet of Curtik. "Where are the military personnel? Who's in charge? Where are the civilians? Keep your hands up."

Curtik said, "We mean you no harm."

"You move and we'll blow you away so fast you ain't gonna know how you died. Now tell me what's goin' on."

"Don't hurt us," Curtik said. "We're unarmed. We're just kids. It was those evil Escala—those pseudos—who did it. They took over the

Moon. They're the ones you want. They made us stand out here 'cause they were afraid you'd start shooting. God, I hate them."

"Pseudos, huh?" Captain Bailey lowered his Las-rifle fractionally. "Don't think so. We heard it was you kids."

"That's what they wanted you to think. They threatened to eat us. They're gonna kill us all, and they're gonna kill you."

"If it was the pseudos, how come they ain't around?"

"Hiding," Curtik said. He pointed toward the plas-glass ceiling. "Up there."

As Captain Bailey and the rest of the Elite Ops troopers glanced up, Curtik and his fellow cadets moved—so swiftly Lendra almost missed it. Eight arms shot out, eight fists striking the Elite Ops troopers at the junction where their helmets met their body armor. The troopers fired their Las-rifles wildly, while the cadets ripped the troopers' helmets from their heads. Curtik snapped Bailey's neck. Two other cadets—Phan and Benn, Lendra noted—did likewise, while Aspen and the other cadets pressed their palms against the remaining troopers' cheeks. The troopers fell to the floor, obviously victims of some sort of knockout cocktail.

"Anyone hurt?" Aspen asked.

The cadets all shook their heads.

"Just these three," Curtik said, gesturing to the dead troopers at his feet.

Benn and Phan laughed.

"You weren't supposed to kill them," Aspen said.

"Oops," Curtik replied. "A small accident. They're more fragile than they look. Besides, we gotta do it sooner or later. Plus they smell funny. Can I kill the rest? Please? I'm askin' pretty."

Aspen shook her head. "Zora wants to question them."

* * *

Escorted by Aspen, Lendra walked beside Truman, feeling almost as light as air. Her stomach, which hadn't bothered her while she was wearing a mock-gravity flight suit, attempted a series of somersaults. She clamped her jaw tightly and glanced over at Truman, who wore a frown.

When they reached Admiral Cho's office, Aspen directed them inside, following them in. Standing beside Cho's desk was Zora. She, like the other cadets, projected innocence and beauty. If anything, she appeared even more angelic than her peers, with curly blond hair and deep brown eyes, bronze skin and an athletic figure.

But Lendra's interface had provided a great deal of information about Zora and the cadets. She knew Zora was the smartest, just as Curtik was the most violent, while Aspen, standing behind her with a Las-rifle, was perhaps the most unpredictable. Lendra wondered whether it would be possible to manipulate these kids or if she would have to destroy them.

Zora carried no weapon and couldn't be hiding one under her clothes either. Her white shimmer cloth coveralls clung to her shapely body. Yet strangely, despite her obviously blossoming maturity, she exuded little sexuality. Or was that just the fact that she was female? No, now that Lendra thought about it, Curtik and the male cadets also were oddly asexual.

"Welcome, Miss Riley," Zora said. "It's so good to meet another of Eli's minions. And a pregnant one at that."

"How did you—"

"Our scans picked it up," Zora explained. "I can see by your bodyguard's surprise that he didn't know." She looked past Lendra to Aspen. "I think you can leave us alone. Check on Curtik. He's certain to do something stupid soon."

"May I see Jeremiah Jones?" Lendra asked.

"Is he the father of your child?" Zora asked. When Lendra didn't reply, she added, "Does he know?"

Lendra shook her head.

"Well, that can wait," Zora said. "We have a few things to take care of first."

She moved behind Admiral Cho's desk, took a seat, and indicated that Lendra and Truman should sit as well.

"I want you to call Eli," Zora said, pointing to the PlusPhone on the desk. "I've lowered the dampening field temporarily. Tell him I've taken command, not Curtik. And we're going to do things my way from now on."

"Why don't you call him yourself?" Lendra asked.

"He doesn't want to talk to me," Zora answered.

"How do you know?"

Zora leaned forward, her intense eyes focusing on Lendra's face. "Do I seem like an idiot to you?"

Lendra's head jerked back a few inches. "Of course not. I'm sorry. Did I say something to offend you?"

"I called him," Zora said, leaning back in her chair. "Or at least I tried to. He didn't answer. His tech assistant, Jay-Edgar, told me he'd only talk to Curtik. Wouldn't even take a message from me. Why do you think that is?"

Lendra shrugged. "Perhaps he doesn't know how to deal with you. Before I left, he briefed me on the program and how he intended Curtik to lead the attack against Earth."

"What does it matter which of us leads?"

"I think he feels more comfortable with Curtik's brand of aggression. And I suspect he's a little afraid of what you'll do."

Zora laughed. "The great and powerful Oz? He isn't afraid of anyone. I think he's just trying to piss me off so I'll attack right away like Curtik would have."

Lendra shrugged. "He knew what to expect from Curtik, where the attacks would come, how to counter them. You're an unknown entity. You could win."

"Oh, I intend to win," Zora said. "But I don't think I want to attack Eli's targets. If I fire on the governments he chose, they'll just set up new ones. So instead, we're asking every government to dismantle its nuclear and bio-chemical weapons, stop all aggressive actions. You do that and we'll let your people live. Simple, no?"

Truman shook his head, as if marveling at her naiveté. He said, "That will never happen. Even if the United States complies, no one else will. And there's no way the United States will comply."

Without taking her eyes from Zora's face, Lendra said, "She doesn't expect them to comply, Colonel."

"That's true," Zora said. "But I want to at least make the offer. Who knows? Maybe you'll surprise me."

"And how long do we have?"

Zora's face went blank, accessing her implant, no doubt. Lendra looked up at the screens lining the walls—light cloth fabrics made from conductive metamaterial. On each screen a different scene was displayed: a few from the Moon but most from Earth. Washington, DC; Paris; London; Beijing; New Delhi; Rio de Janeiro; Jakarta. After a moment, Zora said, "I think forty-eight hours is about right. That seems fair, doesn't it?"

"Two days?" Lendra said.

"Impossible," Truman said. "No nation will be able to make a decision about that in forty-eight hours."

Zora turned to face him, her brow furrowing. "Let me explain something, Colonel. The old days are gone. Whatever quaint notion you might have about how to deal with a problem like this—how to wriggle out of complying—forget it. We'll deliver a mass transmission to every nation outlining my ultimatum with instructions on how to relay the codes verifying that weapons systems have been disarmed."

Zora swung her chair from side to side like a little girl. Lendra found her fascinating—a militaristic version of herself. This girl was what Lendra might have become had Eli begun his program a few years earlier. Lendra pushed that thought aside and said, "Why offer terms we can't possibly meet?"

Zora stopped the chair and leaned forward. "Shall I tell you what will happen?"

Lendra sat back in her chair with a grim smile. "Why not?"

"Your governments—and even the great and powerful Oz—will beg for more time, insisting that a decision can't be made so quickly, that others must be consulted or that the technological requirements are too complex for my demands to be met within the deadline. At the same time, behind the scenes, they'll prepare to launch attacks at us—shielded missiles and rockets with nuclear warheads, not to mention attempts to align the Las-cannons on our position. They will fight to the death for the freedom to pursue their policies of madness and violence. They are convinced their way is the only correct way to rule, so everything else must be wrong. And they will never, ever give up the power they so desperately desire."

Zora smiled sadly. "But if I start killing them, they'll just create new leaders, resolved to stop us. So they have to voluntarily step down." She pointed to the PlusPhone again. "You have forty-seven hours and fifty-eight minutes left."

Lendra placed the call to Elias Leach. "You need to speak with Zora," she said. "Curtik's out of control and she's in charge. And if you don't listen to her, she'll simply cut you out of the loop."

"Fine," Eli said after the three-second lag. "I'll conference in the President."

When President Hope appeared onscreen, sitting next to General Horowitz and Secretary of Defense Raskov, Zora outlined her demands. President Hope said, "That's impossible. We can't even reach the leaders of every country in forty-eight hours."

"Oh, don't worry," Zora said. "We're already taking care of that for you—broadcasting to every country even as we speak."

During the lag time, President Hope's expression changed from resolve to surprise and then anger, while General Horowitz and Secretary Raskov looked off camera. "Hold on a moment," the President said as the sound muted and she too looked off camera. The screen went blue for a few seconds. When President Hope reappeared, she said, "It's not as simple as flicking a switch. We can't just disarm ourselves instantaneously."

"No, it's way more complicated than that," Zora agreed. "There are buttons to push and dials to turn and control bars to adjust. Why, the whole process could take many hundreds of seconds."

President Hope began to frown even before Zora finished speaking. Again, General Horowitz and Secretary Raskov looked off camera.

Again, the screen went blue for a moment. Then President Hope said, "This is not a game. This is thousands, maybe millions, of lives at stake. We can't just eliminate our defensive systems because you ordered it."

"Oh, it's a game, all right," Zora replied. "Just like all the wars started for illogical and unjustified reasons. Wars are philosophical games. I've just increased the stakes. You can argue about it among yourselves if you want, but I'm done talking. I've given you my terms. You can either do as I ask or see if I'm bluffing—makes no difference to me. Thank you for your attention and have a nice day."

Zora cut the connection. "That went well," she said.

"May I see Jeremiah now?" Lendra asked. "Or at least Dr. Poole."

"Ah." Zora smiled. "You're tense. Nervous. I think you mean to harm our good Dr. Poole. Why would Eli want to do that?"

Lendra stared back at Zora, hoping her face betrayed nothing, but shocked that Zora had figured out why she'd been sent.

"You've never killed anyone before, have you," Zora said. She stood, indicating that the conversation was over. When Aspen entered the office, Zora said, "Show these two to their room. Something cozy, with a view of Earth and their very own bathroom."

"I know just the place," Aspen said. "It's only got one bed though. You'll have to share. Don't worry. You'll have complete privacy."

Chapter Fifteen

Taditha Poole sipped her cup of tea, fighting back the nausea, while Rendela sat beside her, as if content to wait all day. Why did she feel so ill? She turned to Rendela, who shook her dark hair and said, "Zora's still busy. But your request is important to her. She'll be with you shortly."

Rendela laughed.

"No, it's not that," Poole said. "I was wondering if I can run a blood test on myself—see if I'm coming down with something."

Rendela shrugged. "It's your blood."

Poole took a sample and placed it in the diagnosticon. While she was waiting for the machine to display its report, she focused on one of the screens, which showed an image of Earth. She ramped up the magnification until she could see Naples, Florida, her hometown. How she longed to return there. But she sensed that she'd never touch Earth again. God, she was tired of the Moon. For a while, Jack Marschenko had made it bearable, but now it was only a cold and desolate rock again. After a moment of staring at her hometown, she broke the silence:

"I hope you didn't kill anyone on that LTV."

"We all know you have a thing for Elite Ops troopers, Doctor," Rendela replied.

"I'm concerned about your well-being. What is Zora up to?"

"About five-feet, six inches. Now sit back and enjoy the tranquility. It's only going to get worse."

Rendela was right. It was bound to get worse. Nothing was going according to Eli's plan. Curtik was supposed to be in charge. He would have attacked the governments Eli dictated should fall. Or would he? Maybe he would have been even more out of control, attacking civilian populations. And perhaps that was Eli's plan all along. Perhaps that was why he insisted Curtik lead the attacks. Curtik's rash arrogance would have led to his downfall. Zora was much more careful. Did Eli know what sort of battle he was in for now? Did he care?

And how could these kids be better than the data indicated? She'd been monitoring them for two years. Was there some hidden human element that didn't register on her scans? Or had they been holding back from the beginning? Was there some pre-capture component to their minds that she hadn't anticipated, some essentially human imprint that didn't show up on any scan?

Their forced evolution had been so carefully calibrated. Then again, so had the Escala, and yet a few of them had become insanely violent. So if in fact there were some atavistic human condition buried in the cadets, perhaps it only affected a small number of them. Perhaps Damon's devolution was tied to this same phenomenon.

"What's up, Doc?" Zora said.

When Poole turned to face her, Zora chomped down on a large carrot, which made Rendela roar with laughter. Poole had been so focused on her thoughts that she hadn't heard the door open. She kept her voice under control, saying, "I'm glad you finally have time to see me."

"Are you upset?"

"Frankly, yes. And disappointed."

"Well, you raised me. So any criticism of me is really an indictment of your abilities. Perhaps, to keep you from making the same mistake again, we should take your child off your hands, just like Eli took us away from our families."

"My child?"

Zora pointed to the diagnosticon. "Take a look. You're pregnant."

Poole glanced at the diagnosticon. Sure enough, she was. "You connected to the diagnosticon with your implant. But how can I be . . . "

"I'm afraid I have no time to explain the birds and bees to you, Doctor."

Poole opened her mouth, but no words came out. She glanced at Rendela, hoping for help of some sort, but Rendela only smiled and looked away. "Please," Poole finally managed to say. She wasn't sure why she was saying it, what sort of favor she was after; she only knew she needed help.

"I've been busy," Zora said, "going over the strategy mapped out by Eli and Cho, and looking over your notes on our progress. I've asked Devereaux to join us. Would you come with me, please?"

Rendela grabbed Poole's arm and steered her along, following Zora toward what used to be Cho's office. As they passed Curtik in the hallway, he smirked at Poole and stuck out his tongue at Zora. Neither Zora nor Rendela saw it. But Curtik noticed Poole watching and chuckled.

When they reached Cho's office, Devereaux was already inside, seated in front of the desk, Aspen standing behind him, her Las-rifle pointed at the floor. Devereaux wore the same calm expression he brought to every occasion, unsurprised and indulgent. He nodded to Poole, Zora and Rendela, including each in the warmth of his smile. Poole smiled back, her muscles relaxing.

"What's up, Doc?" Aspen said as she too lifted a large carrot to her mouth and chomped down on it. She laughed, as did Rendela, Zora and even Devereaux.

Zora moved around the desk and sat in Cho's big chair. She had to know she looked faintly ridiculous sitting there. Zora pointed to the other chair. "Have a seat, Doctor."

Devereaux said, "I had hoped to be able to study the Susquehanna Virus further."

Zora leaned back and cocked her head. "You'll get your chance. But this is more important. Did you look at that data I forwarded?"

Devereaux nodded. "Your genetic and nano-tech records. Fascinating material. But you didn't tell me what specifically you want me to check."

"I want to know what they've done to us," Zora said. "I don't trust Dr. Poole, so I want to hear it from you. What's the matter with us? We're adults now. Yet we're . . ."

"Why don't we want sex?" Aspen said.

Devereaux looked at Poole, his dark eyes fixing her to her chair like pins in a butterfly. She'd met him before, of course, but she'd never before noticed how singular his gaze could be, how unwavering. She resisted an urge to squirm. Yet his voice, when he spoke, was gentle enough: "You didn't explain it to them?"

"I haven't had the chance," Poole replied. "Zora hasn't condescended to speak with me since the takeover."

"All right." Zora placed her palms on the desk and turned her attention to Poole. "Tell me."

Poole took a breath, gathering her thoughts. "You obviously know about the controls that keep you from harming me. And you overrode them somehow or you wouldn't have been able to murder Admiral Cho. I still don't know how that was possible."

"Simple, Doctor. We treated it like a game. We just put him in the airlock like he was a naughty boy—which he was."

"But Curtik opened the outer doors."

"Yes," Zora agreed, "but he was wearing a QuikHeal bandage. And he's Curtik. I don't think any of the rest of us could have done it. He has something extra in him that allows him to go beyond where we're supposed to go. That's why we need him. He can do things—terrible things—that we can't. I'd hate to turn him loose on you. So talk."

"We created a series of psychological and chemical barricades to sexual development as a means of furthering aggressive behavior."

"So we would attack Earth."

"Yes. And even though you've technically gone through puberty, the parts of your brain stimulated by thoughts of sex—the pleasure centers—receive electrical impulses that interfere with their normal circuitry and divert the expected responses away from the urges that cross your mind."

"In other words, when we have thoughts of a sexual nature, we don't derive pleasure from them the way we should."

"Correct. Instead, your brains divert your thoughts to images of conquest, keeping you on task for your mission. And of course the boys receive a chemical cocktail that prevents them from maintaining erections."

Zora nodded. "How soon can you reverse it?"

"I don't know if—"

"Perhaps I should rephrase the question," Zora said. She looked over Poole's shoulder. "Rendela, what's the status of the airlock?"

"It's lonely," Rendela answered.

Aspen giggled; Zora smiled; Poole's throat dried up.

Devereaux said, "I wouldn't recommend what you're thinking of doing."

Zora stabbed a finger at Poole. "Putting her in the airlock? It's plenty roomy."

Devereaux shook his head. "This is the biggest thing that will ever happen to you. It will change you irreversibly. I suspect that you weren't designed to be sexual beings. You're not emotionally prepared for your adult bodies. If you become sexually charged, the experience could overwhelm and ultimately destroy you."

Zora shook her head. "I don't care. I want to be a real person. We all do. Even Curtik, though he probably won't admit it. Besides, don't you want us to fail? We're the bad guys. And according to the vids, bad guys don't win. It's frustrating."

Poole said, "You're not bad guys."

"Aren't we?" Zora turned to Devereaux. "Are we bad?"

Devereaux shrugged. "What you're planning is wrong." He turned his dark brown eyes to Poole and stared at her with disconcerting intensity. "You may have meant well, Doctor. But Eli's plan cannot work over the long term. Cooperation, not competition, is the only lasting solution for Earth's problems."

Zora looked at Devereaux. "You know about Eli's plan?"

"Jeremiah told me about it. But it assumes that humanity cannot change—that we're destined to think and act a certain way, and that we'll destroy ourselves without an external guiding force—like God. Or you."

"Well spoken," Zora replied. "We are certainly Eli's greatest achievement—transgenic and nano-modifications, intellectual and physical enhancements."

"And stunted emotional growth," Devereaux finished.

Zora leaned forward, her shoulders hunched as she glared at Devereaux. Poole knew how intimidating Zora could be when she focused all her energy on you. Yet Devereaux looked calm. Zora nodded slowly and said, "Why aren't you afraid of us? Dr. Poole is."

"Dr. Poole is a sensible woman," Devereaux said. "She knows you're angry with her. And you have every right to be. But you have no reason to be angry with me. Even if you were and you decided to kill me, I couldn't do anything about it. I'm powerless." He pointed to his head. "This is the only thing of value I possess—my only weapon. And whether I live or die, my ideas will continue for a while, which is about as much as anyone can ask. Still, if it makes you feel any better, you do perturb me."

Zora snorted as she slammed her hand on the desk. "I like you!" She turned to Poole. "Why couldn't you be more like him?"

Poole shook her head. "There is no one like him."

"Well," Zora settled back into the chair again, "if you fix us, Doc, I'll give you a shiny new nickel." Zora smiled broadly. "Rendela will assist you. Professor Devereaux will double-check your work. And if you're good, maybe we'll let you keep your baby. Now off you go."

Rendela lifted Poole out of her chair and pulled her toward the doorway. Poole said, "It would go faster if I had my interface."

"But I'm not done playing with it yet," Zora replied.

* * *

As the hours progressed, Poole's endurance evaporated. Nausea fought with exhaustion for control of her body, though exhaustion was winning. What were the odds of becoming pregnant for the first time at forty-two?

Rendela reached over and touched her shoulder. "You gonna puke again?"

"I'm just tired," she answered. "I've been working on this almost nonstop for the past thirty hours."

"I can give you another stimulant."

"No. Please. That might harm the baby." Poole pointed to the screen in front of her as she struggled to regain her composure. "So far, I've mapped everything from the nano-analyzers to the psychometric controls. I've outlined the progression of steps necessary to retrograde the implant override technology. It's easy to eliminate the chemicals you were receiving, but the genetic component is trickier. I just need a few minutes to collect my thoughts. What's going on out there? When are you planning to attack Earth?"

"Soon."

"What does that mean?"

Rendela sighed. "Standard operating procedure, Doctor. You know that. Keep hostages ignorant as much as possible. Don't tell me you've forgotten a tactic you yourself taught us. Besides, Zora will be here any moment. She'll tell you what she wants you to know."

As if on cue, the door opened and Zora stepped into the room. "Maddening, isn't it?" she said. "For years you kept us in the dark about why we were in your program and what you'd done to us. We just had to trust that you knew best."

Emotions flooded Poole: relief, fear, hope, despair. Why was she suddenly so vulnerable? "I'm sorry, Zora. I was only doing my job." Even as she spoke, she realized that with Zora, only absolute truth would work. "I believed in our mission—"

"Yes, and now you're having doubts."

"I also have a baby growing inside me. That changes a woman."

"You look the same to me. Now, we've got to figure out which targets to hit. Eli picked such boring ones."

Poole said, "Why do all this? You've got the Moon. You figured out our plan. You overrode the controls that prevented you from harming Admiral Cho. Can't you do the same with the controls that dictate you attack Earth?"

"Maybe we want to attack Earth anyway."

Poole said, "You've got some other agenda. But I can't figure out what it is. I'm tired. I need sleep, Zora."

"Later. Devereaux says your work has no serious flaws."

"If you trust him so much, why not have him do the work?"

"Then we wouldn't need you, would we?" Zora smiled. "Believe me, I thought about it. But I have my reasons for choosing you."

"You're afraid he wouldn't do it. Or you think he might sabotage the process so cleverly you won't be able to find the flaw until it's too late."

"Very good, Doctor." Zora clapped her hands, mimicking one of Poole's habits. "I'm also reviewing everything the two of you do. So don't think you can slip a harmful change past me. In fact, that's why I'm here. There are a couple things I don't understand in the process of modifying our genetic structures. And I don't intend to take that action until we've discussed exactly what the changes will do and why."

Zora stepped to Poole's tablet and opened the files Poole had been using. For the next two hours, she grilled Poole on each proposed alteration and what it would do to the cadets' psychological makeup. Zora's intensity kept Poole's fatigue at bay. She explained each step, unsurprised at how quickly Zora grasped each one. Zora had always been the brightest student but, like Curtik, she must have been holding back her full potential in classes and tests. Now that she was no longer under Poole's command, she obviously felt free to display the magnitude of her incredible intellect.

"Were all of you this way?" Poole finally asked. "Did you all hide the full extent of your abilities from us?"

Zora shrugged. "A few of us thought we might need an edge. Our way of rebelling, since we couldn't do so outwardly."

"But how did you hide it? You were monitored constantly. There would have been no way to do it, unless . . ."

"I see the bulb lighting up over your head. Go ahead, Doctor."

"You would have had to hold something back from the beginning."

"No—just from when you took over the project. By that point, we all dreamed of freedom. And some of us—the smartest ones or the most determined ones—realized that if you knew how gifted we really were, we would lose whatever edge we had. But that's not the scary part." Zora stopped talking, a faint smile touching her lips.

"What's the scary part?" Poole asked.

"We apparently reached that decision independently at almost exactly the same time, which is why you never caught it."

"Amazing," Poole said. "How could that be?"

"You came in to finalize our development just as we were reaching physical maturity. We knew from your reaction to our abilities that we could go beyond anything that came before. You saw what we could become, while Dr. Hack'emup never saw us as anything but experiments—freaks."

"So now your plan is what?"

"If I tell you," Zora said in a stage whisper, "I'll have to kill you." Rendela laughed.

"I will tell you this," Zora said. "Your interface has been fascinating. We never knew how passionate you are."

Poole's face flushed with anger and embarrassment. "You've been reading my personal journal?"

Zora took Poole's interface from her pocket and handed it over. "Your password was Naples4Me. Anyone could have hacked that. And I'm afraid you were right about one thing. You'll probably never return to Earth. We need you here on our side. Isn't it nice to feel wanted?"

Poole attached her interface. "I'm sorry, Zora—for everything."

Zora shrugged. "Too late. They took away our memories, our families, everything we knew and loved—to make us into perfect little fighters. Do you know who my mother is? My father? Do I have brothers or sisters? Does Rendela?"

"I'm sure it's on record. Eli must know."

Zora shook her head. Her eyes narrowed. Her nostrils flared. And her face hardened. "You told us Damon devolved because his body rejected the treatments. Is that true or did you make it happen so you could give him to Jones? Are we going to devolve too and get the cancer Damon has? You don't know, do you?"

Poole shook her head. She found herself blinking back tears. "Dr. Hackett's team did the nano-surgery. I just refined the neuropsychological components. I thought I was doing . . . we made the hard choices because no one else would. I know it was awful. And I could never do it again. But look at what's happening on Earth. India and China at war. Nuclear weapons. Environmental disasters. Our intent was to make that better."

Zora held up her hand. "I'm not judging you, Doctor. I am what I am. I don't know if I'm happy about that or not. But I can live with it, as long as you give me back my humanity. One thing I've learned from all this though—one thing you and Eli taught me that really sank in—is not to make value judgments about good and bad. The world will think of us as evil unless we win. Then we get to write history."

Nausea suddenly flooded Poole again. She bent over and retched into the recycler.

"She's been doing that a lot lately," Rendela said.

"Poor pregnant Poole," Zora said.

As Poole lifted her head, Zora grabbed a tissue from the desk and wiped Poole's mouth. "Don't worry. Rendela here will take good care of you." Zora suddenly went still, accessing her implant. "Excuse me. Curtik is being a bad boy again."

Zora left the room. Poole couldn't help but admire her force of will, her intelligence, her amazing ability to handle every situation with aplomb far beyond her years. She terrified Poole. And yet she was so damned hard to hate. Even now Poole found herself wanting Zora's respect and admiration.

Rendela said, "Okay, Doc, let's get you cleaned up and back to work."

"I can't. I'm exhausted. If you need to kill me, kill me, but I need to close my eyes for a while." Poole leaned back in her chair and glared at Rendela.

Rendela put her hands up. "Well, you win, then. I surrender. You've got twenty minutes."

171

Chapter Sixteen

Under the changing colors of a bacteria-filled glow globe hovering above him, Jeremiah sat in his wheelchair, his joints feeling like they'd been implanted with burrs. Even sitting still, he felt a constant dull throbbing. And when he moved, a fiery agony struck, making him want to lash out—an instinctive animal response that he recognized but only barely controlled. The Susquehanna Virus intensified his pain, though Dr. Wellon didn't yet know why.

Adding to his discomfort was his suspicion that Zora intended to attack Earth soon, but she had cut off communication with Lunar Base 2, so he couldn't be certain. He wondered if she would attack the Escala too.

Across the room, sitting up in his bed, Damon stared from Dr. Wellon to Zeriphi to Krall and Oggie with a frown of intense concentration, as if he could see their worry. Krall and Oggie, assigned to guard against any sudden attack, stood against the far wall, tense, aware of Damon's attention. He remained under the influence of sedatives and painkillers, no longer showing murderous tendencies now that Dr. Wellon had refined the blend of chemicals and hormones pumped into him. But his body was aging rapidly and Dr. Wellon could do nothing to stop it. Jeremiah noted the gray hair at Damon's temples and felt a hollowness in his chest that made breathing difficult.

With each passing hour Jeremiah found himself growing more attached to the boy, who insisted on being called Damon. "I don't remember Joshua," he said. "And no matter how many stories you tell, I'll never remember him."

Perhaps the greatest frustration for Jeremiah was that his son hadn't smiled at him even once since they'd been reunited.

Dr. Wellon crouched down beside Jeremiah and said, "Biologically, he's about fifty now. Seven years older than you. If we stop giving him the sedatives and painkillers, he'll attack us. The pain would drive him insane. And the nano-cancer inside him will overpower his bloodstream in less than a week." She flexed her hands into ham-sized fists. "On the other hand, keeping him on the sedatives and painkillers will age him more and more rapidly unless we can find a way to slow it down." Her face sagged with sorrow. "It's more than just the WRN protein, more than the RecQ homologs. It's a variable degradation of the small nucleotide polymorphisms in conjunction with the nano-analyzers and filters."

She lifted her hands as if asking Jeremiah to understand the difficulty. He said, "So there's no hope?"

She shrugged, looked down at the floor. "Devereaux is helping, but I fear . . ."

Jeremiah nodded. "It's okay," he said. "You're doing the best you can. If a cure comes in time, it'll be because of your efforts."

Dr. Wellon gently touched his shoulder and turned away.

"Talking about me again?" Damon asked. He tilted his head and looked at Jeremiah with a resigned expression that Jeremiah wished were a smile. "I don't have a lot of pain. But I have no energy." He turned to Dr. Wellon. "You're worried about Zora attacking you. All of you are. But I can't see how it will come out in the end. She's . . ."

He shook his head. "My brain feels wrong. I can't concentrate. My head feels like it's about to explode. Maybe it'd be better just to die and get it over with."

"Don't say that." Jeremiah lifted his hand, wincing as he did so. "There's always hope. Always."

Damon shook his head. "Don't you ever feel like life isn't worth it anymore? Before the sedatives and painkillers I often begged for death. Now it doesn't hurt as much, but I can feel the pain lurking." Damon reached up to scratch his face, caught himself, stared at his hand as if seeing it for the first time and forced it back down. "And if it ever comes back like before, kill me."

"Damon," Dr. Wellon said, "I just got a transmission from Devereaux."

"More treatments," Damon said as he lay back on the massive bed. "Come on, boys. Strap me down."

Dr. Wellon nodded to Krall and Oggie, who secured Damon with wide straps. The bed, designed for the Escala, made him look like a little boy. A glow globe shone a white light on him, washing his color away. Jeremiah trembled, dreading the thought of losing his son now that he'd finally found him. He could almost see Joshua in a hazy future, graduating from college, then medical school, becoming a famous psychiatrist, known for his empathic gifts.

The door chime sounded.

"Greetings," Devereaux said as he stepped into the room, his hands full of vials and his PlusPhone. Dr. Wellon backed away from her station, allowing Devereaux access, while Krall and Oggie stepped to the wall, following Devereaux with their eyes. Even Damon watched Devereaux, twisting his head to keep the great man in view. Zeriphi slipped outside after a brief nod to Devereaux.

Jeremiah said, "You're not wearing your mask."

"It's okay," Devereaux said.

"What about the virus?" Jeremiah asked.

Devereaux shrugged. "Masks won't prevent the spread of the virus. It's already escaped its containment and permeated the air of the settlement. It's done the same on Earth, though that has been kept secret by those governments aware of it. There were multiple strains in the sample sent up here—some transmittable by air, some by water. They present as essentially identical prior to infection, only demonstrating their differences upon attaching to a human host. That's one of the reasons we can't predict how and to whom it will spread in a given case."

"So anyone up here could be infected at any time?"

"I'm afraid so. But don't worry about Damon. Like the Escala, he's immune. It's only the older humans who are at risk."

"Including you," Jeremiah said.

"Don't worry about me. I'm fine. Now let's get to work." He looked at Damon and stopped, saying, "You're interesting. You see us clearly, don't you?"

Damon nodded. "You're afraid."

"Yes, we are," Devereaux replied. "We don't want to lose you. So we're going to try again to slow the aging process. I've modified two more amino acids and fabricated a new nano-trigger for delivery into the WRN protein. The insertion will be painless, but I don't know how your body will react to the changes."

"I'm not afraid," Damon said.

As Devereaux huddled with Dr. Wellon, explaining the nature of his experiments, Jeremiah braced himself for the agony of movement, lowered his hands to the wheels of his chair and began to roll himself toward Damon's bed. Before he traveled a few feet, Krall quickly slid-hopped over and pushed him to Damon's bedside.

When he reached the bed, Damon said, "What about Lendra? Want me to ask Zora if you can see her?"

Jeremiah shrugged, a tiny gesture that nevertheless hurt. "Don't trouble yourself."

"We're already in contact via implant."

"Oh," Jeremiah didn't know why that surprised him. Of course Zora would maintain contact with Damon. For a moment, he wondered if Zora was using Damon as a spy. He decided he didn't care. He said, "I don't know if I trust Lendra."

"Why not?"

"It's complicated. From the beginning of our relationship I suspected she was doing Eli's bidding—spying on me. I didn't really worry about it because I thought I'd left that life behind. But now, with everything going on up here, it feels like I'm being dragged back in."

"Do you love her?"

"I thought I did," Jeremiah said. "I've never been good at reading women. I loved Julianna and she betrayed me. Then I didn't believe her when she turned her life around, which got her killed. As for your mother, I didn't see her suicide coming. I should have, but somehow I didn't. And Lendra, well . . . as much as I care for her, without trust . . ."

Damon reached out with his fingers as far as the straps would let him: a few inches—the first time he'd made any move toward Jeremiah. A lightness found Jeremiah's heart. My son! He fought the pain and tears as he took Damon's hand. It felt cool and comforting. "What I'm trying to say," Damon said, "is that you shouldn't avoid her on my account. I don't remember my mother and I don't remember you. I wish I did. You must really be my father because I can tell that you love me."

Jeremiah's vision blurred. "I do."

"I wish I loved you back."

Joy infused Jeremiah and for a moment he felt no pain at all. "That's okay. I'm not as worried about that as I am about you getting better. And as Devereaux says," Jeremiah looked over at Devereaux, "you can help yourself greatly with a positive attitude."

Devereaux stepped forward and placed his hand on Jeremiah's shoulder. "True. And while we're waiting for the results of this latest transfusion, you and I need to talk." Devereaux grabbed the handles of Jeremiah's wheelchair and backed him away from the bed. "It might take a couple of hours. May as well use the time."

"I'll keep you up to date," Dr. Wellon said.

Devereaux wheeled Jeremiah out the door and toward the personal transportation cars that would take them to the main hangar of Lunar Base 1.

As they entered an empty car, Devereaux paled slightly, a bead of sweat forming on his brow. He wiped it off, glancing at Jeremiah.

"You're infected with the virus too," Jeremiah said. "That's why you're not wearing a mask."

Nodding, Devereaux started the car moving. "I didn't want the Escala to worry, but I deliberately infected myself so that Zora couldn't limit my time researching a cure."

"You shouldn't have done that."

Devereaux said nothing as the car slid forward on its track. All Jeremiah could hear was the rush of air hitting the car and the faint whine of the motor as the tunnel lights approached and receded, the ever-present oxygenating vines sliding by on the sidewalls.

As the car neared LB1, Devereaux said, "We live in a crazy world, Jeremiah. Look at the insanity in India and China. Not to mention that Zora intends to carry out Eli's plan to attack Earth soon."

"That's why we need you alive. You're the most important person we've got."

"Agh." Devereaux waved his hand carelessly. "Don't worry, I'll find a cure. Besides, have you forgotten that you saved my life last year when you gave me some of your blood?"

Jeremiah flashed back to Minnesota: Devereaux stabbed in the stomach; Jeremiah cutting himself, letting his healing blood drip into the wound. He'd forgotten that detail in the ensuing year.

"Odd, isn't it?" Devereaux said. "Your blood made my immune system much stronger than it used to be. And now your blood is so weakened by the virus that it can't even heal your broken legs, while my blood should protect me for a good long while." Devereaux winked. "But don't tell Zora."

The car stopped and Devereaux wheeled Jeremiah off. He halted them just inside the tunnel to the main hangar.

"Meanwhile," Devereaux said, "I can run comparisons of our blood samples, examine the progression of the virus. Hopefully that will lead me to the most likely means of eliminating it. It's a tricky virus—constantly evolving, hiding in multiple locations throughout the body, not just the immune system as was previously thought. And it doesn't always attack the same genomic sequences. It has a familiar look to it, even though I'm sure I've never seen it before. More importantly, for the moment, is Zora's intent to attack Earth."

"Do you think she'll attack the Escala too?"

"I don't know. Why do you ask?"

"The Escala seem to be expecting it. They're worried. I could tell. Damon picked up on it too."

"A perceptive young man. I hope the Escala will do what they must to survive. You and I, however, have a duty to stop the cadets. We can't sit by and watch them murder thousands of innocents. If we did, we would be forsaking whatever humanity we claim to possess. Having climbed the ladder of enlightenment, we must do what we can. Even if it means our deaths."

"I don't know how I can help," Jeremiah said.

"You're a strategic thinker. A warrior. If you put your mind to it, you may find a way. But for now, we ought to speak with Zora—see if we can convince her to change her mind."

Jeremiah nodded. "I'll try, but I doubt she'll listen."

"That's all I ask," Devereaux said as he wheeled Jeremiah to the main hangar, where half a dozen cadets roamed while the big one named Curtik sat atop the military desk, idly kicking it with his heels. He slid off as they approached, smirking at Jeremiah.

"Pappy!" Curtik said. "How delightful to see you."

Jeremiah felt a shock, like he'd just been plunged into an icy bath. "What are you talking about?"

"Didn't anyone tell you?" Curtik's grin widened. "I'm your real son, not that spookster, Damon."

Could it be true? Fear struck Jeremiah in the gut. He shook his head. "I don't know what your game is, kid. But I'm not playing."

"No game," Curtik said. "You're my Papster. You can do a DNA test if you like."

Curtik might be a gifted liar, yet his voice, his facial expression, his body language all spoke of veracity. Jeremiah looked up at Devereaux, who shrugged. Dr. Wellon's DNA test had resulted in an eighty-six percent likelihood that Damon was Joshua, though with all the transgenic and nano-modifications, complete verification was impossible. "Why do you call him a spookster?" Jeremiah finally said.

"He's spooky," Curtik said, "the way he reads people when he's healthy."

"I hear you're a master manipulator."

"Thanks," Curtik said. "But this isn't manipulation. I'm just confused. Part of me hates you for abandoning me and part of me hates myself for feeling that way. I think maybe I killed Mouthy Man out of hatred for you."

"What are you talking about?"

"I knew he was your friend," Curtik said. "Every time I saw him I thought of you. And that made me angry. You see, Pappolini, I remember some of my past. The programming didn't erase it completely. I get these flashes—images of you and Mom. And sometimes they make me feel warm and happy. But then I remember that you just vanished one day. And I get angry again. Why did you do that, Papyrus? Why did you leave me?"

No, Jeremiah thought. He's just playing me. It's all part of his game. And yet Jeremiah couldn't shake the feeling that he was hearing the truth. He said, "Do you remember the song your mother used to sing?"

Curtik closed his eyes for a second and began to hum that familiar tune: *Children's Moon.* Jeremiah shivered. He felt like screaming. If this was a game, it was brilliant. And if not, this monster was his son.

When Curtik finished humming, he scrunched up his face as if he were struggling not to cry and said, "I wish I didn't have to kill all those people. I know it's wrong, but I feel this need to do it. I've been programmed to kill—we all have—and I don't know how to stop myself. Am I a bad person, Paprika?"

"You don't have to be," Jeremiah said.

"I'd like to be good—just like you, Papsy Wapsy."

Devereaux interrupted: "There's no secret involved in being good. Do good things. You don't have to be a monster."

Curtik glared briefly at Devereaux, turned back to Jeremiah and said, "I've been ordered to fire the Las-cannons at specific targets on Earth. Thousands will die. I don't even know those people. I've got no reason to hate them. Yet I do. Why should that be?"

Again Devereaux answered, "Why the pretence to something you're not?"

Curtik jabbed a finger at Devereaux. "You take a lot of chances, old man."

"That's my nature," Devereaux said. "Just as your nature is to lie and scheme to gain advantage. I wonder if there's anyone here or on Earth you actually care about."

179

Curtik stared at Devereaux for a moment before turning his attention to Jeremiah. "Why are you with the spookster? Aren't I good enough for you?"

"I was told he's my son," Jeremiah replied. "But even if he's not, he's more man than you. You're simply a brutal killer."

Curtik grinned. "Ah, just like you, Pappy."

"Be thankful I'm in this wheelchair," Jeremiah said.

Curtik laughed. "Would you teach me a lesson like Mouthy Man did? He sure showed me. Rammed his face into my fists, over and over until I understood."

Jeremiah struggled to his feet, took a step and crumpled in agony.

Above him Curtik roared, slapping himself on the knee as tears ran down his face. He said, "Oh, do it again."

Curtik brought his leg back as if to kick Jeremiah in the ribs. He launched his leg forward, stopping his foot a few inches shy of Jeremiah's chest, his face wrinkling in surprise.

"Congratulations, Curtik," Devereaux said as he helped Jeremiah back into the wheelchair, struggling only a little with Jeremiah's lunar weight of thirty-five pounds. "That's a promising sign. You have great potential."

Curtik said, "What are you doing here, anyway?"

"Zora's expecting us," Devereaux lied. "And we're already running late."

"Oh," Curtik said. He backed away with an elaborate bow. "Mustn't keep Zora waiting. Go, go, go. Run along, children." He clapped his hands three times. "We'll chat later."

Devereaux rolled Jeremiah past Curtik and down the corridor toward the command office, patting Jeremiah's shoulder. What was the truth? Jeremiah wondered. Could Curtik be my son? And if he is, how can I love him? And what of Damon? He believes I'm his father. He actually wants me to be his father. How nice that would be. But somehow, Jeremiah knew that Curtik hadn't lied.

Zora sat alone inside, staring blankly into space when Devereaux opened the door. When she saw them, she raised a hand to tell them to wait, then stared off again for a few more seconds. Jeremiah studied the screens along the walls, the capitals about to be demolished. Was there any way to stop Zora from launching her attack? He couldn't think of one. And any plan would require many, if not all, of the Escala to die.

"Okay," Zora finally said, "what can I do for you gentlemen?"

"We have some things to discuss," Devereaux said.

"We do, do we?" Zora pursed her lips. "Very well." She looked at Jeremiah. "Problems with Curtik?"

Jeremiah realized from her expression that she already knew what had happened. She'd probably been monitoring the whole incident. "He claims to be my son."

"So I heard. We're completing a DNA comparison. He may be telling the truth. It looks like there's a ninety-two percent chance he's your son. Of course, there's also a sixteen percent chance that I'm your son." Zora laughed. "Aspen is fetching your friend Lendra."

"You can't attack Earth, Zora," Devereaux said.

Zora looked at Jeremiah. "Is that what you were going to say?"

Jeremiah nearly said yes, but one glance at Zora's face convinced him that any attempt to dissuade her would fail. He said, "I wouldn't try to tell you what you can and can't do. But I will point out that attacking Earth is what Eli programmed you to do."

"You worked for him."

Jeremiah nodded. "I'm no longer his servant and I never will be again."

The door opened and Aspen showed Lendra in.

"Jeremiah!" Lendra said. For an instant her face carried a look of pain. It might have been his imagination. Lendra glanced at Zora, smiled briefly at Devereaux, then threw herself at Jeremiah, bending over and wrapping her arms around his neck. The faint and familiar flowery aroma of her perfume mingled with her sweat and fear. She clung to him, squeezing hard—hurting him—and yet he found her embrace comforting. He reached up and touched her arm.

She said, "I missed you so much."

Her voice carried at least some truth. Jeremiah, in agony, said, "Please let go."

Lendra released him and stood, her brow furrowing. She looked as lovely as ever. "Wait a second. You have the Susquehanna Virus." Lendra backed away. "Why aren't you wearing a mask?"

Jeremiah looked at Devereaux, who said, "It wouldn't guarantee your safety. The virus is already in the air."

"An absolute tragedy," Zora said.

Lendra looked from Jeremiah to Devereaux to Zora and back. Her jaw set, eyes narrowed. "What are we going to do?"

"Nothing," Jeremiah answered.

"I refuse to accept that. You never give up."

"Sometimes surrender is the only alternative."

"Lose to win," Zora said, keeping her eyes on Jeremiah, her smile broadening to let him know she understood he would continue to oppose her and that she didn't mind. "The willow bends while the oak breaks."

Aspen giggled.

And Jeremiah realized the enormity of the task before him. How could he fight this little girl who was so much smarter than he was, always a few steps ahead?

Lendra's face hardened. To Zora she said, "Can we have some privacy, please?"

"We're all friends here," Zora said, "aren't we? At least, I'd like to be. Won't you be my friend, Lendra?"

Aspen laughed. Lendra folded her arms under her breasts and scowled.

Zora grinned and said, "Aren't you going to tell him you're pregnant?"

"*Thank you!*" Lendra turned back to Jeremiah and reached out as if to take his hand, but then pulled back. "We're going to have a baby."

"A baby?" Jeremiah said. "When did that happen?"

"Just recently," Lendra said. "Aren't you happy?"

"In vitro?" Jeremiah said.

"Darling." Lendra shot him a warning glance.

"It's just that for the past year I've been using a contraception," Jeremiah explained to Zora and Devereaux. He looked back at Lendra.

"You probably knew that since you've been spying on me for Eli."

"Ooh." Zora leaned forward. "Tension."

"Heavy," Aspen added.

Zora and Aspen began to giggle. Lendra glared at them.

"If it makes any difference," Zora said, "this child's a girl. Lucky kid. Damon says you're a great father. And that Kyler girl likes you too. Even Curtik didn't attack you when I was sure he would. What is it about you that makes people worship you?"

"Ooh, ooh, ooh," Aspen raised her hand, waving it frantically. "I want him to be my daddy too."

"We all do," Zora said. "He's the absolute coolest."

"Yes, he is," Devereaux said. "The best man I've ever known."

Jeremiah said, "I'm not a good man."

"Oh, but you are," Zora said. "We're all going to fall madly in love with you because you're so noble and kind and handsome. And we're all going to hate the wicked witch who spied on you for the great and powerful Oz."

Lendra grasped Jeremiah's hand. "What I did doesn't change how I feel about you. I love you, Jeremiah." She kissed his forehead. "Let me take care of you."

Her words, her tone, her body language and scent rang almost perfectly true, yet Jeremiah sensed the falseness behind them. What a gifted liar she was. How many had she gotten away with? He'd always found her difficult to read—almost as tough as Julianna. And what was the lie? That she loved him? No, maybe that part was true.

Zora said, "You're clever, Witchy Poo. You come up here to kill Poole or at least take over her duties." Lendra cringed and Jeremiah knew Zora spoke the truth. "How do I know you won't attack Jeremiah, or team up with him to attack us? You may not be one of Eli's ghosts but you're devious and twisted."

"I've never killed anyone," Lendra said, "as you so accurately pointed out."

"Oh, but you could," Zora said. "You're a mean one, Witchy Poo. Besides, I don't think Jeremiah should play with you." She looked at

Jeremiah. "What do you think? Do you want to have funzies with Witchy Poo?"

"I'm concerned about you," Jeremiah replied. "I've carried the burden of killing for a long time. I don't wish that on you."

"You're just too precious to be believed," Zora said. "I'm definitely going to fall in love with you. Let's go. It's time to start the party."

Aspen reached down, pulled Lendra to her feet and said, "Come on, Witchy Poo. I've heard the Las-cannons make beautiful holes. Nice deep craters. If you like, we just have time to stop for popcorn before the show." She grinned at Jeremiah and gestured to Devereaux to wheel him out.

Chapter Seventeen

From a hospital bed, Elias looked up at Dr. Hassan and tried to remember how he got here. "What happened?" he asked, his tongue thick.

"You suffered another stroke, Mr. Leach," Dr. Hassan said. "You're under a lot of stress and your body is breaking down. The stem cell therapy hasn't worked. Without the nanobots, you will die."

"Become a thyborg," Elias said. He frowned at the lisp in his voice and shivered at the thought of becoming a freak, like an Elite Ops trooper or even one of the cadets on the Moon.

"Nanobots are merely a healing mechanism." Dr. Hassan nodded.

The strokes scared Elias, though not as much as the idea of putting thousands of microscopic computers inside his body, turning himself into a machine. It wasn't just a pathological fear of carrying nanotechnology in his body; it was also because he knew how such technology might be used against him.

Dr. Hassan continued: "You'll have another stroke soon. The next one may be fatal. I don't understand your reluctance to utilize nanotechnology. Even Manyara thinks you should accept the nanobots."

Manyara. Where was she?

"You've ill-treated your body for eighty years," Dr. Hassan continued. "Now it's falling apart and we can fix it with a simple injection."

Dr. Hassan leaned back in his chair and waited. Elias tried to take a deep breath. When was the last time he'd inhaled without pain? He couldn't remember—a year, maybe—right before Jeremiah left him.

Nanobots would allow every movement he made to be monitored, spied upon by doctors or computers, making him vulnerable, perhaps making him programmable. Elias had used information derived from

ID chips to create the program on the Moon, to find the perfect children to kidnap and alter. How much more data about himself would be floating around—interceptible by some unscrupulous hacker—if he agreed to the nanobots?

His body, his brain: these were his last bastions against the invasion of technology. By accepting the nanobots he would lose whatever semblance of privacy he retained in a world that offered next to none. ID chips were implanted in virtually every baby. The wealthy used nanobots not only to heal but also to transmit medical information.

But more than that, if someone somehow hacked into the nanobots, he might be compelled to do anything—his will no longer his own. He might be like the cadets he created, just a tool performing a task for a puppetmaster far away.

Elias wanted to live, but not with the nanobots.

He opened his mouth to inform Dr. Hassan he wasn't willing to accept the nanobots when Jay-Edgar, his technology assistant, entered the room and said, "They just hit the Toninato-Huxley facility in Nevada."

"What?"

Jay-Edgar projected a vid onto the wall. One moment the facility stood in the desert, looking like some insignificant factory; the next it was bathed in red light. Seconds later the cluster of buildings exploded, leaving behind a jagged crater.

No! How had Zora even known of the XV4 program? Clever girl—so unpredictable—so dangerous. They were supposed to attack dysfunctional and hostile governments, then threaten the rest, not take out America's most advanced rocket facility.

"Get me to my offith," Elias said.

Jay-Edgar and Dr. Hassan helped him up. His left leg didn't work right. It wouldn't hold his weight. And his left arm was numb. But with a man on either side of him he managed to make it down the hall to his office. He slumped onto the sofa and watched other attacks follow. Reports came from Russia, China, India, Brazil and dozens of other countries. In every case, the facility destroyed harbored a secret military program. Elias had known about them, of course. But how had Zora found them? Elias' stomach roiled. This was all wrong.

But was it a bad thing? Ultimately these children wouldn't be able to take over Earth. All they could do was cause massive destruction—more than Eli had intended, and to different targets. But the plan wasn't necessarily ruined. The three Las-cannons orbiting the Equator would run out of fuel eventually. And the cadets themselves couldn't succeed over the long-term. Elias had made certain of that. Still, the world needed to see that a future of ever-escalating violence awaited unless people changed.

"The President's calling," Jay-Edgar said.

"Put her through," Elias answered.

Angelica Hope's image appeared through the holo-projection, her coiffed blond hair surrounding her head like a halo. She sat at a large conference table with General Horowitz, Chairman of the Joint Chiefs on her right, Secretary of Defense Raskov on her left, and National Security Advisor Epps beside Raskov. The walls around them contained a bank of screens showing the same scenes of devastation Elias had witnessed via holo-projection. He could tell they were in the command bunker deep beneath the White House.

Elias said, "Madam Prethident."

"He's suffered another stroke," Dr. Hassan explained.

President Hope said, "I'm sorry. But I warned you this would blow up in our faces. Secret programs destroyed, foreign governments accusing us of instigating the destruction. And what can I tell them? They're right. This is your fault. Do you know how many people are dying as we speak? Not to mention that we've lost our most secret rocket base. What were you thinking?"

Elias' heart began to race. "I don't know how that happened. Thereth no way Thora could have found out about that program." It came out as an indecipherable mess of syllables.

President Hope stared at him. General Horowitz shook his head. Raskov lifted his hands to indicate he couldn't understand. Cursing silently, Elias used a tissue to wipe the saliva from his lips and nodded to Jay-Edgar, who translated for him.

"And yet she did." The President glared at him. "She also destroyed similar programs around the world. Was that part of your plan too?"

"Abtholutely not," Elias answered. His breath came in gasps. "I didn't—"

"So it's out of control."

"Temporarily." Sweat formed on Elias' brow. He wondered if the air conditioning was working. "But . . ."

"You don't have any way to stop this madness."

Dr. Hassan handed him a small cup. He swallowed the bitter liquid and struggled to keep it down.

President Hope looked at Horowitz and Raskov. "So what do we do now?"

Raskov said, "We still have plenty of firepower. And our deep-space program hasn't been hit yet. Nor have the Russian or Chinese LTV programs."

General Horowitz said, "Those aren't military options."

"We could load an LTV with nuclear weapons," Raskov said.

"And wipe out everybody on the Moon?" Epps asked. "Maybe destroy the Moon itself?"

"Would you rather have them wipe us out?" Raskov sneered.

"What about the Las-cannons?" President Hope asked. "How do we regain control of them?"

Everyone turned to Elias. He stared back, waiting for his racing heart to slow, his breathing to return to something approaching normal. He felt himself thinning—that was the only word he could think of to describe it—stretching into vapor. Becoming lighter. "I don't know," he finally said. "Itth pothible my people could figure out a way to do it, but it would take weekth, maybe month."

Again they failed to understand him. Jay-Edgar translated for him once more and flashed the emergency signal. Elias glanced over to see what was so important. More attacks—Elite Ops Bases 1 and 2; Britain's Ultra Fighter Academy; China's Future Warrior Group; Russia's Great

Soldier Program. Elias couldn't help but feel a little delight at those losses. Just thinking about Elite Ops troopers and other countries' equivalents made him shiver. Then came a direct hit on Singapore and another on Istanbul. Why those cities? Did they have secret programs he didn't know about? The President and her advisors looked on, stunned into silence. President Hope was the first to recover.

"Singapore and Istanbul. How many millions is that?"

Elias shook his head as he watched two more holo-projections. All he could see was scorched rubble as the satcams pulled back—huge craters in the ground that extended for blocks. Only a few square blocks in each city were completely destroyed: a million lives? What could Elias say that wouldn't set the President off?

"This program of yours, Elias," President Hope said, her cheekbones flush with anger, "is a disaster. We have to find a way to stop those kids. What are our options?"

Her four companions swiveled around to Elias.

A terrible headache suddenly struck him, then numbness in his face. General Horowitz snorted and said, "Any bright ideas?"

Raskov said, "I think we have to load an LTV with nuclear weapons, launch it at the Moon and take out the entire settlement."

Elias blinked several times. So tired. So hard to see clearly. Everything depended on Lendra. He remembered that. But he couldn't let anyone know about that option or it could leak to the cadets, who then might be able to stop her. He tried to say, "What's to keep them from blowing the LTV out of the sky? All they have to do is train the Las-cannons on it. It's got no evasive ability."

Jay-Edgar translated for him.

"What about taking out the Las-cannons?" General Horowitz suggested.

"How do we do that?" Epps asked.

Raskov said, "Particle beam cannons."

"Insufficient range," Horowitz said. "We have a few dozen XV4 rockets remaining. Fortunately they were shipped out before the attack on the Toninato-Huxley facility. We could modify them. It'd be a long shot trying to evade the Las-cannons, but I'm afraid it's the only thing that has a chance of getting through."

"Hot air balloons," Elias said just as an explosion shook the building, rattling the plas-glass windows. It felt like an earthquake. The image of President Hope and her advisors vanished into blackness.

"The White House," Jay-Edgar spoke calmly.

"Madam Prethident!" Elias said as a holo-projection came up showing the hole where the White House had stood. A black crater fifty feet deep replaced it. Elias tried to get to his feet and failed. "Jay-Edgar, whatth going on over there?"

"Switching to backup," Jay-Edgar said. "Oh-oh."

"What?"

Jay-Edgar flushed with embarrassment or anger. "That last transmission was monitored."

"How?"

"A decoder piggybacked onto the scrambling program—very clever. Must have been the cadets. I'm reconnecting, running my new hexi-algorithmic scrambler program. Let's see them tap into this."

Jay-Edgar worked his controls while pain filled Elias' chest. Suffocating pain. He closed his eyes. How easy it would be to just give up, let the darkness come, make someone else handle the world's problems. No, this was his mess. He had to handle it. When he opened his eyes, Dr. Hassan stood beside him, passing a med-scanner wand over his head. Elias heard explosions via holo-projection and saw corpses littering burnt craters. Smoke filtered the images, hiding details. Elias could almost smell the fires burning. The thinning became more pronounced, but the pain receded.

Fog enveloped him. An Elite Ops trooper somehow appeared and picked him up. He tried to scream but nothing came out. The trooper carried him down a hall and placed him on a bed. He felt a hypo pad against the back of his hand. A tingling spread across his chest and face. He had an almost uncontrollable urge to scratch himself, as if the nanobots were itching the inside of his skin, tormenting him. He screamed again but heard nothing. The room went dark.

He awoke some time later—no fogginess in his brain now. An intravenous tube ran from the back of his hand to a large machine at the side of the bed. Electrodes had been placed on his head and chest. Near the door, huddled in close conversation, were Jay-Edgar, Dr. Hassan, President Hope and General Horowitz. Two Elite Ops troopers flanked them, their armor making them look like shadows in the dim lighting.

"Are we alive?" Elias asked.

"Yes, we are," President Hope replied.

When Elias looked at Dr. Hassan, the doctor answered his unspoken question: "Yes, Elias we've hooked you up to the rejuvenator/amplifier. How do you feel?"

Elias lifted his arms and moved his head. No pain, no discomfort for the first time in years. "Very good," he said. "I feel . . . young." No slurring to his voice. "So I'm full of the little things?"

"Yes. Thousands of nanobots are cruising through your bloodstream even as we speak, repairing damage, restoring youth and vitality to your vital organs."

"I never gave my permission," Elias said.

"You're alive. We can probably remove them later. You should have a few days before they integrate fully."

"I'll think about it," Elias said. Almost against his will he smiled. He didn't want to feel this good. It was wrong. And yet he wanted to live pain-free for a good many more years. Perhaps privacy and self were overrated. And what were the odds someone would be able to hack his nanobots? He looked at President Hope. "What's happening out there?"

The President shook her head. "There've been hundreds of attacks on military facilities by the Las-cannons and a dozen attacks on cities. By conservative estimates, there are at least thirty million dead worldwide. In addition to the White House, 10 Downing Street and a dozen other official residences are gone—all allies of America. Fortunately, most had been evacuated as a precaution upon hearing from Zora that attacks were coming. But our ability to respond militarily is pretty much gone. The only good thing is that China and India have ceased hostilities for the moment."

General Horowitz nodded his agreement. "They're focused on the Moon instead of each other. But nobody has the capability of attacking the Moon. We've got plenty of Las-rifles, shields, troops. But no way to get to the Moon or the Las-cannons."

"What about the hot air balloons?"

"What hot air balloons?"

"We could use three of them—one from Asia, one from Europe and one from here. Coordinate their launches so they reach the upper atmosphere just as the Las-cannons are passing by. Put an Elite Ops trooper in each balloon. When they get to maximum height, they can take out the Las-cannons."

"Hmm." General Horowitz nodded slowly. "Interesting. Low-tech—might give us an element of surprise. Still, there's no guarantee it would work and we might not be able to send up Elite Ops troopers."

"Why not?"

"Those kids have locked on to our satcom technological weaponry. They reprogrammed the Las-cannons to target high-value military and energy components. An Elite Ops trooper might draw too much attention to himself."

"Not if he wasn't armored up."

General Horowitz shrugged. "It's possible. If we send someone up without the particle beam cannon converter loaded, it might escape detection."

"What about packing an emergency LTV with nuclear weapons or sending up the XV4s?" President Hope asked.

"LTVs are too slow," General Horowitz said. "We could use them for an attack against the Moon after we destroy the Las-cannons. But with the Las-cannons orbiting the Earth, sending up an LTV would be suicide. However, we might be able to use the XV4s as decoys."

"I agree," Elias said. "The XV4s aren't fast enough to evade the Las-cannons. Zora would destroy them before they got anywhere close to detonation range."

"Do you think these hot air balloons could work?" Hope asked.

"They're low-tech, as the General said. I don't know what made me think of them. But Zora won't be expecting that kind of attack. They'll be so far beneath the Las-cannons she probably won't even see them if they go up without the converters loaded."

"Any chance they'll succeed?"

Elias looked at General Horowitz. They both shrugged. "I think they're all we have," Elias said.

President Hope took a deep breath and stared at the far wall. For the first time since she'd arrived, Elias noticed the dust on the shoulders of her jacket—leftovers from the attack on her bunker—the lines on her face and the darkening of the skin under her eyes. When was the last time she'd slept? After a moment she said, "Who can we send?"

"I know just the man," General Horowitz said. "Our most experienced Elite Ops trooper."

"Major Payne?" Elias said with a glance at the Elite Ops troopers by the door. Were they standing up just a little straighter? They looked huge, almost too large to fit through the doorway.

"Captain Payne now. No one's better with a particle beam cannon. And that business in Minnesota wasn't his fault. Carlton programmed him the same as the other Elite Ops troopers. Plus, he's eager to atone for his misdeeds."

"He's too dangerous," Elias said. He turned to the President. "We retired him from active duty last year, cut off communications between him and his fellow Elite Ops troopers. He's been serving as a weapons instructor for special forces ever since."

"And from all reports," General Horowitz said, "he's been doing a fine job."

"He damn near took over the government."

"We both know that was Richard Carlton's doing. The programming and conditioning made him Carlton's pawn. That's all been corrected. And we don't have to worry about him organizing another coup because his communications implants have already been removed. That'll save us a lot of time."

"I don't think we have any choice," President Hope said. "If he's the best man for the job, we have to use him. You'll have to accept that, Elias. Oh, and one more thing. I'm taking over your office for the time being. I need the communications access." She turned to the door. "You can join us when you feel up to it."

Elias glanced again at the Elite Ops troopers beside the door. His pulse had quickened, he noticed—his breathing too. Once again he felt the urge to scratch himself, to get at the nanobots inside his skin, pull them out before they took over his mind, his soul. He nodded. "I'll be there in a moment." He lifted the tube connected to his hand and looked at Dr. Hassan. "Take this off." The President and General Horowitz left, trailed by the Elite Ops troopers; Dr. Hassan removed the intravenous tube; and Elias beckoned Jay-Edgar over. "I need a summary of what's happened while I've been out."

"I've got it," Jay-Edgar said. He projected another vid onto the wall and began manipulating the feed. "This is just a sampling."

Images appeared from around the world: a Chinese Air Force base loaded with jet-copters lit by red light, then a massive hole where the jet-copters had stood; Britain's newest nuclear submarine, the behemoth Dreadnought, shown cruising the North Atlantic, the picture taken by another vessel, turning red as the water around it began to boil, exploding outward as the image went black; CIA headquarters at Langley, where people could be seen running, replaced by the familiar red light, which filled the projection for a few seconds, after which the buildings blew apart, leaving behind a massive crater. More images followed—rocket bases in Korea, Pakistan, Iran, South Africa. About every tenth attack was on a populated area—a city or a landmark. One attack hit the center of what Jay-Edgar noted was Syracuse, Sicily. Another struck Pascagoula, Mississippi. Strange.

Millions were dying—most of them instantly, mercifully. The plan was a total disaster. If only Curtik had taken charge like he was supposed to. Or would that have been even worse? Would he have avoided attacking governments and gone after civilian targets? Eli had to stop thinking that way. He had a job to finish. He'd set the wolves loose among the sheep because that was the only way to save the sheep—only now he had to figure out a way to stop the wolves.

"There's something missing," Elias said as he stared at the holo-projections, a numbness spreading over him: a numbness that wasn't physical.

"Missing?" Jay-Edgar asked.

"The pattern is wrong. It should be all strategic targets or all civilian ones, maximizing the terror. This blend is . . . perhaps Zora's not completely in control up there." Elias put his head in his hands.

"Are you okay?" Dr. Hassan asked.

"It had to be done," Elias answered. "There was no other way."

Dr. Hassan and Jay-Edgar stared at him, as if unsure how to reply.

"We're destroying our world," Elias continued. "Such a fragile place. Such fragile people. We're committing unspeakable acts of violence upon each other, becoming more barbaric rather than less, refining our tools of death so we can more accurately hunt down and kill our enemies. All of us are to blame. You, me, the President, even Manyara."

"Manyara?" Dr. Hassan said.

"We all did it by refusing to condemn it. You see that, don't you?"

"Of course, sir," Jay-Edgar said. "You did what had to be done."

"I wonder how harshly I'll be judged."

"Pardon?"

"Never mind." Elias hopped out of bed, his joints flexible, his muscles strong. He felt fifty again. While the Earth deteriorated, its defenses dying, his body revitalized itself. The fountain of youth swam in his bloodstream.

* * *

Shaking with laughter at the memory of Eli's slurred words, Curtik fired his Las-cannon. He ignored the targets Zora had designated, leaving those for Wee Willie and Aspen, instead going after populated areas with ess sounds in their names. With each hit his delight grew. "Thufferin Thingapore! Thilly old Ithtanbul. Thayonara, Thithily! Whoopth, I almotht mithed Pathcagoula, Mithithippi. How thad."

Curtik's boys shouted encouragement, calling out targets for him to hit next. Too bad Benn and Addam had guard duty. They would have enjoyed the killing. Instead they'd have to experience it through their implants. But it wasn't the same. There was nothing like a good kill to bring out the thrumming delight at the center of him. He glanced over at Zora. The bitch just didn't have a sense of humor. She stood next to Pappolini Jeremiah in his wheelchair while Phan and Shiloh trained their Las-rifles on the Papster. Lendra and Devereaux— God Himself—stood to the other side of Pappy. God Himself never took his eyes off Curtik, ignoring the carnage on the screens. Let him look. Curtik didn't care as long as Zora didn't pull him off the Las-cannon.

"Come on, Thora," Curtik said, "thith ith fun." He winked at Pappy and God Himself, who just stared back without saying a word. They hadn't spoken since the attacks started.

"You're nutth, Curtik," Wee Willie said. "But you're right. Itth fun to talk like thith."

All the boys joined in the mockery, lisping at each other. But the girls kept an eye on Zora. And most of them only smiled or giggled— waiting for the bitch to give them permission to laugh. She was too damn hard on them—too hard on everybody. Life should be fun. Enjoy the kills—they might not last.

Zora shook her head. "You're hitting far fewer targets than Wee Willie and Aspen. Don't you think you should concentrate on the people who can hurt us instead of innocent civilians?"

"Innothent thivilianth?" Curtik said. "I thought we were thuppothed to terrorithe them."

"That's why I haven't stopped you so far," Zora said. "But I don't want you running your Las-cannon dry. We need to maintain a charge of at least fourteen perthent."

"Perthent!" Curtik laughed so hard he nearly fell over. All the cadets howled with delight at that. Zora smiled and Curtik realized she hadn't made a mistake after all. She'd deliberately misspoken. Clever, clever bitch.

Zora's smile tapered off. "Just remember we need that reservoir of power. Okay?"

"Yeth, ma'am," Curtik said as he put his hand to his forehead. "I thalute you. Hey, I've got an idea. Letth call Eli. I want to hear him talk again. Only from now on letth call him Thylvethter—you know—like the cartoon character."

"Thylvether!" Wee Willie hooted. Curtik's boys doubled over, slapping themselves on the legs, poking each other, even poking the girls, some of whom broke out into actual laughter.

God Himself continued to stare at Curtik, doing his best to ruin the fun. Why didn't the scary old bastard leave him alone? At least Lendra provided some pleasure. Her face was pinched, her hands clenched, her body shaking, which gave Curtik an ecstatic warmth in the pit of his stomach. Then he noticed Pappy staring at the Earth with a stone face, his expression unreadable, as if he didn't care. Curtik followed his eye out the plas-glass ceiling toward Earth. No sign of the laser strikes was visible from here. The planet continued to spin, looking like some giant marble against a background of black velvet, little pinpricks of white light visible behind it. Curtik wished Pappy was down there. He wanted to kill Jeremiah most of all.

Pulling his attention back to God Himself, Curtik sprang to his feet and yelled, "Boo!"

Both God Himself and Lendra jumped and Curtik laughed. "Thcared you, didn't I?" Neither Aspen nor Wee Willie joined his laughter this time. Only a handful of cadets—the ones Curtik terrorized—bothered to laugh. The tension built as Curtik returned to his seat. Damn, it was just a joke. Maybe God Himself needed to vanish. If Zora continued to let him wander around freely, he might accidentally find his way out an airlock. Imagine killing the greatest human of all.

"Down to thirty perthent," Aspen said. She looked at Curtik with a slight smile before catching God Himself's eye and turning serious. "Enough for a couple dozen strikes per Las-cannon before we reach the fourteen percent mark."

"Make them count," Zora said, feeding coordinates to Curtik and the others through her implant. "Only high-quality targets from here on out. I mean it, Curtik. No more fooling around."

"Okay, okay. I got a little carried away."

"I don't want them to be able to retaliate. And if we waste all our ammunition on unimportant targets, they'll mount some sort of attack against us."

"Bring 'em on," Curtik said. "We gotta fight 'em sooner or later."

"Just do your job," Zora said. "Take out the targets I've indicated."

Pappy finally spoke: "Are we done here?"

Zora turned to face him. "Ah, Jeremiah. How do you feel? Do you hate me now?"

Pappy shook his head. "You're doing what you were programmed to do. I've killed before too. Blown up things . . . people. The only difference is one of degree. But I've seen enough."

Zora bent over and grabbed his hand, her eyes focused on his. "What would it take for you to hate me? How many more would I have to kill?" She turned her head toward Lendra. "What if I killed Witchy Poo?"

Pappy grimaced as he shrugged. "I don't think I could ever hate you."

Curtik said, "You hate me though, right?"

"Sorry," Pappy answered. "I feel sorry for you and I wish I could help you, but I suspect you're beyond help."

Curtik rose to his feet and took a step forward, the urge to kill overwhelming him. He brushed someone's hand aside but found himself surrounded by girls—Zora's pets. Somehow he had to figure a way to take control.

Curtik raised his hands and backed into his chair. "Good one," he said with a laugh. "Got me there. Tweaked my buttons good. Love you too, Papster."

Chapter Eighteen

The motion of the jet-copter gave Captain Windol Payne an overwhelming urge to urinate. He grabbed the chem-urinal, unzipped his coveralls and used it, cleansing his system of deactivated nanobots. After zipping up, Payne took a long drink of nutri-water. Important to stay hydrated if he didn't want to cramp up. He found it hard to believe that it wasn't the pseudos who'd taken over the Moon. He still thought of them as abominations, even though he was no longer programmed to hate them.

He remembered kidnapping two kids for the cadet program, years ago, back when he was under Richard Carlton's spell. He'd only done what Carlton ordered, what he'd been compelled to do. But he still felt tremendous guilt over his actions. Payne particularly remembered one cute little blond girl. He couldn't recall her name. She'd been living in Iowa—an easy target. Payne had taken her after she got off the bus. Dressed like a police officer, he'd told her that he was taking her to her parents. Such a trusting, innocent face: when she discovered he had lied, she cried for only a short time before staring at him with a wisdom beyond her years. He wondered what became of that five-year-old, shrugged that thought aside.

A helium balloon.

Payne shook his head. Shooting down a Las-cannon from a balloon: were they kidding? At least they were giving him a particle beam cannon instead of a bow and arrow. There was a time he'd have sworn he couldn't miss any target he aimed at with a particle beam cannon. Then came Minnesota and Jeremiah Jones—another pseudo.

By God, he was fast! Faster than anyone Payne had seen before or since. Were the kids that fast too? Faster? Hard to believe. Nanobot technology made sense. It supplemented the body's own systems—a pure enhancement that left one fully human. But the idea of inserting animal DNA into people struck him as obscene, no matter how many times they told him that the only real difference between human and animal DNA was which genes were activated.

He shivered, feeling cold for the first time in years: no nanobots to regulate his metabolism. Even such details as fine motor control were now exclusively in his fingers: no assistance from nano-connectors.

Payne felt empty. He volunteered for this mission because the guilt of his actions had been building to an almost intolerable burden. And he felt lonely after being cut off from his men for the past year. He needed to redeem himself. Maybe, if he survived, he could even return to active duty. Once an Elite Ops, always an Elite Ops.

Below him, in the waning light of day, what used to be the CIA's headquarters in Langley was mostly charred ground and rubble. A crater, wide and shallow, stretched over an area of several hundred meters, demonstrating the amazing power of Las-cannon technology. The weapons could either send narrow beams of unprecedented power, or wider, less-potent rays that still unleashed a destructive force almost without parallel—much more powerful than a particle beam cannon.

The flight took half an hour. The view outside—a sunset of orange mellowing to pink and purple—was beautiful. Circling a small meadow, the pilot landed on a concrete pad next to a metal hangar, where General Horowitz stood waiting under a floodlight with a short black man and an Elite Ops trooper. Payne felt a pang of self-pity.

He stepped out of the jet-copter, which immediately took off, vanishing into the growing darkness. The pilot and copilot had said not a word to him on the way out. Payne approached the General and saluted, then recognized the armored trooper behind him as Adrian Lye, a former student, now the new commander of the Elite Ops.

"General," Payne said. "Adrian."

"Windol," Lye replied, clapping Payne on the shoulder. "Good to see you. Thanks for volunteering. We need you."

"Captain," General Horowitz said, gesturing to the short black man, "this is Ned Jefferson. He'll be going up with you."

Payne looked the short man over. He wore a clean white shirt tucked into dark pants. His sneakers looked ancient in the dim lighting. Next to the heavily armored Elite Ops trooper and even General Horowitz, he looked tiny. His face had at least a week's growth of gray hair on it. Otherwise his head was bald. He could be anywhere between fifty and eighty. Lean as a greyhound, his face was impassive as stone until he flashed Payne a smile, exposing bright white teeth.

"Ned is one of the best balloonists in the country," General Horowitz said.

Payne said, "Does he know the mission?"

"Yes," General Horowitz said.

"Am I in command, sir? Or is he?"

Adrian said, "You're a team, Windol. Ned will get you into the best position possible. You'll take the shot. You leave as soon as we coordinate with two other teams—one in India and one in Spain. It has to be perfectly timed, so we hit all three Las-cannons at once. We won't get a second opportunity. I'm in contact with Mukesh Mangeshkar and Pedro Castanos. They're the equivalent of Elite Ops troopers in India and Spain. They'll each be going up with a professional balloonist— some woman named Saronjini Bharanarrayan and a guy named Escobar Manolillo."

Ned Jefferson's eyebrows lifted.

"You know those people?" Payne asked.

Jefferson shrugged. "Heard of Escobar," he said in a raspy voice. "Never met him, but he's a world-class balloon racer. Won the Paris-to-Beijing Race last year. Saronjini I know. She holds the world record for the highest elevation by a balloonist."

"How high is that?"

"Thirty-one miles."

"And how high have you flown?"

"Eighteen miles."

Payne turned to General Horowitz. "Aren't the Las-cannons about 60,000 miles up?"

"Approximately," the general replied.

Payne shook his head, stared at Adrian. "So I'm firing at a target 60,000 miles away in the middle of the night? What am I missing?"

"If you can get up to forty miles, you'll have almost no atmosphere to shoot through," Adrian said. "So you'll get almost no distortion or resistance. And with Mr. Jefferson's fancy balloon, you should be able to get to nearly forty miles up, so your target will only be 59, 960 miles away. Plus, the Las-cannon puts out an electronic signal you'll be able to track."

"Oh." Payne flung up his arms. "Well, then it's easy."

"We'll be diverting the Las-cannons by firing a dozen XV4s at them," General Horowitz said. "When the Las-cannon above you fires, you'll be able to load the converter and lock onto its signal. Major Lye tells me the shot can be made."

"With all due respect," Payne said. "Major Lye doesn't have to make the shot."

Adrian took a step forward. "I did volunteer for the mission."

"I know, Adrian." Payne lifted his hands in apology. "I'm just saying that it's going to take one hell of a shot. And what if the Las-cannons don't provide enough of a signal for the particle beam cannons to get a full lock? If we're off even one degree in any direction, we could miss the Las-cannons completely."

"We picked you because you're the best," General Horowitz said.

"Again, with all due respect," Payne said, "I was the best when I was armored up. If I can't get a strong signal, I'll have to use manual override. The odds against hitting a target that far away . . . well, they'd be astronomical."

"Not with a scatter setting, full power," Adrian said.

"That would give me only one shot."

"Yes, but your odds of hitting it would be much better. At least fifty-fifty. Maybe sixty-forty with your skill."

"And with a scatter setting, even at full power, how much damage would I inflict? Would it be enough to destroy the Las-cannon?"

"That's an unknown," General Horowitz conceded. "But it's still our best shot."

Payne looked from General Horowitz to Adrian to Ned Jefferson, who had listened to the conversation quietly. Brave little man. Payne said, "And what happens afterwards?"

"If you fail," General Horowitz said, "I imagine you'll be shot out of the sky, in which case you'll have a," he turned to Jefferson, "ten percent chance of survival?"

Jefferson shrugged. "Near enough."

"So, hit the Las-cannon," General Horowitz said, "and bring the balloon back down safely and we'll pin a medal on you."

"Excuse me," Jefferson said, "Got some work to do. What's our ETD?"

"Two hours, ten minutes," Adrian said.

"Right," General Horowitz said. "Let's go over the details, see if there's anything we can do to improve our odds while Ned gets the balloon ready."

"Who is he really?" Payne asked.

"An old friend," General Horowitz said. "I'd trust him with my life."

For the next hour and a half, as night swallowed twilight, they discussed how they planned to coordinate the strikes. To avoid detection of the comm system, Payne and Ned Jefferson would be using a modified walkie-talkie to speak with Adrian, who would maintain a comm-link with the bases in India and Spain. General Horowitz would deploy the XV4s in three separate launches, timed so that they approached the Las-cannons just as the balloons reached their upper limits, forty miles up.

Payne had already urinated one last time, then slipped into his pressurized suit and donned his parachute. He left his helmet off for the moment. Jefferson wore the same equipment, laughing as he struggled to fit his parachute over his suit.

When the ground crew wheeled the balloon out from the hangar, the floodlight showed three balloons atop the basket, barely visible in the night. Did these people know how much a longshot this was? They certainly spoke optimistically enough. But then, Payne himself had done the same on more missions than he could remember. Never let the troops know you have doubts.

Adrian approached Payne and held out his particle beam cannon. "I want you to use mine," Adrian said. "It's perfectly calibrated and balanced, fully charged."

"Thanks," Payne replied. He snapped open the cannon, unloaded the converter and placed it in his pocket. "I'll do my best."

"Good hunting," General Horowitz said.

Payne put his helmet on and climbed into the basket, where Jefferson already stood encased in his suit. Payne grabbed a handhold on the basket and waited for Adrian to give the go signal. Minutes ticked by. Payne studied the basket. Beside the helium tank was an electronic console. He and Jefferson had little room for themselves. When Adrian pointed at them, Jefferson released the balloon. It rose rapidly, the people on the ground shrinking. It was like being in an elevator. Payne's stomach dropped only a little in response to the acceleration. Higher and higher they drifted into the blackness, moving east as they rose toward the Las-cannon.

"Gonna be a long flight," Jefferson spoke through the walkie-talkie comm system, his voice sounding strong. "Might want to relax."

"How do you know I'm not relaxed?" Payne said.

Jefferson shrugged inside his suit. "Quite a death grip you got on that handle. Might need to save your strength to fire that particle beam cannon. They got a kick."

Payne stared at the little black man. "How would you know . . . who are you?"

"Friend of the general's."

"Special Forces?"

Jefferson checked the instrument panel and adjusted a dial. Payne looked down and saw the lights receding. He realized they'd already climbed at least a mile. It was a beautiful sight from up here, so quiet and peaceful.

"Check your systems," Jefferson said.

His eyes adjusting to the darkness, Payne found the helmet controls and made sure everything was working properly, then said, "So who are you really?"

"Jack of all trades, master of none. Actually, I'm a friend of Jeremiah Jones."

Payne's stomach dropped. His throat dried up. He managed to croak: "You're a CINTEP ghost."

"I retired this year," Jefferson said. "That's a young man's game. We just hit two miles, by the way. Might want to let them know."

Payne keyed the external link and gave the information to Adrian. Then he said, "Are you like Jones?"

"Not exactly. I've been enhanced, but not to his level." Jefferson adjusted the flow of helium to another balloon. Payne studied him, wondering if the man intended violence after the mission. Jefferson kept his attention on the console. After a time, he looked up at the balloons. Payne again looked over the side of the basket. Already the lights below looked incredibly far away. Payne thought he could detect the faint outline of a river. Then they hit the clouds, which blanketed the view. For a time there was only silence and a few faint stars in the distance. But as the clouds thinned the stars brightened, becoming multitudes.

"Seven miles," Jefferson said.

Payne relayed the information to Adrian, then flexed his fingers inside their gloves as he contemplated the difficulty of the shot he'd have to make.

As if able to read his mind, Jefferson said, "You ever fire a particle beam cannon without armor before?"

"A couple times," Payne replied.

Jefferson nodded, said, "You can brace your shoulder against my back when you take the shot."

"Okay," Payne said. "I'm sorry about what happened in Minnesota—with Jones."

"Not your fault," Jefferson said. "We all know Carlton programmed you to attack those innocents. Besides, it's not me you owe the apology to. It's Jeremiah."

"I tried. Left a message for him with Elias Leach."

"I don't think Jeremiah got it," Jefferson said. "He left CINTEP before I did. In fact, that's why I left. Don't tell him that though. Wouldn't want him to get a big ego. Eight miles."

"You think I'll get the chance to say anything to anybody afterwards?"

"We're not going to die, Captain," Jefferson said. "You just focus on the shot and let me worry about getting us down safely."

As Jefferson returned his attention to the console, Payne visualized the shot ahead. He pictured it in his mind, imagining himself braced against Jefferson's back, using the particle beam cannon's tracking mechanism to lock onto the electronic signal of the Las-cannon. It wasn't a foolproof system, especially from a range of thousands of miles. He didn't care how little atmosphere the ions had to travel through. A shot of 60,000 miles was a hell of a shot no matter what. Could he make it, even if he were wearing his armor? He wouldn't want to take that bet.

The miles dropped away beneath them. Twelve, then eighteen, which was as high as Jefferson said he'd ever been in a balloon. Jefferson kept his attention on the instrument panel, which at first seemed odd until Payne realized that he had to worry about their direction as well as their height.

The miles passed more slowly as the atmosphere thinned—twenty, twenty-two, twenty-four. The suit kept Payne warm, but he sensed the extreme cold outside. Jefferson leaned over his console, studying gauges and dials. "Thirty miles," he said.

Payne relayed the information to Adrian.

Jefferson grabbed Payne's free hand and put it on the helium tank's regulator. "Keep the flow at three."

"Is there a problem?" Payne asked.

"We're losing helium," Jefferson said. "A small leak."

As Jefferson adjusted dials, he slowly rocked his head from side to side like a metronome. It was probably his way of panicking. Payne looked out over the basket at the stars, at the Moon, which was nearly full but partially hidden by the balloon. The kids were up there along with the pseudos. Was the blond girl one of them?

"Windol," Adrian's voice came through the walkie-talkie, "you at thirty-four yet?"

Payne asked Jefferson, who shook his head. "Thirty-two," he said.

When Payne relayed the information, Adrian said, "You should be at thirty-four."

Payne told Jefferson, who grabbed the now-empty helium tank and tossed it overboard. He opened his toolbox, pulled out a T-wrench and loosened the bolts holding the console to the basket. Reaching again for the toolbox, he found a wirecutter and clipped the wires leading from the console to the balloons, then lifted the console and dropped it over the side too. Finally he put the T-wrench and wirecutter back in the toolbox and tossed it overboard. Looking up at Payne, he said, "No more helium. And I never liked that console."

Payne jerked his head to indicate the lost items. "Does that mean we can't take the balloon back down?"

Jefferson grinned through his mask. "Getting the balloon down is easy. When's the last time you parachuted?"

"Four years ago."

"Don't open the chute too soon. You want to be well into the atmosphere first."

"You think we're going to survive this?" Payne asked.

Jefferson shrugged. "I'm an optimist."

Payne laughed. "I like you, Ned."

Once again Adrian's voice came over the walkie-talkie: "Where you at, Windol?"

Payne looked at Jefferson, who said, "Tell him to give us a heads up when the XV4s are fired."

"Saronjini's at thirty-eight miles," Adrian said on hearing Payne's report. "Escobar's at thirty-seven. We fire the XV4s in twelve minutes."

"Roger that," Payne replied.

Jefferson shook his head. "We're not going to make it above thirty-six miles. With the extra atmosphere to fire through, you'll get about a two-percent greater distortion, which means that to maximize your chance of hitting the Las-cannon, you'll have to adjust the dispersal pattern to approximately ninety-two percent of full scatter while keeping the power setting at full. And your aim will have to be perfect. No margin for error."

Payne stared at Jefferson, stunned by the man's expertise. "Maybe you should take the shot. Jones was as good with a particle beam cannon as any Elite Ops trooper."

"I'm just the pilot," Jefferson said. "You're the marksman."

Payne nodded as he reached for the converter. Adjusting the settings on the particle beam cannon, he jacked open the back cover and began to take slow, even breaths, closing his eyes and again visualizing the shot while attempting to relax his muscles. He was too tense. He needed to reach that fine point at the edge of indifference where his muscles would respond almost instinctively, without interference from his emotions, aiming without guiding, letting the shot come of its own accord; that was the difference between taking the shot without armor and making it with the assistance of the mechanicals embedded in his Elite Ops exoskeleton.

"XV4s are away," Adrian's voice came through the walkie-talkie. "Repeat, XV4s are away. Acknowledge."

"Copy that," Payne replied.

He slapped the converter into the back of the particle beam cannon and closed the cover. Jefferson clapped him on the shoulder and held him for a moment, nodding. Payne found that reassuring. He nodded back. Jefferson braced himself against the side of the basket, leaning into it hard. In the silent night, Payne knelt down, snugged his shoulder against Jefferson's back and sighted along the weapon. It felt good in his hands.

A small rushing sound announced the approach of the XV4s. Payne had been expecting a roar but they were almost soundless in the thin air, their exhaust flames piercing the blackness as they hurtled into the heavens. Payne swung the particle beam cannon through a lazy arc until the green targeting scanner light came on. At the same instant a red light shot through space, a narrow beam that originated in the exact spot the scanner had located. Before Payne could fire, the scanner lost its signal.

One of the XV4s blew apart—yellow and red and white fire that split the sky like some silent fireworks show.

Another red beam just as Payne acquired another signal lock. One and a-half degrees higher, half a degree left of the previous one. Another XV4 exploded just as the signal vanished again.

Damn! Too slow.

Payne had to act more quickly. He held the weapon almost steady, moving it only centimeters to the left and upwards. Another red beam, another signal lock and Payne fired.

The recoil would have knocked him backwards out of the basket if Jefferson hadn't grabbed him. The shot made the muffled sound of mittens clapping in the snow. A searing bolt of red lightning struck the balloon and he began to fall, his sight suddenly gone.

All he could feel was an intense burning sensation on his face, chest and arms. He thought he screamed but he couldn't hear anything. The searing pain in his upper torso took every thought from his head. His face hurt like hell. Consciousness faded.

He awoke, gasping, to the feel of hands on his body, the rush of air past his face. His helmet must have been damaged. Still no vision, but he heard a roaring in his ears. His face felt like it was on fire, his chest as if he'd been struck with a sledgehammer. Terror overwhelmed him. Payne fought against the creature holding him until he realized it was Jefferson. Somehow the smaller man had caught him in free fall and placed a mask over his mouth and nose, allowing him to breathe. But if he'd given Payne his mask, how was he breathing? Payne tried to relax as the smaller man clung to his suit—the two of them still falling, locked in the inexorable grip of gravity.

"It's okay," Jefferson yelled. "Just relax and take a deep breath."

After Payne inhaled, Jefferson pulled the oxygen mask away. Payne almost panicked and grabbed for the mask. But he managed to control himself and a few seconds later it was clamped over his mouth again.

They soon fell into a rhythm of breathing alternately. After a few minutes, Payne's breathing grew easier.

"Did I hit the Las-cannon?" he yelled as he reached up to feel his face.

"Don't know," Jefferson replied. He pushed Payne's hand away from his face. "Don't touch it."

"I can't see."

"The Las-cannon burned your face pretty badly. We're lucky it was a glancing blow or we'd be dead. Don't worry. They'll grow you new eyes, better than the old ones. I'm more concerned with the damage to your chest and your suit."

"How bad is it?"

"You'll still get some flotation from the suit, but trying to swim will hurt." He grabbed Payne's hand and guided it to his parachute's handle. "When I let go, wait ten seconds, then open the chute. Okay?"

"Okay." Payne didn't want Jefferson to let go.

"Remember, the chute will beep as you approach the ocean. The beeps will get closer together the nearer you get. When you hear a continuous tone, bend your knees and prepare for impact. Got it?"

"Got it. Ned?"

"What?"

"Thanks."

"I'll find you."

Jefferson let go. Payne counted to ten and pulled the handle, feeling the lurch in his stomach as the chute caught. He was drifting in total blackness, a mote in the currents of the atmosphere.

A beep sounded from his parachute's harness. Then another. They began to come more frequently, finally melding into one continuous note. Payne felt for the release catch on the chute, kept his hand there, bent his legs in preparation for landing and braced for impact. When he hit the water, it took his breath away. He swallowed two huge gulps before clawing his way back to the surface, his arms and chest hurting so badly he thought he might pass out. Coughing up water, he popped open the release catch, kicked his way out of the chute and began clumsily treading water as the ocean rose and fell around him. He'd never felt such pain before. His face itched and stung, piercing him with a thousand burning needles, yet that pain paled beside the agony in every movement of his arms and chest.

"Ned!" he yelled as a wave struck him. He swallowed more water. It was all he could do to stay afloat. No way would Jefferson be able to find him. He wondered if there were sharks nearby. When something brushed against his leg, he thrashed away from it before realizing it was just his parachute. He couldn't recall ever being this scared before.

His face fell beneath the water and he swallowed another mouthful of brine. He fought back to the surface and coughed heavily. He kept treading water, his strength dissipating. Several times his face slipped beneath the waves, making him swallow more of the sea. Jefferson wasn't coming to save him.

He thought about the little blond girl he'd kidnapped a few years ago—how calmly she'd accepted her fate. How brave she'd been. Somehow that gave him courage to accept his death. He deserved to die for what he'd done to her and her family. "I'm sorry," he yelled. "I'm sorry!"

A splashing sound came from behind him. A shark? How much would it hurt to be killed by a shark?

"I got you," Jefferson called out as he grabbed Payne and wrapped his arm around Payne's chest, keeping Payne's head above water. "Took a while to find you. You're doing great. Stay calm. The jet-copters are on their way. Can you hear 'em? They're almost here. You made it, buddy."

Payne strained to hear their familiar whomping sound, and when he did, he began to cry.

Chapter Nineteen

Curtik waited for the Earthlings to counterattack. And waited. And waited. As his orbiting Las-cannon passed over England, he fired a shot at Stratford-Upon-Avon. But it didn't fill him up. He felt an uncontrollable hunger to kill.

"What are you doing?" Aspen asked from her Las-cannon station.

"Bloody Shakespeare!" Curtik said.

Wee Willie chuckled.

Aspen said, "Quit wasting ammunition. Your Las-cannon's already down to thirteen percent."

"I'm bored."

"They'll attack soon. Be patient."

Curtik glanced over at Wee Willie, who stuck his thumbs in his ears and waggled his fingers, making Curtik laugh. "Whatever," Curtik said. "I'm going to get something to eat. Let me know when they launch their rockets." He went to the mess hall to get an ice cream bar, then wandered toward the hotel where the tourists were locked up, thinking he might kill a few after his snack.

He walked past Shiloh and Phan, the cadets on guard duty, and down a long carpeted hallway, where he heard a dim knocking. It grew louder as he reached the end of the hall, coming from the last door. Excellent—someone to murder. Curtik's pulse began to race. He searched his implant for the access code, unlocked and opened the door. A blond woman stood before him. "Please," she said, "our daughter is sick."

"What? Are you joking?" Curtik took a bite of his ice cream sandwich, savoring the cold, sugary vanilla taste.

"She's very ill."

Curtik shoved the woman against the wall as he stepped into the

212

room. He glanced at the bed, where a girl of about ten lay. Kneeling next to the bed, holding her hand, was a man with dark hair. By his side stood a younger girl. The man and the younger girl looked up at Curtik, their fear keeping them silent.

Curtik glared at them.

"Please," the woman said as she struggled to her feet. "You can do whatever you want to us. But help her."

Curtik nearly punched her. But she presented no challenge. She just stared into his eyes and said, "please" over and over.

"Shut up!" Curtik barked.

The woman closed her mouth and cowered down next to her husband, wrapping an arm around the younger girl, who began crying. Curtik took another step forward, looked down at the girl on the bed. She had blond hair like her mother but dark eyes like her father. Her face was bathed in sweat, her face flushed. Her feverish eyes followed Curtik.

I can kill her, Curtik thought, and Zora can't blame me because I'll just be putting her out of her misery. He snarled just a little to scare the girl. Her father cringed away; her mother moaned; her little sister cried even louder; but she didn't blink. She just stared at him.

Curtik shoved his half-eaten ice cream bar into his mouth as he stared back at the girl. His cheeks bulged with the frozen treat. The girl started to smile, then cringed in pain. Curtik quickly swallowed the ice cream, picked the girl up and pulled her away from her father's grasp. She was lighter than he expected. Should he break her neck? Rip her arms off?

"Can I go with you?" the mother asked, rising to her feet.

"Down!"

The mother sank to her knees, put her hands together in front of her as if in prayer. "You'll help her, won't you?"

"Stay!" Curtik ordered as he backed toward the door. He closed it behind him and locked the family inside. As he held the girl in his arms, the rage inside him subsided. Inexplicably, he found himself heading for the exit. As he walked, the girl continued to watch his eyes.

213

He found her gaze unsettling. Before he reached the lobby, Wee Willie informed him via implant that the attacks were starting.

"I'll kill you later," Curtik said to the girl. He handed her off to Shiloh and Phan, and told them to take her to the hospital.

"Wait for me," Curtik told Wee Willie as he slid-hopped over to his station.

"I got the Chinese missiles," Aspen said from her station.

"I got the Russian ones," Wee Willie added.

"No fair," Curtik said as the other two began firing. "Save some for me."

He settled into his station. "I call these eighteen." He highlighted the missiles he'd chosen for himself and began to laugh as he shot rockets out of the sky. This was more like it! He took his time, savoring each shot, tightening the beam with each strike, putting progressively smaller holes in each missile, while still blowing them apart. Before he completed all eighteen, Aspen destroyed the three nearest her Las-cannon.

"Hey!" Curtik yelled. "Those were mine. Get your own."

"I called them first," Aspen replied.

"But I highlighted them. Now look what you've done. There's nothing else to shoot at. What am I supposed to do?"

"Why don't you try to figure out what their next strategy is going to be?"

"Duh. The next thing on the agenda is multiple countries coordinating attacks and launching a massive attack."

Aspen said, "Is that what you'd do?"

Curtik shrugged. "Of course. But I'd also reprogram the rockets so they all looked identical to our sensors, so we wouldn't be able to distinguish between the more sophisticated ones and the older ones that wouldn't have a chance of reaching the Las-cannons anyway. So we wouldn't be able to target the greatest threats."

"You think they'll do that?" Aspen said.

"Those morons?"

Wee Willie said, "Here come some more."

"Fancy ones," Aspen said. "Radar avoidance, multi-shielding, fast."

"And what is that way down there?" Wee Willie asked. "It looks like a balloon. Awfully high in the atmosphere for a balloon."

"Where?" Curtik asked. "Oh, now I see it. That *is* odd." He destroyed an oncoming missile. "Hey, there's a balloon below my Las-cannon too."

"And mine," Aspen said.

"Damn!" Curtik said. "Take 'em out. Now."

He fired his Las-cannon. Wee Willie and Aspen did likewise. But even as he fired he knew his Las-cannon had been hit. The display went dark. He began sifting through available cameras until he found one on an adjacent satellite. All he could see was the Las-cannon hurtling out of orbit, its power circuitry gone black.

"Son of a bitch!" Curtik yelled. "What the hell was that?"

"Particle beam cannons," Aspen said. "They got yours. Damaged Wee Willie's. Mine's still okay."

"Give me yours," Curtik said.

"No."

"Dammit, Aspen, give me control."

"Go to Earth!"

"You can have mine," Wee Willie said as he punched in the codes to transfer control of his Las-cannon.

Curtik took the controls, checked the power reserve—nine percent—and saw that the Las-cannon, heavily damaged by the particle beam cannon, had begun to fall out of orbit. He tried to line up targets as the Las-cannon spiraled downward. "Son of a bitch! You cheating rat bastards!"

"Curtik," Aspen said. "Calm down."

"Shut up!"

"Wee Willie, what did you do?" Aspen asked. "You locked me out of the controls. Get me back in."

Every time Curtik acquired a target he lost it again as he fired. The damn thing would be useless in a few seconds, accelerating out of control. Crap, it was over Thailand. What the hell was there to hit in

Thailand? He found Bangkok, deactivated the targeting mechanism and powered the levels to maximum. Moving his head in a small circle, becoming simpatico with the downward spiral of the Las-cannon, he judged its spinning orbital decay until he was certain he could aim it properly. He fired, individual pulses every four and a-half seconds while the Las-cannon was pointed at Bangkok. He kept firing until the Las-cannon had been emptied of every last ounce of energy. Hopefully, the city was a barren crater.

Curtik slammed his fist into the control board. It wasn't enough. He needed to kill more and more of them to feed the emptiness. "We gotta kill 'em all. Rotten cheats. Gimme control of the last Las-cannon."

"Curtik!" Zora's voice stopped him.

Curtik turned to face her. Shiloh and Phan stood behind her, their Las-rifles aimed at him. "You know what those bastards did?" Curtik said. "They took out two of our Las-cannons. How the hell are we supposed to kill them without the Las-cannons?"

"We don't," Zora said.

"What? Come on, Zora." Curtik heard the whine in his voice but couldn't stop himself. His body shook with frustration. "We've got to kill 'em."

"That's over," Zora said. "We move on to Plan B now."

"Plan B? What the hell is Plan B?"

"Survival."

"No." Curtik launched himself at Zora. He never reached her. Las-rifle pulses struck him in the chest and back, knocking him to the ground. The burning agony took his breath away. A stinging numbness followed. He began to laugh as tears filled his eyes. Fighting the pain, he turned onto his side and looked back at Aspen, who kept her Las-rifle pointed at him.

She shook her head. "I knew I'd have to stun you today."

Curtik rolled onto his back. Slowly he forced the laughter down, glanced at Zora and tried to speak. Instead, he vomited ice cream.

"You just won't play nice, will you?" Zora said.

"Shoot, me, again," Curtik finally managed to say.

"Look," Zora said as she bent over him, "you're the best fighter we've got. The best at reacting and improvising. The way you handled that Las-cannon as it died. That was great. I don't think anyone else could have pulled that off. And realizing the hot air balloons carried weapons. Impressive. Why can't you just follow orders?"

The stinging numbness spread throughout Curtik's body, amplifying the desperate need to kill. He giggled and started to get to his feet. Aspen fired again, knocking him back to the ground. This time the pain hurt so badly it almost felt pleasurable. Once more Curtik lost the ability to speak. He worked his jaw for a few seconds and said, "I'm afraid, I have to, kill you, now." He marveled at the words coming out of his mouth—not that he didn't mean them, but why was he saying them out loud? "Nothing personal. But you all, have to die."

"Off to the hospital with you," Zora said. She beckoned Shiloh and Phan over. "Put him with that sick girl," she said as they picked him up.

"You're dead, Zora," Curtik yelled as Phan and Shiloh dragged him away. "We have to keep killing or we'll die." He tried to struggle against Phan and Shiloh but his body refused to obey his commands. The residual bioelectric echo kept his muscles from working properly. "You're gonna have to kill me to stop me," Curtik yelled.

Shiloh dug her Las-rifle into Curtik's side. "I never liked you, Curtik. Just give me an excuse to zap you."

* **

Dr. Poole and Rendela stood beside a pair of hospital beds, one of which held the girl Curtik had brought in earlier. "Kill you too," Curtik shouted, wondering why he was shouting and who he planned to kill. Rendela shook her head and aimed her Las-rifle at Curtik as Phan and Shiloh dumped him on the bed next to the girl, where Dr. Hack'emup stood. Off to the side, Dr. Wellon conferred with Devereaux, God Himself. Hack'emup met Curtik's eye for only a moment before looking away while the other two spared Curtik only a glance. Phan and Shiloh fastened the restraints around Curtik's wrists, ankles and chest, then moved to either side of the door.

"Well, Curtik," Poole said as she waved a scanner from side to side. "You seem to be having trouble playing with others. Tell me, are you furious right now?"

Curtik forced a grin. "As a matter of fact, Piscine, I'm planning a party."

"Your nerves stretched thin?"

"A Las-rifle can do that."

Poole shook her head. "I think you're out of balance, possibly devolving."

"Not a chance, Piscine. I'm not like the spookster."

Poole studied her scanner. "Do you have an uncontrollable urge to kill?"

Curtik clenched his hands into fists, imagined them around her neck, squeezing until her head popped off. "I can control it. Come here and I'll show you."

"An inability to concentrate on anything other than killing for more than a few seconds?"

"I could just maim a few people."

"This feeling that if you don't kill someone soon you might explode?"

Oh, yes! "Seems to me you're the one obsessed with killing."

Poole turned away, said to Rendela, "I'll need some time to study these results. Something's definitely changed in his neural pathways."

Curtik shouted, "I got shot, you stupid bitch!"

Rendela turned to Shiloh and Phan. "For now he's not one of us. Remember Damon and how squirrelly he got? Show no mercy. If he somehow finds a way out of those restraints, shoot first, call for help later."

"Love to," Shiloh said with a smile. She aimed her Las-rifle squarely at Curtik's chest. "Give me a reason," she purred.

"Now who's the psycho?" Curtik said. He shivered, his body feeling cheated, pushed to the edge of ecstasy, then pulled back. He wasn't devolving. He couldn't be devolving. He just needed to kill. He giggled again. "I'm going to murder you, murder you, murder you," he chanted, unable to control himself, surprised at the words coming out of his mouth. "Kill you all as hard as I can."

Poole pressed a relaxant pad to his neck. He fought it, clenching his fists, pounding them on the bed as Poole shook her head. The wrongness of the relaxant ate at him, making him nauseated and even more on edge. It tried to steal the tension from his muscles. Curtik refused to let it. He drummed his heels on the bed. "Kill, all. Gotta do it."

"That's not good," Poole said as she checked her scanner again. "The relaxant isn't taking hold. Just like with Damon." She prepared another relaxant and gave it to Curtik. A temporary blackness enfolded him. When he opened his eyes, Poole stood beside his bed. God Himself was gone. Dr. Wellon sat at the room's only desk, looking through a powerscope. Hack'emup stood on the other side of the girl's bed, adjusting the settings on a pharmodispenser. Phan and Shiloh stayed by the door, accessing their implants. Curtik's implant indicated that several hours had passed.

"Do you feel better?" Poole asked.

"A bit," Curtik replied.

"You're devolving," Poole said. She gently touched his arm. "However, the nanobots are reacting differently with your neural pathways than they did with Damon."

"What does that mean?"

"You'll have periods of lucidity and periods when all you want to do is kill everyone around you. I think the stress of this situation brought it on. The sedatives I gave you helped, but I can't give you too much without risking major organ failure or extremely rapid aging."

"Why are you being so nice, Piscine?" Curtik asked. "You should hate me for killing Mouthy Man."

"I helped make you what you are." Poole squeezed his arm. "I share the blame. Don't worry. We've learned a lot about devolution from studying Damon's condition. We'll do everything we can to save you." She touched her interface. "I have to go."

As she left the room, Curtik turned toward the girl in the next bed. She lay on her side, staring at him.

She said, "Are you going to kill me?"

"Not yet."

"Do you like being mean?"

"Sure."

"Sometimes I'm mean to Kaylee. My parents like her more than me."

"My Dad hates me."

"Oh." The girl seemed to think about that for a moment. She said, "You can yell at me if you want."

Curtik snorted. "Maybe later."

"Okay," the girl said. "Do you feel bad? After I yell at Kaylee I sometimes feel bad."

"No," Curtik said. "Actually, I feel better."

"I'm glad. My name's Kyler."

"I'm Curtik."

"Do you have the Susquehanna Virus too? I have it. I'm going to die."

"Who told you that?" Curtik said. He glared at Hack'emup, who refused to meet his eyes, then stared at Dr. Wellon's back. "Hey, Beef Wellington, tell her she's not going to die."

Dr. Wellon looked up from her work and shook her head. "Sorry. I don't know."

"Well, what are you doing about it?"

"Dr. Hackett is adjusting her medication as we speak and I'm preparing a series of treatments that might enable her body to recognize the virus as harmful, so it will fight the virus on its own."

"Hack'emup'll kill her if you don't keep a close eye on him. He's an idiot."

Dr. Wellon bit her lip. "Dr. Hackett is a competent surgeon."

"He damn near killed Wee Willie a few months ago. If they hadn't called you, he would have died."

Hack'emup finally met Curtik's eyes. "You've done nothing but ridicule me since the first day we met."

"That's because you've been nothing but a moron since the first day we met."

"And you've been a little bastard. You know nothing about nano-medicine. Wee Willie's nanobots created a feedback loop that—"

"Blah, blah, blah. What about a transfusion for Kyler? You can use my blood."

Dr. Wellon seemed to contemplate his offer before shaking her head. "I doubt it will be effective but I'll take a sample to study."

"Why won't it work?"

"The nanobots inside you were designed specifically for your body. Any attempt to transplant them to Kyler might result in a battle between them and Kyler's immune system. Much like the problem Dr. Hackett encountered with your friend. I'm sorry."

"What about regular medical nanobots?" Curtik said. "They're not targeted for a specific metabolism or biochemical output."

"True," Dr. Wellon conceded. "Dr. Hackett's already given her an injection of those. But they're having trouble recognizing the virus. Perhaps Devereaux will find a solution."

"Devereaux!" Curtik spat out the word. "God Himself doesn't care about Kyler. He's worried about humanity. Like that diseased species can be saved."

"Aren't you trying to save one of them?"

I am! Why? For some reason he'd connected with her emotionally. She wasn't like that bitch Zora. She was just a brave little kid. Had she been whining or crying like her parents and sister he'd have killed her. But she possessed a strength Curtik admired. If only all humans were like her. She watched him, a sickly child about his own natural age, even though she was infinitely younger, drawn up in a fetal position, beads of sweat on her forehead, damp curls trailing across the pillow, her brightly feverish eyes tracking his.

Curtik suddenly flashed back to one of the few memories he retained from his old life—sitting at a water park with his parents, eating ice cream on a hot summer day. Why did that memory pop up now?

He glanced at Hack'emup, who sucked in his breath with a hiss as he continued making adjustments to the pharmodispenser. If anything was certain, it was that Hack'emup couldn't save Kyler. When the computer on the desk beeped, Dr. Wellon bent to the screen and adjusted the audio receiver so no one else could hear what was being said. After a few seconds, she said, "I'm on my way." She got to her feet, huge and scary and yet somehow comforting, and said to Hack'emup, "I'll be back soon."

Another beep sounded, this time from Hack'emup's machine. Dr. Wellon stopped and looked at Hack'emup, who nodded and said, "Her lungs are shutting down. Activating auto-respirator. Heart function at thirty percent."

"You can't leave her to that idiot," Curtik said.

"There's only so much we can do." Dr. Wellon grabbed a small vial off the desk where she'd been working and handed it to Hack'emup. "This isn't quite ready, but I don't think we can wait any longer. Administer this immediately."

Hack'emup took the vial from her and began preparing a hypo pad.

Dr. Wellon looked at Curtik and said, "I'm sorry, but I have other patients."

As she passed between Phan and Shiloh, another beep sounded from Hack'emup's machine. Kyler closed her eyes. Curtik struggled against his bonds, flailing away helplessly. "Let me out of here," he shouted to Phan. "I promise I'll kill you quick. Please."

Phan frowned. "What kind of promise is that?"

"Come on!" Curtik roared. He caught Hack'emup's eye. "If she dies," Curtik yelled, "you're next."

Hack'emup moved up close, bent over Curtik and whispered, "You're devolving, you murderous bastard. You're going to die, screaming in agony, until you're nothing."

Curtik tried to lunge at Hack'emup, but his restraints held.

"You're a dead man," Curtik yelled.

"Wake up, Kyler," Curtik shouted. "Wake up! You've got to fight it."

Kyler opened her eyes. She stared at Curtik, peaceful and calm, as if she'd accepted her impending death. "Tell my . . . love them."

"Fight it, Kyler," Curtik urged. "Don't go to sleep."

Kyler blinked a few times, then closed her eyes again. Curtik continued to call her name as Hack'emup injected her with the substance Dr. Wellon had prepared.

"Wake up, Kyler," Curtik pleaded. "Come on. Wake up."

The unconscious girl took no notice. Would she slip away without a fight? How could she not battle to survive? Again Curtik struggled with the bonds that held him. "Goddammit! Let me out of here." Phan shook his head almost imperceptibly; Shiloh ignored him. Even if Curtik were to somehow break free, nothing he did would save her. Killing, it appeared, was not the solution to every problem. For the first time in a long time, almost as far back as he could remember, Curtik felt afraid.

Chapter Twenty

Lendra paced in one of the infirmary's exam rooms, waiting for Zora, telling herself that the walls weren't closing in on her. *This is not a coffin. Does she know about my claustrophobia? And does she know my true mission?* Three small steps, turn around, three small steps—Lendra fingered the glass bulb containing her neo-dopamine. If she didn't get out of this room soon, she'd have to take a dosage regardless of the risk to the baby.

She'd had no opportunity yet to access Eli's hidden program to accelerate devolution in the cadets. How was she supposed to activate the program when she couldn't get near the encrypted system?

A loud crash sounded through the walls, and an anguished cry that sounded familiar. *Jeremiah?*

Lendra opened the door just as Rendela and Dr. Poole approached. Rendela grabbed her, pushing her down the tunnel toward a hospital room a few meters away. Inside the room, Damon lay on the bed, his hair completely white. Jeremiah sat in his wheelchair at the bedside, bent over and sobbing. A broken monitor lay on the floor.

Lendra's stomach dropped. She'd never heard Jeremiah cry before. She wanted to rush forward and hug him. But Rendela held her arm tightly.

Damon lay unmoving. On the other side of the bed, Zora stood quietly, her eyes on Jeremiah, frowning. Something about her looked different today. She was still a beautiful young woman, but suddenly more mature. Dr. Wellon lifted the broken monitor off the floor and beckoned Dr. Poole over, whispering to her.

Lendra looked from Rendela's hand to Zora and said, "Please."

Zora nodded and Rendela released her arm. Yet, now free to embrace Jeremiah, Lendra hesitated. She knew Jeremiah was still angry with her, so she eased over to his side and tentatively placed a hand on his shoulder. God, she loved him! She couldn't remember a time in her life when she'd felt like this toward another person, as if Jeremiah were both lover and son. She knew this protective feeling was likely hormonal in nature but she didn't care.

Jeremiah's shoulders shook as he cried. He didn't turn toward her, but he didn't push her away either. She rubbed his back gently until he quieted and his shoulders stopped moving.

Finally he said, "Everyone I love . . ." and placed his head in his hands.

Lendra wanted to say that Damon wasn't his son, though she knew that wouldn't make it any better. He'd chosen Damon for his own, which only made Lendra love him more.

Yes, she had betrayed him. But she'd done it for his good as much as hers. They deserved a chance to make a family together. And he would love her the way she loved him if they shared a child.

Jeremiah straightened himself and took a deep breath, then looked across the bed at Zora. "I'm sorry," he said. "I don't know what got into me."

Zora said, "You really are the sweetest man, aren't you."

"No, I'm not." Jeremiah lifted his hands and studied them for a moment. "I guess I deserved that. I've killed enough people that I can't complain when the ones I love die."

Rendela said, "What happened?"

Dr. Wellon said, "Massive systemic failure—brain, heart and lung function all ceased at the same time, along with kidney, pancreas, thyroid and . . . a coordinated attack by the nanobots. We couldn't stop it. I'm sorry, Jeremiah."

Rendela said, "Is this going to happen to Curtik too?"

"Curtik?" Jeremiah said.

Dr. Poole shrugged. "It looks like devolution has begun for him as well. He's in the next bay."

Another cadet devolving! Lendra might not have to get into Dr. Poole's system after all. Perhaps all the cadets would devolve—their nanotechnology attacking them faster than Eli expected.

Zora glared at Lendra. "Why are you so happy, Witchy Poo?"

"What? I'm not happy."

"You're practically glowing."

Lendra dug her fingernails into her palms. She'd thought her face was a mask. How could Zora have read her so easily?

Jeremiah twisted his head to look up at Lendra. "That's why you were sent here, isn't it? You were supposed to ensure that the cadets devolved."

Lendra went still with shock. Her face flushed. She marveled at Jeremiah's intuition even as it frightened her. "How could you say that?"

"Ooh," Zora said. "Look, Rendela. See how angry Witchy Poo is? Think she'll attack us?"

Rendela aimed her Las-rifle at Lendra. "Please do."

Lendra eased behind Jeremiah, using him as a shield.

Jeremiah shook his head. "Eli didn't send you up here just for me. You're his insurance policy. What did he tell you to do?"

Lendra glanced over at Zora, noted the hatred on the young woman's face, and grabbed the handles of Jeremiah's wheelchair to keep from collapsing. She realized she was dead now if she didn't do something. "Please," she said, putting a hand on her stomach, "I'm carrying Jeremiah's baby."

"Some computer program, no doubt," Zora spoke quietly, the menace in her voice clear, "you being a computer genius and all. I'll want the access codes to that program. Now."

"It's hid—," Lendra's voice cracked. She cleared her throat and tried again: "It's hidden in Dr. Poole's system—an encrypted program designed to accelerate devolution to a childlike state in forty-eight hours. It wasn't supposed to be lethal. At least, that's what I was told. And I swear I wasn't going to activate it."

Zora turned to Dr. Poole, who raised her hands and said, "I didn't know anything about it, Zora. I promise. Otherwise, I could have activated it at any time."

Lendra said, "Eli knew she would think of you as her children, so he didn't tell her about the failsafe. I was sent up here to initiate the devolution."

Dr. Poole's eyes widened. Zora looked at Rendela for a long moment, neither of them saying a word, before turning to Jeremiah. "When are we going to die?"

"I don't know," Jeremiah answered.

"But we're going to devolve."

Jeremiah shrugged, wincing as he did so. "Almost certainly."

Rendela scowled at Lendra.

Would she fire? Will my daughter die right now?

Jeremiah grabbed Lendra's arm and pulled her down beside him, putting his body in the way. "You're either behind schedule," Jeremiah continued as if nothing had happened, "or matters have accelerated so that Eli needs you to devolve sooner that anticipated." He turned to Dr. Poole. "You saw nothing in Curtik's analyses to indicate that this might happen?"

"No," Dr. Poole replied. "Everything was normal the last time we looked. My guess is that stress accelerated both Damon and Curtik's devolution. Their cortisol, GH and norepinephrine levels were extremely high. Damon was too sensitive. He caught every nuance. And Curtik expected to be in charge, so when Zora took control, he felt enormous pressure."

"You're also under tremendous stress," Jeremiah said to Zora. "So you have to take care of yourself. Let Rendela and Aspen help you. Above all, fight the urge to commit violence. If you were programmed to devolve, then . . ."

Zora nodded slowly. "With a little creative hacking, we might be able to reverse the process."

Rendela shivered and said, "I don't want to die, Zora."

"You're not going to die yet," Zora said.

"I'm going crazy," Rendela said. "I need to kill someone." She aimed her Las-rifle at Jeremiah.

"Not him," Zora said. "Are you crazy?"

"Then Witchy Poo."

Lendra trembled as Rendela's Las-rifle centered on her chest. In a blur of movement, Jeremiah launched himself out of his wheelchair.

227

He hit Rendela's stomach with his shoulder, grabbing the Las-rifle out of her hands as she fell back against the wall. They both cried out in pain as Jeremiah fell on top of her. She fought against him, punching him over and over. But he just absorbed the blows, holding the Las-rifle away from her. Dr. Poole and Dr. Wellon backed against the wall, while Lendra stayed crouched near the bed.

"No more killing," Jeremiah shouted. "No more killing!"

Rendela stopped struggling as Zora took a step forward. When Zora held out her hand, he simply gave her the Las-rifle. What was he thinking? Or maybe, Lendra realized, he was far ahead of her. He couldn't fight them all with a single Las-rifle. Whatever chance they had of survival, they now needed these cadets. Why hadn't she thought of that?

Zora lifted Jeremiah off Rendela and held him up while Wellon rolled the wheelchair over to them. As Jeremiah settled into the chair, he said, "Killing will only add to your stress levels. Believe me."

Zora handed the Las-rifle back to Rendela, who stood against the wall breathing heavily and rubbing her stomach. She aimed the Las-rifle at Lendra again. She said, "I gotta shoot somebody. I could just stun her."

"Please." Dr. Poole raised her hands. "You have to control yourself."

"Why?" Rendela said, swinging her Las-rifle to cover Dr. Poole. "If we're going to die anyway, why not kill you all now?"

Dr. Poole backed up to Damon's bed. Jeremiah rolled his wheelchair forward until Rendela turned her Las-rifle on him.

"Zora," Jeremiah said.

When Zora focused on him, Jeremiah said, "What you're feeling right now isn't real. This anger was programmed into you—to be your default reaction to stress. But it's not who you are. It's something external. You can fight it. You just need to focus on other things—your friendship with each other, pleasant memories."

"We haven't had a lot of happy times up here," Zora said.

"But you've had a few. You and Rendela are friends—and Aspen. Surely the three of you have some good memories. Like rescuing me from that crater. Didn't it feel good to help someone else?"

Zora shook her head and took a slow breath. "You keep surprising me. You should want to kill me. Why are you being so nice?"

"You were created to become a weapon by a man who never saw you as a person, but as a tool to be bent to his will."

Zora sneered at Lendra. "And designed to break when we'd accomplished our mission."

Lendra shivered. She realized that her fear had kept her from thinking straight, whereas Jeremiah was playing it perfectly, getting Zora to trust him. The question now was whether Zora would let her live. Lendra had to find a way to make herself indispensable.

"Eli has to be stopped," Jeremiah said. "He probably showed you the old vids that he grew up watching—alien invaders, cyborgs with restricted life spans to prevent world domination. It all ties into his master plan of uniting the world into one force for good. But he twisted it so badly that it's something unrecognizable."

"Well, at least you don't have to worry about us blowing up the Earth. That's not really an option anymore. Only one Las-cannon remains. The other two were destroyed."

"Perfect," Jeremiah said. "One's just enough."

Zora's mouth twitched in what might have been a smile. "So," she said, "this desire to kill you . . . or kiss you . . . is programmed?"

What? Lendra thought. She wants to kiss him? The father of my child?

Jeremiah smiled tentatively, that shy smile that drew women to him, and said, "If you want to kiss a man like me, it must have been programmed into you. Just mark that as another urge to avoid."

"I'll try," Zora said, with a hint of a smile. She looked down at Damon and the smile vanished as her jaw tightened.

Jeremiah said, "The urges will probably get worse as the stress of our situation increases. I assume Curtik became uncontrollably violent like Damon?"

"Not exactly like Damon," Zora said. "But he definitely got aggressive."

"Which means any cadet who displays aggressive behavior should be monitored carefully."

Rendela scoffed.

Jeremiah said, "You might not want to leave any of your people alone. I'd suggest you put everyone in pairs, if not in threesomes. Watching each other."

Zora looked at Rendela. "Spread the word. Everybody in twos and threes until further notice. And tell them why."

Rendela nodded as her eyes took on a glazed appearance. Obviously notifying her fellow cadets via implant.

Zora turned to Dr. Poole and said, "Can you test us for devolution? Find out whether we're likely to suffer the same fate as Damon?" She glanced down at the dead boy and touched his hand briefly.

"I'll try, Zora. But until the devolution begins, I may not be able to spot any anomalies. I suggest you examine Eli's program to see if that holds any clues. And it would help if we can autopsy Damon." She looked down at the body on the bed.

"I can do that," Dr. Wellon said. "I'm sure Quekri will agree. She'll be here any moment."

Jeremiah and Zora looked at Damon, then stared at each other. They appeared equally distraught, having bonded over the dead boy. Lendra felt like hitting someone. And yet when she looked upon Jeremiah's face and saw the loss there, a heavy sadness came over her.

She put that thought aside and concentrated on Zora. How soon would she devolve? Zora was no Curtik. In this kind of stressful situation, if Curtik were in charge, he'd have attacked anything and anyone, strewing random destruction about him like a tornado until he devolved into an unreasoning animal—until his excesses destroyed him—whereas Zora just might have the emotional control necessary to survive.

Dr. Poole said, "I'll get started. I need another sample of your tissue. Rendela's too. We'll compare it to Curtik's and Damon's."

She opened a small case on the desk beside her, removed a collector pad and pressed it to Damon's hand, obtaining a small quantity of cells. She did the same for Zora and Rendela.

As Rendela escorted Dr. Poole out, Zora walked around the bed to Jeremiah's side. She said, "Will you help us?"

"If I can," Jeremiah said. His focus on Zora, if anything, intensified. Lendra's stomach lurched, whether from the growing baby or the scene before her, she couldn't say. She felt an urge to reach out and grab Jeremiah, but she was afraid to draw Zora's attention.

So she only watched as Zora's hand reached out tentatively toward Jeremiah, then withdrew. The bitch! Obviously she was sending subconscious signals to Jeremiah. But Zora's sexuality had not yet awakened. Had it? Was Jeremiah being drawn to her even without that? And if her sexuality was awakening, could Jeremiah resist her? Could any man?

Zora said, "What do we do now?"

"We survive," Jeremiah said.

"We want that too," Quekri said from the doorway as she stepped into the room, Quark trailing her. Lendra hadn't heard either of them approach, they moved so silently.

Zora turned to face her. "We need your help. We believe we're going to devolve like Damon. Curtik has already shown signs of it. And we don't have the scientific expertise to run every permutation, test every genetic possibility, to determine if it's going to happen or how to stop it."

Dr. Wellon said, "If I autopsy Damon, I might get some answers into the systemic collapse of his organs."

Quekri nodded. She stepped over to the bed, looked down at Damon and said, "Damon, I remember you."

Quark and Dr. Wellon echoed her words, paying respect and saying a final goodbye.

"Wellon will help you," Quekri said, "but the rest of us are trying to prepare for our journey to Mars, which you promised we could undertake. And we need the rest of our team working on that."

"I'm sorry. But we can't survive without you."

Quark stepped around Quekri, scowling, his body seeming to grow even more massive and threatening as he pointed at Zora. "You intend to force us?"

Zora put out her palms in apology. "We have the Las-rifles."

Quark's hands clenched into fists as he glared at the young woman. His body tensed, a coiled spring. Zora looked back at him—unarmed, unafraid. For a moment Lendra thought Quark was going to break her neck. She had no doubt he could do it, no matter how fast Zora was. A voice in the back of Lendra's brain shouted to Quark to do it. Zora stared up at him with a look on her face that said she didn't care whether she lived or died. She certainly made no move to escape. Was she calling in backup via her implant? Somehow Lendra doubted it. What a brave girl. What a dangerous rival.

"Quark," Jeremiah said.

Quark glanced at Jeremiah, unclenched his hands and stepped back a pace.

"We're all in this together," Jeremiah said. "We fight the rage too, Quark. Don't forget that. These kids aren't so different. They've been altered and programmed and made into what they are. They weren't even given a choice like you were."

Quekri said to Zora: "Eli's war will be here soon. You know that, don't you?"

Zora nodded. "Earth will try to destroy us. They'll take out the entire lunar colony if they can. Don't worry, we'll get your ship ready in time."

Jeremiah looked at Zora, sadness and pain written on the frown lines of his face. He said, "We're no match for their power."

Zora nodded. "True, but we may be able to force them to a draw." She leaned forward, hands on knees, compressing her breasts as they came level with Jeremiah's face. His eyes dropped briefly to her chest. If this was a clumsy initial attempt at seduction, Zora was going to be a world-class temptress. "With the last Las-cannon, we can at least defend ourselves until we figure out a strategy. How much time do we have?"

"Maybe a couple days before they come for us."

Zora straightened and caught Lendra's eye. "I ought to kill you, Witchy Poo," she gestured to Jeremiah, "even though he doesn't want me to. Give me a reason to keep you alive."

"I understand nanotechnology," Lendra said. "I can analyze the nanobots. And I'll help deconstruct Eli's program. As Jeremiah said, we're all in this together. For some reason, that never occurred to me before. But I give you my word I won't try anything."

"What's your word worth," Zora said, "after what you did to him?"

"I'm sorry I betrayed you, Jeremiah," Lendra said. "But I'm not sorry I'm carrying your daughter. I do love you in my own confused way."

"Touching," Zora said. "Let's go. You've got a lot to do to buy your life." She took Lendra's arm and walked her out the door. Lendra looked back at Jeremiah as they left. But his eyes were focused on the beautiful Zora. He wouldn't. He couldn't. She's a child.

Chapter Twenty-One

Taditha Poole tried to concentrate on the twisting double helix of Zora's DNA under her Powerscope, but Curtik continued to babble from his bed in the next room and Rendela and Kammilee refused to close the door, insisting that they needed to watch him as well as guard Poole.

"I looked at your neck but it wasn't bent, so I thought I would give it a strangle," Curtik sang out. "Then your arms would go limp and you'd be a big gimp and your head would suddenly start to dangle."

Poole glared over at Curtik and shook her head. She felt like she was close to discovering something, but found it difficult to concentrate. It didn't help that Curtik's rhymes were all just that little bit off.

"You want another stimulant?" Rendela asked.

With a broad grin, Kammilee jumped off her stool, a hypo pad held high.

"No," Poole said.

At a gesture from Rendela, Kammilee sighed and returned to her stool. Poole bent back over her Powerscope, comparing Zora's DNA sample to an older one she had on file. The computer had found no major discrepancies in any alleles, so Poole was now checking minor differences. She hadn't slept in over 24 hours. Probably no one had. An urgency had come over the Moon. Every time Poole took her allotted break—walking around the main hangar to relax her mind—cadets watched her with accusation in their eyes. And why not? She deserved the blame, at least partly.

Each cadet reminded her of what her baby might become, should she survive long enough to give birth. How she missed Jack Marschenko—despite their short time together.

Poole stared at the same sequence of Zora's DNA she'd been studying for the past few minutes, her mind drifting with fatigue, unable to process what she was seeing. Again she looked up, her eyes wandering past Rendela and Kammilee to the open door, through which Curtik's bed was visible. He caught Poole staring at him. His mouth ticked up in an uncontrolled twitch as he chanted: "I looked to the Earth and saw its great girth and decided I have to be cruel, but my Las-cannon's broke and my body's a joke and my doctor's just Piscine in the pool." He giggled, while the girl in the bed beside him slept on.

Poole arched her back until it cracked, took a deep breath and returned to her Powerscope.

She retrieved the data on Curtik's DNA, noting the cellular degeneration and increasing molecular dissimulation: indicators that Curtik would devolve like Damon. She flipped back to Rendela's sample. Like Zora's, it showed virtually no change. Even the nanobots surrounding the cells behaved the same—snowflakes, submarines, eels and clusters—the four nanobot shapes. Curtik's nanobots showed some variance from earlier samples—moving at a much more rapid pace. But that was likely due to their efforts to repair the damage to his DNA. So the problem apparently wasn't in the nanobots. But it had to be. And somehow it had to express itself in the genetic code. She went back to Zora's sample.

For a moment Poole lost the allele she was working on. It took her a few seconds to find it again. She adjusted the view and that was when she saw a mutation in one protein. She'd missed it before, or maybe the mutation hadn't occurred yet when the computer analyzed Zora's DNA. That little change was enough to alert Poole that the stress of the situation would eventually take its toll.

Zora would devolve.

Poole quickly slipped Rendela's slide into the Powerscope. At the same gene sequence she saw nothing out of place. How could that be? Had she not seen what she thought she had? Why wasn't the problem occurring in Rendela's DNA? She had to be missing something. She checked a neighboring sequence and then another, and there it was: a similar mutation.

Which meant that all the cadets would devolve. She looked up at Rendela, who frowned briefly and said, "What is it? What did you find?"

"A mutation," Poole replied.

"Hold on," Rendela said. Her eyes lost their focus for a moment. "Zora's sending Devereaux."

Less than a minute later Devereaux entered the room with Dr. Wellon. "You okay?" Devereaux asked.

Poole nodded. "Just tired."

Dr. Wellon said, "I could give you a mild stimulant."

Again Kammilee jumped off her stool, hypo pad at the ready.

"Back off, bitch!" Poole raised her hands as Kammilee and Rendela giggled. "Why does everyone keep pushing those?"

"Maybe because you don't look well," Devereaux said as Rendela gestured for Kammilee to return to her seat. "What have you found?"

When Poole explained the mutations she'd spotted, Dr. Wellon bent over the Powerscope and confirmed the find. "There's something else," Dr. Wellon said in her deep rumble. "I can't quite place it. But something's different about the sample."

Devereaux took a turn at the Powerscope; he spent a long time hunched over the eyepiece, his hands fiddling with the controls as he manipulated the various slides. Curtik, his arms and legs secured by the straps, sat up in his bed looking on from the next room.

"Piscine in the pool has spotted the trap," Curtik sang, "Beef Wellington has narrowed the gap. God Himself will find the solution or else we will all enjoy our devolution."

"God," Poole said, "I wish you would get the rhythm of your rhymes right."

"He's doing that on purpose," Rendela said. "Trying to annoy us."

"He's succeeding," Poole replied. She wondered at the mechanism that caused Damon, the least aggressive cadet, to spiral into near-constant violence during his devolution while Curtik, the most aggressive, was turning to poetry. That deviation should be explored. She made a note to herself in her interface.

"Interesting," Devereaux said. He straightened, rubbed his lower back and pointed to the Powerscope. "It looks like the nanobots may be engineering the mutations rather than simply issuing directives to the cells to mutate. We have to get this information to Zora right away. Perhaps Dr. Hackett can assist us. He's an expert on nanotechnology."

"Hack'emup, whack 'em up," Curtik sang. "Soon we'll have to pack 'em up. In coffins, get it?" He cackled. "Hackett'll kill us, unless that's his aim. Then we'll survive, though we'll all become very lame."

"Curtik," Rendela said, "get some sleep." She closed the door to Curtik's room, then gestured for Poole and Devereaux to precede her to the lab.

"We've analyzed the results of Damon's autopsy," Devereaux said as they walked, "and we confirmed that the nanobots caused the deterioration. But we couldn't ascertain how it was being done. This finding of yours, however, looks promising."

"What progress has Zora made?" Poole asked.

"She just broke the code on the encrypted program hidden in your files," Devereaux said. "Apparently Lendra was able to crack the algorithms. Now they're examining the devolutionary commands."

When they reached the lab, Poole saw a dozen Escala sitting hunched over Powerscopes along one wall, Quekri among them. On the opposite wall, Dr. Hackett and his team worked at another bank of Powerscopes. Aspen stood in the middle of the room with a Las-rifle. And closest to the door, Zora also stood at a Powerscope, Lendra by her side. Zora looked up at their entrance. "You found something," she said.

Devereaux nodded and gestured toward Poole. "Actually, Dr. Poole spotted it first. A mutation."

"Where?" Zora asked.

Poole handed over the slide. "In the L-6 quadrant."

As Zora studied the slide, Devereaux said, "Dr. Wellon noticed something odd. So I looked and saw a confused pattern among three nanobots—all clusters."

"The coordinators," Zora said.

"Exactly," Devereaux replied. "I reconfigured them, activating their transmitters. This is where it gets interesting. When I uploaded the most current data from them, I got a corrosive signal."

"We didn't get any corrosive signals," Zora said. "We reconfigured a dozen nanotransmitters an hour ago."

Devereaux nodded, a smile spreading across his face. "I didn't get it on any of my samples either. It only happened with the three nanobot clusters in the sample Dr. Poole was studying. This is guesswork now but I believe the sabotage programs were designed to awaken in only a small percentage of the nanobots implanted in each of you. It's brilliant. Makes the sabotage almost impossible to find. A further guess is that the selected nanobots were programmed to attack the DNA before they corroded, so any study of tissue samples would yield a negative result for devolution until after the process had begun. Which means we're not going to find corrosive signals until after the mutations occur. So we're going to have to fix the nanobots systemwide."

Can't we just eliminate them?" Poole asked.

"No," Zora and Devereaux said together. Devereaux motioned for Zora to continue. Zora tilted her head in a slight bow.

"Our nanobots are different from the ones in the Elite Ops," she said. "Theirs are completely external, functioning as a supplement to the body's natural processes. Most of ours, however, act essentially as symbionts, attaching themselves to various organisms and becoming part of the lungs, liver, brain, all the major organs. Ours can evolve. The Elite Ops' nanobots can't. And that's how ours could be programmed to devolve."

"Exactly," Devereaux nodded, looking on like a proud father.

"So how do we fix them?" Poole asked.

Devereaux and Zora looked at each other. Zora said, "We need time to deconstruct Witchy Poo's program."

"It's not my program," Lendra said. "I had nothing to do with it. I was only supposed to activate it."

"You keep saying that," Zora said, "but I can't think of a reason to believe you."

"I wasn't even working for Eli five years ago."

"Who said the program was created five years ago?" Zora turned to stare at Hackett. "And how do we even know the corrosive nanobots were implanted when we were abducted? They could have been injected any time in the past five years by any of our medical team."

Hackett paled. "No, Zora. I'm a doctor. I took an oath."

"Hm," Zora said. "You're the one who handled all our nanotechnology. You're the logical choice.

"I . . . I wouldn't do such a thing."

Poole caught the tiny squeak in Hackett's voice and figured he was lying. Lendra caught it too, for her eyes widened slightly, but Zora seemed not to notice. More likely, she decided to let Hackett think he got away with it.

Zora said, "We'll worry about that later." She turned to Poole. "For now, Lendra, Devereaux and I will work on a fix while you, Dr. Hackett and the other members of his team will treat any cadets who exhibit symptoms of devolution. I've already received several requests for medical assistance. Probably just nerves. Psychosomatic symptoms. But you will treat them promptly and you will put their minds at ease. Understood?"

"Yes," Poole replied. "Thank you."

"I probably ought to kill Witchy Poo, you and Hack'emup. You make any mistakes and I won't have any reason to keep you alive."

Poole felt her insides stirring, wondered if she were about to vomit again. Bile rose up in her throat. She swallowed it down and said, "We won't make any mistakes."

Quekri said, "What about us?"

Zora said. "You will continue to assist us."

"Under armed guard? I hardly think that's necessary. I promise we'll work on this as long as it takes."

Zora smiled. "I've been promised many things by many people. I don't remember any of those promises coming true."

"But if you all devolve," Quekri said, "you may kill everyone on the Moon. Do you want to take us out with you?"

Zora walked over to Quekri, a petite doll confronting a giantess. "When do you stop working on the problem? When you know the final breakdown is inevitable? Or when you realize we can't stop you from completing your spacecraft? And even if you make the promise, what's to keep your fellow Escala from honoring it? They might decide they no longer want your leadership. They may lock you up and kill us themselves. They might . . ." Zora shrugged, turned away. "They might do a lot of things. I don't trust anyone anymore."

"What about me?" Devereaux said. "What if I promised to keep the research going as long as it takes, until you're cured or dead?"

Poole cringed at his bluntness. Zora went still. She stared at Devereaux for a moment, smiled sadly and said, "Get to work."

* * *

Poole said nothing to Hackett and his team as they prepared hypo pads of euphoramine, neo-dopamine and a muscle relaxant. Before they finished, Shiloh entered the admitting room, Phan at her heels. Shiloh was trembling, her finger twitching beside the trigger of her Las-rifle. Phan didn't look much better. He shifted from foot to foot, jittery.

Hackett said to Shiloh, "Could you at least put your weapon down? I don't want to be shot while examining you."

"You aren't touching me," Shiloh said.

Hackett raised his hands. "The complications arising from my treatment of your friend were not my fault. Wee Willie's system isn't really human anymore. None of your systems are. The nanobots combined with the animal DNA create original problems that a doctor can't necessarily comprehend. Perhaps a vet—" Hackett paled as he stopped himself.

"A veterinarian?" Shiloh said, her finger going to the trigger as her Las-rifle came up, the weapon shaking in her hands. "Somebody who knows about lizards and snakes?"

"I meant no offense," Hackett said, backing away, stopping only when he ran into Dr. Maria Immaculata Garcia Delgado, a tall

Argentinian with flowing black hair that dangled to her waist. She grabbed Hackett's arm and pulled him aside in a protective gesture, her body shielding him. Poole had almost forgotten that she and Hackett were lovers. Garcia was the kind of spitfire who was willing to lose her life in a grand gesture. Poole hoped she wouldn't do anything stupid. Behind her, Dr. van Wyck, the blond South African, and Dr. Lee, the short, stocky Korean—both recently rotated up to the Moon—backed against the wall, while Drs. Nakamura and Srinlangshiran—the married nanotech experts who should have rotated out by now—sat tensely in the corner.

"Get away from me," Shiloh said. She aimed her Las-rifle at Poole. "You. Piscine. Fix me."

"Calm down," Poole said. How she hated that nickname. "Try not to get excited. This is not true devolution. It's a temporary condition driven by stress. You've got weeks before you begin to break down. Maybe months."

"Yeah," Shiloh said as she poked Poole in the chest, "you sure diagnosed Curtik real well."

Poole rubbed herself where Shiloh's Las-rifle had hit her. "I didn't know your nanobots had been sabotaged. My information was limited and mostly wrong. So I had no way to diagnose the problem."

"I don't care. Just fix it. Fix me. Now!"

Poole reached for a hypo pad and pressed it to the back of Shiloh's hand. The cadet's body twitched as the drugs took effect. Her face suffused with blood, her head jerked back and forth, her hand tightened on her Las-rifle.

"What the hell did you do to me?" Shiloh asked, lifting the Las-rifle and aiming it between Poole's eyes. Phan stepped back toward the door, bringing his Las-rifle up and pointing it at Hackett.

Poole wanted to scream. It took all her self-control not to. She couldn't even open her mouth for fear that a scream would come out. I'm not going to beg, she thought. I will die with dignity.

Garcia stepped forward and said to Shiloh, "Your body is fighting the drugs."

"Particularly the nanobots," Hackett added.

Shiloh swung around, her Las-rifle moving with her, lining up on Hackett. Poole shuddered with relief and began to breathe again.

"I don't think so," Shiloh said. "It should have . . . oh." She smiled broadly. Her eyes widened slightly. "Okay, now it's working. You gotta try this, Phan."

"You all right?" Phan asked.

"Oh, yeah. It's good."

"I'm next then," Phan said.

"But you're not—" Hackett began, then stopped as van Wyck grabbed his shoulder.

Poole waited for her hands to stop trembling and pressed a pad to Phan's hand. Since he wasn't as agitated as Shiloh, he didn't twitch as badly while his body fought the drugs. He began to laugh—a crazed, almost demented giggle that erupted into a bark every few seconds.

"You were right, Shiloh," he said. "This is unbelievable."

Together, the two of them drifted out of the room.

The hours became a blur after that. Poole, Hackett and his team saw cadet after cadet, each of them in varying stages of anxiety attacks. They were eager to experience the drug-induced pleasure and impatient to the verge of violence until the euphoramine kicked in. Each had a frightening reaction to the injections: some spasmed; some became angry; Benn actually fired his Las-rifle at van Wyck. Fortunately, the stun setting saved the South African's life. Dr. Lee took him to his quarters after that. Of all the cadets, only Zora, Rendela and Aspen stayed away.

The last cadet to arrive was Wee Willie. When he stepped into the room, Poole held her breath. Hackett glanced down at Wee Willie's Las-rifle and trembled. Once again, Garcia slid in front of him, putting herself in the line of fire. This time, Hackett nudged her aside. He said, "If you want to kill me, kill me. But I didn't do anything wrong."

"It's okay, Doc," Wee Willie said, his expression bland, his body relaxed. "I know it wasn't your fault. In fact, why don't you give me the injection?"

Hackett looked at Poole, his eyes wide, mouth open.

Wee Willie nodded reassuringly. "I just wanna see what all the fuss is about." He held up a hand to stop Poole from approaching him and sidled over to Hackett. Garcia stared at him but backed away.

"Are you sure?" Hackett asked.

"Positive." Wee Willie looked at the far wall as if afraid to watch the injection. He waited while Hackett selected a hypo pad. Poole couldn't help but imagine Wee Willie twisting around and breaking Hackett's neck or firing his Las-rifle into Hackett's face, but Wee Willie just stood motionless.

As Hackett administered the hypo pad, his hands shook so badly he missed Wee Willie's hand, placing the pad on the cadet's wrist. Wee Willie smiled encouragingly. For a moment it looked like he wouldn't have a reaction to the euphoramine. He blinked repeatedly as his jaw snapped open and closed. After maybe half a minute the tension in his face eased.

"Good," Wee Willie said. He smiled—a crazy, lopsided smile that Poole suspected was only partly due to the euphoric. "No hard feelings, Doc?" Wee Willie held out his hand and Hackett reached out tentatively. Grabbing his hand, Wee Willie shook it while Hackett winced.

Wee Willie let go. "It's gonna be fine, Doc. We're all in this together." He turned and walked out the door.

Poole realized her heart was racing: breaths rapid, hands clenched into fists, sweat trickling down her sides. Her coverall suddenly felt cold from the moisture.

"I thought he was going to kill me," Hackett said. "Did you see his eyes?"

Poole nodded, slowed her breathing. Garcia grabbed Hackett's arm. As Poole slumped into a chair the room began to blur. Why was she crying? Exhaustion? Relief? She reached for a tissue and wiped the tears away. "He didn't seem nervous," she said. "I wonder why he—"

Hackett clutched his chest. His face turned purple—mouth opening in a rictus of agony as he fought for air, making choking noises, lurching toward Poole. Garcia reached for him but missed. He toppled as Poole struggled out of her chair. It took ages for him to hit the floor.

Garcia screamed, while Nakamura and Srinlangshiran rushed forward to help. They turned Hackett's rigid body onto its back and tore the top of his coverall open. His eyes stared blankly past them.

"No, no, no," Garcia said as she dropped to her knees beside Hackett. She grabbed his hand while Poole did chest compressions and Nakamura hooked Hackett up to the AutoLife machine. Within seconds, Srinlangshiran activated the heart/lung functions and Poole was able to stop her work. She sat back on her heels as Hackett's face turned a grayish white.

The AutoLife machine whirred as it pumped blood and oxygen through Hackett's body but even though Hackett's chest rose and fell, Poole could tell it wasn't enough. The brainwave activity monitor showed nothing. All the AutoLife machine was doing was keeping his organs fresh.

Using her interface, Poole contacted Zora and told her that Hackett was dead.

"Are you sure?" Zora asked.

"Wee Willie gave him some sort of poison. He's got zero brain function."

"He never had any brains. So how can you be sure he's dead?"

"Zora," Poole said.

"I gave Wee Willie permission," Zora said. "It was Hack'emup who sabotaged our nanobots."

"Are you certain?"

"It was either Hack'emup or you. Should I kill you too, just to be sure?" She disconnected without waiting for a reply. Poole shivered. While treating these cadets, she'd almost convinced herself that everything was going to be fine. But Hackett's death served as a reminder that they wouldn't be safe until . . . when? Maybe not until all the cadets were dead.

Chapter Twenty-Two

While President Angelica Hope enlisted Jay-Edgar's help in connecting with a group of the world's leaders via holo-projection, Elias Leach moved out of range of the holo-camera. He noted that China had been excluded as he activated his PlusPhone's sound filter so he could speak with Dr. Hassan.

"I'm telling you," he said, "my skin still itches."

"But it's better than it was, right?" Dr. Hassan replied.

"A little, maybe."

"And it will keep getting better if you just don't think about it. It's not unusual to have itching for a few days after implantation. Your body is still adapting to the 'bots. But we ran all the tests and your body will not reject them. This is just your well-known Frankenstein complex triggering your imagination. I can prescribe neo-dopamine to alleviate your anxiety. You'll be fine. Try to relax."

"Relax!" Elias disconnected and deactivated the sound filter so he could listen to the mostly pompous asses discussing what to do about the problem on the Moon.

The Russian President, Piotr Navrakov, said, "Russia will never yield to threats." The metallic voice of the translator sounded oddly calm contrasted with the redness of his face. It didn't synchronize with his lips, making the holo-projection look like some ancient movie that had been poorly dubbed into English. "We will not disband our government. We have been freely elected. And we will not walk away because of the threats of a few terrorists on the Moon." He turned to stare directly at President Hope. "Everyone knows your country created this mess. One of your agents is responsible."

The French President chimed in next, wearing a scarf in compliance with her Islamic beliefs. "France will not disband our government.

We've sent these infidels on the Moon a dozen messages, warning them that any attack on France will be met with overpowering force and reminding them that any dispute they have with Earth is with you."

President Hope nodded to Jay-Edgar, who overrode the audio circuits and allowed her to speak next: "Blame is not important right now. Staying out of it isn't an option. These children see the whole Earth as their enemy. And I didn't endorse the idea of dismantling our governments. I merely pointed out that Zora and her cadets had demanded it. I'm sure none of us intends to comply with that demand. What we have to figure out is how we're going to stop them before their next attack. We don't know where they'll strike. Frankly, given their personalities and your warning to them, France might be the next target they choose."

The Great Pomposity, as Elias thought of Brazil's President, came next: "If there was any justice in the world, they would hit the United States. Frankly, the world would be better off without your bullying and ubiquitous cultural presence. Perhaps if we attacked you as well, those Moon children would accept that we mean them no harm and back off."

Jay-Edgar gave President Hope the audio again: "Fighting among ourselves is what they want. We have to unite against this threat, not claw each other to death. These children will engage any and all of us. They haven't discriminated between friend and foe to date and there's no reason to believe they will in the future. We must band together for the sake of our planet and work toward a unified goal—defeating our common enemy."

England's Prime Minister, Gwendolyn Pryce-Jones said: "I agree. We must move beyond our fractured past."

"But America caused these deaths," the Italian Idiot said. "You are responsible for them as much as if you pulled the trigger. Someone in your country created these warrior children."

"It was irresponsible," the Arrogant Argentinian added. "More importantly, it was the wrong goal. We all know the world's falling apart. Look at what Brazil has done to its rain forest." Brazil's Great Pomposity turned red and began stabbing at the audio icon but the Arrogant Argentinian ignored him. "Look at the terrorism birthed by the Middle East. Look at the pollution caused by the growth of Asia."

"Let's stay on course," India's Prime Minister said, beating the Great Pomposity to the icon. "We don't need another discussion about how we're destroying the world and how we need to prepare the planet for our children's children. China has attacked us. Now the Moon has attacked us. We need help, not more Devereauxnian platitudes."

"It's not off point," Pryce-Jones said. She'd become more a Devereauxnian each passing year. Three people to her left in the holo-projection, Brazil's President Penela was yelling silently as he stabbed at the audio icon. Elias laughed softly. "It's a vital discussion essential to the viability of our planet's ecosystem, which we have not stewarded properly. And one of the reasons is the competitive nature of our governments toward each other. Grasping what we can before anyone else can seize it. Perhaps this threat can bring us together."

"Russia's needs are Russia's needs," Navrakov said. He glanced sideways at Brazil's Great Pomposity, the trace of a smirk on his face. A few other participants moved their hands over their audio icons, prepared to stab downward and keep the Brazilian from the audio as long as possible. A game they'd played before whenever one of their number became severely agitated. "They cannot be sacrificed for an uncertain future. I applaud the goal of cooperation but not at the expense of my people. We lost thousands in those attacks. Someone must pay."

India's Prime Minister said, "No one has suffered more than India. China's claims that a rogue military cell attacked us are not credible. We launched a counter strike, of course, but we need a global response to that aggression."

"Please," President Hope said. "Even though China may have preemptively attacked you, we have a more immediate global problem."

"If you will not help us, we will not help you." India's screen went blank.

Elias pushed his chair another three inches away from the holo-camera. He wondered if all his planning had been for naught. Would the nations of Earth learn to work together? They had to. Some day, when Earth was stronger, safer, more secure, history would thank him. And yet, he had a dread feeling that something awful was about to happen. Too many uncertainties lay before him. His anxiety had been building since Zora took over the Moon and began doing unpredictable things. She had an agenda he couldn't discern. And she was overdue for an attack.

Brazil's Great Pomposity finally hit the audio, his face red with anger. Elias engaged his sound filter to silence the coming rant. Shaking his head, his eye landed briefly on the Elite Ops trooper beside the door. Elias felt an itch between his shoulder blades. He grabbed a pen and used that to scratch himself.

Activating his PlusPhone, he tried once again to reach Zora. This time, instead of a refusal to answer, he was routed to a prerecorded message: "Hi, this is Zora. Sorry, we're busy taking over the Moon right now but please know that your call is important to us. We'll get back to you as soon as we've finished plotting your destruction. Thanks for calling and have a super day!"

Elias laughed. This Zora was quite the comedienne. He'd never anticipated someone other than the blunt and brutal Curtik would be leading the cadets. A stupid mistake. The possibilities a subtle leader like Zora offered were intriguing. But they were also moot. The cadets would soon be destroyed—either by Earth or their programming. Despite Lendra's failure to activate the self-destruct virus, they would still devolve. It would just take a little longer.

He noticed that Brazil's Great Pomposity had finally relinquished the audio and tuned back in to the conversation.

". . . That's why America must attack first," Navrakov said. "We will stand in support. When they destroy your missiles and deplete the Las-cannon's reserves, we will launch our few remaining missiles."

"How courageous of you," President Hope said. "As usual, everyone seems content to let America lead. Of course we'll do so. As if we haven't done it enough over the past two centuries. But we need support. We don't have enough rockets to break through their defenses, even assuming the power reserves on the remaining Las-cannon are as depleted as projections show."

President Hope kept control of the audio and turned to General Horowitz, who said, "That's why any attack would require the use of multiple rockets—as many as we can fire—to confuse the enemy, giving the few missiles with the range to reach the Moon the opportunity to slip past the defensive curtain of the Las-cannon."

Australia's Prime Minister, Cynthia Howard—a poor man's Angelica Hope: not as blond or as good looking, but still attractive—said, "Even if we managed to succeed, you're asking us to destroy the one outpost we've created in our attempt to leave this planet. If we can't create something as neutral as the Moon without destroying it, where are we as a species?"

The Nigerian Nincompoop said, "The Moon is a threat to us all. If we have to destroy that outpost to survive, that's what we'll do. We must kill these terrorists. We must band together. Only an iron hand can prevent future attacks on our governments. We must become that hand."

"No," France's President said. "That's exactly the wrong approach. The iron hand is what got us into this mess in the first place. We must lift the downtrodden, educate the masses, provide the means for everyone to reach the level of progress we First World countries have reached."

"There isn't enough." England's Pryce-Jones got the audio again. "We all know it. Devereaux made it clear. We continue to replay the tragedy of the commons, depleting commonly held resources, plundering shared wealth because, as common users, there is no mechanism in place to prevent over-reaching by any individual user. Everyone takes from the ocean because no nation owns the ocean. Everyone pollutes the air and water, perhaps only minimally, for the sake of economic gain. Everyone says, 'If I don't take what I want, someone else will and it won't be available for me.'"

Pryce-Jones spoke with a familiar passion. Elias wondered if the nations that were using the universal translator could tell she was on a favorite topic.

"Our ethnocentrism," Pryce-Jones continued, "has sown the seeds of our destruction. Every decision that emphasizes individual ahead of community, community ahead of nation, nation ahead of world, diminishes us."

"Earth is not a zero-sum game," the Nigerian Nincompoop said. "There are plenty of resources to go around."

Pryce-Jones shook her head. "Cooperative regression is the only solution to our problems."

A direct quote from Devereaux, Elias recalled, and a sage bit of advice, but useless given the reality of the world's desires.

The Nigerian Nincompoop buzzed in again. "If you want to take less, take less. We won't stop you. But don't ask us to settle for less than you have. You built your civilizations on the backs of Africans. It's our turn."

General Horowitz stepped away from the camera's range and sidled over to Elias. "It's going well," he said quietly.

"It's a disaster," Elias replied.

"Not at all. Of course we're shouldering a lot of the blame. But at least they're talking. Discussing a common problem and slowly marching toward a solution. I think we're on the way."

Jay-Edgar stood up and waved at President Hope. "Incoming call," he whispered loudly. "Zora."

"Bring her in," President Hope said.

Zora's image popped up on the far wall. "Greetings, Earthlings," she said with a broad smile. "Take me to your leader."

"I'm talking about Eli," Zora clarified. "Elias Leach, for those of you who don't know. He's the one who set all this in motion, creating us to attack Earth so that you all would unite against us."

Elias felt a thunk in the pit of his stomach as Zora's words settled. This was the attack he hadn't seen coming—the overdue, brilliant assault: a wedge to drive the leading countries of the world apart. She was outing him.

"He's the one to thank for the destruction we've rained down on you," Zora continued. "Is he there, President Hope?"

President Hope pushed her audio icon without results.

"Just nod if he is," Zora continued. "I'll keep control of the board for the moment. Otherwise we'll have to put up with that annoying three-second delay. Eli, come out, come out, wherever you are. Come and stand next to the President so the world's leaders can get a good look at you."

President Hope nodded to Elias. He stood, keeping his face calm, his jaw relaxed. His knees shook a little as he walked to her side. All his years as a puppet master vanished as he stepped into camera range—a tiny man—a child beside the majestic President Hope. He could almost see the cartoons in the leading papers, the caricatures of him that would inevitably appear. The midget with the *idée fixe* that killed millions. He could feel the hostility through the projections.

"Ah, there you are," Zora said after an interminable three-second delay. "Good to see you. Sorry I missed your call. No doubt you're all plotting your revenge. Multiple missiles fired our way with the hope that a few will make it past the Las-cannon, wiping out the lunar settlement with one massive nuclear explosion. It's a good plan, the best we've been able to come up with. Curtik articulated it before he began to devolve. But let me warn you against such a hasty strategy."

Zora's gaze swept from left to right as she looked at each world leader. "Our options are not as limited as you might imagine. Although we were engineered to fail, to devolve into unreasoning, berserk warriors, we were not supposed to know that was coming. Now we have time to prepare for it.

"It's a brutal, horrifying way to die." Zora's eyes locked onto Elias. Rage emanated from her—and implacable will. "Agonizing and without dignity. I wonder if you truly understood how terrible this death is. Are you that much a monster? I wish I knew for certain."

Elias blushed. He hadn't known. No one had. When Dr. Hassan, Dr. Hackett and their team had put together the program, they'd only been able to speculate on possible outcomes. There'd been no opportunity to test the system. The necessity of speed, of creating the cadets while he had the opportunity to do so—before President Hope took office—had forced Elias to approve the devolution of the children, but he'd always regretted the uncertainties it demanded. And now the itching began again, between his shoulder blades. He shrugged, hoping to quell the desire to scratch.

Zora, who had paused for a moment, continued: "On with the business at hand. You people make certain assumptions about our defensive abilities vis-a-vis the Las-cannon. Were I you, I would not be so convinced of my conclusions that I would fail to consider various unpleasant alternatives. In other words, we might decide to do something unexpected, something similar to what Eli planned when he created us, but different enough to alter the landscape of the world. We might fire a burst at Yellowstone, for example, or Iceland."

Zora paused for a moment. "Remember that we have nothing to lose, so we don't feel the necessity to play by your rules. What started as a compulsive attack on irrational and selfish governments has changed. That goal is unattainable. You will never cede power to anyone else. It's your *raison d'etre*. So we're no longer even going to try to change you. We're focused simply on survival. You can keep your godforsaken planet, for all the good it will do you.

"Here's what we propose. You leave us alone, we'll leave you alone. If you choose to attack us, you *will* regret it. When I finish this call, I'll transmit the facts we've gathered so far, including the data that show the inevitability of our devolution, the cruelness of our creation for destructive purposes. Ask yourselves if this is the kind of unification you want. Do you really want to ally yourselves with a regime that would do what Eli and his cronies did to us?

"One more thing," Zora said, "and I'll let you get back to your squabbling. Someone out there may be able to come up with a solution to our devolution problem. Your countries all have advanced genetics and nano-technology programs. If you find a solution for us before we devolve, we will reward you to the best of our ability. If you fail . . . and if we fail . . . well, I can't guarantee we won't attack you in our dying rage. Let me apologize for such an eventuality in advance. Sending data now. Toodles."

Zora grinned as her place in the holo-projection went dark. The world's leaders began to jostle for audio. Elias backed away.

"This is all your fault," Brazil's Great Pomposity said. "We should fire a rocket at them just so they'll blow up Yellowstone and destroy your nation. You deserve to be wiped out."

"No," Cynthia Howard said. "It would create volcanic winter, filling the sky with tons of ash, darkening everything, killing off plant and animal life. The air would become foul—even fouler than it is now—contaminated with fatal levels of hydrogen sulfide. The water would be undrinkable. And the world would become a tremendously cold place—for years."

"Exactly," Pryce-Jones said. "The previous attacks have already started us on that path. If a single massive volcano erupted, billions would die. It would be devastation on a much larger scale. You would not be exempted from the fallout."

"Having the Las-cannon trained on us is unacceptable," Navrakov said. "Though I fear there's not much we can do about it at the moment. In the meantime, we must exact some measure of vengeance to appease them."

"Yes," the Nigerian Nincompoop agreed. "Your man must be charged with crimes against humanity. And you should be arrested too."

General Horowitz lunged forward and stabbed the audio icon. "President Hope knew nothing about this program. It was enacted before she was elected, put in place by her predecessor and this man who was once a trusted advisor."

Elias felt a surge of anger and fear rising up inside him. And the itching between his shoulder blades worsened. He watched the faces staring back through the holo-projection, noted the hostility on every one of them. These fools dared to judge him?

"Give us Elias Leach," the Great Pomposity said, "and we will see to it that justice is done."

"We will arrest Mr. Leach," President Hope said. "He will be tried in America. We will not hand him over to a lynch mob."

She nodded to General Horowitz, who nodded to the Elite Ops trooper by the door. Together they advanced on Elias.

Elias stepped forward into the range of the holo-camera again. He could feel the nanobots eating away at his skin from the inside. Rage overwhelmed him. "So this is how it ends?" he shouted. "I get arrested, tried and convicted of crimes against humanity, perhaps even executed, all because I tried to save the world from your endless infighting—your stupid wars. You people are cowards. You don't deserve to live."

General Horowitz and the Elite Ops trooper reached down and grabbed Elias' arm.

"I never should have tried to save you. You can all blow yourselves up!"

Together they marched him away. Elias held his head high, righteous anger quelling his fear.

They escorted him to the room Elias had often used for holding prisoners in the past—an eight-by-ten cell with toilet and sink, and a hard narrow cot. The Elite Ops trooper let go of Elias' arm and halted outside the door. Elias took a seat on the cot as the metal door shut with a clang, the bolts engaging with a snick. The itching grew worse. It took over his arms and legs. He felt an uncontrollable urge to scratch.

"Sooner or later," he yelled at the cameras that monitored his every move, "you'll need my help."

Stay calm, he reminded himself as the itching spread. He scratched the top of his head, then his belly. "You can't keep me in here forever," he yelled. "I'm the only one who knows all the details about the project."

Even his eyeballs itched. His breathing quickened. He closed his eyes and rubbed his eyelids, then his cheeks. Falling onto his back, he squirmed back and forth on the cot as he scratched his arms and legs. Stop it! he ordered himself. It's all in your head. But the itch didn't listen. He scratched and scratched.

Chapter Twenty-Three

Jeremiah reveled in his dungeon, free of pain. But something called to him urgently—a warning. He couldn't stay any longer. Fighting the desire to remain, Jeremiah pulled himself to a fully awakened, agonizing state. Lendra and Zora stared down at him.

"Thank God," Lendra said.

"What happened?" Jeremiah asked as he sat up slowly, the knife-like pain in his joints making every movement torture. He noticed Devereaux, Quark, Dr. Wellon and Dr. Poole. The two doctors were studying a scanner.

Devereaux said, "We found you unresponsive. Nothing could wake you."

"I was in a self-hypnotic state when I felt this sense of danger."

Zora said, "Devereaux suggested that Quark tap an SOS on your broken legs in Morse code and after a couple of minutes, you came to."

"You scared us," Lendra said.

Jeremiah looked from Lendra to Zora, who frowned at him, her hands clenched into fists that trembled. Behind her, Aspen stood in the doorway, a Las-rifle gripped in her hands. "You weren't coming back," Zora said. "You wanted to stay there, didn't you?"

Jeremiah shrugged, wincing at the movement. "What's our situation?"

"Nothing from Earth yet. I had Wee Willie set all the Las-rifles to stun to prevent deadly accidents. Three cadets shot people this morning. We're becoming edgy waiting for them to attack."

Dr. Poole said, "We may need to increase the dosage of euphoramine to keep them calm. But that may hasten the onset of devolution."

"How's Curtik doing?"

Devereaux said, "He's still devolving. We gave him a small transfusion of your blood and the good news is that your lymphocytes—part of your white cells—have begun to cluster around Curtik's nanobots. In particular, your T cells and B cells are interacting extremely well."

"What does that mean?" Jeremiah asked.

Dr. Poole said, "We don't know whether your blood will prove to be an effective antidote to the devolution, but the fact that your T cells have recognized the nanobots is a good sign."

"That's great." Jeremiah caught the frowns on the faces surrounding him. "Isn't it?"

Dr. Wellon said, "We gave him the last of your pre-infected blood. Since you're infected with the Susquehanna Virus, a transfusion may not react the same way, and it will definitely infect him if we proceed. Plus . . ."

She looked over to Dr. Poole, who said, "Your bone marrow isn't producing white cells efficiently right now, due to the virus."

"Surely I'm producing enough to give Curtik a transfusion?"

"Probably. But our calculations indicate that you would need to provide a lot of blood to achieve measurable results in reversing the devolution—at least half a liter."

"And any further blood loss," Dr. Wellon said, "could result in a setback in your recovery. Plus, if your bone marrow fails to produce replacements, your condition might worsen. The virus could get out of hand, overwhelm your immune system. And if somebody else begins to devolve or if a few cadets begin to deteriorate at once," Poole's eyes shifted to Aspen, who twitched, "we would need much more of your blood."

"More than you can safely give," Lendra said.

"Still," Jeremiah said, "if it might save Curtik, it's a chance we have to take."

"It's more than that," Zora said. "Curtik's devolution might be too far advanced already. Your blood might not save him. But for those of us who haven't begun devolving yet, your blood might be used as a preventative. If each cadet received a few hundred milliliters, that could be enough to prevent devolution from occurring at all."

Lendra's mouth dropped. "Each cadet? You'd have to drain Jeremiah of all his blood."

Jeremiah smiled. "Killing the goose that laid the golden egg." He wondered briefly why he wasn't afraid. Was he that willing to seek release from this painful existence? Or did he believe the cadets wouldn't actually kill him?

Devereaux said, "We might not need to go that far. Doctors Nakamura and Srinlangshiran believe they might be able to derive a synthetic or nanotech agent by observing Curtik's progress during the treatment, studying how your white cells target the nanobots and duplicating that process. We could also transfuse some of your blood to one of the cadets who hasn't yet devolved to see how that resolves itself and perhaps duplicate that process as well."

"Do it," Jeremiah said.

"You don't understand," Dr. Wellon said. "The important element here is your white cell count. That's what Curtik needs and that's what you're not making efficiently. Your immune system is dangerously close to failing."

Jeremiah looked at the concerned faces surrounding him. "I want to save my son."

Zora coughed; her face paled.

"You don't look well," Dr. Poole said. "Perhaps your devolutionary process has started as well. She grabbed Zora's hand.

"Get away from me," Zora said. "I'm fine."

"You're not fine," Dr. Poole said. "None of you are fine. You're all about to devolve."

Zora spun about, flailing her arms. "Get back. Stay away from me or I'll kill you."

Dr. Poole raised her hands and stepped back. "I'm just trying to help."

Quark pulled Devereaux behind him, while Dr. Wellon placed herself between Devereaux and Aspen. As Aspen waved her Las-rifle about, Lendra backed into a corner. Jeremiah slid to the edge of the bed and prepared to launch himself forward if anyone attacked. He glanced at Quark, who nodded almost imperceptibly. They needed to make sure both Devereaux and Zora stayed alive and healthy.

Zora shivered. She went still.

"What is it, Zora?" Dr. Poole asked.

"Wee Willie says they've gone quiet—no chatter between the big nations."

Quark said, "They're planning something."

Devereaux nodded. "They're desperate to retain their power, and they don't like having a gun pointed at their heads, threatening global nuclear winter. Already there are signs that the Las-cannon strikes you made earlier have begun to alter Earth's climate, vastly increasing the amount of particulate matter in the atmosphere."

"What are they up to?" Lendra asked.

Zora scoffed. "You probably know. Maybe we should persuade you to tell." She shivered again, then sat on the floor. Dr. Poole took a step toward her, but Zora glared at her until she backed away.

"I don't know anything," Lendra said.

"Let's kill 'em all," Aspen said, her hands shaking.

"No," Zora said. She continued to shiver. "We need to conserve power in that last Las-cannon. If we lose that, we'll have no defenses."

Dr. Poole removed a blanket from a shelf and draped it over Zora's shoulders. "No point in freezing," she said.

"Don't touch me," Zora said.

"We have to find out if you're devolving."

"Fine." Zora stood, her blanket falling to the floor. Her whole body shook as if she were having a seizure. When Dr. Poole reached for her, Zora grabbed her hand and threw her across the room. Dr. Poole screamed as Jeremiah launched himself off the bed. He caught her, but her momentum drove them both into the wall with such force that the wind was knocked out of him. Wincing, Jeremiah lowered Dr. Poole to the floor. He spun around to face Zora. But before he could move, Aspen hit him with a blue laser pulse.

A burst of intense heat struck Jeremiah's chest. He fell.

"Quark," he managed, "the rage."

Quark stepped in front of Zora. He made no aggressive moves, simply keeping himself between Zora and Poole. Aspen moved to the side and fired at Lendra, who cried out and dropped. Zora, looking up into Quark's face, tightened her mouth into a grimace and flung herself at him, her tiny fists blurring as they pummeled his stomach and chest. Quark grunted under the onslaught but held his ground, letting her punch him, protecting his groin and face with his hands while she hit him again and again. Lendra writhed in pain, screaming.

"Yeah!" Aspen yelled. "Kill him! Kill him harder!" She aimed her Las-rifle at Quark as Jeremiah struggled to his feet. He knew he had to distract Aspen long enough for Quark to calm Zora down. Without Zora in control, the cadets would destroy everyone. He mentally prepared himself for another Las-rifle burst, psyching himself up to withstand a laser pulse long enough to disarm Aspen. After all, he wouldn't actually be burning alive.

He lunged at Aspen.

She fired at him again. It felt like someone had hit him with a flamethrower. He couldn't breathe. He tried to focus on anything except the agonizing blaze encompassing him—Zora's slowing punches; Lendra's quieting screams; Dr. Wellon shielding Devereaux. Though he knew he wasn't actually on fire, he felt like he was. He managed to stay on his feet and even take a couple steps towards Aspen.

Zora stopped punching Quark and turned to stare at him.

Aspen yelled and took a step forward, jamming the Las-rifle into Jeremiah's stomach as she continued to fire. That gave Jeremiah the opportunity to yank the Las-rifle from her hands.

With the laser pulse gone, a cool wave overwhelmed him. All his pain vanished. He began to laugh and realized almost immediately that he couldn't stop. He felt invincible, dancing on the edge of a cliff, aware of the danger below yet unable to back away.

Aspen shook her head. "How did you do that?"

"Whoa!" Zora's eyes grew wide, her nostrils flaring. "That's the most amazing . . . nobody should be able to . . ."

Devereaux stepped around Dr. Wellon, who lifted her scanner and pointed it at Jeremiah. "You continue to astound me," Devereaux said. "I wouldn't have believed it if I hadn't seen it with my own eyes."

Quark gave Jeremiah a little bow, while Lendra brought herself to a sitting position and put her hands on her stomach.

Dr. Poole said, "What you did just isn't possible."

Jeremiah shook his head as his laughter died down. "I know. But I feel great. I could almost . . ."

The pain returned, worse than before—totally incapacitating. His body tensed with agony as his chest constricted tightly. He froze, sensing that the slightest movement would cause him to black out. Yet standing still created too much pain. He needed to do something. So he dropped the Las-rifle and sat on the floor, bending over to clutch his stomach. He struggled to breathe, taking ragged gasps of air.

Aspen retrieved the Las-rifle while Dr. Wellon continued to study her scanner and Dr. Poole checked on Lendra.

"Your white cell counts rose dramatically," Dr. Wellon said, "as if your immune system was triggered by the laser pulses your body absorbed, though I don't know how that's possible. Leveling off now though. Pain levels . . ." She shook her head. "How are you still conscious?"

"A tad uncomfortable," Jeremiah acknowledged. He took a few more ragged breaths. "What happened?"

"I'm not sure yet. Apparently that laser strike created some sort of temporary overload. For a little while there, you were making T cells at an accelerated rate."

Devereaux and Zora looked at each other.

"What?" Jeremiah asked.

"This may be a solution to the problem of transfusing your blood," Zora said. "If you got shot a few more times, maybe you could produce enough blood for more transfusions."

"Unlikely," Devereaux said. He stepped over to Dr. Wellon's side. "I think this was an aberration. There's no guarantee that shooting him again would produce a similar result."

"There are other problems with the laser strikes," Dr. Wellon said. "Decreased lung function, muscle tetany, and your heart nearly stopped. Another laser strike might kill you."

Jeremiah coughed. He glanced down at Lendra, whose eyes were wide open. Jeremiah said, "How do you feel?"

"Tired. Jeremiah, what kind of creature are you becoming?"

"I don't know." Jeremiah turned to Dr. Poole. "How is she?"

"She'll be fine. So will the baby. They just need some rest and electrolytes."

"Okay," Zora said, in control of herself again. "Let's all head to the lab. We'll get some blood from Jeremiah—test it on Curtik and maybe Aspen."

"No," Devereaux said. "We need to give it to you."

"I don't have time. I have to check on Earth. We need to monitor them—be ready to attack—because they're doing something sneaky. They'll be coming after our Las-cannon. And if we lose that, we're dead."

"Let Rendela or Wee Willie handle that," Devereaux said. "You're about the only indispensable person we've got up here. You're the one keeping the cadets under control. If something happens to you, who knows what they'll do?"

"He's right, Zora," Dr. Poole said. "You have to be the one."

"I still don't like it," Dr. Wellon said. "We don't know how much Jeremiah can safely give, especially in his weakened state."

"You can't kill yourself, Jeremiah," Lendra said.

As Quark lifted Lendra, Jeremiah said, "I'm not trying to kill myself. We need Zora more than me right now. Take what you need."

Dr. Wellon eased Jeremiah into his wheelchair, then pushed him, while Quark carried Lendra, the others trailing behind. Jeremiah sat as still as possible, trying to minimize the pain in his joints, taking shallow breaths.

When they reached the lab, Jeremiah saw Curtik thrashing about in the next room, tugging at his bonds and practically levitating off the bed. Curtik didn't say a word as he threw his body against the restraining straps over and over. My son! This brutal and twisted beast is my son. For an instant Jeremiah wished Damon had been his real son. What a terrible thought! How could I have considered that? Maybe that's why Curtik is so homicidal, because he inherited my facility for killing.

Stop it, Jeremiah told himself. You're his father and you'll act like it and eventually you'll find the good in him.

On the bed beside Curtik, Kyler lay unconscious, an oxygen tube running to her nostrils. She looked so tiny and vulnerable. Jeremiah rubbed his eyes. Why did he feel so much more concern for her than he did for Curtik? What kind of father was he? He wheeled himself into their room, his self-directed anger stemming the pain.

"Hello, Curtik," Jeremiah said.

Curtik stopped thrashing and stared at Jeremiah. "Shh," he whispered. "I'm hunting wabbits."

Aspen laughed as Curtik resumed his fight against the straps, flinging his arms and legs about while Quark settled Lendra into a chair.

Dr. Poole said, "We're going to give you a transfusion of your father's blood, Curtik. Hopefully that will reverse the devolutionary process."

Again Curtik stopped moving. He jerked his head in Kyler's direction. "Give it to her."

"We'll give her some too," Jeremiah said.

"You're not a vending machine," Dr. Wellon said.

Jeremiah looked at Devereaux, who said, "She's already infected, so she can't be harmed by the virus. It might work. We've already put her on the whole package of anti-virals, but she's not progressing as well as we'd like."

"I can't be responsible for your health if you do this," Dr. Wellon said.

"We could shoot him again," Aspen said. "See if that helps." She aimed her Las-rifle at Jeremiah.

"No!" Lendra yelled.

Jeremiah tensed, expecting Aspen to fire, but Zora raised her hand.

"I'll shoot him," Curtik said. "He looks like a wabbit." Curtik reached toward Aspen. "Give me the gun. Gimme the gun. Gimme the Goddamn gun!"

He began screaming unintelligible sounds of outrage as he stretched against the restraining straps. Dr. Poole moved over to his bedside and reached for a hypo pad as he continued to roar. Within a few seconds he grew quieter, struggling less as the sedative kicked in. In under a minute he was asleep.

Dr. Wellon began transfusing Jeremiah's blood. She ran it through a filter-analyzer and into Curtik's arm, while engaging the monitors so Doctors Nakamura and Srinlangshiran could study how his body reacted.

As the blood drained out of him, Jeremiah felt increasingly weak and cold. The room began to spin and the people in it grew blurry. He struggled to keep his eyes open as fatigue overcame him.

It almost felt like he was falling. His mind began to wander. He visualized the response he would make if given the ultimatum the cadets had given Earth and suddenly realized what the politicians there must be doing.

"Las-cannons," he said as Dr. Wellon moved to Kyler's side and gave her some of Jeremiah's blood.

"Las-cannons?" Dr. Poole said.

"They're building Las-cannons."

"Impossible." Lendra shook her head. "That would violate the Berlin Treaty."

"It makes sense," Zora said from her chair beside Kyler's bed, where she waited for her turn at a transfusion. "I should have thought of that before." She shivered as she looked down at her shaking hands. "I didn't realize how anxious I was. I guess I need your blood after all."

"But building Las-cannons would be suicidal," Lendra protested. "It would start an arms race. And all it would take would be one faulty Las-cannon to set off an explosion greater than any nuclear bomb. That's why the only ones allowed are in orbit."

"It should be easy enough to check," Jeremiah said, his breathing returning to normal. "You can monitor the sat-feeds.

As the Las-cannons get closer to completion, the scanners should show spikes in radiant energy consumption levels. I estimate the levels would at least quintuple at the military bases where they're building them."

Devereaux nodded. "And a radio-spectrum-assay analysis should confirm the electro-chemical reactions of the charging process, though we would have to wait until they're essentially completed before we could detect that emission."

"I'll get Wee Willie on it," Zora said as Dr. Wellon initiated the transfusion into her arm. Dr. Wellon gripped Zora's arm tightly to keep it from shaking while she inserted the needle. The two of them grew more distant as the transfusion progressed. Jeremiah thought Zora was no longer shivering, though his vision had become foggy, as if he were seeing everything through a gauzy curtain. Even sound began to diminish.

"Jeremiah," Lendra said. "Jeremiah, you have to stop. Doctor!"

Jeremiah tried to answer, but he felt too weak, too indifferent. He struggled even to breathe.

"He can't give anymore," Dr. Wellon said as she cut off the flow. "His heart is in fibrillation." She attached an external pacemaker to his chest and he began to breathe easier.

"I'll get Jeremiah some blood," Dr. Poole said. "It won't be special like his, but it will help replenish what he's lost."

Devereaux put his face down close to Jeremiah and said, "How do you feel?"

Jeremiah blinked his eyes a couple times and opened his mouth, but no words came out.

"Well done," Devereaux said. He laid a hand on Jeremiah's shoulder. "How about you, Zora? How do you feel?"

"It's too early. I wouldn't feel any . . ." Zora stopped and nodded. "Oh, I see. You're wondering if there's a psychological benefit from just knowing I've got his blood in me." She lifted her hands and stared at them. They shook slightly but not as badly as before. "But I don't feel any different. How long do you think it will take?"

Devereaux shrugged. "I don't know—maybe hours or days. But I was hoping that with the nanobots in your system, it would take effect more rapidly."

"And if it doesn't help?"

"We might still find a cure. And Earth will be looking too. Besides, you might have weeks before you fully devolve."

Zora got to her feet and shivered. "I can feel the pressure building. All of us can. Apart from myself, the only cadets I can trust with the Las-cannon anymore are Wee Willie and Rendela." She shot a glance at Aspen. "I'm afraid anyone else might start shooting."

"Isn't that where we're headed anyway?" Lendra said, her voice sounding higher than normal. "It's inevitable. Earth will attack. You'll fire the Las-cannon. We'll all die. What difference does it make if you fire first?"

Dr. Poole said, "Are you okay, Lendra? You seem distressed."

"No, I'm not okay." Lendra looked at the walls and ceiling, then took a deep breath. "We're all going to die up here. This place is going to become a mass of cinders when Earth is done with it. When they finish building their Las-cannons, we die—as simple as that."

"Calm down," Dr. Poole said.

"I can't." Lendra got to her feet and moved toward the doorway. "I feel like the walls are closing in on me." She stepped over to Jeremiah's wheelchair. "Help me, Jeremiah." She reached for him.

Zora said, "Sorry, Witchy Poo. We need him to find out who's building Las-cannons."

Aspen grabbed Lendra by the arm and walked her back to her chair.

"That's not it. You just want to drain him again. You vampires!"

"If you don't relax," Zora said, "I'll strap you down like Curtik. Do you want that?"

Jeremiah found the energy to speak: "You can't strap her down. She has claustrophobia and a mild case of obsessive-compulsive disorder, which she used to be able to control with neo-dopamine. But now that she's pregnant she can't take it. Perhaps Colonel Truman can be of assistance."

"Witchy Poo is claustrophobic?" Zora said.

"Jeremiah!" Lendra said as she stared at him.

Jeremiah shook his head. "I'm sorry, Lendra. Would you rather they strap you down?"

Lendra shook her head and scrunched back into her chair as far as she could. "How could you? They're going to lock me in a tiny room."

Aspen grinned. "I hadn't thought of that."

"No," Jeremiah said. "You will not torture her. She can help you."

"You can't stop them," Lendra said. "They're insane and they're getting worse. We're all going to die. And there's nothing you or your precious Zora can do about it."

Jeremiah must have looked confused, for Lendra said. "Don't bother to deny it. I've seen the way you look at her. And she's totally smitten with you too. You disgust me, both of you. She's a child."

Zora laughed. "You're a crazy one, Witchy Poo. Get some rest. We'll let Colonel Truman visit you." She suddenly stretched out her arms and lurched toward a chair. Grabbing the back of it, she said, "Whoa! Unbelievable. This feels bizarre." She looked over at Jeremiah. "Is this what it's like to be you?"

Dr. Wellon aimed her scanner at Zora. "Are you feeling the effects of the transfusion?"

"I feel great," Zora said. "Full of energy, but sort of off-kilter—like I might jump into the ceiling. And my joints feel kind of warm and itchy."

"Me next," Aspen said. "Do me."

"Not yet," Dr. Wellon said. "Jeremiah can't give any more blood right now. Plus, we have to study this and see how it progresses. We'll need to check with Doctors Nakamura and Srinlangshiran to see if they're tracking the changes as well. There may be side effects we haven't foreseen. It would be better if we can synthesize a cure that will align more closely with your nanobots."

Chapter Twenty-Four

Lendra walked through the main hangar, Colonel Truman by her side. Phan followed them, Las-rifle in hand. Every few meters she stopped to smell a raspberry bush or an orange shrub or a row of the hybrid beans that did so well on the Moon. She could almost pretend she was out for a stroll and not trapped here waiting to be killed. Without meaning to, she found herself looking up through the plas-glass window at Earth. She told herself her claustrophobia wasn't getting worse while fingering her glass bulb of neo-dopamine.

"Are you thinking what I'm thinking?" Colonel Truman asked.

"Probably not," Lendra replied. "I wonder where Jeremiah is. Zora hasn't let me see him for two days. Do you think they're still draining him of his blood?"

"Whatever they're doing, it seems to be working. The cadets are calmer. They're still jumpy, but I don't get the sense that they might attack any second."

"Is Jeremiah even alive?"

"I'm sure he's fine." Colonel Truman draped his arm around her shoulders and hugged her gently.

She smiled in gratitude and said, "So what were you thinking?"

"I was wondering about Earth. The latest news reports indicate that the Susquehanna Virus has become more aggressive in the past few days. They think it has something to do with the Las-cannon strikes stirring up particulate matter in the air."

"Are you worried about your wife?"

"Actually, I was worried about my daughter. She's in Portland. And they said the Virus hit Seattle hard."

"Zora won't let you call her?"

Truman shook his head.

STEVE MCELLISTREM

"At least she doesn't hate you," Lendra said. "I haven't been permitted to do anything more than simple calculations. Zora forwards a problem to my interface to solve within an hour. Then I'll get a break for an hour or so before she provides another challenge. Every time I finish one, I expect her to kill me."

Lendra glanced across the hangar at Wee Willie, who manned the military desk. He alone seemed to be immune to the devolutionary process, so Dr. Poole occasionally took samples from him. Lendra had double-checked various tests on the samples Zora provided but so far she'd found no real difference between his samples and those of the other cadets. Lendra suspected that he was simply less stressed because he'd been allowed to kill Dr. Hackett and now was placed in a position of relative importance but with little responsibility for making difficult decisions.

"The Escala," Colonel Truman said, "except for Dr. Wellon and Quark, seem to have vanished."

"They're working nonstop on the Pilgrim," Lendra replied, "hoping to get it ready for the launch to Mars before . . ."

Colonel Truman looked up through the plas-glass ceiling toward Earth. "It's frustrating being kept in the dark. I wonder what Zora's planning."

"She's engaging in classic captor-hostage behavior, keeping us in the dark." Lendra caressed the glass bulb. She refused to give in to the temptation to take a dose. Her baby's well-being was more important than her discomfort.

"Do you think she's planning to leave for Mars with the Escala?"

"It's possible." Lendra accessed the information available on the Pilgrim from her interface. "But the ship wasn't designed to transport that many people. In addition to the vast amount of equipment and biological material necessary for long-term survival on Mars, the ship might accommodate up to seventy-five people."

"There are less than sixty Escala."

"Fifty-seven," Lendra replied. "But adding almost forty cadets plus the extra supplies needed to sustain them would severely overtax its resources."

"Unless Zora's planning on taking the Pilgrim herself, leaving the Escala behind?"

"Perhaps," Lendra conceded.

"But incorrect," Zora spoke through Lendra's interface, startling Lendra.

Colonel Truman reached out to steady her. "What is it?"

"Zora just told me that she's not planning to steal the Pilgrim."

"She's still monitoring us?"

"Of course," Zora said through the interface.

Lendra shivered. She felt an anxiety building in her depths, a tension that spilled over into a nervous tic in her right eye. *I will not take neo-dopamine.* "How can I help you? More calculations?"

"No. Jeremiah wants to see you. Turn around."

Across the hangar Jeremiah stood next to Zora. Lendra hurried toward him, Colonel Truman by her side, Phan following.

When she reached Jeremiah, Lendra noticed dark circles under his eyes and lines of fatigue creasing his forehead. Zora appeared exhausted too—thinner and paler than Lendra remembered. She longed to wrap her arms around Jeremiah, breathe in his masculine scent. But the stiffness in his posture told her he didn't reciprocate her feelings.

"Are you all right?" Jeremiah asked. "Are they treating you well?"

"Yes. They just wouldn't let me see you. You're out of your wheelchair."

"It helps that the Moon's gravity is only one-sixth that of Earth." Jeremiah turned to Colonel Truman. "How is she?"

Colonel Truman nodded. "She told me about her claustrophobia. They've let her stay out here in the main hangar when she's not working."

"Good. You look after her. We've been busy monitoring developments on Earth."

"The Las-cannons?" Colonel Truman said.

"Several nations have neared completion, though none have finished. When they test the components, the distinctive power signature will let the rest of the world know that they've violated the Berlin Treaty. So they'll be cautious. Plus," Jeremiah rubbed his forehead, "as Lendra pointed out,

269

one mistake in the calculations or connections or converters and they'll have a disaster on their hands. They'll wait until they're absolutely certain they've made no mistakes before they attack."

Lendra reached toward Jeremiah, pulling her hand back when Zora's eyes narrowed. "You look tired. Are they still taking your blood?"

"No. The doctors were able to concoct a treatment based on how my blood interacts with their devolving nanobots."

Lendra turned to Zora, noting the pain lines etched in that young face. "You don't look well either."

"I'm fine, Witchy Poo," Zora said. "But his white cells have begun attacking my joints, just as they did his."

"Don't pain medications work?"

"Not yet," Zora said. "Dr. Wellon thinks they will in time. My body has to adapt to this intrusion. Besides, I need to experience his pain. He saved us."

Zora grabbed Jeremiah's arm and leaned into him. He allowed it, showing nothing. Did he like her attention, her obvious worship of him? Or was he doing what needed to be done to try to save them all, letting her think she was getting through to him? Again Lendra felt a tic in her right eye.

"Are you healed?" Lendra asked. "No longer devolving?"

Zora let go of Jeremiah and glared at Lendra. "Why are you so interested?"

Lendra took a half step back and bumped into Colonel Truman, who rested a hand on her shoulder. "I'm concerned about you. We need your intelligent leadership."

"As much as we need your ass-kissing?"

"I've already apologized for my role in what happened. What more do you want?"

"Zora," Jeremiah said.

"Okay," Zora said. "I don't think I'll ever be healed. But the damage to my DNA has been halted and the rage is almost gone. I don't feel like killing you anymore." Her lips ticked upward briefly. "Maybe maiming you a little. But that's not because of the devolution."

"Then why?"

Zora tilted her head toward Jeremiah. "Because of what you did to him. You betrayed him, like the great and powerful Oz betrayed us."

Zora's scowl felt heavy, almost like a physical blow. The hair on the back of Lendra's neck stood up. Was Zora in love with Jeremiah? Probably.

Lendra said, "May I speak to Jeremiah alone?"

Zora looked up at Jeremiah. When he nodded, she said, "A few minutes. Then we've got to get back to work." She looked at Colonel Truman. "Come on, Colonel False-Girl, let's give them some pretend privacy."

Zora said nothing aloud to Phan but he moved back a dozen paces, while she and Colonel Truman walked across the hangar. She whispered to Colonel Truman, who bent down to hear what she was saying, and a flicker of jealousy ran through Lendra. Stupid! Lendra thought to herself. Get a grip.

"How can I help you?" Jeremiah said. He stood motionless, as if trying to maintain his balance or minimize the pain of movement. Yet the look on his face was unyielding.

"Look, I know you're angry with me for doing the in vitro fertilization."

"That's not why I'm angry. I'm angry because you conceived a child without my knowledge or consent, as if I had no say in the matter. If this was the first time you'd betrayed me, I might be able to forgive it."

"I didn't . . ." Lendra wondered how much Jeremiah knew, which betrayal he was referencing. "I was doing my job."

"I know. You want to run CINTEP some day. But there's a price to pay for your ambition."

"I still love you," Lendra said, feeling her connection to Jeremiah slipping away. Her right eyelid twitched again. She reached up to massage it. The smallest dose of neo-dopamine would take the tic away. How frustrating that she couldn't risk even that.

"I think you'll find that you don't. You love the idea of being in love with me, and you think I could help you run CINTEP, but you don't love me. So what is it you want?"

"We have to save our daughter, Jeremiah. You have to help me. She's your child too. We should take an LTV—you and I, Devereaux and Colonel Truman. Zora will let us go if you ask her." She realized even as she spoke that she needed to phrase it differently if she wanted Jeremiah's help. "We can fly back to Earth where we can work diplomatically to save the cadets. We can't do anything for them up here. But back there, we can save them."

"How?"

"We'll speak with President Hope, let her know that things have changed up here and that the cadets are no longer a threat. She'll be able to convince the world's leaders to abstain from violence."

"And in the meantime you'll be safe."

"I'm not concerned about myself. I'm worried about our child."

"Please," Jeremiah said. "If you're so concerned about our child, why haven't you asked me how my son is doing?"

Lendra dropped her hand as the last bond between them broke. She glanced over at Zora and Colonel Truman, who had circled the hangar and were heading their way. Zora had her hand wrapped around Colonel Truman's bicep. Did she know what she was doing? Was she deliberately flirting or was this just something she mimicked from vids? After all, as bright as she was, as adult as she looked, she was still just a girl.

"It may not be tactically critical information," Jeremiah said, "but he is my son and therefore important to me. You might have at least asked."

"I'm asking now. How is he?"

"Since he had already begun the devolutionary process, his recovery will be much longer, but I believe he'll survive."

"Will he need more of your blood?"

Jeremiah shook his head. "They can use nanobots to complete the treatment."

Zora and Colonel Truman approached, Zora no longer clinging to Colonel Truman.

"Before you get your hopes up," Zora said, "you should know that I won't let you take an LTV back to Earth."

Lendra said, "What's your plan, then?"

Zora frowned. "Still hoping to sabotage us?"

"No," Lendra said. Despair hollowed her chest and stomach. "I know you don't trust me, but we're all on the same side now. Earth will attack soon. And we won't be able to stand against their combined arsenals."

"Of course not," Zora agreed. "All I can do is destroy them back. They used to call it MAD a long time ago. Remember?"

"Mutually assured destruction? That's your plan? We all die up here because you're angry at what was done to you?"

Lendra immediately regretted her words. She looked to Jeremiah for help but he only shook his head. Zora smiled, as if she'd just won a small victory.

Truman, clearing his throat, stepped around Lendra, shielding her from Zora, and said, "We've all been under a lot of stress."

"You don't think we have the right to be angry?" Zora said.

"Of course you do," Lendra replied. "But killing millions of innocents isn't the answer." as the

"Which ones are the innocents again?"

"The children."

"Which children? The ones used to further the grandiose ideas of a megalomaniac or the ones who haven't yet been used?"

"You're not children anymore," Lendra said. "When you took over the Moon, every life here became your responsibility. Jeremiah understands that even if you don't."

Again Jeremiah shook his head. What was he trying to tell her?

"So we surrender?" Zora said. "We hope they decide not to blow us to smithereens but instead let us rot in some prison for the rest of our lives, all because we were acting under a compulsion programmed into us by a monster? Or do you think they'll let us go?"

Lendra wanted to reassure Zora that things would work out, but she saw from the set of Zora's jaw that a lie wouldn't work.

"Seriously," Zora said. "After what we did, do you think they'll let us go?"

Lendra took a deep breath and said, "No."

Zora nodded, then she and Jeremiah looked past Lendra's shoulder. Lendra turned to find Devereaux and Quark approaching.

"Jeremiah," Devereaux said when he reached them, "it's good to see you up and moving."

"Hurts like hell," Jeremiah replied.

"I suggest we retire to the patio," Devereaux replied, pointing toward the Marriott's lobby.

Quark rearranged chairs and Lendra took a seat, flanked by Jeremiah and Colonel Truman. Zora sat on Jeremiah's other side, Devereaux in the final chair. Quark opted to stand beside him, his hands on the back of the chair as if ready to pull Devereaux out of the way should any hazard present itself. Phan moved off a few paces and stood at ease.

"A couple of items," Devereaux said. "First, the Pilgrim is essentially completed. The engines test-fired perfectly. The ship will be ready for departure to Mars in a few days. We can begin loading immediately, with your permission."

Zora nodded. "Will you be going with them?"

Devereaux glanced up at Quark and shrugged. "That decision has not yet been made."

"And the second thing?" Zora said.

Devereaux held up his PlusPhone. "I've been monitoring the sat-feeds, examining the data. The scanners show that energy consumption levels at three locations on Earth have quintupled in the past two hours."

"Las-cannons." Zora said.

"Indeed. The radio-spectrum-assay analysis confirms the electro-chemical reactions of the charging process."

Zora shifted in her seat, her movements stiff, as if to minimize the pain in her joints. "How long before they attack?"

Devereaux looked at Jeremiah, who said, "A few hours if they're willing to risk firing a Las-cannon without running the final safety checks—testing components and calibrating the converters. Otherwise, a couple of days."

"Which nations?" Lendra asked.

"Does it matter?" Zora said.

"It does if you're going to fire the orbital Las-cannon at Earth. You shouldn't punish nations who are not in violation of the treaty."

"If I fire the Las-cannon, it will be to take out the entire planet, hitting geological hot spots like Yellowstone, Iceland and the Azores. I'll spread a nuclear winter over the world that will wipe out eighty percent of the population—give the planet a long time to recover from the infestation of humans."

Stunned, Lendra opened her mouth to respond, then shut it. Anything she said might trigger Zora's wrath, tip her over into firing the Las-cannon. And yet something in Zora's tone suggested that she would only fire the Las-cannon as a last resort.

Zora sat still, staring straight ahead. At first Lendra thought she'd become catatonic. Then she realized Zora was using her implant to review the data Devereaux had retrieved.

Jeremiah smiled at Lendra.

"What?" she said.

He looked down and she realized that she had grabbed Colonel Truman's hand. When had she done that? She pulled her hand free. Perhaps her subconscious had sensed that their lives were about to come to an end and the desire for human contact had overridden her conscious mind.

Reaching up, she grabbed the glass bulb of her necklace, feeling an almost uncontrollable urge for neo-dopamine. What were the odds that a tiny dose would harm the baby? What she needed in the absence of the drugs was a good massage. Jeremiah's strong hands had been especially good at kneading her muscles, draining away her tension.

Inexplicably she found herself aroused, then embarrassed. How could she even consider sex at a time like this?

Zora shivered as she turned to Jeremiah. "I want to fire the Las-cannon."

"I know," he said. "That's the programming. That urge to violence results from the pain of transformation." He gestured to Quark. "We feel it too. But lashing out isn't a viable long-term solution. We can't destroy them before they destroy us. Even if we take out these three targets, more Las-cannons will be built and we're running out of fuel. Eventually, nuclear winter or not, they'll win."

He looked at Devereaux, who nodded. "A hostile action is unlikely to advance our cause. Any hope of leniency demands that we now demonstrate restraint."

"Still," Zora said, "if we destroy their Las-cannons we might buy enough time to depart."

Devereaux shook his head. "The Pilgrim won't carry us all to Mars. And even if we somehow crowded on, many of us wouldn't survive the journey. Nor would we live long or pain free on Mars. It will take years for the Escala to modify the planet enough for humans to thrive there."

Zora took a deep breath. "Fine. We'll go with your plan. I want everyone in the hangar in ten minutes." Looking up at Quark, she said, "I'd appreciate it if you, Dr. Wellon and any other Escala who can be spared would join us. And you should expedite the loading of the Pilgrim so you can take off as soon as possible."

Lendra said, "What are you going to do?"

Zora spoke to Phan: "Rendela, Aspen and Wee Willie keep their Las-rifles. Everyone else disarms. Let's wheel Kyler and Curtik out here too. I want their beds in the middle of the hangar."

"Jeremiah?" Lendra asked.

"We're going to ask for clemency."

"That's your plan?"

"Have you got a better idea?"

Lendra nodded. "We could take the Pilgrim and the LTVs to Earth."

"How does that save three hundred and sixteen people? You can't fit everyone aboard the ships. And how does it ensure that they won't blow us out of the sky as we approach?"

Lendra said, "If they believe we're escaping from the cadets, that we're innocents, they'll let us through. We load everyone we can into the Pilgrim and put a few people in each LTV to fly behind the Pilgrim. We send out distress signals that we verify with a vid feed. Then we sacrifice the LTVs, blowing them up with the Las-cannon as we near Earth. They'll believe the Pilgrim is escaping from the cadets. We land safely."

Jeremiah shook his head. "So we should sacrifice people on two LTVs and everyone on the Moon who can't fit into the Pilgrim?"

"We could fit almost everyone into the Pilgrim for the short journey to Earth. We'd only have to sacrifice a few people on each LTV and one person to stay behind to fire the Las-cannon."

Zora said, "Earth would think it was some kind of trick."

"Maybe. But it's better than sitting here doing nothing. I think we could pull it off. Jeremiah?"

Jeremiah shrugged. "They'll expect a ruse like that."

"So we wait for some rogue nation to fire a rocket at us?"

"We have more time up here. The closer we get to Earth, the more vulnerable we become. And if you're wrong, everyone dies."

Quark said, "Plus, even if we made it, the Pilgrim couldn't take off from Earth's gravity, so the Escala would be trapped there. Earth would never finance another journey, which means the Escala would die there."

"I promise you," Lendra said, "once we get there, I'll make sure you get the funding you need to build another ship—one that can take off from Earth."

"That's quite a promise," Quark said. "We've heard it before from people with a lot more authority than you."

"Trust me," Lendra said. "I'll find a way to make it work."

Zora nodded. Was she considering it? She said, "Tell me something, Witchy Poo, are you willing to take one of the LTVs?"

Her stomach clenched as if she'd been punched. "I'm pregnant," she said. "I have to worry about more than just myself."

"Of course," Zora said. "We'll go with Devereaux's idea. But that was a good try."

Lendra turned to Jeremiah, but she found no comfort in his cold stare. Instead, Colonel Truman put his hand on her shoulder and squeezed gently. "It's okay," he said. "We'll be fine. This'll work."

But Lendra couldn't dispel the premonition of death. This was a crazy plan. Someone on Earth would attack; someone would send up a rocket. Didn't they know that? Did they not care that they were all about to die? She smiled at Colonel Truman and nodded as if in agreement while gripping the glass bulb of neo-dopamine. She thought she might explode if she didn't ingest some soon.

Chapter Twenty-Five

Elias Leach paced in his eight-by-ten cell. He knew the walls were stationary even though chips in the swirling, white-gray paint gave the illusion of movement. So he knew he wasn't going crazy. He had used the room many times in the past few years, driving several detainees mad in a matter of hours. Last year a detainee named Eldridge Cunningham had even managed to kill himself by running headfirst into a wall when no one was monitoring the vid feed. Still, the ceiling appeared to be dropping, the walls closing in. It would have been nice to close his eyes but every time he did his eyelids scraped like sandpaper. He began to understand the claustrophobia that plagued Lendra.

The sink and toilet sat to the right of the door, made of a plasticized rubber coated with metallic shimmer fabric, appearing to move whenever he stared at them. The narrow cot on the far wall away from the door actually did move—small portions of its electric mattress randomly prodding and pricking its occupant, making sleep all but impossible except for the truly exhausted.

He'd tried to sleep on the floor several times in the past two or three days, but he couldn't turn his mind off. Yet he also couldn't focus his thoughts. He blamed the nanobots for that. Except for the itching, he couldn't recall the last time he'd felt so good physically or been so frustrated at his inability to act on that feeling. The nanobots acted like a fountain of youth, giving him increased energy and a healthy appetite such as he hadn't possessed in ages. He bounced; he paced—wall to sink, turn, sink to wall, turn. Was that just the nanobots?

The coveralls they'd given him to replace his clothes—which they'd feared might contain microtechnology that could aid an escape—contained a sweat and odor absorbent that kept him reasonably fresh.

But the isolation in this cell on the top floor of the CINTEP building tormented Elias more than he would have guessed possible. For the few days he'd been locked up, he'd seen no one and no one had spoken to him. Nutri-water came from a tube that dangled from the ceiling. Energy bars slipped one at a time through a window in the door, randomly. He hadn't received one for hours.

He hammered on the door and yelled, "Hey, anybody there?"

Nothing—just a slight echo.

"Frustrating, isn't it?" a raspy voice spoke from behind him. He spun around but no one was there. That voice, though, sounded like Eldridge Cunningham. Was Elias just imagining it or did one of his jailers know about the Cunningham incident? Were they playing with him, feeding him drugs in the food or water, or was he going crazy?

Scratching his arms and legs, he reached around and clawed at his back. Goddamn nanobots! They were both gift and curse. He hated himself for feeling better, knowing he'd never give up the nanobots now. The itching was merely the cost of his rejuvenated body.

He shadowboxed briefly, dancing left and right, clumsy but with vitality. Why couldn't he concentrate on anything? Was that what had happened to Curtik? Was that why Zora had been able to take over the Moon?

He ceased his movements, came to a complete rest, determined to fight the anxiety. It's nothing more than a hallucination, he told himself—a false feeling amplified by the nanobots. Yet his breaths became more rapid and ragged as he stared at the walls.

"I did what had to be done," he said to the cameras. "I acted in the best interests of the United States—hell, the world. You know that. Do you really believe I deserve to be imprisoned?"

His words echoed.

"Me too," the raspy voice said.

"Shut up!" Elias said. "You're not real. I'm just exhausted."

He moved to the cot and lay on his back. As the bed poked and prodded him, he stared at the central camera. Was anyone watching at this particular moment? Could he kill himself like Cunningham had?

No. He refused to succumb to their tortures. The bed is comfortable, he told himself. This is like a massage. And when it pokes me in the middle of the back, it scratches my itch.

A familiar tiny click came from the screen on the wall. He directed his attention to it just as the screen lit up. This time the audio came through so softly he almost couldn't hear it; other times it had blared so loudly it gave him a headache. As usual, they showed him news channel summaries of the previous day's events. Scenes of destruction played on the screen. Was this their way of blaming him for what was happening or were they preparing him for interrogation?

"What do you want to know?" he yelled. "Just ask. I have no secrets."

A lie. Although he'd kept President Hope informed of much that he'd done, he hadn't told her everything.

"Why not just pump me full of truth juice and be done with it?" Elias knew he shouldn't be speaking. He ought to have more self-control than that. "Or do you have a sadistic streak?"

"Like your sadism?" the invisible Cunningham asked.

"I told you to shut up."

"I bet they drugged you," Cunningham said. "How much you wanna bet?"

Elias ignored the voice and closed his eyes, wincing as sandpaper lids scraped his eyeballs. It had to be the nanobots, devilish little machines zipping back and forth across his eyelids until the pressure built to an uncontainable explosion. He opened his eyes. Damn! His stomach growled a protest. He thought about banging on the door again. No, that was what they wanted. They wanted to break him. He could outlast them.

He just had to accept the fact that he was utterly powerless. Turning his attention to the screen, he watched every story. India continued to dig out from the effects of a series of bombings in Hyderabad, while China cleaned up Guangzhou, hit by retaliatory strikes, and ramped up preparations for a full-scale war against India, while simultaneously blaming the United States for the Las-cannon strikes it had endured.

Bangkok had switched from rescue to recovery efforts following the massive strike by the orbiting Las-cannon. Dozens of other cities, also hit by Las-cannon strikes, struggled with their own debris. The skies around the world had become increasingly dark with soot and ash residue. Temperatures had already plummeted seven degrees on average. Water supplies, now largely contaminated, led environmentalists across the globe to call for U.N. leadership, while the Secretary General of the U.N. jetted from city to city pleading for humanitarian efforts from nations more focused on their own problems than the world's.

None of this was going the way Elias had imagined it. The world's shortsighted leaders continued to engage in self-preserving nationalism. "You people still don't get it," he yelled.

In America, civil unrest continued its rise, mostly in reaction to shortages or price hikes. Every state had called out the National Guard to keep order. Curfews had been instituted throughout the country. Local terrorist attacks had spiked too. And many hospital emergency rooms had filled to overflowing, igniting fisticuffs and worse over scarce medical resources. One hospital in Seattle had lines going around the block, while police officers and firefighters kept order and helped with triage.

The broadcast ended with an update on the Susquehanna Virus. The network anchor reported that seventy-eight Americans had died since yesterday, while three hundred more were infected. Thousands more had been infected worldwide. The Centers for Disease Control and Prevention had confirmed that the virus was approaching a global pandemic.

Elias shook his head. He hadn't taken that damned virus into account. Perhaps that would obliterate the human species despite his efforts to save it. As the images of death and destruction replayed across the screen, Elias wondered what Earth was doing about the cadets. Were the nations of the world coming together behind the scenes as he'd predicted? Were they even now hatching a plan to take down the cadets? And what were they doing about the virus?

It was so frustrating being out of the loop.

As the TV shut off, the center of Elias' back itched again, despite the poking and prodding of the mattress. He moved to the floor and sat with his back against the rounded corner of the bed so he could scratch the spot and get some temporary relief. He raised and lowered himself against the bed, but the scratching soon became painful.

"Goddamnit!" Shaking with fury, he jumped to his feet and shouted, "I had the courage to act. The world was falling apart. This was the only solution. I'll never apologize for that."

Another echo.

"Maybe they're all dead," Cunningham said. "Maybe they all died from the virus and you'll rot in this cell."

"Go away," Elias said. He moved to the sink and splashed water on his face, then took a drink of nutri-water from the dangling tube before resuming his pacing.

He walked from sink to wall, wall to sink, his mind drifting from problem to problem. There was so much he could be doing. They were wasting his talents in this cell. A high-pitched whine sounded just outside the door.

This was different.

Elias tensed, turned toward the door, straining to listen. Yes, definitely a whine—the kind that emanated from the power packs of the Elite Ops. So a trooper was outside. Was he coming to kill Elias? The Elite Ops knew of his contempt for them, which made his transformation from the infusion of nanobots all the more ironic.

The lock buzzed and Elias backed into the corner as far away from the door as he could get, his hands up in a defensive posture. The Elite Ops trooper outside would have to travel an extra eight feet to break his neck.

But when the door opened, President Hope entered the room, followed by General Horowitz. Elias felt both relief and fear. He glanced at the Elite Ops trooper, who stayed outside.

"Hello, Elias," President Hope said.

"Madam President." He tried to keep the anger and hostility out of his voice.

"I know you're upset," the President said. "I don't care. I told you I didn't want this program proceeding while I was in office. And you went ahead with it anyway."

"I didn't intend to defy your orders, Madam President. The cadets just—"

The President raised her hand. "It doesn't matter how it happened. What matters is that this disaster occurred on my watch. I'm the one who will be judged a failure by future generations . . . if there *are* any future generations. Some of my people are saying this could be the end of humanity."

"We needed a disaster like this, Madam President. To save us."

"So you still think it's a good thing," President Hope pointed to the now-dark screen, "after everything you've seen?"

"Not good," Elias corrected. "Necessary. It was the slow build-up that was killing us, the creeping toward the tipping point, where every nation would reach critical mass around the same time, putting a massive strain on our planet's limited resources and ability to heal itself. This kind of premature action will allow us to focus on the dangers that await should we continue our militaristic ethnocentrism."

"Fancy words," President Hope said.

"That's your insecurity speaking."

General Horowitz took a step toward him, his face reddening, but President Hope grabbed his arm.

She said, "You like to imagine you're the smartest person in every room, but you're not always right. You know that the United States will never surrender her military superiority. And China will never accept a subordinate role in the world. Russia still hungers for the old days when it could make a claim that it had the greatest might. And Brazil craves recognition as one of the top nations. At least half a dozen others pursue some sort of global power. Did you really think your actions would change that?"

"It's still possible."

"You don't get it, do you? You're so convinced you're right that you can't even acknowledge your mistakes."

"What was going to change without some external force? How were things getting better before this happened? We were headed for a long and painful extinction."

"We still may be."

"Ah, but now we're forced to take action. The clock is ticking and if we don't act swiftly and correctly, humanity will die."

General Horowitz said, "We've talked to every leading nation a handful of times in the past few days. None have even remotely suggested that disarmament is a possibility. They're all afraid this is just a ploy by the United States to increase our dominance as the planet's greatest superpower. They think you engineered this scenario to control the Moon and force them to back down. Now they're building up their arsenals even more rapidly than in the past."

"And we," President Hope said, "have no choice but to continue our development of weapons to defend ourselves. Your plan failed."

"Fools," Elias said.

Horowitz said, "Are you calling the President a fool?"

Elias shook his head. This was all falling apart. Badly. If only Curtik had led the cadets, attacked mercilessly, given the world barely enough time to react and no more, the result might have been different. Damn that Zora!

Elias felt exhausted. He sat on his bed. He'd forgotten how much fatigue could impact the mind, how difficult it became to think when he was exhausted. For the moment he couldn't keep a single thought in his head. Jumbles of images and ideas flitted past, darting in and out of consciousness, eluding capture.

"Elias," President Hope said.

He looked up. "Sorry," he said. He made himself stand again. They were here to punish him. And he deserved their reprobation. Everything he'd worked for about to be ruined because one little girl reached a potential far beyond what he'd predicted for her and one little boy didn't achieve to the level Elias had expected. He straightened his back, stood to attention, looked into his President's face and said, "I am, of course, very sorry, Madam President, for letting you and this great nation down. Whatever course of action you choose to take, I will . . ."

His voice trailed off as General Horowitz, his finger to the earpiece he wore in his left ear, bent close to the President and whispered something behind a cupped hand. President Hope raised her hand to stop Elias' speech.

"Put it on," President Hope said. "You should see this," she explained to Elias.

The TV came to life again. On the screen was an image of the main hangar of Lunar Base 1, filled with people standing together, looking toward the cameras. In the center of the screen stood Devereaux and Zora. Flanking them were Lendra, Colonel Truman, Quark, Dr. Poole and two hospital beds, one holding a little girl and the other carrying Curtik. Behind them were cadets, tourists and workers—and standing in the back, a number of Escala, dwarfing their companions. Dr. Hackett's team stood off to one side, though Elias didn't see Dr. Hackett among them. But Jeremiah stood near the edge of the crowd and at the limit of the camera pickup. His face looked pinched with pain. Elias searched Lendra's face for any message she might be trying to send. But before he could read anything the cameras focused in on Devereaux.

The great man said: "Friends, the Moon was supposed to be neutral, owned by every nation and none. But one man, over the past few years, built forty weapons here to attack you, to create mass panic and horrific loss of life. These forty weapons are children—" Devereaux gestured toward Zora and another cadet behind her whom Elias didn't recognize— "kidnapped from their families, genetically enhanced, infused with nanotechnology, whose growth was accelerated, and whose minds were conditioned to hate and destroy you. Their bodies achieved near perfection even as their minds were poisoned. But they are just children. The man who did this—an American named Elias Leach—made these children into fighting machines in an attempt to unite the oft-warring countries of the world, heedless of the human costs. His program lifted them up to great heights, then tried to crash them by causing unspeakable pain, by attacking their DNA, mutating their bodies and minds so they would feel compelled to obliterate you without knowing why. They are the weapons fired upon you by him, by Elias Leach."

Elias turned to the President. "This went out everywhere?"

Tight lipped, she nodded.

Devereaux continued: "And so they attacked you just as he planned. With his help, they took control of the orbiting Las-cannons and fired upon your cities and your military bases out of unreasoning rage. They killed millions, all because they did not see that they were mere puppets, dancing to his tune, acting out his play, until it was too late.

"We know now the full extent of the damage caused, the pain and suffering, the anger and despair. We managed to cut the strings that held them. They no longer dangle from his insidious fingers. So we come here today to apologize for the harm he programmed them to inflict upon you, the harm we wish we could take back. We understand, however, that apologies are not sufficient. As much as we desire your forgiveness, we understand the barrier to such a plea. You wish justice, retribution, revenge, and who can blame you?"

Elias glanced at President Hope and General Horowitz. They ignored him, focusing on the screen. Only the Elite Ops trooper at the door paid any attention to him. And the trooper's Las-rifle was aimed at his belly.

"Your leaders," Devereaux continued, "are even now conspiring to exterminate us, at the cost of destroying the Moon itself. Several nations have nearly completed work on illegal Las-cannons, which they will be able to fire at us within a few days if not a few hours. We come before you now to tell you, you need not wait. Control of the last remaining Las-cannon is at this moment being rerouted back to the United Nations. We put ourselves at your mercy. What we did to you . . ." Devereaux paused.

"Clever bastard," Elias mumbled, "inserting himself into the position of an attacker."

". . . gives us no moral authority to beg for our lives. Perhaps we deserve to die for the sake of the greater good, even though it was Elias Leach who pulled our strings.

"But we nonetheless ask you to contact your governments and plead with them on our behalf, for we believe we can help you greatly if spared your vengeance. You see, we have found what we believe is a cure for the Susquehanna Virus. It's not perfected yet, but it seems to be a cure. And it will likely be destroyed if your leaders choose to attack us."

Again Devereaux paused to let everyone know just how big a mistake an attack on the Moon would be.

"If we are spared," he continued, "we will give you the serum. Even if you choose to destroy us, we will attempt to preserve the serum as a means of protecting the future of humanity. But the task may be insurmountable given the might of the forces directed against us. Our cameras will continue broadcasting from this point forward, allowing you to see us in what may be our final moments.

"Remember, we're just like you—people struggling to survive in a harsh world. And now that we're no longer under Elias Leach's control, now that we're no longer compelled to lash out by the rage that was implanted in us from the outside, we wish no harm to anyone. We await your decision. If you choose to exterminate us, we cannot stop you. But mercy is the greatest human quality. Mercy elevates us. Thank you, and goodbye."

Devereaux held up his hand and the cameras pulled back, the sound diminishing, generalizing to the buzz of dozens of people chatting in one large space. A few seconds later Devereaux strode away, slowly and somewhat stiffly in the lower gravity of the Moon. Zora, Quark and the Escala followed him out of the hangar. Two cadets wheeled the beds away. Those left behind mingled among themselves, occasionally glancing up at something in the ceiling Elias couldn't see—Earth, he realized, would be visible through the plas-glass window in the roof. Elias saw no one carrying a weapon. Jeremiah had vanished as well. He must have slipped away before the camera panned out.

"Well?" President Hope asked.

"Well what, Madam President?" Elias said.

"This is your mess." The President glared at him, red blotches on her cheeks, her lips a thin harsh line. "Any suggestions? Any ideas?"

Elias shrugged. "Some idiot is going to fire a Las-cannon or a rocket at them. That's a given. We have to find a way to stop it."

"Yes," President Hope waved her hand impatiently, "but how?"

General Horowitz said, "Giving up that Las-cannon to the U.N. was suicide."

"Not necessarily," Elias said. "You need to call an immediate meeting of the U.N. Security Council, get everyone on board with the idea that the Las-cannon must be used to thwart any aggressive action taken against the Moon. Sell them on the cure for the virus. Offer them whatever you have to—just get them manning the Las-cannon."

President Hope said, "We're already negotiating that with China and Russia."

"There's no time for negotiations," Elias said. "Concede whatever they want. Just get that Las-cannon operational."

President Hope nodded toward the general. "That's what we thought as well. I just wanted confirmation from you, because you're part of it." She pointed at Elias. "They want you."

"Who wants me?"

"Everyone." She turned for the door, the general behind her. "We'll let you know which country wins the sweepstakes, which country gets to prosecute you for your crimes and imprison you for the rest of your life."

A trial at The Hague?

The door slammed shut. The lock buzzed. Son of a bitch! He might be locked up for the remainder of his days. On the other hand, a trial at The Hague would allow him to explain why it had been necessary to act as he had. He could attack the fools in China and India who continued their march to war. He could show the world the idiocy of its leaders. And if some fool did attack the Moon, that would only bolster his arguments. He might still be able to win.

Chapter Twenty-Six

As she stepped into the main hangar, waiting for yet another analysis of the cadets' nanobots, Taditha Poole noted that the place was alive with cadets, tourists, workers, soldiers and Elite Ops troopers—all savoring their last few moments of tranquility. Zora claimed the attack would come soon. There was even a pool to predict which nation would strike first. Poole had selected Argentina as the most likely of those nations remaining when her turn came. She almost laughed: how ludicrous to bet on which nation would be the first to try to kill you.

Rendela walked beside her, a Las-rifle in her hands. Zora's lieutenant seemingly watched everyone and no one, her eyes shifting from person to person while her face showed no expression. On the far wall streamed a news feed from Earth describing the ongoing crisis. A dozen people sat in front of the screen while twice that many stood behind them, shuffling their feet back and forth, their attention shifting from the screen to the view of Earth through the plas-glass roof window, to the military desk where Wee Willie and Crazy Vigg monitored the nations below, and back to the screen.

She saw no Escala.

They'd been finalizing the Pilgrim's preparations for hours, loading it even as they continued fine-tuning the electrical and life-support systems. Zora had asked a few cadets to assist them, speeding up the process. No one could blame them. Why stay for a possibly fatal attack when a means of escape, however dicey, existed?

But the Pilgrim would only be taking the Escala and Devereaux. Those left behind faced a high probability of death. At least it was likely to be quick and painless.

The scanner completed its analysis of data and Poole checked the results, then transmitted the data to Rendela's implant.

After a moment, Rendela said, "It looks like we're almost better."

"Not quite," Poole replied. "Actually, if you examine the neuro-nano configuration, you'll see that the destabilization has only been halted. Although the new nanobots have already begun to repair the devolutionary damage, you've got a long way to go to be cured. However, your emotional states are far better than before the nanobots were implanted."

Rendela smiled. "The mind is an amazing thing. Just knowing we have these new nanobots inside us is enough to make us feel . . . healed."

"The doctors did a fabulous job," Poole said.

"What about our sexuality?" Rendela said.

"I'm scanning that aspect now."

"Is it true that our devolution was caused by the same nanobots that created the rage?"

"Probably, though Doctors Nakamura and Srinlangshiran would know better than I. All I know for certain is that unless we make some changes, full puberty will hit hard. It might even be fatal."

"Why? It's just sex."

"It's more than that. The nanotech inside you altered your normal development, accelerating physical and intellectual growth while stunting emotional conceptualization and internalization. Your brains were rewired. We can't just let your sex drive out all at once. That will overwhelm you. I fear many of you would commit suicide. The intensity of desire could also erupt into murderous violence once you begin to lust after each other—some of you may retreat into that comfortable homicidal violence rather than deal with unrequited passion or jealousy."

"You'd probably be the first one we killed," Rendela said. She spoke almost without emotion, as if simply stating a fact.

"I didn't know the full extent of what I was doing," Poole said. "I realize that sounds lame, but I didn't know you'd been programmed to die. I thought we could fix you after you accomplished your mission, after you stopped these endless wars on Earth. I'm sorry."

STEVE MCELLISTREM

Rendela shrugged.

When the last scan was completed, Poole transmitted the data to Rendela's implant. "As you can see," she said, "we'll have to ramp up your sexual drives gradually once we eliminate the corrosive nanobots from your systems. We will fix you. I promise."

"Of course you will," Rendela said with just a hint of sarcasm. "I sent a summary to Zora. She wishes to see us now."

"I know you've been lied to a lot. I've lied to you a lot. But this time I promise I'm not."

"Time will tell."

"What about visiting the graveyard? Zora promised me I could."

Rendela nodded. "We need your advice first. Please."

As Poole walked, she noted how the dynamic on the Moon had changed the past few days. Orders were no longer given; requests were made, options given. One no longer had to eat at a specific time or gather in a specific place. The run of the entire settlement—except for Lunar Base 2, where the Escala were transferring their possessions to the Pilgrim, and the hospital, where Curtik and Kyler still fought for life—was available. Yet for all the friendliness and light-hearted banter, and despite the fact that few of the cadets were armed anymore, everyone knew the cadets were in charge.

A dozen Escala lined the tunnel to Cho's office. Rendela led Poole past them and into the crowded office. Several Escala stood by the open door. Zora stood behind Cho's desk. Beside her, Jeremiah sat in the admiral's chair, while Devereaux stood with Quekri, Quark and Dr. Wellon off to the side. The blond Escala Zeriphi held Celestia facing Jeremiah. Poole felt a sudden connection to the young mother, who caught her eye and smiled. The child seemed fascinated by Jeremiah's visage: pale, gaunt, lined with pain. Finally Zeriphi pulled the baby back, looked down at Jeremiah and said, "Jeremiah, I remember you." The traditional goodbye of the Escala.

Poole's stomach fluttered. "Are the Escala leaving already?" she asked.

"Soon," Zora said.

"The Pilgrim's ready?"

Quekri shrugged. "As close as we can get it. We can make any final adjustments during the flight."

Zora said, "Military installation activity around the world has increased dramatically. Jeremiah and Devereaux predict an attack within the next few hours, although we're not certain what form it will take—whether it will be rockets or a Las-cannon. If it's a Las-cannon, the Pilgrim needs to be gone. And if it's a rocket, we don't know if the U.N. will be willing or able to stop it."

"And even if it killed only some of us," Quekri added, "we don't have many people to spare. We need everyone on Mars."

Poole looked at Devereaux. "And you're going with them?"

Everyone turned to face Devereaux, who glanced at the baby in Zeriphi's arms. The child sucked her thumb, her free hand wrapped around her black curly hair. She stared into her mother's eyes with an intensity and focus that gave Poole a fleeting moment of jealousy.

"I've decided to stay on the Moon a while longer," Devereaux said.

A collective gasp came from the Escala at the door, who passed the word down the hallway. Quekri, Dr. Wellon and Zeriphi looked stunned, Zora elated. Only Quark and Jeremiah showed no expression. Poole wondered if Devereaux had already told them or if they had figured it out. Of all the Escala, Quark knew Devereaux best. And Jeremiah could make his face show only what he chose.

"We've already packed your things," Dr. Wellon said. "All your equipment, your personal files."

"There are too many problems that need to be resolved here," Devereaux said. "And I am an old man. Losing me would not be a tragedy."

Quekri shook her head. "You're the one person humanity can't afford to lose."

"You're only seventy-three," Zeriphi protested.

"I feel much older," Devereaux said as he leaned over and patted the baby's head. The child stared at him. Her eyes, exceptionally wide and bright, flickered with intelligence. "I liked Doug," Devereaux said, apropos of nothing, "but I wouldn't call him a handsome man. Yet Celestia here is the cutest baby I've ever seen."

"Thank you," Zeriphi said.

"And her IP is extremely high."

Poole glanced again at the baby. They'd already done an Intelligence Potential test? She was only a few months old.

"Take good care of her." Devereaux lifted his hand away and stepped back. "She might become . . . anything she wants. No need to offload my things. They can make the trip with you."

"So you're coming to Mars later?" Quekri said, her voice rising with hope.

Devereaux nodded. "I hope so. I would love to see it. The sooner you build the necessary infrastructure, the sooner I can visit. Perhaps in a few years."

Quekri pursed her lips, said nothing. She looked at Quark, who had maintained silence throughout. He stood like a statue, a great behemoth. He smiled at Quekri.

"Oh, no you don't," Quekri said to him.

"What?" Dr. Wellon asked.

"Quark intends to stay behind with Devereaux," Quekri said.

"You don't need me," Quark said.

"The hell I don't."

Quark sighed. "I'll follow along with Devereaux."

"How will you survive without the radiation lights?"

Quark gestured toward the ceiling. "I'll simply stand out there, on the surface of the Moon. Plenty of radiation there."

"So you've got it all figured out." Quekri pointed a finger at him. "We agreed. I'm in command now that Zod is dead. You're bound to my orders."

Quark bowed his head. "I am."

"And you think I'll just let you stay?"

"It's the logical decision."

"When were you going to tell me?"

Quark shrugged. "When I knew for certain Devereaux was staying behind."

Quekri shook her head, flinging her hands in a gesture of disgust. "Men!"

A giggle escaped from Poole. How delightful that men, no matter how constructed, presented the same problems to women they always had . . . and apparently always would. She caught a glimpse of Quekri's thunderous face and bit the inside of her cheeks until the urge to laugh was replaced by pain.

Devereaux cleared his throat. "I have a favor to ask of you, Quekri."

"Something equally delightful, I'm sure," Quekri answered.

"I'd like you to take some of the cadets along."

"Cadets?"

Devereaux nodded. "They're the only people of their kind. To lose them all would be unthinkable. And they'll stand a much better chance of surviving on Mars with their nanotech systems than ordinary humans."

"They would be subject to my authority."

Zora said, "That would be made clear to them."

"So you're in on it too," Quekri said.

"We discussed preserving our subspecies, or whatever it's called, yes."

"Who would we bring with us? And how many?"

Zora turned to Poole. "That's why I asked for Dr. Poole. Do you have any recommendations, Doctor, as to who would be best prepared for such a journey? Four, maybe six people."

Poole took a deep breath, blew it out slowly as she perused the files in her interface. "Well," she said, "the best candidates would be you, Rendela, Wee Willie and Addam."

"I can't go," Zora said. "Neither can Wee Willie or Rendela. Who's next on the list?"

"That gets more questionable," Poole answered. "Aspen is a possibility. So is Benn, but only because he and Addam are in the same tong. Shiloh also might do reasonably well with the Escala. But then you would probably have to let Phan go as well."

Zora nodded. "We'd need one more girl to balance it out. Who?"

Poole studied the psych-profiles as they played down her visual cortex. There wasn't a lot to distinguish one from the next. Most of the girls and boys fell within the bell curve—just your average super-intelligent, super warriors. "Maybe Indee," she finally offered. "Or Kammilee."

"I think Kammilee," Zora said. "I'm sending for them now. I'd like you to observe—make certain we've got the right people."

She gestured for Poole and Rendela to follow her and led them to the main hangar, where Addam, Benn, Phan, Aspen, Shiloh and Kammilee waited. Zora must have notified them by implant, for they were discussing the trip in excited voices as Poole approached.

"Are you all okay with this?" Poole asked them.

Six heads nodded. Six implants sent data to her interface consistent with her analysis.

Aspen said, "We promised Zora we'd obey Quekri."

Poole touched Aspen's shoulder. "I'm concerned that because of your close ties to Zora, you'll feel homesick."

"We'll still be able to communicate by implant—tapping into the comm system of the Pilgrim. And we'll be fine as long as we stay in the graphene-aluminum room they've designed to protect us from radiation. We'll meet again some day."

Zora said, "I hope so, if we survive."

"You'll make it, Zora," Aspen said. "I know you will."

"You'd better get ready," Zora said. "Say your goodbyes. The ship will be leaving as soon as you're packed."

"Good luck to you all," Poole said. She looked at Zora. "I sense no major problems with any of them."

"Good," Zora said. "You can visit Jack Marschenko's grave now, though I don't know why you want to. It's not him anymore."

"Humans need closure," Poole said, "and I wasn't allowed to attend his funeral."

* * *

Poole donned a spacesuit and stepped through the airlock doors onto the surface of the Moon. Several hundred meters away she saw the Pilgrim standing erect, a huge gray ship with a tube connecting it to the tunnel below. Footprints formed a path to a small crater off to the left, which served as the graveyard. As she walked, she looked up at Earth—the giant blue and white disc hovering in the star-speckled darkness of space and felt an oddly hollow thumping in her chest. She wished Jack Marschenko could see the beauty of that sight. She wished she could take him back with her some day.

Poole stopped at the edge of the crater and looked down at the capsules that made up the graveyard. Blue, yellow, red and green: each about a foot tall and several inches in diameter: they stood upright on the lonely barren land, like tulips in the spring. And the top few inches of each capsule contained an image of its occupant. From here, Poole couldn't ascertain which capsule contained Jack Marschenko's remains. She stepped down into the shallow crater and shuffled forward, noting the otherworld stillness of the place. With no atmosphere, the spot was undisturbed by wind or rain. It felt like sacred space, as if the souls of the dead could reside here forever.

She noticed the capsules for Admiral Cho and Sorokin—the big worker who'd been the first to die. And there, near the top of a red capsule, was Damon's smiling face: from a time before his devolution. Next to him was a blue capsule with an image of Jack Marschenko's face. He looked back at her with the beginnings of a smile, as if he'd just noticed her.

Poole fell to her knees.

She looked from Jack's face to Earth and couldn't help but imagine what their life might have been. Her stomach clenched. Was that her baby saying goodbye? She put a hand to her belly and stared at Jack's face for a long time, trying to memorize every detail. Then she reached into her exterior pocket and grabbed a sheet of paper she'd torn from a notebook. It was a simple lined page, on which she'd copied a poem from a church service long ago, when her parents had been memorialized. The comm deactivated so no one could hear, she read the poem aloud:

Into the great eternal, past the weeping grasp of Earth,
through the porthole of infinity to the place where angels dwell,
I commend thy spirit with a heavenly prayer;
hopeful, ever hopeful, that we shall one day meet again,
beyond the pain and sorrow, in the pastures of love.

Tears filled her eyes. She blinked them away and picked up the capsule, opening the top and placing the poem inside, letting her gloved fingers linger over the individually wrapped tissue samples stored there. She sealed the capsule again and placed it back precisely on the circle in the dust where it had stood before. But she turned the capsule, so that Jack could look toward Earth, toward home. Poole cried for a long time then, sobbing into her helmet. She didn't try to hold back the grief. It burst past the dam of her control, flooding her.

* * *

Opening the inner doors to the main hangar, Poole set her face in the professional mask of doctor and psychologist. Rendela waited for her.

"You took your time," Rendela said. "Lots happening. Only seven hours left. The Escala are leaving. Nigeria shot a rocket at us."

"Nigeria?"

"You didn't win the pool, if that's what you're wondering," Rendela said. She took Poole by the arm and steered her toward the tunnel that led to LB2. "We have to hurry. Dr. Wellon has some last-minute ideas for our treatment. Have you checked your messages?"

Poole accessed her interface and noted a dozen new files. She glanced at them as the car sped along the rails. When they reached their destination, she followed Rendela to the central hub, where Zora, Devereaux, Quekri, Dr. Wellon, Jeremiah and Quark had gathered. They were staring at a large screen on the wall, which showed an image of the Pilgrim. The ship stood vertically, three flanges decorating the outside—no doubt for when the ship arrived at Mars and needed to maneuver in the planet's thin atmosphere. The tube that allowed access for loading was still attached but there were no gantry cranes or support arms to hold it in place. There didn't need to be in the non-atmosphere of the Moon. No storms or wind could threaten its balance. And it was so big that only the most careless of loading efforts would topple it. Near the top of the ship a dozen windows reflected the light of the sun.

"You're late, Doctor," Zora said.

Dr. Wellon reached into a pocket and pulled out a data cube, which she handed to Poole. "A backup. I also sent the files to your interface. It may give you some ideas for treatments." She gestured to Jeremiah. "I took some samples from him to study on the way to Mars."

"Why Nigeria?" Poole asked.

"Are you upset that you didn't win the pool?" Zora asked.

Rendela grinned. "Phan picked the winner."

"Why are you just standing here doing nothing?"

"Well," Zora said, "we already paid him before he boarded the Pilgrim. He used the money to buy a full case of Nummy Bars."

"That's not what I'm talking about and you know it."

"What would you have us do, Doctor?"

"Call somebody on Earth. The U.N., Eli, anyone." Poole looked from face to face, but they all looked calm.

Zora said, "They're aware of the launch. They'll either stop it or they won't."

"We have to go," Quekri said. She turned to Quark, who leaned forward so she could put her forehead against his. They each put an arm on the other's shoulder and stood that way for half a minute, neither one speaking. When she pulled her head away, he reached into a pocket and pulled out a small multi-colored statue of Emerging Man, which he handed to her.

"For safekeeping," he said.

"It will be waiting for you," Quekri said. She nodded to Devereaux, as did Dr. Wellon.

"Don't say it," Devereaux said. "We'll meet again."

"We'd better," Quekri said. She and Dr. Wellon turned to Jeremiah and in unison said, "Jeremiah, I remember you."

"Quekri, Wellon," Jeremiah said, "I remember you."

The two Escala lumbered down the tunnel that led to the Pilgrim. Everyone turned to stare at the large screen on the wall. No one spoke. After a few minutes the tube connecting the tunnel to the Pilgrim detached from the ship and retracted into the ground, leaving the black hatchcover and the mirrored windows as the only things breaking up the gray of the Pilgrim. Poole knew there was another hatch on the opposite side and farther up, an emergency exit.

"Thirty seconds," Rendela said.

Poole glanced at Quark. The Escala revealed nothing of his thoughts, as if he had no more than an academic interest in seeing the Pilgrim launch. But he kept his eyes on the screen. Poole felt herself drawn to him, to his bulk and his damned self-control—dark, silent and strong as they come. Not that Poole would ever act on her feelings, but it felt good in a way to have someone sexy to look at, to remind her that life goes on when a loved one is lost. The baby inside her helped too. Little Jack Marschenko Poole. She suddenly noticed Zora staring at her. Feeling the heat rush to her face, she turned back to the screen.

Within seconds, a cloud of dust exploded outward and upward, turning yellow with the exhaust of the giant Toninato-Huxley engines. Poole felt a vibration in her feet as the golden cloud enveloped most of the ship, leaving only the top exposed to the cameras. The ship emerged from the cloud, gathering speed as it departed. The vibration vanished as the dust cloud lost its coloring. Three small yellow flares poked out from behind the capsule and the black hatch slid out of view when the ship began to spin. The vessel grew smaller as the Pilgrim accelerated away. Slowly, the dust cloud began to settle to the ground.

"Such a small moment," Devereaux said, as if picking up on Poole's thoughts, "and yet that ship carries the promise of humanity's future, for if anything is certain, it's that Earth isn't big enough to hold us. Our survival requires at least some of us to leave the nest."

"Speaking of survival," Poole said, "how long until the rocket reaches us?"

"Seven hours," Zora said, "give or take a few minutes."

"So we might have only seven hours to live?"

"Less, if they fire a Las-cannon," Zora said.

"How much time would we have if they do that?"

Zora looked at Jeremiah, who said, "Less than a minute if they fire the orbiting Las-cannon at us. Two, maybe three minutes if they fire one through Earth's atmosphere. Either way, we won't have enough time to escape."

Poole looked at Devereaux, who shrugged. "We still have options. Remember there are two LTVs outside."

"How many people can they hold?" Poole asked.

"Not enough," Jeremiah said. "So we're hoping not to use them. But if we have to, eighteen—maybe twenty—could be packed inside each one and sent back to Earth."

"It's a risky strategy though," Zora added. "The closer we get to Earth, the more we come into range of their remaining weapons."

"I see," Poole said. "So you plan to take off if the rocket looks like it won't be stopped, fly around for a bit and land back here."

Zora nodded. "That's one option. We might also try for Earth."

"And who picks the LTV passengers?"

"I do," Zora said. She glanced at the screen, where the Pilgrim had become only a yellow dot, receding into blackness, then turned to Jeremiah with a sad smile. "I can't let anyone else take that responsibility." She looked at Poole. "The LTVs might be just as dangerous as waiting here—even more so. Here at least there are tunnels and the base at LB3. Don't worry, we'll try to keep your baby as safe as possible."

Don't worry. Did that advice ever work for anyone? Poole had dispensed it many times to her patients, but she'd never before realized just how trite it sounded. She knew she was likely to die, whether in an LTV or on the Moon. She wasn't sure she minded, as long as they put her in a capsule next to Jack, turning her face out like his so they could look upon the Earth together.

Chapter Twenty-Seven

For the first time in her life Zora felt afraid. She found the sensation interesting but unpleasant, and she wondered if the reason she felt fear was because every joint hurt. Pain and fear often traveled in tandem. She sat behind Admiral Cho's desk, while Rendela, sitting across from her, cleaned her Las-rifle. Zora had dismissed everyone else so she could think, but the fear and pain took all her concentration. She jumped a little when Rendela said:

"Talk to me, Zora."

"We're going to die."

"So?"

"Don't you get it? No matter what I do, I won't be able to get us out of this situation."

Rendela frowned as if she didn't understand.

Zora said, "China won't allow the U.N. to fire the orbiting Las-cannon at the rocket because of their ties with Nigeria. If we stay here, we die. And if we take the LTVs, we become vulnerable. If we try for Earth, they blow us out of the sky. And if we try to land back here, the blast will have destroyed too much of the settlement for it to be livable. And even if it somehow survives, they can just come after us again. We're powerless."

Rendela said, "You're tired and you're hurting, so you don't see it. You should let Dr. Poole help you."

"What don't I see?"

Rendela shook her head. "That we were never meant to survive."

"You think I don't know that?"

"Not really," Rendela said. "You're acting like one of them. But we're warriors. All we get to decide is how we die."

"I'm afraid, Rendela. Aren't you?"

Rendela nodded, smiling sadly. "Of course. You'd have to be stupid not to be afraid. But I'm a cadet. They picked us because we're special. And you, you're the smartest of us all. We need your leadership. Why don't you let Dr. Poole give you something for the pain? They've tweaked the anesthetics. They'll work now."

"What if the medicine changes me, makes me weak?"

"You're not strong now. You're not decisive. How can you lead us? As long as you're scared and hurting, you can't be what we require."

"Jeremiah doesn't need painkillers to think."

"Well, goody for him."

"You don't find him attractive?"

Rendela's face wrinkled. "He's ancient!"

"No, Devereaux's ancient. But they're both smart and kind."

"If they're so bright, why kick them out of the office?"

"Deciding the fate of the colony is my decision, not theirs."

"Then make a decision."

"I can't. I need more experience. We weren't created to solve problems like this. We were only built to attack. What do you think I should do?"

"I think you should take a painkiller and hear what they've got to say. Otherwise we might as well shoot ourselves now."

Zora grinned. "When did you get so smart?"

Rendela sniffed and turned her head away. "If you're just now figuring out how intelligent I am, maybe we can't be friends anymore."

"I never liked you," Zora said.

"Does that mean you'll take your medicine?"

Zora laughed, feeling better despite the sharp twinge in her shaking shoulders. "Fine, I'll take the damn medicine. And then we'll see what Jeremiah and Devereaux have to say."

"Good, I'll fetch them. Dr. Poole's outside with the new anesthetic."

Zora laughed again. "You sneaky little bitch."

Rendela grinned as she slid-hopped out the door, but Zora caught the sorrow behind it and realized that Rendela still believed they were all going to die. We won't, she promised silently. I'll get us out of this. I swear.

Dr. Poole entered the office. "Rendela said you'd take an anesthetic?"

Zora nodded. "I need something to take the edge off. It's too hard to concentrate."

Dr. Poole stepped forward and pressed a hypo pad to the back of Zora's hand. "I don't understand why you waited so long. That's something Curtik would do."

The pain quickly diminished, making Zora feel like she could think again, like she no longer needed to concentrate on keeping the pain in check. She breathed in the familiar floral odor Dr. Poole always wore and felt slightly comforted by the older woman's presence.

"How are you feeling?" Dr. Poole asked as she lifted Zora's chin and stared into her eyes.

"Better, thanks. Did you add a stimulant?"

Dr. Poole shook her head as she released Zora. "You're just able to focus on something besides the pain now. I could give you a little more, but I'm afraid that might inhibit your clarity of thought. No matter what you think of me, I'm rooting for you, Zora."

"I'm not as scared as I was before."

"I am," Dr. Poole said. "I don't see a solution. We're counting on you to find one."

"No one's dying just yet."

Dr. Poole pointed to her interface. "Have you seen the reports from Earth? The Nigerian rocket was made by China, and with the head start it has, no nation has a rocket fast enough to overtake it. It'll take a Las-cannon to bring it down. Plus, no one seems to know if it's carrying a nuclear weapon. The Nigerians aren't saying. Neither are the Chinese. Not that it matters. Any reasonably large explosion will take out much of the settlement. Only a few pockets deep in the tunnels might be safe."

"There's plenty of time for the United States or Russia to fire a Las-cannon at the rocket."

As Zora spoke, Rendela entered the office, trailed by Devereaux and Jeremiah, whose face was pinched in pain. He put his hands on the back of a chair as if casually leaning on it, but Zora knew he was using it to support himself. She felt a flash of guilt at having eased her pain so quickly. But she also felt relief at having these men here to help her; she no longer had to make every decision herself.

Devereaux held up his PlusPhone and said, "I'm in contact with General Horowitz, who tells me we can't count on that happening—at least not with respect to America's Las-cannon. They still haven't finished testing all the components, and if they fire it and it's defective, the resulting explosion would be catastrophic."

Dr. Poole said, "You think they'll let the rocket destroy this colony, after all they've invested here? Not to mention all the innocent people who will be killed."

Zora looked at Jeremiah, who smiled at the irony. He shrugged, wincing as he did so. "President Hope ordered the Las-cannon shipped out to sea so it can be fired more safely. They should have time to destroy the rocket before it reaches the Moon. However, they still have to calibrate it correctly. And the longer they wait, the closer the rocket gets to us, making it that much more likely the beam will hit us—either in addition to the rocket or instead of hitting the rocket."

Devereaux held up his hand, listening to the PlusPhone for a moment, and said, "General Horowitz confirms that they're continuing to test components. They're hoping to calibrate the Las-cannon some time in the next three or four hours, assuming no problems."

"That still brings the timing pretty close," Jeremiah said. "And from what I've heard, Las-cannons are much trickier to build than particle beam cannons, so it's unlikely they'll get through the testing without finding a few glitches."

Devereaux said, "I agree. I've examined the schematics and studied the process. I estimate they won't be able to calibrate the Las-cannon for at least five hours."

Zora said, "Which puts the rocket so close to us that any effort to blow it up might destroy us too."

"I'm afraid so," Devereaux said.

"Are any other nations close to completing a Las-cannon?"

"Russia and China," Devereaux said, "though their signal traffic isn't as open as the Americans' and my guess is that neither nation will consider blowing up the rocket—China because of their formal alliance with Nigeria, and Russia because they always felt slighted by the Americans' greater presence on the Moon."

Zora turned to Jeremiah. He looked tired, almost old. But he smiled at her and nodded.

"What should I do?" Zora asked. "What would you do?"

Jeremiah frowned. "Nothing different than you. I'd prepare to launch the LTVs soon, with maybe a dozen people in each. I wouldn't want them too crowded in case you have to keep them in space for a while. Everyone left behind should be sent to LB3 or LB2 with portable oxygen generators. Those facilities are farthest away from the main hangar and so more likely to withstand an explosion. Plus, the Escala continued tunneling as a means of working off stress, so their tunnels go deeper than any in LB1. I'd also seal off LB1 from LB2 and LB3, with explosives if necessary, to prevent the spread of radiation, because it's likely that missile carries a nuclear warhead. But you know all that."

"Of course she does," Rendela said.

Zora smiled, glad of Rendela's faith in her. "Who would you put on the LTVs?"

"I'd take the people I most needed to save. The LTVs offer more flexibility. They can make for Earth if the worst happens here. And if the colony isn't destroyed, they can return to the base. I'd certainly take Devereaux, Quark, Dr. Poole and Lendra, as well as the Verloren family and any other families with children, if there are any. And I'd fill out the LTVs with a few cadets and doctors. I'd leave behind the military personnel, the workers, and me. Not that our lives are less meaningful necessarily, but we understood the risks when we signed up and we're in the best shape to survive."

"Children and families," Zora said. "I knew you'd be rational and noble." Rendela laughed.

How odd that Jeremiah would consider children to be important. It was so selfless—the kind of thing Zora wouldn't have even considered.

She wasn't sure she agreed with him on that front, but at least she understood a little why he'd chosen the people he had. Just as she began to appreciate what it meant to be fully human, she was about to die.

Devereaux said, "I have to disagree with Jeremiah in one respect. You have to take him with you. His blood may hold the key to defeating the Susquehanna Virus, so he should be placed in a position of maximum safety. Also, Quark and I intend to stay behind."

"Of course," Zora said. "I would expect no less from the great Devereaux. But you're the one with the best chance of finding a cure for the virus."

"There are many gifted scientists working on that problem."

"Okay," Zora said. "I'll let you know what I decide when we have the LTVs ready. We've got less than six hours. Let's work on LB3 and LB2. I want to be able to close them off from LB1 in case the worst happens. And keeping everybody busy will distract them from what's to come. Rendela, you get the LTVs ready. We'll have Crazy Vigg and Wee Willie work with the Elite Ops to find the best way to seal off the two bases." She looked at Jeremiah. "Perhaps you could help with that as well."

Jeremiah nodded.

Devereaux said, "When are you going to announce who will be going on the LTVs?"

"I think I'll wait until the last minute—make it easier on everybody."

"Good idea," Devereaux said. "That's exactly how I would do it. Remember, no one is guaranteed survival. So no matter what you decide, we'll support you."

Dr. Poole held up her hand. "I just got a transmission. Lendra overdosed on neo-dopamine. She's in the infirmary."

She slid-hopped out the door.

"Crazy old Witchy Poo," Rendela said.

Jeremiah sighed. "I have to check on her."

"I'll come with you," Zora said. She walked Jeremiah to the infirmary, wondering if he actually loved Lendra. Perhaps he's falling for me, Zora thought. Part of her wanted that. Part of her found the notion idiotic. He's Curtik's father, she told herself—an old man. Not as old as Devereaux, but still . . . Yet he was kind and handsome and fiercely intelligent: a warrior.

When they reached the infirmary, Jeremiah quaintly gestured for Zora to precede him. Dr. Poole studied a scanner at the foot of Lendra's bed. Curtik and Kyler lay awake beside her. Lendra, her face tight with tension, caught sight of Jeremiah and managed an embarrassed smile as she held out her hand.

"The great Pappolini," Curtik said. "Are you here because you're sick too? Please say yes."

Jeremiah shook his head. "Hi, Kyler," he said as he ruffled the youngster's hair. "How are you?"

"It doesn't hurt so much anymore," Kyler said.

"I'm glad," Jeremiah said. He turned to face Lendra. "What were you thinking?"

"Go ahead and ignore me, Papster," Curtik said. "Hey, Zora, I wanna get outta here. Piscine said I had to ask you."

"In a minute," Zora said. She turned to Dr. Poole. "How's Lendra?"

"She'll survive," Dr. Poole said. "I'm more worried about the baby. So far, my scanner shows no significant damage, though defects may emerge later."

Jeremiah took Lendra's hand. "Why would you take neo-dopamine? You know how dangerous it can be."

"I couldn't think," Lendra replied. "We're going to die up here unless I can find a solution. And I couldn't concentrate. They wouldn't let me see you. I needed you to hold me."

"Oh, me too!" Curtik said, raising his hands as far as the restraining straps allowed. "Hold me, Pappy."

Kyler giggled and lifted her hands also.

Zora bit the inside of her lower lip. She looked at Curtik and when the urge to laugh subsided, said, "What makes you think you're ready to be released? You can't control yourself at all."

"Oh, come on, Zora. That was funny. I'm just messin' with his head. I'm not violent anymore. Ask Piscine."

Jeremiah sat on the edge of Lendra's bed. "You're not going to die up here," he said, raising his voice to include Curtik and Kyler. "You're all going on the LTVs. It's still going to be dangerous, but you'll survive. Zora will see to that. Won't you, Zora?"

Zora nodded. "Rendela and I will fly the LTVs. We'll make sure you're safe.

"Oh, now that's too much," Curtik said. "I should be one of the pilots."

"If you were healthy, maybe," Zora said.

"I am." Curtik looked at Dr. Poole. "Tell her."

Dr. Poole said, "He seems to have stabilized. I don't see any further nanotech deterioration. No psychotic rages. No delusions. And I see improvement in a few areas. Jeremiah's blood is doing its job in conjunction with the new nanobots we implanted."

Zora glanced at Jeremiah, who was caressing the back of Lendra's hand with his thumb. Lendra smiled at him, seemingly content now that she had his attention. She glanced at Zora and a hint of smugness touched her expression. Zora fought the urge to grab Jeremiah's hand away and slap Lendra's face, instead focusing on the problem of Curtik. "So is he safe?" she asked Dr. Poole. "Or is he going to go on a murderous rampage?"

"Oh, please," Curtik said. "I don't want to kill anybody anymore. Not even Paprika. That was just the devolution. You have to let me out at some point. Besides, I'm the best pilot you've got."

"Rendela's better."

Curtik held up his hands. "Okay, fine, she's better. But she's a freak. And I'm better than you. So are you gonna let me outta here?"

"I'll leave that up to Jeremiah. Ask him."

"Oh, that's cruel. Putting my fate in his hands."

"Where it belongs," Zora said. "After all, he's your father."

Jeremiah had been following their conversation with a small frown, as if bemused by the whole thing. He released Lendra's hand and got to his feet. He walked toward Zora and for a moment she thought he was coming to her. But he paused for only an instant before veering over to Curtik's bedside.

"We're all in this together," he said. "We've only got a few hours left to figure out how best to save everyone." He removed Curtik's straps. "We could really use your help, son."

Curtik sat up. "You expect me to thank you?"

"I expect you to help us figure out the best way to isolate safe areas so that if the rocket reaches us, we'll have pockets of air that will allow us to survive."

"Okay, just so you know, I'm not gonna thank you." Curtik swung out of bed and stepped over to Kyler's side. "And you. You get better or I'm gonna send in the tickle monster, okay?"

He made a fierce face, scowling and growling until Kyler began giggling again.

"I will, Curtik," Kyler said.

"Good." Curtik turned to Zora. "Where do you want me?"

"Help Wee Willie and Crazy Vigg."

"Right." Curtik straightened to attention and saluted Jeremiah. "Pampolicious!" He waved furiously at Lendra. "Witchy Poo. Later."

As he slid-hopped out the door, he sang out, "Here I come to save the daaaay!"

Lendra said, "Are you sure about this? He seems crazy to me."

"I think it was the right move," Jeremiah said. "Besides, how much worse could things get?"

"Can you sit with me a while?" Lendra reached out her hands again. And again she glanced at Zora with a slight smile. Did Jeremiah see the obvious manipulation? Was this how all women behaved when they targeted men? Or was Lendra playing her?

Zora shook her head and watched Jeremiah. When he edged toward the door, Zora felt a lightness infuse her whole being, as if she weighed nothing at all. She almost felt as if she could fly.

Jeremiah said, "We'll get Colonel Truman in here to sit with you if you like."

"I want you, Jeremiah," Lendra said. "I've always wanted you."

"I've got work to do. Don't worry, you'll be fine on the LTV."

"Are you staying behind?"

Zora said, "That hasn't been decided yet." A small lie, but she wanted Lendra to suffer.

"I'll do whatever you do, Jeremiah," Lendra said.

"You'll go on the LTV," Jeremiah replied. "As you're so fond of reminding me, you have a baby to think about now."

When Jeremiah walked out, Zora stayed behind for a moment. "Actually, I'm leaning toward leaving you on the Moon and taking Jeremiah with me."

"You can't do that," Lendra said. "He belongs with me. You think you've won? You think he could love you? You're a child." She gestured toward Kyler. "You're no older than her."

"I'll send in Colonel False-Girl," Zora said as she slid-hopped out the door.

This is so weird, she thought to herself. We may all die up here in the next few hours and I'm worried about whether some man loves me or not. And yet she couldn't deny the power of her emotions—the anti-gravity joy, the rage-inducing jealousy, the gut-wrenching anxiety. No wonder Dr. Poole was worried about bringing them to full adulthood. How would Curtik handle all this?

Still, whether they lived or died, whether Jeremiah chose her or not, at least he hadn't returned to Witchy Poo. It took all her effort not to laugh as she entered the main hangar.

Chapter Twenty-Eight

Colonel Truman directed the transportation of emergency stores to LB2 and LB3: ready meals, portable oxygen generators, medical equipment, backup batteries, spacesuits, heaters and all the water they could carry. But his mind kept drifting to Lendra Riley. He'd gone to visit her at Jeremiah's request a few hours ago and found her scared and alone in the infirmary. Even Kyler Verloren had been released from her bed, reunited with her family. Truman had sat beside Lendra and taken her hand as she struggled to maintain her composure.

"I realize it's silly," she said, "pining over a man who no longer loves me, if he ever did."

"I'm sure he did," Truman said. "I'm sure he does." Lendra squeezed his hand, making his heart jump. God, he longed to hold her. How idiotic to fall in love now!

"No, he doesn't," Lendra replied as her hand retreated. "Not anymore, anyway. You've seen the way he acts around Zora. You've seen the way he's pushed us together."

Truman didn't know what to say to that, but something must have shown in his face, for Lendra said, "I didn't mean to imply that I found your company tiresome. Far from it. You've treated me far better than Jeremiah has this trip. It's just that . . . I thought if he knew I was pregnant, he might change his mind about us. But that's not going to happen."

She reached for her glass bulb necklace, which reminded him of one he'd given his daughter McKenna a few years earlier.

"That's a pretty necklace," Truman said. "You wore it in Minnesota last year, didn't you?"

"You remember that?" Lendra held the necklace out for Truman to see. "Jeremiah barely notices what I wear."

"Does it have a secret compartment that twists open?"

Lendra's eyes widened as she pulled the glass bulb away.

"My daughter's necklace does. She keeps lip balm in it."

Lendra reached behind her neck and unclasped the necklace. She pushed it toward him. "Here, you take it."

"Excuse me?" Truman asked.

Lendra said, "I keep my emergency supply of neo-dopamine inside. And I can't take any more without harming my baby." She pressed the necklace into his hand. "Am I a terrible person?" she asked.

"Of course not." Truman covered her hand with his. He noted her strong fingers and the smoothness of her skin. "You're just under a lot of stress. We all are."

"You really are the sweetest man."

Truman felt the warmth of blood rushing to his face. "Why don't you get some rest?" he said. "I'll stay here until you fall asleep."

As she closed her eyes, Truman studied her face. She was a beautiful woman. But there was more to her than that. Intelligent, inquisitive, caring—no matter what her troubles with Jeremiah, Truman was certain she had only good intentions. And if Jeremiah couldn't forgive her minor transgressions, whatever they were, then he was a fool.

"Hey, Laaady!" Crazy Vigg said in a nasally voice, interrupting his thoughts.

"What?" Truman said.

"The last of the water containers," Crazy Vigg said. "To LB2 or LB3?"

"Oh, sorry," Truman said. "LB2."

"What's your problem, lady?"

"I don't like that," Truman said.

"I don't like being called crazy either. But everyone does it just the same."

"Have you told them you don't like being called crazy?"

"You don't know much about kids, do you. Why are you so distracted? Is it Witchy Poo?"

"It doesn't matter," Truman said.

"She likes you," Crazy Vigg said, "even though she's still into Jeremiah."

"You think?"

"They call me crazy because I see things they don't. I'm not always right, but . . . Like you're into Witchy Poo, who's still into Jeremiah. And Wee Willie's into Rendela, but she's into Zora, who's also into Jeremiah. And Piscine is into Quark, but Quark is into Devereaux in a weird, protective, brotherly way. And Shiloh's into Curtik, but she can't deal with it so she pretends she hates him. Now she's on her way to Mars and she doesn't have to worry about Curtik because she'll never see him again. He'll survive, but he'll never leave Earth."

"And what about you?"

"I'm into you, lady." Crazy Vigg laughed. "I'm totally into you. And rockets." He looked up through the plas-glass ceiling.

Truman followed his gaze. The approaching missile loomed large, magnified so that it looked much larger than Earth—as if it would be here any minute. Stay calm, he told himself. Yes, you're probably going to die. So are we all, one day. Your day just happens to be today.

"Are we going to survive, Vigg?" Truman asked.

Crazy Vigg just smiled.

Jeremiah made his way over to the military desk, nodded at Crazy Vigg and said, "How we doing?"

"We just finished moving the last of the supplies," Truman replied.

"Good. We've got about an hour before the rocket hits. The first LTV leaves in ten minutes. You'd better get Lendra. She'll be on the second LTV." Jeremiah raised his hand as a signal to Zora, who stepped onto the staircase leading to the first LTV. Elite Ops troopers and a group of cadets formed a wall between the staircase and the crowd.

"Now boarding," she said as Truman headed toward the infirmary, "Rendela, Wee Willie, Roze, Salma, Doctors Nakamura and Srinlangshiran . . ."

Her voice tailed off as Truman entered the tunnel leading to the infirmary but he knew his name wasn't on the list. He stepped into Lendra's room and sat beside her on the bed, touching her shoulder.

She awoke, frowning until she saw his face. Then she smiled. God help him, she smiled.

"Yes?" she said.

"Time to go," Truman said. "You'll be on the second LTV."

"Really?"

Truman nodded, and Lendra sat up, hugging Truman fiercely. He put his hand on her back, inhaling the flowery aroma of her hair. He couldn't help but recall that he and Emily hadn't made love in years, and he realized now that although he had blamed her for the loss of their physical relationship, it had been just as much his fault for belittling her protests as a desperate search for meaning.

When he stiffened, Lendra released him and sat back, staring into his eyes. "What is it?"

"I just realized that I sort of abandoned my wife. Ever since my brother Ned disappeared during a CIA mission fifteen years ago, I've been sinking into my work, withdrawing from my family. Maybe that's why McKenna moved to Portland."

"Well, it's not too late," Lendra said. "It's never too late for love."

She smiled, a sad smile that acknowledged the falsity of her words, and Truman returned it. Is it too late, he wondered, when you realize that you're in love with someone else? We'll both love people who don't love us back and we'll go on with our lives as if it doesn't matter.

"We should get you out to the main hangar," he said.

"Are you coming on the LTV?"

"No." Truman kept his voice calm. "All military personnel and lunar workers are staying on the Moon." He reached into his pocket and pulled out Lendra's necklace. "Here." He tried to hand it to her, but she shook her head and pushed it back.

"You keep it. If people start to panic, it will serve as a relaxant, keep them calm."

"What about your claustrophobia?"

"It's not so bad on the LTV. There are windows and screens to look at. I'll be fine. I don't think I could handle being stuck in one of those tunnels. Besides, I can't take any more."

315

"Thank you," Truman said. He pulled Lendra to her feet and guided her out the door. She was a little unsteady, so he held onto her arm above the elbow. When they reached the main hangar, the first LTV door was already closed, the ship's engines humming as it prepared to depart. Almost everyone on the Moon stood watching as the airlock sealed off the ship, although Crazy Vigg remained seated at the military desk, muttering to himself as he checked the screens before him.

Truman scanned the crowd, keeping his breathing under control, only a tight smile showing. Everyone was so accepting. Scientists, soldiers and even the lunar workers: they all understood the impossibility of their position and yet maintained discipline. Apparently the psych evaluations of the lunar workers were accurate.

Truman wondered if he was more afraid than the rest of them. Because his lunar visit was an emergency and not intended to last long, he hadn't undergone a psych evaluation. How would he hold up? You're a professional soldier, he told himself. You chose this life. You will not tolerate fear.

And yet he wanted to live. He wanted the opportunity to tell Lendra how he felt about her. And this wasn't the time to do that, so if he died, she would never know how he felt. That scared him almost more than dying.

He turned to one of the large screens as the LTV backed away from the hangar, then lifted into the air, a small yellow dust cloud exploding outward as its engines accelerated.

One down, one to go.

People began moving around again, most of them shuffling about and chatting quietly. Jeremiah emerged from the crowd. He nodded at Truman and said to Lendra, "We put your bag on the second LTV. You leave in fifteen minutes."

"Aren't you coming?" Lendra asked.

Jeremiah shook his head. "We'll be fine up here—maybe even safer than you. We'll be deep in the tunnels with oxygen generators, food, water, medicine. We'll be able to last for weeks, if necessary."

"Assuming the tunnels are properly sealed," Lendra replied.

"The Elite Ops know what they're doing."

"I could stay with you."

Jeremiah shook his head. "With your claustrophobia?"

"So this is the end for us?"

Jeremiah glanced at Truman. "We've been over for awhile, Lendra. Your decision to have this baby doesn't change that. I'm fond of you, but I don't love you."

Lendra sagged. Truman wrapped an arm around her shoulders. How could Jeremiah be so cruel at this moment? Jeremiah looked at Truman again. "Take care of Lendra," he said.

"What do you mean?"

"I want you to go in my place. I'll ask Zora to take you."

Hope surged in Truman's chest. "You can't—"

The loudspeaker clicked on and Zora spoke to the crowd: "Final boarding—Curtik, Lendra Riley, Racine, Doctors Poole, Westin, Remar, Floyd and Garcia Delgado, Devereaux, Quark and Jeremiah Jones."

Jeremiah's eyes widened. "What about Kyler's family?" He turned to face Zora, who looked at him over the crowd. She caught his eye and shook her head.

Lendra, meanwhile, looked from Jeremiah to Truman and back, frowning. Her hand lifted, as if she wanted to touch one of them, but she lowered it without making contact.

"She won't let you stay," Truman said to Jeremiah.

"I can convince her."

"No," Truman said. "I can't let you remain behind. There's a better chance of survival on the LTVs."

"I'm not being noble," Jeremiah said. "I hate flying. And if I have to fly, I'd rather wait until something larger comes to rescue us. Besides, I'd rather stay behind with Kyler and her family."

Truman struggled to maintain his composure as his emotions warred within: fear, hope, anxiety, relief. Would Zora let him take Jeremiah's place? And could he go even if she did? How could he live with himself if Jones died? Jeremiah and Devereaux were the only indispensable men up here.

Truman noticed that he'd begun staring at Crazy Vigg, who grinned and shook his head before returning to monitor his screens, still talking to himself. Had the cadet seen this coming? And why wasn't he going? He was one of the most talented cadets, if one of the least predictable. He showed no fear, as if he'd known all along he wouldn't be among the chosen.

As the doctors climbed the staircase, a few of them waved at the crowd. A dozen or so people waved back, making an effort to smile. Even Truman caught himself smiling. With his peripheral vision, he saw Jeremiah and Lendra doing the same.

Zora waited until they'd passed inside before nodding to Curtik. The cadet approached Devereaux and Quark, a Las-rifle in his hands.

Devereaux said, "I'd rather not go."

Zora smiled. "I know. Everyone here knew you'd volunteer to stay behind. But I'm in charge. You either board under your own power or we carry you up." She gestured toward the stairs. A stillness settled over the hangar. Devereaux shrugged and headed for the LTV, Quark following.

Zora and Curtik moved toward Truman, Jeremiah and Lendra. She pointed at Lendra. "You're next, Witchy Poo."

Lendra hugged Truman, her body shaking as she did so. Truman glanced at Jeremiah, who smiled and nodded, as if he knew how Truman felt about Lendra. Perhaps he did. Then Lendra released Truman, turned to Jeremiah and opened her mouth. But instead of speaking, she turned away and walked to the LTV's stairs. When she reached the top, she gave a brief wave and stepped inside.

"And now you," Zora said to Jeremiah.

"How can you leave the Verlorens behind?" Jeremiah said.

"I can't justify taking tourists in place of scientists. And I need Racine as a backup pilot. Besides, as you pointed out, we don't know if the LTVs will be safer."

"Let me stay. I'll help take care of the kids."

"I'm sorry. I wish I could let you. But I can't. They'll be as safe as we can make them. We'll put them at the back of LB3—the deepest tunnel."

"Can Colonel Truman take my place?"

Zora looked at Truman, but he shook his head. "Jeremiah has to go."

"I agree," Zora said. "You're the right man to lead these people, Colonel. I trust you. Sorry, Jeremiah. You go."

Curtik raised his Las-rifle and pointed it at Jeremiah's chest. "Well, Papster," he said, "do I get to shoot you?"

"I'm coming," Jeremiah said. He turned to Truman. "I wish you were going. You're good for Lendra. I think the two of you would make a fine couple."

"What . . ." Truman shook his head. His stomach roiled. "I'm married."

"But you're in love with Lendra. I wish you could be there to take care of her."

"Well," Truman said, "I guess you'll have to do it for me."

Jeremiah held out his hand. "Get as deep as you can. Protect the Verlorens. Good luck."

Truman shook his hand, then watched Jeremiah walk away, still favoring his injured legs. Passing the Elite Ops troopers who guarded the stairway, who ignored him as if he were nothing, their hatred of him still obvious, he climbed to the LTV and disappeared inside without a backward glance.

"Let's go," Zora said to Curtik. She handed her Las-pistol to Truman, butt first, and said, "You might need this. Hopefully you won't. Get to LB3 and LB2 as soon as you can. Seal everything behind you. Crazy Vigg will remain out in the main hangar."

"But he'll be killed," Truman said as he secured the Las-pistol to his belt by its magnetic connector.

Zora shrugged. "The best way to ensure the tunnels seal properly is from the hangar side. He'll also be able to implement any last-second ideas we may come up with for how to save you."

Truman looked over at Crazy Vigg. The young cadet continued muttering to himself as he checked the screens in front of him. But otherwise he seemed calm.

Zora followed Curtik to the LTV stairs and up to the platform. Raising her hand, she spoke to the assembled crowd: "We'll do everything in our power to assist you, but there's not much we can do. Obey Colonel Truman and his designees. There aren't enough spacesuits to go around, so find small rooms as far from here as possible and seal yourselves in. Hopefully someone on Earth will realize the stupidity of blowing up this place and will stop the missile." Then she entered the LTV and sealed the door.

Truman, as the ranking military officer, knew he ought to get the people moving out of the main hangar, but he had no desire to order them out. Like everyone else left behind, he wanted to watch the LTV take off.

The LTV's engines hummed. Less than a minute later it backed away. On the screens, another small yellow cloud of dust arose as the LTV lifted off the surface of the Moon.

After giving everyone a few seconds to absorb the finality of it, Truman said, "All right, people. You know your assignments. Remember, Captain Sharon Englin, Elite Ops trooper Wilson and cadet Lydene are in charge at LB2. Elite Ops trooper Mottz and cadet Joffer will work with me at LB3. Let's move."

The exodus began. Every carload would carry an Elite Ops trooper or a cadet to ensure order. Yet all their precautions appeared unnecessary. All the workers acquitted themselves with dignity, which helped Truman keep his composure as well.

"How much time until the missile hits?" a woman asked.

"Forty-four minutes," Mottz replied.

Truman stood beside Crazy Vigg at the entrance to the military area so he could look down the tunnel that led to Cho's office, where the tunnel to LB3 began. From this spot, he could also see the tunnel to LB2 across the hangar. As the rail cars sent people to their bases, Truman took a few deep breaths and prepared for what he had to do.

Beside him, Crazy Vigg muttered to himself, too softly for Truman to understand what he was saying. Was he going over his final instructions from Zora? Or was he really crazy? Either way, Truman admired him.

Joffer hopped on the second to last railcar with the Verlorens, leaving only Mottz and Truman behind. Mottz quietly said, "Thirty minutes."

"Right," Truman said. He turned to Crazy Vigg. "You go with them. I'll stay behind to check the seals."

Crazy Vigg laughed. "I don't think so, madam."

"Excuse me?"

"What is it with you humans? Why are you so eager to sacrifice yourselves? Do you think it's noble, Colonel False-Girl?"

"It's my duty as senior officer to ensure the safety of everyone on the Moon to the best of my ability, particularly the civilians. That includes you."

"If you want to save everyone, I'm the logical choice to stay behind. I know the main hangar's weaknesses and strengths better than you. And I'm smarter and way more handsome. You might screw up and kill us all."

"I can't allow you to sacrifice yourself."

"No one's asking you to." Crazy Vigg shook his head. "Can you calibrate the necessary shock wave of a secondary plasma detonation? Do you know precisely where to place a charge to ensure the integrity of a seal? Can you do it all in your mind without the help of a computer?"

Truman felt a rush of gratitude at Crazy Vigg for giving him an out, allowing him to live, if only for a little while longer. But he wondered if the young cadet knew death was inevitable. "I just . . ."

"I'll be fine," Crazy Vigg said. "I'm tired of people anyway. I'm not crazy, just . . . Besides, I'd only get on everyone's nerves if I was locked up with all of you. Anyway, I'm curious as to what's on the dark side."

"Thank you, Vigg," Truman said.

"Go on, get outta here. I've got work to do."

Truman raised his hands in surrender. He walked to Cho's office with Mottz, Crazy Vigg following. When Truman boarded the last car with Mottz, Crazy Vigg stood beside the airlock. As the car pulled away, Truman held up his hand in farewell, and just before the car rounded a corner, he saw Crazy Vigg's face fall, as if the cadet finally understood that he was about to die alone. Then the curve of the track took them out of view.

They rode to LB3 without speaking, the hum of the car on the rails the only intrusion.

When they reached their destination, Truman led them away from the car, past the training court and down a long hallway through another airlock to the cadets' quarters—a group of eight rooms where they would make their last stand. Dozens of people were crowded inside. All the doors were open, the people staring out.

"Time?" Truman asked.

Mottz said, "Twenty-two minutes."

Truman pointed back at the airlock they'd passed. "Seal that up. Let's see what's happening on screen."

Truman entered the farthest room—a storage room about twenty feet deep and fourteen wide with a pile of supplies stacked against the back wall beside a portable chem-toilet. The Verlorens stood inside the door, the parents holding their daughters' shoulders. Truman smiled at them and looked up at the screen, where the rocket continued to grow.

Joffer slid-hopped down the corridor to the airlock and hit the button to seal them off. Then he returned to the group, where everyone stood watching the rocket, shuffling about.

"Eighteen minutes," Mottz said.

Truman stepped out into the hall and activated the general broadcast intercom so he could speak to the people at LB2 as well:

"The cadets and the Elite Ops have done everything they can to protect us. I trust their work to keep us safe. We may have to dig our way out when this is all over, but we've got plenty of food and water. We've got oxygen generators to keep the air fresh. A rescue will come from Earth eventually. We just have to hold on, maintain our composure and we'll be fine."

Switching off the general broadcast function, he stepped back inside the first room to watch the incoming missile, which loomed impossibly close, seemingly still accelerating, as if eager to destroy them. On another screen Crazy Vigg, ignoring the warhead that was about to obliterate him, welded the seals to the main hangar, ending any chance of saving himself.

Did he understand the finality of his actions? Yes, he was smart. But did he fully grasp the significance of what he'd done? Did he not care whether he lived or died? Perhaps his teenage brain, unfinished as it was, benefited him as he prepared for death.

"Fourteen minutes," Mottz said.

Truman wondered how safe they'd be back here in the tunnels. Since no one knew for certain how large the detonation would be, no one could say if they were within the kill zone. Oddly, he no longer felt afraid. Perhaps that was because there were no more decisions to make, no more possible avenues of escape. All he could do was wait for the missile to strike. He wished he'd told Lendra how he felt about her. What a strange thought to be having as a bomb rocketed toward his head.

Chapter Twenty-Nine

President Angelica Hope stood beside General Horowitz in the middle of Elias Leach's office gazing at the screens that Eli's tech specialist, Jay-Edgar, displayed. Her stomach burned and her knees felt rubbery, like she'd just played a three-set tennis match in ninety-degree heat. She'd run out of time trying to convince China to allow the U.N. Security Council to fire the orbiting Las-cannon at the missile. Even though Russia had finally granted its approval, the launch codes couldn't be activated without a unanimous vote. And there were less than fifteen minutes until the missile struck the lunar colony. She reached up a hand and massaged herself just below the sternum as if she could fight back the acid externally.

"Twelve minutes," Jay-Edgar said.

"The LTVs?" President Hope asked.

"On the far side of the Moon," Jay-Edgar replied. He pressed the panel in front of him and a screen showed the two LTVs orbiting the Moon. Another screen displayed the inside of one of the LTVs. President Hope spotted Quark, Devereaux, Zora, Lendra Riley and Jeremiah Jones.

On yet another screen, she saw the main hangar of Lunar Base One and the cadet Jay-Edgar had identified as Crazy Vigg. The cadet straightened from his inspection of the seal on the tunnel to LB3.

"Both tunnels sealed," Crazy Vigg said. "No air flow, no weaknesses to structural integrity. These babies will withstand a nuclear bomb."

"They'll have to," Rendela said from her LTV.

From the other LTV, Jeremiah Jones said, "What if we blow up the main hangar before the missile strikes?"

Zora answered: "What are you thinking?"

"If we could detonate the hangar roof a few seconds before the missile arrives, the outward explosion might divert enough of the blast to increase the odds of survival for the people at LB2 and LB3."

Zora shook her head. "Slim odds of that. What do you think, Crazy Vigg?"

Crazy Vigg grunted. "It's so skinny it's invisible." He laughed. "But what the hell, I've got nothing better to do."

Zora said: "Let's try it. Assume a two-second differential."

"Can we contact them?" General Horowitz asked.

"We can try," Jay-Edgar said. "They're broadcasting to every nation."

"Do you have a suggestion?" President Hope asked.

General Horowitz opened his mouth to reply, but then shook his head.

"Perhaps we should just observe," the President said.

Jay-Edgar switched the primary image to a room at LB3. Inside were dozens of people—Colonel Truman standing beside what had to be an Elite Ops trooper and a cadet, surrounded by a number of people, including a family with two young girls. They were staring at the camera, or more likely at the screen next to the camera. Another room showed a similar scene—then a third and a fourth. Jay-Edgar dropped those images to secondary status and returned the image of Crazy Vigg to primary status.

Crazy Vigg moved in a curious slide-hopping gait down a tunnel, where another camera picked him up as he reached the armory. The cadet lifted two cases of plasma charges and slid-hopped back to the main hangar. He placed the cases in the center of the hangar. "May as well clean out the armory," he said, turning away. As he passed his computer station, he punched in a command.

"Six minutes, twenty-three seconds," a female computer voice said.

Crazy Vigg slid-hopped back toward the armory, where he grabbed two more cases and a Las-rifle, then exited the door and turned back toward the main hangar.

On the way back he slid too far and crashed into the military desk, dropping the cases, the Las-rifle flying out of his hands. President Hope cringed as she waited for the explosion. It never came.

General Horowitz said, "Plasma charges are extraordinarily stable. It'll take a laser pulse to ignite them."

"How many cases do we need?" Zora asked.

"Too many variables to know for certain," Jeremiah replied. "We don't know how powerful the missile is, so even though we know its speed, we can't determine precisely how much counterforce is necessary to alter its trajectory."

Crazy Vigg got to his feet laughing, picked up the cases and maneuvered his way around the military desk over to where he'd placed the first two cases. He stacked them beside the other two and slid-hopped back to the armory yet again.

The computer voice said: "Four minutes, nineteen seconds."

Curtik laughed. "Leave it to Crazy Vigg to set the timer for odd seconds."

President Hope felt like she was being stabbed in the stomach. As if he were reading her mind, General Horowitz handed her an antacid. "Thanks," she said as she watched Crazy Vigg moving rapidly through the tunnel. "Is this plan at all viable?"

General Horowitz shrugged. "It's as good an idea as any."

As Crazy Vigg returned to the main hangar with two more boxes, the voice said, "Two minutes, seventeen seconds."

"That's probably enough," Zora said.

"One more trip," Crazy Vigg said.

"You'll never make it in time," Rendela said.

"He'll make it," Zora said as Crazy Vigg slid-hopped to the armory one last time. He picked up two more cases and returned to the main hangar. Skirting the military desk, he set the cases down atop the middle two, looked around and said, "Oops."

Zora said: "Under the orange bush."

"Thanks," Crazy Vigg replied. He reached under the orange bush and came up with the Las-rifle.

"Thirty-one seconds," the computer voice said.

Crazy Vigg adjusted the settings on the weapon, approached the cases he'd placed on the floor and raised his Las-rifle.

For an instant, President Hope was there in his body, aiming at the plasma charges, seeing the inevitability of her death. "Could I do that?" she whispered.

"What did you say?" General Horowitz asked.

"Nothing." My God, this kid has courage. Don't think about it. Focus.

"Fifteen seconds," the computer voice said as Jay-Edgar brought up another image, this one of the Moon as seen from an orbiting satellite.

The voice counted down the remains of Crazy Vigg's life. "Eleven, nine, seven . . ." Crazy Vigg didn't try to shield himself from the explosion. Standing only a few feet away from the cases, he shook his head and muttered to himself in time with the voice: "five, three . . ."

Crazy Vigg fired a red burst at the cases. Instantly the view of the main hangar went black. President Hope felt a fist grabbing her lungs, squeezing the breath out of her. She shifted her attention to the projection of the Moon. At the bottom of the image, near the south pole, there was a tiny white flash—a flicker—a brightening almost more imagined than seen: quickly gone. But the bottom of the Moon became fuzzy. Jay-Edgar magnified the image until the haziness resolved itself into a giant cloud of dust and debris, shot out from the Moon by the explosion, slowly drifting back to the lunar ground.

"Vigg," Quark said in his deep rumble. "I remember—"

The LTV connection died.

President Hope's eyes welled up. She blinked away the water. I will not succumb to sadness. I will not succumb to despair and anger. Later—when this is over.

The audio channels lit up with a cacophony of voices. Before she could tell Jay-Edgar to silence them, he did it.

"Increase magnification," General Horowitz said.

The image of the Moon grew larger still. Beneath the dust and debris, the lunar settlement had largely vanished, a jagged crater taking its place—a dark circle destined to become a permanent feature of the lunar landscape.

"What about the people at LB2 and LB3?" President Hope asked. "Are they still alive?" Please let them be alive. Let Crazy Vigg's death not be in vain. Unbidden, she heard Elias Leach's voice in her mind: You know, if they're alive, you might be able to use that to your advantage.

Jay-Edgar brought up image after image, all black. "Cameras are no longer transmitting," he said. "All power lost. All satellite transmissions offline. And both bases are buried under tons of rock. But if we superimpose the schematics of LB2 and LB3 onto the crater formed by the bomb . . ." Jay-Edgar brought up several images and placed one atop the other on the screen. "If we adjust for geographic elevation . . ." He manipulated another schematic, and pointed at the screen, where two pockets had been highlighted. "We can see that both LB2 and LB3 survive in parts."

"The LTVs?" President Hope said.

"Nothing. We're not seeing any signs of a crash, but if they went down on the far side of the Moon, we wouldn't."

"Any way to scan LB2 or LB3 without satellites?" General Horowitz asked.

Jay-Edgar shrugged. "We can try with an Earth-bound satellite, but it will be hard to verify life forms over that much distance and beneath that much rock. Madam President, we're getting urgent calls from all over the world."

"Try a scan. Let them wait."

President Hope had to know if there were survivors first, before she could deal with the rest of it.

"I've got multiple life signs," Jay-Edgar said. "Not sure how many, but there are at least some survivors."

"Excellent," President Hope said. She felt like pumping her fist, having won a big point. "Get that information out to every nation." She shook her head. "Odd, isn't it?"

"What's that, Madam President?" General Horowitz said.

"This stupid plan Elias concocted to bring the nations of the world together. It might actually work now. China, Russia, Brazil, India: they all have citizens up there that need to be rescued."

"A rescue mission would take days. Anyone still alive up there," General Horowitz shook his head, "won't be for long. And we can't just dock up there. We'll have to dig them out."

"We'll find a way," President Hope said. "The whole world saw this footage. People will pressure their governments to help. I want to make sure that young man's sacrifice wasn't wasted. I don't care what we have to do. I also want those LTVs to return safely. A great many nations harbor ill will toward us—if not for our ideas, then for our pre-eminent place in the world—but we might be able to bring them together to accomplish this rescue mission. Imagine a truly global initiative. If we do it right, if we push hard enough, we can still salvage something from this mess. Let's set up a conference. I want every nation with spacefaring capability on the line."

"Yes, ma'am," General Horowitz said.

While Jay-Edgar activated multiple screens with images of foreign leaders—China, Russia, India, Brazil, France, Germany—President Hope sat for a moment and closed her eyes, saying a prayer for the soul of that brave child.

* * *

China's President, Chen Hui, led off the discussion after glaring at India's Prime Minister: "Our country has suffered the worst. We've lost more people than any other nation. And we demand justice. We will not discuss any rescue mission until you transfer this Elias Leach to us for prosecution. If you refuse, be advised that we haven't ruled out a military response."

"According to our records, China has twenty-three people on the Moon," President Hope replied. "Don't you want to save them? And Elias Leach has been arrested. We haven't decided what to do with him yet. He's caused deaths across the world, not just in China. We lost thousands here as well. What's to be done with him is a question for another time. What we need now is a multi-national rescue effort to save those innocents."

"Perhaps we should just rescue our own people," Russia's Navrakov said, his voice metallic as the translator converted his words into English. "We have eighteen citizens on the Moon. They're innocent. How many of your people can say that?"

"Most of the people on the Moon are innocent," England's Pryce-Jones said. "Britain has sixteen citizens trapped there. And we will attempt to rescue them, no matter the cost. But their nationalities are irrelevant."

She paused for a moment. "Unfortunately, our joint program with Australia has suffered some setbacks recently and we cannot launch for at least one week."

President Hope turned to General Horowitz. "How many days will it take us?"

General Horowitz repeated the question into a PlusPhone. After a few seconds, he replied, "We have two companies with LTVs that could launch a rescue mission in the next week, but neither can be ready in the next forty-eight hours."

"Not soon enough," President Hope said. "Can anyone launch earlier? President Chen Hui?"

The Chinese President shook his head. "I have not yet decided whether China will assist," he said, the translator making his voice sound exactly like the Russian President's. "If we choose to help, we might rescue only our personnel. And since you refuse to hand the mass murderer over to us, we feel no obligation to extract your people."

"This is an easy decision," President Hope said as her stomach continued to burn. "The people trapped on the Moon aren't the people who attacked us. Even the cadets are victims of Elias Leach's machinations. Regardless of the fact that some maniac created this problem, we all have an obligation to save them."

"Of course we are concerned," Chen Hui said. "But the cost of such a mission would be extremely high. I am inclined to let you deal with the Moon. China will focus its energy on our more immediate problems. If you were to hand this Elias Leach over to us, we might reconsider assisting with a rescue."

"This is partly your fault," President Hope reminded him. "You chose not to destroy the Nigerian missile. You voted against UN action. And even though you completed work on a ground Las-cannon, you still didn't destroy the missile. So this problem is not just of our making. You contributed to it as well."

The Chinese President shook his head. "Our Las-cannon has not been properly tested. What about yours? You didn't fire on the missile either."

"Enough," Pryce-Jones said. "We must act swiftly. We can debate culpability at a later date."

"You're right," President Hope said. "What about you, President Penela?"

"We can launch a lunar transit vehicle in seven hours," the Brazilian President said.

"Seven hours? That's fantastic."

"We will of course take the lead."

"Of course," President Hope agreed. "And is this the LTV with the drilling equipment onboard?"

President Penela's eyes narrowed. "You know about this?"

President Hope nodded. "But we were not aware you'd tested the system yet."

"We've only tested it locally. Not on the Moon, obviously."

"What help can we provide?"

"Brazil requires no assistance," President Penela said. "Except for your money."

"We too," India's Prime Minister Sitmandesh said, "have been developing such a system. We could launch an LTV in two days. Our engineers could coordinate with your people. We could send an LTV to the other base."

President Penela nodded. "Very well."

France's President Montesquieu said, "We will be happy to contribute to the rescue effort to help subsidize costs, but we don't have an LTV ready."

"We will also contribute to the costs," Pryce-Jones said.

"Russia will pay too," Navrakov said.

"President Chen Hui?" President Hope said. "Can we count on your assistance as well?"

The screens went quiet as everyone focused on the Chinese President. It was a measure of China's economic might and its tenuous connection to the world's other superpowers that no one broke in to try to further persuade him.

"Fine," he finally replied. "We will help. But this matter of Elias Leach is not over."

With the rescue flights agreed to, President Hope disconnected, then called her cabinet together via holo-conference. "Let's focus on assisting the two companies that can launch an LTV the soonest. Get them whatever help we can to speed up the process."

"Madam President," Jay-Edgar interrupted her, "I've got one of the LTVs calling."

"Connect us," President Hope replied.

Zora's image came through. Behind her, Curtik manned the controls.

"Well, howdy," Zora said. "Beautiful day for a bombing, isn't it?"

"Are you all right?"

Seconds passed without a response. For a moment President Hope thought Zora was ignoring her. Then she remembered the delay in transmissions.

"We're just doing a little sightseeing," Zora replied.

"The other LTV?"

Another pause as the signal traveled across half a million miles. "They haven't been able to restore communications but we're keeping in contact via implant."

"Are you able to contact anyone on the Moon?"

Though she understood that the laws of physics demanded the three-second delay, President Hope still wished she could have instantaneous communications. She glanced at Jay-Edgar, who raised his hands in apology.

"I'm afraid not," Zora said. "Their communications were damaged in the blast. And they've lost all power, so they're on batteries only. But our scanners show that quite a few people survive."

"We're sending up a rescue mission," President Hope said. "Brazil and India will lead. The United States can send up reinforcements in a few days."

After the delay, Zora said, "We can't wait here for you to rescue us."

"You may be shot down if you try to land on your own. A number of rogue nations might decide to take advantage of the situation. And many nations have the capability of launching missiles into low-Earth orbit. Your chances are much better if you wait for us to retrieve you."

"That might work," Zora said eventually, "if we hadn't sustained electrical damage in that explosion. Even though we were on the far side of the Moon, there was a massive electromagnetic pulse in that explosion. That's probably what destroyed the power cells on the Moon. It also wiped the satellites."

"Are your LTVs safe to fly back to Earth?"

President Hope looked at General Horowitz, who said, "Perhaps you could start for Earth and offload Devereaux and Jones to one of the rescue LTVs at the halfway point."

This time the delay lasted almost a minute. President Hope saw Zora speaking with people outside the range of the vid pickup, but the audio had been turned off.

When she turned back to the camera, she said, "So you can save the important people? I'm afraid neither Jeremiah nor Devereaux is willing to leave the LTV. They say either we all live or we all die."

"We could transfer all of you to the rescue LTV," President Hope said.

Again Zora turned away. More time elapsed. President Hope, after a glance at General Horowitz, stared at the screen.

"That might get other people killed," Zora finally said. "As you pointed out, there are no guarantees. We'd rather take our chances alone than jeopardize the brave folks coming to rescue the survivors. We'll be there in two days. Either we'll see you then or you'll get a fantastic fireworks show."

The connection severed, the screen going black.

"What do we do now?" General Horowitz asked.

"We try to convince the world not to shoot them down," President Hope replied. She felt another twinge of nausea and put her hand to her stomach. Devereaux and Jeremiah Jones had to survive. Surely even rogue nations like Nigeria understood that. Didn't they? This was about saving humanity, not revenge. Pressure would have to be exerted, not just by the United States, but by the entire developed world. "We've got two days until they reach Earth," she said. "We need to convince everyone that these LTVs must be allowed to land safely. Contact every nation with the capacity to strike against them. I want all our diplomats on this. We' got a lot of work ahead of us."

Chapter Thirty

Colonel Truman coughed as dust saturated his throat. The ground felt cold. He heard his companions coughing and sneezing as well. The two little girls were crying, their parents comforting them. The room was pitch black. When he reached for his PlusPhone, he felt like he'd been stabbed in the back. His right knee hurt too. Some of the rocks from the ceiling collapse must have struck him. The damn PlusPhone was dead, so he couldn't use its flashlight setting. He managed to stop coughing long enough to say:

"Anyone's PlusPhone working? Any lights at all?"

"Hang on," Joffer said, his voice thick. "There's an emergency light somewhere by me."

As he waited for Joffer to find the light, Truman pictured Raddock Boyd, the man he'd killed in Minnesota last year—the mole on Boyd's cheek, the Semper Fi tattoo, the crew cut. Whenever he was alone in the dark he thought of Raddock Boyd. How he wished he could erase that memory.

A yellow light suddenly shone through the dust. More than half the space was covered by a pile of rubble—boulders and jagged rocks that stretched almost to the ceiling at the back end of the room, twenty feet away. The Russian tourists, Gregor and Maria Dmietriev, lay beside Truman, partially covered by rocks. They appeared to be unconscious. "How many people are buried under that pile?" Truman asked.

"Ten," Joffer said. "Besides those two. Your knee is bleeding."

Truman nodded. He looked up at the people standing by the door: the Verloren family; Hicks, the Australian power plant worker; Mishra the Indian tech; Li Huan and his wife Li Chen, engineers both; and Mottz and Joffer. Joffer pulled the Dmietrievs clear and Li Huan and Li Chen began ministering to them. Mottz knelt beside Truman and tenderly squeezed his knee. Truman winced. Taking off his shirt, Mottz tied it tightly around Truman's knee.

"Might be a broken kneecap," Mottz said. "That will at least stop the bleeding." He lifted Truman and set him with his back to the tunnel-side wall. It felt like a knife was twisting inside Truman's back, but he managed not to scream.

"We're all gonna die," Hicks said. He coughed. "Look at that mess. We're dead."

"Shut up," Mottz said as he glanced at the Verlorens. He moved toward the pile of rocks. "The medical supplies are buried along with the doc. We'll have to see if we can dig them out. Everybody quiet. Hello!" he called. "Anybody alive under there?"

Truman heard a soft whirring sound that might have been ringing in his ears. He heard the muffled voices of people in the room next door. Somehow their voices made it through the solid rock wall.

Hicks grabbed the door handle and pulled, but apparently the force of the explosion had warped the heavy metal door and sealed it tight. "Get us out of here," Hicks yelled as he pounded on the door. "Somebody give me a hand with this door."

"Leave the door shut," Li Huan said.

"We gotta get outta here." Hicks continued pounding on the door.

"We don't even know if the tunnel's structurally intact," Brian Verloren said. He hugged Kyler while his wife Roanne held Kaylee in her arms and rocked her side to side.

Joffer grabbed Hicks and pulled him away from the door, then shoved him toward the pile of rocks. "Help Mottz dig."

Hicks stared at Joffer, his hands clenched into fists, while Mottz straightened from his work and looked at Truman.

Truman shook his head, signaling Mottz to leave Hicks alone for the moment, and said, "Joffer, see what you can find out about our neighbors. Are they okay? Are they in contact with anyone on the outside?"

Joffer walked over to the wall and ran his fingers along a crack. Putting his mouth close to the crack, he called out:

"You okay in there?"

"We're fine," someone called back. "Lost all electrical power though. Emergency lights—batteries only. All our PlusPhones and interfaces are fried. No communications with anybody on the outside. How are you?"

"Half the room collapsed. We're digging people out now. Can you get out into the tunnel?"

"When we opened the door, a bunch of rocks spilled in. Now we can't get it to close."

Truman said to Joffer, "Tell them to stack the rocks inside the room and re-seal the door. There might be a leak out in the tunnel."

Joffer relayed the instructions and stepped over to help Mottz pull rocks clear of the pile. Mishra moved into position to take the rocks from Mottz and Joffer and stack them in the corner. Brian bent over to face his daughter. "You stay with Mommy, all right? Daddy's gonna help move these rocks."

"Okay," Kyler said. She looked at Truman as she backed into her mother.

Truman smiled at her. "Everything's going to be fine, Kyler."

Hicks shook his head. "You're all crazy. Those people are dead. Why waste time digging them up?"

Mishra said, "What do you want to do, Hicks? Stand around bitching?"

"I'm not helping dig up a bunch of corpses. Let 'em stay buried."

"The food and water are under that pile as well," Truman said. "Not to mention the medkit and the oxygen generators. You don't dig, you don't eat. And you don't drink."

Hicks stood for a few more minutes, muttering to himself, then began to help Mishra, taking rocks from the Indian tech and placing them atop the pile beside Truman.

Every few minutes, Mottz would hold up his hand, they'd stop digging, and Mottz or Joffer would call out: "Anybody alive under there? Anyone?"

Roanne sat with her back to the door, her daughters on her lap. They kept quiet, thank God. Truman wasn't sure he could handle crying children. He felt nauseated. His throat burned with dust. He smelled urine and bile. Sitting there with nothing to do, he recalled the moment the blast hit—the ground shaking under his feet, people screaming as the lights went out and the ceiling collapsed. Truman had been standing beside the Russians. He'd fallen, pummeled by debris. It had taken him a few seconds to realize that he was screaming too and only then managed to stop himself.

He shook off the thoughts and concentrated on staying calm, smiling in as reassuring a manner as he could at the two girls. Boulders scraped against each other as they were pulled free and stacked in the corner. In a few minutes Mottz and Joffer pulled three bodies clear, their heads and chests bloody and misshapen. Roanne turned the girls' heads away so they wouldn't see the devastating injuries. Hopefully, the fallen had felt no pain.

Truman felt useless sitting against the wall but every time he tried to move he nearly fainted. So he just watched as Mottz and Joffer led the rescue effort.

He thought about the weirdness of how the room next door had survived the blast and how only part of this room had collapsed— the part of the room that was structurally the weakest. There must be tiny fissures running all through the Moon, created by the continual hammering of asteroids over millions of years.

He tightened the bandage on his leg, grunting as he did so. Every movement of the knee felt like someone was sawing across it, ripping tendons and muscles.

"You okay?" Mottz asked.

"Just a little discomfort," Truman replied, his raspy voice betraying his thirst. He wanted to scream—give in to the fear and agony, but he was afraid of starting a panic. I have to be strong, he told himself. These people are my responsibility. He heard a couple people in the other room ranting about death. And for their voices to carry through the crack, they must be shouting. Truman was thankful that his charges were more composed. He caught Kyler's eye and winked at her. She offered a tentative smile.

Mottz stopped working, held up his hands and said, "I got someone here."

"Alive?" Truman asked.

"Can't tell. Joffer, give me a hand."

The cadet joined him in lifting the rock while Hicks and Brian pulled the body clear. It was a woman, her skull an oddly misshapen mass of bloody tissue. Brian kept her mutilated head hidden from his daughters' view. After Mottz and Joffer lowered the boulder to the ground, Mottz handed Brian a dirty cloth, which he placed over the woman's head with a nod of thanks.

"I think I found water," Mishra said.

"Excellent," Joffer said. "We could use a drink." He moved over to Mishra's side and helped remove boulders. "Under here. Mottz, give me a hand."

Mottz stepped to Joffer's side and together the two of them grabbed a massive boulder that would have weighed well over a ton on Earth. They lifted it off the ground and carried it toward the pile of rocks in the front corner where they carefully leaned it against the pile.

Meanwhile, Hicks rushed over to the five-gallon water container and pulled it free. He scraped away some loose dirt and tried to twist the cover off, but it was jammed. "Son of a bitch!"

"Please," Brian said. "That's not going to help."

"Give it to me," Mottz said.

Hicks handed the container to Mottz, who drew his Las-knife and cut the top off. He poured some water into the upside-down cap and handed it to Roanne. First Kaylee, then Kyler took a drink. Mottz filled the cap for them again and passed the container to Truman.

Truman drank slowly, savoring the moisture. He hadn't realized just how parched his throat was. "Thanks," he said. "Let's take a ten-minute break."

Truman didn't want the break—or more precisely, the thoughts that were bound to come with it—but these people couldn't keep working at this feverish pace. The sound of screaming came from the next room. Everyone looked over at the crack in the wall. It lasted for maybe a minute. The ranting died away. Truman recalled that Dr. Lee was next door—probably a tranquilizer.

In the quiet that followed, Truman thought about McKenna and Emily, then for some reason flashed on an image of his older brother Ned, who had disappeared in South America while working for the CIA fifteen years ago. Why was he thinking about Ned now? He had a few old photos of Ned on his broken PlusPhone, but he hadn't looked at them in a while and he was having trouble recalling Ned's face.

Raddock Boyd's face, on the other hand, was clear in his mind. And he could hear the ex-Marine pleading for his life. No, he told himself. That was an accident. You didn't know the stimulants and painkillers in the truth serum would kill him. You were just following orders. Right, tell that to God when you die.

He forced his mind to focus on Emily and McKenna and Lendra. Was it too late to reconcile with Emily? Probably. He wasn't even sure he wanted to. The truth was, he loved Lendra. Perhaps that was stupid, for she wasn't his to love. But if he was honest with himself, he had to admit that he had stronger feelings for her than he did for Emily. McKenna he loved completely, wholly. But she was no longer his little girl. He glanced at Kyler and Kaylee. My God, they were calm—sitting there with their mother's arms around them. They reminded him of McKenna when she was young.

He found his fingers stroking the outline of the glass bulb of neo-dopamine Lendra had given him. Of course! He pulled the necklace out of his pocket. It took him only a few seconds to figure out how to unscrew it. Inside sat a silvery paste. Touching it with his finger, he pulled away a small dab and placed it on his tongue. Within seconds a comforting warmth engulfed him, a rush of optimism as the pain in his back and leg receded. He felt like he could accomplish anything. His mind seemed to expand, slowing down and speeding up at the same time so that every problem presented a solution.

"What's that, sir?" Mottz asked.

"Neo-dopamine," he replied. "Since the pain medication is buried, I thought it might help."

"Good idea," Mottz said. "I could use a hit as well."

"Me too," Joffer said.

"We should all get a hit," Hicks said.

"Okay," Truman said. "Just a tiny dab. It's highly concentrated. Not the girls though."

He allowed the adults to put a finger in the glass bulb and touch it to their lips. For a moment the room was quiet, as people absorbed the drug.

Joffer yelled, "Hoooweee! That's good stuff!"

Mottz nodded. Hicks just smiled, his eyes narrowing. Perhaps he'd taken too much. Roanne began to hum; Brian hugged his daughters and kissed the tops of their heads. Mishra bobbed his head over and over, while Li Huan looked at his hands as if seeing them for the first time. His wife Li Chen appeared unaffected. She pointed to Gregor and Maria. "Them too?"

"Ask the doc next door," Truman said.

Joffer called out the request to Dr. Lee.

"You just gave it to everyone?" Dr. Lee yelled. "This isn't some recreational drug. It's serious medicine—only to be prescribed after a thorough neurological examination. I recommend that none of you take another dose. The risk of addiction is extremely high. The risk of brain damage from overdose is extremely high. And it has an accumulating effect. It builds up in your system over time. It can even change neural pathways—sometimes after a single dose."

"We'll be careful," Truman called back. He screwed the cap on the glass bulb and put the necklace back in his pocket. "All right," he said. "Joffer, tell Dr. Lee to find whatever they can to start enlarging the opening between these two walls. We want it big enough that people can get through if necessary. Also, get them working on trying to fix the communications equipment so we can contact the people at LB2. Maybe those folks are still in touch with someone on the outside. We'll continue our rescue efforts here. We'll need to reach the portable chem-toilet at some point. Okay, let's get to work."

Mottz and Joffer jumped back to the pile and began lifting large boulders, which they passed to Hicks and Mishra, who assisted Li

Huan and Brian in stacking them beside the bodies. The neo-dopamine had given them increased energy and strength. Wow, Truman thought, we'll find those buried people in no time.

And in less than a minute they found two more bodies. Li Huan and Brian stacked them atop the others while Mottz and Joffer continued to dig. Hicks, however, began to slow down, his movements less coordinated. He fell at one point, causing everyone to stop and stare. Laughing, he got to his feet and said, "Whoopsie. Don't know what happened there. I just fell over."

"Maybe you should sit for a while," Truman said.

"I'm fine. Let me gurg. I mean, let me work."

"Okay," Truman said.

They returned to their digging. Glancing up at the ceiling, Truman wondered what else he should be doing, what else he should be taking into account. His eye tracked a reddish dust mote that swirled up and around in a tiny whirlpool of air. Another dust mote did the same. And suddenly Truman realized there was a leak.

The spacesuits were buried in the back of the room next to the oxygen generators—no telling how badly damaged they were. And there was no way, without functioning sensors, to determine just how quickly the room was losing air. Truman studied the rising dust motes, wondering if it was possible to determine by their speed just how much time they had left. He almost laughed. Maybe Lendra could do it, or Devereaux, but Truman's grasp of advanced mathematics was practically nil.

Should he tell his fellow survivors about the problem? Or should he wait until he had no choice? Let them enjoy the moment. Besides, if the oxygen generators and the spacesuits aren't damaged, it won't matter. And it's a slow leak. If that holds true, perhaps we can replace any missing oxygen with airflow from the room next door, which still has its oxygen generators intact.

"Got another body," Mottz said as he reached down into the pile and placed a hand on someone's neck. "Dr. Melsinto. The medkit must be here too."

He and Joffer moved two rocks and pulled the corpse clear, coming up with the medical supplies, which they set beside Li Chen. Mishra removed a large QuikHeal bandage from the medkit and wrapped it around Truman's knee, adjusting the anesthetic to high. He pulled out a back wrap, and when Truman gingerly lifted his shirt, the Indian tech settled it around him.

Truman adjusted the anesthetic on that to high as well and within seconds his back pain vanished. He got to his feet.

"Careful, sir," Mottz said. "You might have serious damage to both your leg and back. Just because they don't hurt anymore doesn't mean you're not making things worse by moving around."

"I'll take it easy," Truman said. "Three more people to find. Then we'll dig up the food, the chem-toilet, the oxygen generators and the spacesuits. Li Huan, perhaps you can move to the crack in the wall and get instructions from Dr. Lee. Hicks and Mishra, help Joffer and Mottz with the heavier boulders. Brian, continue stacking rocks and bodies. I'll help where I can."

"Lork the lagpolly," Hicks said. His face scrunched up in frustration. "Fahgenny oggpoggin wallagoddy." He jabbed his finger in Truman's direction.

"What did you say?" Mottz asked.

"What the hell?" Hicks flushed, his breathing coming quicker, raspier. "Sorry. Don't norg what gort into me."

"Must be the neo-dopamine," Truman said. "We'd better run a scan on you. Come over here."

Hicks rubbed his face with his hand, leaving black smudges on his nose, cheeks and forehead. "You might be right. I feel kinda weird."

Truman found the scanner in the medkit and turned it on. Running it above Hicks' head, he checked the readout, but it presented a series of graphs and lines that made no sense to him. He didn't even know how to translate what he saw. Nevertheless, he walked over to the crack in the wall and called out to Dr. Lee, telling him what he'd found.

Dr. Lee made him run the scan twice more, each time changing the parameters to access different information.

343

"I can't be sure without running the scans myself," Dr. Lee said, "but it sounds like the neo-dopamine is altering his neural pathways. That's not uncommon."

"Should he rest?"

"No," Hicks said. "I can work."

"It probably won't hurt him to work," Dr. Lee called out. "It might even be better for him—get the neo-dopamine out of his system quicker. Just don't let him strain himself."

"There," Hicks said as if he'd just proven some point. "Don't stop me." He grabbed another boulder.

Mottz looked at Truman, who shrugged. "He seems okay."

"Curse I yam," Hicks said. "Butter than you."

Truman reached down and fingered the Las-pistol Zora had provided. It was set to medium—a high stun setting. Hicks hadn't shown any tendency to violence so far, but he'd been hostile and uncooperative. And for some indefinable reason Truman suspected he might erupt.

Joffer apparently agreed for he placed his back to the wall so he could hand rocks off without turning his back on Hicks.

Meanwhile Li Huan relayed instructions from Dr. Lee to Li Chen, who gave Gregor and Maria the prescribed medication. The scanner showed head injuries to both Russians, and Dr. Lee felt that their best chance for survival was to remain unconscious.

Truman moved to Mishra's side, where he could keep an eye on Hicks while helping stack rocks.

Within ten minutes, Mottz, Joffer and Hicks had dug up the remaining three bodies. Although Truman had figured they'd be dead, the certainty that came with their discovery dealt him an almost physical blow.

"Okay," he said. "We'll need food, more water, spacesuits, the chem-toilet, the oxygen generators and any tools we can find. Let's hold off on trying to open the door. Most likely the tunnel has collapsed all down its length." He glanced up at the dust motes, still swirling and rising toward the ceiling. "And we shouldn't dawdle trying to find the oxygen generators either. I think we've got a small leak."

"A leak?" Brian said.

"Narg!" Hicks said. He punched the wall hard, not even wincing as he did so.

"How do you know?" Roanne said.

Truman explained about the rising dust motes and said, "So we'll want to get the oxygen generators started if we can. If not, we'll pull oxygen from next door. And we've still got the spacesuits. We have twelve suits for thirteen survivors, assuming the suits aren't too badly damaged."

"Who doesn't get a suit?" Hicks said. "I vote one of the Russians."

"We'll worry about that if and when we have to," Truman replied.

Joffer said, "I'm kinda surprised you told us about the leak—expected you to keep that quiet. I've been checking it and I estimate we have fourteen to sixteen hours before the pressure enlarges the leak to a point where we're losing more oxygen than we can get from next door."

"Can we patch it?" Mishra asked.

Truman shook his head. "I'm not even sure we can find it." He looked up at the dark ceiling, jagged and cracked, maybe eight feet above his head. He saw multiple fissures, any one of which might lead to the outside. "And even if we do, how do we reach it?"

Mottz said, "Let's get those oxygen generators and see if they're still functional."

Hicks lifted a rock the size of a basketball and began turning it over in his hands as if studying it.

"Hicks," Truman said.

Hicks ignored him.

"Hicks!" Truman said. "You okay?"

"Sharg," Hicks said. He flung the rock at Mottz's head. Mottz, only a few feet away, raised an arm in defense. The rock struck him a glancing blow as Kyler and Kaylee screamed. Before Truman could grab his Las-pistol, Joffer launched himself at Hicks. The cadet dove horizontally, landing a punch that caused Hicks' head to snap backwards. The force of the blow pushed Hicks into the wall, his head striking it with a thud that made Truman cringe. Hicks fell to the ground, where he lay unmoving. Once again Truman was reminded how ordinary he himself was. Mottz—an Elite Ops trooper—had almost escaped unscathed, while Joffer was even faster than Mottz. He'd knocked Hicks out before Truman could unholster his Las-pistol.

Kaylee began crying again. Her mother clutched her tightly and began humming to her. Kyler patted her sister's arm and said, "It's okay, Kaylee. He won't hurt you."

Mottz touched his forehead, where a gash bled profusely. Joffer meanwhile bent over Hicks to check on him. Mishra and Brian waited, clearly frightened and unsure what to do next.

"Here," Li Chen said as she reached for Mottz. "Let me put a QuikHeal bandage on that for you."

As Li Chen bandaged Mottz, Joffer dragged Hicks over to the pile of corpses and placed him atop it.

"He's dead?" Truman asked.

"A little bit," Joffer said. "Guess I hit him too hard."

Truman sighed. Everyone turned to him, looking for his reaction. Was that murder or self-defense? And did it matter? It was probably necessary given the circumstances. He recalled Boyd's death and almost wished he'd been charged with negligent homicide or involuntary manslaughter. He deserved to be punished. But Joffer was just a kid. Truman couldn't lay that kind of guilt on him.

"Okay," Truman said. "That's an unfortunate accident. But we've got more important things to worry about. We need to dig up the oxygen generators and the spacesuits. Mishra, you and Brian give Mottz and Joffer a hand."

"Should we say something?" Roanne said. "A prayer?"

"We can take a moment of silence," Truman said. He bowed his head and noticed the others doing the same—even Joffer.

But a few seconds later Joffer said, "You hear that?"

"What?" Truman asked. Then he heard it. "That hissing sound?"

Joffer nodded. "The leak's getting worse."

Truman studied the dust motes spiraling upward. Yes, they appeared to be moving faster.

"Stop what you're doing," Truman called out to the next room. "We've got a leak here to the outside. You need to seal off your room from ours. Do whatever you can to patch that crack. Got it?"

"Got it," Dr. Lee called back. "Good luck."

"You too," Truman called. He lowered his voice. "All right, let's see if those oxygen generators are working and let's dig up those spacesuits just in case."

It took them ten minutes to find the first oxygen generator. But it was smashed and useless. The second one looked hardly any better. Mishra tried to start it, but it only made a small coughing sound. The third and final oxygen generator looked less damaged, but it too wouldn't start.

"Looks like we need those spacesuits," Mottz said.

Truman turned to Mishra. "Can you look at the oxygen generators?" he said. "Maybe get one of them working?"

"I'll give it a shot," Mishra said. "But even if I get one running, it might not provide enough oxygen to offset what we're losing." He grabbed the toolkit that had been unearthed with the third generator and began taking the machine apart. Li Huan and Li Chen moved over to help him, having done all they could for Gregor and Maria.

"Let's get back to it," Truman said. His knee twinged as he stepped to the pile of rocks, but he refused to succumb to the pain.

Mottz and Joffer distributed stimulants from the medkit, but Truman decided to forego taking anything else at the moment. The neo-dopamine combining with the anesthetics left him feeling somewhat detached and he was afraid a stimulant would give him a heart attack. Plus the image of Raddock Boyd solidified his desire to avoid taking more drugs.

They worked more slowly now, pacing themselves as they dug up the spacesuits, stopping every few minutes to look at the ceiling, as if they might be able to determine whether the leak was getting worse. It took a couple hours to get the last suit clear of the rubble. Five of them were ripped in places and another's regulator was damaged beyond repair, which meant they were six suits short.

"We need that oxygen generator," Truman said to Mishra.

"We're working on it," Mishra said. "We swapped out the voltostats and the transducers but we still have a few parts that are shot. We'll either have to repair them or find something to use as a replacement."

Joffer said, "Can I give you a hand?"

"We got enough people. What we need are parts."

Li Chen held up a damaged spacesuit. "What about using parts from this?"

"Good idea," Truman said. "Let us know what we can do to help."

He glanced down at Gregor and Maria. "Mottz," he said, "Can we construct some sort of pocket using tarps that we could fill with air from an oxygen generator?"

"Be hard to seal it off, sir. But I suppose we could use a Las-knife to weld the edges. Put people in spacesuits and have them checking the seals while we wait for a rescue. But who goes inside the tarp and who gets the suits?"

Joffer said, "The Russians go in the tarp. We couldn't take care of them inside suits anyway."

Mottz nodded. "That's logical. I volunteer for the tarp as well."

Truman shook his head. "No. We need you in a suit. Joffer too. And the engineers and Mishra."

Brian said, "I guess that leaves us in the tarp. The girls won't fit in the suits anyway."

Truman said, "I'll go in the tarp with one of you. The other one can have a suit."

Roanne said, "No. We'll stay with our daughters in the tarp."

"We don't have to decide right now," Truman said. He shivered. He also noticed that he was having to take slightly deeper breaths. "It's getting cold in here."

"Because we're losing oxygen," Joffer said. "I think there's a portable heater in the corner over there." He stepped through the rocks toward the back of the room.

"What about trying to get into the tunnel?" Mottz said. "Maybe it hasn't been compromised."

"I'd like to wait until we don't have any choice," Truman said. "If it's got a leak, it'll only make things worse."

A crack sounded from up above.

"More shifting rock?" Truman said.

"Probably," Mottz replied.

"Maybe it helped us," Truman said. "Maybe the shifting rock partially sealed the leak." Though he knew he was likely wrong, he thought it might help morale to accentuate the possibility of something good happening.

Then the oxygen generator started and a cheer went up.

"We've got air," Mishra said as he hooked the generator up to a pile of rocks. "Not sure how long this thing will run. We had to patch a couple of systems. We'll keep it going as long as we can."

"Good job," Truman said. "Now we wait and hope for the best."

Chapter Thirty-One

E lias Leach entered his old office. The Elite Ops trooper who had escorted him stopped outside the door, while his comrade stood inside the doorway—unarmored thankfully. Perhaps the President had taken his phobia into account. Or maybe they just didn't perceive him to be a threat. He might show them differently.

His skin itched—a psychological reaction, he told himself—just fear of the nanobots inside him. If he could only control the fear, the discomfort would go away. President Hope stood beside General Horowitz in front of Elias' desk, almost as if she feared sitting behind it. Or maybe she just wanted a position of power over him. As always, she looked magnificent.

Why had she sent for him? Did she need advice? Had she finally realized that he was right, that this action had been necessary? If so, he was prepared to be magnanimous—to help her out in this difficult time.

"Madam President," Elias said as he came to a halt. "General Horowitz." He nodded to Jay-Edgar, who turned away, devoting his attention to the holo-projections against the far wall: various news reports, all silenced. Was Jay-Edgar still on his side? "How may I help you?"

"I think you've helped us enough," President Hope said.

"Then why did you call for me?"

"We're sending you away."

"To The Hague?" If so, the people of the world would soon hear why he'd created the cadet program in the first place. The failures of their leaders necessitated his actions. He could picture himself speaking out in righteous indignation.

"I'm afraid not," President Hope said. "We've decided to hand you over to the Chinese in return for their assistance."

"The Chinese?" Elias shivered again. How could she hand him over to the Chinese? "But they . . ."

"They won't put you on trial publicly, no." President Hope read his mind. "So you won't get the bully pulpit you seek."

Elias' knees weakened, his chest tightened, his heart raced. Despite the nanobots inside him, he could swear he was having a heart attack, or another stroke. The Chinese would bury him deep, torture him over many years, making sure to keep him alive so that he suffered the maximum amount. How could President Hope surrender him to that kind of future?

"I can still help you," Elias said. "I understand the twisted minds of the Russian and Chinese leaders better than anyone else."

"You probably do," President Hope replied.

"I can get them to pay reparations and promises of future assistance in rebuilding the lunar settlement as a penalty for refusing to allow the orbiting Las-cannon to shoot down the Nigerian missile."

"Go for the jugular, eh?"

"There will never be a better time. This is the last best chance for America to be the preeminent leader of the world. Don't throw it away because of my errors. Don't succumb to some misguided notion that America deserves to do penance."

President Hope smiled. "Now is the crucial time to take charge, to dictate the direction Earth will take for the next century. An Ameri-centric view is necessary to guide humanity's growth properly. Otherwise, the chaos that reigns on Earth will spread to the solar system and the galaxy. There will be a Chinese planet and a Russian one and a Brazilian one. Humanity's future requires a more diverse expansion that benefits all people."

"You say that ironically," Elias said. "But it's true."

"Perhaps," President Hope conceded. "I'm tempted to keep using you—to rely on your vast knowledge of the way the world works, and to take advantage of your many contacts. But that road only leads where we've been. You're a dangerous man, Elias. I'm sorry, but I have to wean myself off you."

An itch developed behind his right eye, deep inside the skin. He reached up and massaged his temple. He glanced at the Elite Ops trooper guarding the door. "When are you planning to turn me over to the Chinese?"

"That's why I've called you here," President Hope said. "The only way they'll guarantee that their allied nations won't fire on the incoming LTVs is if we hand you over immediately."

"So this is the end?" Elias trembled. He couldn't allow himself to be locked away forever, with no chance of escape, no future except pain and loneliness. That would drive him mad. He had no choice. Catching Jay-Edgar's eye, he gave an almost imperceptible nod and moved toward his chair. "May I sit for a moment?"

"Don't get too comfortable," President Hope said. "They'll be coming for you soon."

"If I'm handed over to the Chinese," Elias said as he sat, "they'll force me to tell them what I know about this country's secrets. I don't wish to betray America. You know that. But I won't be able to hold out for long against their truth serums and torture. I will spill what I know, sooner rather than later. Even more terrifying, there are always new drugs, new treatments that can compel obedience. We proved it with the Elite Ops and the cadets. Which means that I might be compelled to work against this country's best interests."

President Hope nodded. "That is certainly possible."

"So how can you do it?"

President Hope blushed. "There are ways to ensure you don't betray us."

No! Elias imagined the worst thing he could think of, the greatest punishment he could ever receive. "You're going to lobotomize me?"

President Hope held up her hands in apology. "I can't in good conscience destroy your mind. However, there are drugs that will destroy your memory and limit your Intellectual Potential."

Breathe, Elias told himself as he pushed the chair back a few inches, putting himself only a couple feet away from the secret exit, wondering what was taking Jay-Edgar so long. Perhaps the young man hadn't noticed his signal. Dare Elias make it more obvious?

"This is your fault," President Hope continued. "You played God far too often. And there's no excuse for that, no matter how noble your intentions. You don't get to choose the future for nine billion souls."

Elias scratched his arms and chest; the itching had become almost unbearable. He felt dizzy, lightheaded. Had Jay-Edgar betrayed him? It wasn't possible. Elias had to struggle not to look at the boy, not to notice his presence.

He waited. He hoped.

The President stared at him, no hostility in her eyes. No warmth either. Just determination. Elias' hands rose toward his face, his fingers curling into claws.

Jay-Edgar said, "Excuse me, Madam President. I'm getting a strange transmission here."

Elias' hands stopped moving. A surge of adrenaline—a tingling—pulsed throughout his body. He'd never doubted the boy.

"What is it?" the President asked.

"It's some kind of—"

Jay-Edgar's voice became a scream of agony as a surge of electromagnetic particles filled the room.

Elias braced himself. Even though he was sitting in the "eye" of the discharge, and despite the fact that he was prepared for it, he was nearly overcome by the intensity of the burst. It pressed on him with physical, almost suffocating force. Disoriented, he blinked rapidly, trying to figure out where he was. The Elite Ops trooper fell to the floor, screaming. The President and General Horowitz collapsed, crying out. Elias hoped they'd be okay. He slid out of his chair and knelt beside the wall. The Elite Ops trooper outside banged on the office door. It would give way any moment. Elias placed his palm on a slightly discolored patch of wallpaper.

A small door opened in the wall and Elias crawled through. When the door snapped shut behind him, the disorienting effect of the electromagnetic particles vanished. His vision and balance were restored. He was on all fours in a small room that was actually an elevator. It dropped, his stomach lurching as he fell toward the sub-basement. This escape route had been designed a decade ago. Elias had never expected to need it.

Taking a deep breath, he fought the fear and surprise that threatened his ability to think. He needed to concentrate on the precise sequence of events that would help him disappear. Jay-Edgar had perfected the system in the past two years but it still required Elias to follow the instructions perfectly.

The elevator reached bottom and the door opened to complete blackness. Elias grabbed onto the handles placed there to help him to his feet and stepped out.

Soon the pursuit would begin: Elite Ops troopers, radar detection, local law enforcement.

The lights came on. A tunnel appeared before him. A few paces ahead, a small electric cart waited. Elias took a seat and reached for the package next to the steering column. While the car drove itself down the tunnel, Elias opened the package and put the neo-skin mask on. It was a perfect match for Manyara Harris' face. He also put on a pair of gloves.

The Elite Ops trooper would be on his way to the basement. Reinforcements would be called, converging on this location. Elias felt exposed. Jay-Edgar's calculations about how much time he would have might no longer be accurate, given the increased number of troopers in the area protecting the President. He expected a yell or a shot with every breath.

After what seemed a long time, the car reached the end of the tunnel, where another tiny elevator stood waiting. Elias ducked inside. The elevator rose to the roof of an old office building, where an MX8 personal jet sat under a temporary shelter. Elias glanced at the CINTEP building he'd called home for so long, ducked under the shelter, climbed into the jet and donned the shabby dress that Manyara had placed in a granny bag just inside the door. He pulled out a gray wig and secured it atop his head with a grungy scarf. Finally he made certain that the Las-pistol and the scatterer in the bottom of the bag were both fully charged before stepping into the cockpit.

A series of commands set the autopilot that would fly the MX8 and initiate the auto-destruct sequence. Next he removed the partial skeleton from its stasis container; the bones—from a dead homeless man of a similar age and with the same measurements as Elias—had been sterilized, then infused with samples of his DNA. The only problem was the recent addition of nanobots to his bloodstream. Would the absence of nanobots in the wreckage alert his pursuers to the fact that he'd not been aboard at the time of the explosion? He had to hope not—nothing he could do about it now. He compressed the stasis container and put it into his granny bag.

His last task before leaving was to ensure that the people looking for him believed he was onboard. He switched on the electronic biochemical radiator that Jay-Edgar had installed last year. A brilliant idea: the radiator would emit a human signature to any scanner—a false positive that would convince his pursuers he was aboard.

Slinging the granny bag over his shoulder, Elias activated the scatterer and stepped out of the plane. He checked the time: ten minutes. Another glance at the CINTEP building: he still saw no one. Was the pursuit coming?

Elias crouched below the three-foot-high safety wall that bordered the roof and scurried toward the fire escape on hands and knees, reaching it in less than thirty seconds. He doubted he would have been able to make this escape unaided had he not been injected with the nanobots. His formerly fragile body would not have been able to move quickly enough. The MX8 hummed as its engines ignited. Without looking back, Elias slid down the chute, clutching his dress to his legs.

When he reached the alley behind the warehouse, he straightened the dress and looked around: empty. Walking slowly, he affected the limp and slouch of Manyara Harris; he tried to remember every detail of the way she moved. His nerves screamed at him to go faster but he knew that would only draw attention. He had to hope that the scatterer would deflect any scanners directed his way.

As he reached the sidewalk, the MX8, having reached full power, took off. From street level it sounded like an old fashioned automobile as it accelerated away. Elias joined his fellow pedestrians and lifted his head to follow the jet's progress. The MX8 arced upward.

After a moment, he continued on his way. His heart raced. How many years had it been since he'd walked down a busy sidewalk? Again he felt an itch behind his right eye. He longed to scratch his cheeks but was afraid to do so with the mask on.

As he walked, he found himself avoiding eye contact, even though he knew no one could recognize him. He was probably the most hated man on the planet right now, so if someone by chance figured out who he was, he'd have to start shooting. He clutched the Las-pistol at the bottom of his bag, forcing himself to move slowly, stay in character. He had to be Manyara Harris, cleaning woman, not Elias Leach, enemy of the people.

He bent over slightly, limped a little—but not too much, as Manyara had coached him, because he didn't want anyone to offer him assistance. And it was working. The pedestrians mostly ignored him as they hurried on by. Occasionally one would glance up at the MX8. The sidewalk, though busy, wasn't as crowded as it was during rush hour.

Elias craned his neck and twisted his head to watch the jet shrink as it flew farther away. Would the charges detonate before the Elite Ops fired upon it?

"Watch where you're goin', lady!" a heavyset man warned as Elias bumped into him.

"Sorry," Elias spoke in a high-pitched voice, his sweaty fingers tightening on the grip of the Las-pistol in his bag.

"These are brand new shoes," the man said. "Cost me nine hundred dollars." He stared hard at Elias, eyebrows drawn together in suspicion, nose wrinkling in disgust.

Anger and fear flooded Elias. Why was this nutcase talking about his shoes? And they weren't new. Scuffmarks were visible. Heart racing, Elias sidestepped the man. He wanted to kill the bastard. I'm a little old lady, you crazy son of a bitch!

Continuing on, Elias made a conscious effort to relax his grip on his weapon. With his peripheral vision he saw the vanishing MX8 blow apart in a fiery explosion. The pedestrians stopped, oohing and aahing, asking each other if they'd seen *that*, exclaiming at how dangerous Washington was becoming before continuing on their way. Elias noted that the heavyset man was still watching him and lowered his head. He walked east.

The moron followed him. Perfect! I'm going to have to kill this bastard to get away. He tried to blend in with the foot traffic. Limping along, his eyes constantly sweeping the area for police officers or Elite Ops troopers, he focused on keeping his head down, avoiding eye contact. His breaths came in rapid gulps. How was he going to dispatch this insane idiot without drawing attention to himself?

He glanced back. The man was still behind him, his intense glare focused on Elias as he maintained pace. Halfway down the next block Elias spotted an alley. He stopped a few paces inside its entrance and leaned against a building wall, waiting for the big man to approach. Heart racing, stomach churning, throat dry, palms sweating: he gripped the Las-pistol and adjusted the setting to medium.

He contemplated what he'd lost—CINTEP—the organization he'd built from nothing twenty years before. Would it survive? Perhaps under the leadership of Lendra?

Hopefully the President would recommend Lendra as CINTEP's new director. That way the President would get a woman she could theoretically control, one who would exercise influence for years to come, right in line with President Hope's oft-stated desire to be more than just a short-term thinker. And Elias might get an ally who could help him in the future, who could bring him back to power once President Hope's tenure was up.

The man suddenly appeared at the alley entrance. He stopped there, glaring at Elias. For a moment neither moved. Elias gripped the Las-pistol tightly. The man raised his arm and pointed at Elias. "God sees you," he said. "You can't hide. He will find you and smite you with his righteous wrath. Blasphemer! God sees everything."

A couple hurried past on the sidewalk, trying to ignore the man as he directed his anger at Elias.

Come here, Elias thought. Step a little closer.

"Only the righteous shall be saved," the man said. "Those like you will burn in eternal hellfire." He turned and walked away.

Elias took a couple of deep breaths. He'd almost fired.

He waited a moment until he was sure he'd regained his composure, then continued on to the hideout—a basement apartment he owned through a complicated series of cutouts. Before he went inside, he gazed at the smoky sky, inhaled deeply the acrid particles that polluted the air. The Las-cannon strikes at dozens of locations across the country—not to mention the many strikes on top-secret military facilities around the planet—had brought an ashy dustiness to the atmosphere. Already meteorologists were predicting that worldwide temperatures would average ten degrees below normal for the next year. Elias wouldn't feel that difference, however. He would experience the world only vicariously, buried underground, hidden away in a cell.

He checked to make sure no one was watching as he entered the apartment building. He made his way down the stairs to his new apartment, accessing it with his thumbprint. The door opened to reveal little more than a cement-lined room—thirty by twenty feet—adjoining a sumptuous bathroom with a whirlpool bath/shower and a red cedar sauna. A dampening field protected the space; it would display an image of an empty apartment to any scanner. Along the far wall hung a series of screens. He wondered if news of his escape had made it to the media yet.

His chair, positioned in the middle of the room, slowly spun around. He scrambled to grab the Las-pistol in his bag as Manyara Harris came into view.

"Well," she said, "not such a big man now."

"What the hell?" Elias said. "How did you . . . Get out of my chair."

Manyara laughed as she climbed to her feet and made her way over. "You make that dress look awful."

"It's not me," Elias answered. "It's the dress."

Manyara cackled. "Took a long time to find something perfect for you."

"Thanks a lot." Elias couldn't help but smile.

"Welcome to your new home."

Manyara stood a few feet away, studying him, her eyes alive with humor and intelligence, and just a trace of sympathy. "Look much better than I remember," she finally added.

"Nanobots," Elias replied. "I had another stroke a while back."

"That's not it." Manyara grinned. "You look good when you look like me."

"How did you know I'd be here?"

"Jay-Edgar sent me a message. Figured you could use a little help."

"I was scared out of my mind," Elias admitted as he removed the scarf and wig. "I'm such an idiot. Almost panicked and killed some nutcase out there."

Manyara stepped in close and pulled the mask free. Holding it up, she said, "You're a brilliant man. Almost as smart as me."

"I wouldn't go that far," Elias said.

Manyara smiled. "Perhaps not. But you got away from them. I bet not even your Jeremiah Jones could have done that." She removed her hand and gestured at his dress. "Why don't you take a shower? I've got to go soon. If I don't show up to clean your office . . ."

"Why don't you shower with me?" Elias asked as he traced her cheek with the back of his hand.

Manyara slapped his hand away. "Stop it. You're a dirty old man."

"I think it's the nanobots." Elias shivered. "That reminds me. Dr. Hassan was going to get me some neo-dopamine for my anxiety. I'll need that as soon as you can get me some."

"It might take a few days." Manyara pointed toward the bathroom. "Go. Shower. Now."

Elias shut off the scatterer, took off his dress and handed it to Manyara. As he stripped out of his coveralls, he wiggled his bottom at her. She just laughed. "Sorry, hon," she said. "I've got to go. I left some food in the oven."

Elias smelled it now—a blend of mild spices. But he wasn't hungry.

As she grabbed her bag and headed for the door, she called over her shoulder: "I'll check on you tomorrow."

Elias still didn't understand why she wouldn't let him get her medical license reinstated. How long could she continue punishing herself for agreeing to euthanize his dying wife?

He entered the sauna, which Manyara had warmed to a comfortable 130°F, and turned on the screen against the wall. As he suspected, a news story was already playing about his escape and death. General Horowitz told reporters that they'd underestimated his resourcefulness but that the jet he'd used had been sitting for so long that an electrical short had likely caused it to explode. Elias wasn't fooled by the report. He knew they'd still be looking for him.

He switched off the news and let his body relax. But now that he was no longer tense, the urge to scratch increased, eventually driving him to the shower, where he stood under the cool water, refusing to scratch, focusing on anything besides the itching. After drying off and changing into fresh clothes, he made his way into the media center and slumped into his chair before the blank screens.

The Chinese wouldn't believe President Hope's story. Would they attack the incoming LTVs or just let various allies do it for them?

The itching intensified. Elias longed to be outside under whatever sky existed, no matter how polluted, walking through a park or along a beach while Jay-Edgar fed him data on Earth's continuing crises, deciding his species' fate, instead of sitting in the dark: an impotent rat in a cage of his own making.

An unreasoning fear came over him: a nightmare scenario wherein he was implanted with nanobots that gradually turned him into something less than human, a machine afflicted by madness. The itch became almost unbearable. It's just a phobia, he told himself, the Frankenstein complex. But panic soon overtook him. He gripped the armrests tightly, fighting the urge to scratch, struggling for breath, rocking back and forth. His fingers dug into the fabric of the chair as his forearms twitched, pulling at his hands. He gripped the chair harder, refusing to succumb to the intensifying impulses.

He needed neo-dopamine.

His head throbbed, itching in a cacophonous symphony of discordant torture. Although the only sound in the room was the hum of the electrical equipment, Elias heard a raucous jangling in his ears. He took deep breaths, half screaming, half moaning, sweat pouring down his forehead, causing him to itch even more. He refused to succumb to it. He suspected that even the slightest touch would compel him to claw at himself.

He closed his eyes and shivered, taking deep breaths.

After a time he was able to control himself. His breathing slowed; his pulse dropped. I can control my mind, he told himself. I don't need neo-dopamine to keep the itch at bay. At least that bastard Eldridge Cunningham didn't follow me here.

"Who says I didn't?"

"You're not real. I just need some neo-dopamine and you'll vanish."

"Too bad you don't have any."

The itch returned, more insistent than before. Reaching up, Elias scratched his cheek tentatively. God, that felt good! But the itch didn't go away completely. Again he scratched himself, more heavily this time, drawing a rivulet of blood. He scratched more harshly, feeling for the nanobots he knew were under his skin. He caught one, or at least something gritty that he removed, squeezing it between thumb and forefinger. And for a moment he felt blessed relief. Then to his horror, the itch returned.

Chapter Thirty-Two

Taditha Poole rubbed her belly, hoping to quell the nausea, and stared at the screen in front of her, searching the northern sector of South America for oncoming missiles. Although she was glad to be heading home, she knew that the closer they came to Earth, the greater the danger became.

Beside her, Lendra alternated between studying southern Africa and the devastating crater on the Moon. She leaned in and said, "It never occurred to me that I could be in love with two people at the same time. It doesn't make sense."

"Love never does," Poole replied, her mind drifting back to Jack Marschenko and the precious few days they'd had together.

Lendra turned to look back at Jeremiah, huddled with Devereaux, Zora and Quark, either discussing strategy or analyzing data in the back of the LTV while Curtik and Racine flew the ship. "Do you think he'll ever love me again?"

Poole shrugged. She didn't care. Lendra was a lesser version of Eli—a seeker after power. Poole suspected that the real reason she loved Jones was because she thought—at least on a subconscious level—that he could enhance her ability to take over CINTEP. And maybe that made her the perfect person for the job. But Poole was tired of the games and strategies. She just wanted to be left alone. No chance of that anymore. Given what she'd done to those kids on the Moon, she was going to be forced to continue working for CINTEP indefinitely.

"Look," Lendra pointed to an image of seven LTVs nearing the Moon. "The rescue ships are almost there."

"Shouldn't you be focusing on southern Africa?" Poole said.

"They're not going to attack us," Lendra said. "The Middle East is the primary threat."

"What about Angola and Zimbabwe?"

"Don't worry, I'm watching them. And you don't have to watch South America at all." Lendra reached over and changed the view on Poole's screen, getting an enlarged image of the LTVs.

The Brazilian vessel—green with a yellow diamond and a blue globe at the diamond's center to represent the country's flag—led the group of seven LTVs as they neared the Moon.

"How many people do you think survived?" Lendra asked.

"I'm sure Colonel Truman is fine," Poole replied as she returned her screen to its view of northern South America. "You saw the overlay of the blast area against the bases. The farthest sections look virtually untouched—just a few cracks. Probably more than half the colony survived."

"But did he go to the farthest room or did he insist on being heroic and place himself in the area closest to the blast?"

"I think we should worry about ourselves," Poole said. "A lot of people want us dead."

From the cockpit, Curtik said, "Eyes peeled, people. We enter orbit in a few minutes."

Poole studied Curtik. He was a new person since he'd taken the helm of the LTV—no longer a child. Maybe that was because his life was at stake now too. Though as soon as Poole had the thought, she dismissed it. Curtik wouldn't be concerned with his own safety. More likely he relished the idea of testing himself against whatever Earth threw at him.

Zora moved to the front of the LTV. As she passed, Poole noted the tension lines around her eyes and the rigidity of her posture. She hadn't slept in the two days since they'd left the Moon. Probably she hadn't slept for a week. Fortunately her implant allowed her brain to mimic sleep when she was resting. Otherwise Poole suspected she wouldn't be able to function at all right now.

Poole wondered how Rendela was holding up in the other LTV. She found that she missed Rendela, her guard and near-constant companion for the past many days. Now that she thought about it,

Poole couldn't remember Rendela ever doing anything horrible. She'd been a remarkably decent captor.

There was a lot to admire about all these kids. Live or die, they'd all excelled in some way or other: Curtik with inventive cruelty, Crazy Vigg with insight and courage, Wee Willie with intelligence, Rendela with steadfastness and calm loyalty, Zora with brilliant leadership. Some day, someone would take note of that fact and use the techniques Poole, Hackett and others had pioneered to design better people.

Poole shifted her attention to Zora, bent over Racine, her back tense as she gripped the handrests on her chair, and stared at the instrumentation in the LTV's cockpit.

Zora pressed the screen in front of Racine. Then she turned around to face the LTV's passengers. She gestured toward the back of the LTV, where Quark, Jeremiah and Devereaux stood. "We've been monitoring communications into and out of hi-tech military facilities. We've sent out distress calls through regular channels, and the camera feed is being broadcast via satellite. No one's threatened us yet. But signal traffic out of a dozen nations is suspiciously quiet. Someone's going to fire on us soon."

Dr. Garcia Delgado said, "You can't blame them. You blew up half the planet."

Curtik spun around. "Oh, come on. Half? Really? A tiny smidgeon. A minute sliver. A fingernail."

"What about Singapore and Istanbul? You've killed millions."

"Under a compulsion," Devereaux said.

"Their actions were still unforgivable," Dr. Westin said. "They knew they were murdering innocents."

"We can debate the question later," Zora said, "like at our trials. Though we won't have to worry about it if they blow us out of the sky."

"The United States is requesting safe passage for the LTVs," Lendra said, tapping her interface to indicate that she'd picked up the transmission. "And President Hope is warning all nations that there will be consequences for firing upon us."

"What does that mean?" Dr. Floyd asked.

"Not much," Jeremiah answered. "It just confirms that the attack will come from countries with poor economic and diplomatic ties to the United States."

"My analysis," Lendra said, "shows that Pakistan is the greatest threat, followed by Nigeria, Sudan, Egypt, the rest of the Middle East, then parts of the Far East and the rest of Northern Africa. They all consider themselves victims of First World oppression. And they all have sufficient military arsenals—mostly purchased from China and Russia—to attack us as we near the planet's surface."

Zora said, "We'll be coming in over the South Pole. That'll make any attack more difficult."

Curtik said, "Entering orbit."

Poole checked her screen. Sure enough, they'd reached Earth's outer atmosphere and were circling the planet, north to south.

"This is when it starts to get dangerous," Rendela spoke from her ship.

"We'll lead you in," Wee Willie added. "Stay on a forty-degree vector to avoid the potential debris field."

"We go in together," Zora said.

"Negative," Wee Willie said. "It makes more sense to maximize our chances of survival. That means separating. Tell her, Curtik."

"He's right," Curtik said.

Zora shook her head. "You make assumptions that may not be correct. There's no guarantee that the first LTV will be the most likely target. There's no guarantee that a forty-degree vector will ensure our survival. I say we go in together. We live or die together."

"Doesn't matter to me," Curtik said. "I'll fly it any way you want. But we need a decision now."

Rendela said, "We have to do it, Zora. Your LTV has the more important people. We'll provide whatever cover we can."

Zora sighed. "Fine."

Rendela said, "Try to keep up with me, Curtik."

"Oh, this is war!" Curtik yelled. "Strap yourselves in, people. We got ourselves a roller coaster."

As Devereaux, Jeremiah and Quark returned to their seats, Jeremiah hobbling painfully, Zora strapped herself in to the chair immediately behind the cockpit and said, "Keep your eyes on the monitors and the areas I've assigned you to. Even though we expect the attack to come from the regions Lendra identified, that doesn't mean we won't see an attack from somewhere else."

Jeremiah said, "There's also the possibility that someone will fire at us from a submarine or a ship, so watch the oceans too."

"Right," Zora said. "Dr. Poole, Lendra, you keep monitoring communications. Curtik, Rendela, Racine, Wee Willie, put on your spacesuits."

Despite the mock gravity flight suit, Curtik practically bounced to the back of the LTV cabin, a huge grin on his face.

"Not the helmets yet," Zora added. "But bring them with you."

After Curtik returned in his spacesuit, Racine donned hers. Because they'd left spacesuits for the people staying at LB3, they only had two per LTV. And the suits were reserved for the pilots, though it didn't matter. Any direct strike against either LTV would mean certain death for the occupants, spacesuit or not. But if there were a small leak, pilots wearing spacesuits might be able to land the LTV. The passengers would simply have to make do with oxygen masks, and hope that the inside of the LTV didn't become a vacuum.

"We're suited up," Rendela said from the other ship, "and rarin' to go."

Zora laughed. "So are we."

Poole suddenly felt love for them all, all these fragile humans struggling to survive. Even Curtik. Even Lendra. Out here in the vacuum of space, they were all equal. Quark, Jeremiah and the cadets—they were just as dependent on the bubbles of oxygen inside their crafts as Poole was. One laser strike, one direct hit by a rocket and they'd all be dead. And that would be a terrible thing, for they were good people; they all had much to offer the world. She herself was the worst of them—or perhaps Lendra. But Poole would change if she got the chance.

Shaking her head, she concentrated on her screen. Beside her, Lendra tensed up. Poole looked around and saw that the other doctors aboard all gripped their armrests tightly, while Quark and Devereaux appeared unconcerned.

"I can't believe they're not afraid," Poole said, tilting her head to indicate Quark and Devereaux.

"Oh, they're afraid," Lendra said. "They're just acting brave for us."

"Maybe," Poole said. But she wondered if that was true. Perhaps they had conquered their fear. She knew Jones was afraid, but she couldn't see him because he was seated directly behind her.

"Helmets on," Zora said. "Prepare to execute de-orbit burn."

"Copy that," Rendela said.

Curtik put on his helmet and began the de-orbit burn to slow the LTV. Poole felt increasing pressure. Her nausea, a constant for two days, lessened as the increased gravitational pull dropped her stomach to its rightful place. No matter how advanced the mock gravity flight suits, they were no match for Earth's gravity.

Thank you, God, she thought. Now just get us down to the ground without some idiot firing at us.

The chatter coming through Poole's interface took all her attention. It increased to where she couldn't track anywhere near all of it, so she had to scan it rapidly, searching for patterns and changes that might indicate a threat. Her work prevented her from catching the beautiful colors of reentry but she heard Quark pointing them out to the doctors across the aisle.

"Okay," Zora said, "We've reached re-entry. Now's when the attacks are most likely. Stay sharp."

"I'm getting increased chatter from Nigeria," Lendra said. "And they're broadcasting telemetry on our position."

"I got a missile launch," Wee Willie said, his voice sounding slightly metallic because of his helmet. "Pakistan."

"I see it," Zora said. "Broadcasting to the U.N. Stay focused. There'll be others."

"Righto," Wee Willie answered.

STEVE MCELLISTREM

"I'm picking up telemetry on our position in Sudan too," Lendra said.

"Correcting course," Rendela said.

"These vehicles weren't built like fighter planes," Curtik said, his voice also sounding metallic. "Should be interesting. Hang on."

As Curtik veered the LTV to the left, a red streak slashed through the air from the orbiting Las-cannon. The missile, miles away, exploded in a jagged burst, flames shooting out in a dozen directions from the epicenter.

"Missile incoming from Nigeria," Lendra said.

"And another from Pakistan," Zora added.

Two more red streaks split the sky. Two more missiles blew up, showering the lower atmosphere with burning shards of metal, looking almost like a fireworks display. Curtik had the LTV yawing, seemingly out of control, but whooping with delight as he flew toward the incoming fire.

"We've got more launches," Wee Willie said. "Saudi Arabia, Turkey, Egypt, Bangladesh. Hell, there's dozens of 'em."

Now the United States' Las-cannon fired as well, in clear defiance of international law, striking missiles before they got near the LTVs. Blown-up rocket parts scattered across the sky. Curtik, dropping rapidly, laughed as the LTV jolted left and right, barely swerving past deadly obstacles.

I am not terrified, Poole said to herself. If my time has come, so be it. Yet she could smell the acrid fear in the cabin and her throat was so dry she had to cough.

"This bird flies better than I thought," Curtik yelled.

Beside them, Rendela matched Curtik's line of flight, a task made possible by the fact that the two cadets could communicate via implant.

Poole gave up monitoring communications and simply stared at the viewscreen in front of her. She could tell Lendra had done the same. Yet the Las-cannons above and below them continued to fire, knocking out rocket after rocket. Curtik continued to holler as he made the LTV twist and dive. Rendela maneuvered her LTV expertly, matching Curtik's flying with perfect synchronicity.

368

As Curtik and Rendela steered past a large chunk of metal, the viewscreen showed a lethal shield of burning debris and incoming missiles ahead—a barrier that looked impassable.

"Oh-oh," Rendela said from the other ship.

"Now it gets a little tough," Curtik admitted.

"We're not getting past that," Lendra spoke so softly Poole almost didn't hear her.

"Hang on!" Curtik yelled.

Poole clutched her armrests and fought to keep herself from screaming. Curtik and Rendela would never be able to penetrate that wall of metal. All this way, Poole thought, from the Earth to the Moon and back, through the rigors of training the cadets, and she was going to die here only a few miles up. Not even the Las-cannons could shoot down all the incoming missiles, for they were so close to the LTVs that a direct hit might detonate them into the LTVs. Yet the Las-cannons continued firing. Missile after missile exploded. But three loomed straight ahead, impossible to avoid.

Poole winced. And now I die, she thought. Where are you, God?

Her viewscreen showed Rendela and Wee Willie at the controls of their LTV, leaning over in their seats as they struggled to turn. Meanwhile, Curtik twisted in his seat, manhandling the LTV sideways as he accelerated up. Poole's body pressed back into her seat. The viewscreen filled with an image of Rendela's LTV leaping forward and down, directly into the path of the incoming missiles, blowing apart. The explosion took out all three warheads.

"Rendela!" Zora cried out.

Rendela! Poole thought. The best and sweetest of the cadets. Is this how you save me, God? By sacrificing the one cadet who absolutely deserved to be saved?

"I remember you, Rendela," Quark said. "Wee Willie. Toma." Each name came separately, distinctly. "Yulee. Dr. Nakamura. Dr. Srinlangshiran. Hong. Dobbitz. Roze. Salma."

Poole shook her head. Quark hadn't even known those people and he mourned them. Poole knew she ought to grieve too, but instead her mind recalled Jack and his gentle touch, so incongruous compared to his phenomenal strength.

Curtik put the LTV into a dive, straight down.

Another missile came at them. No escape. Then a laser strike pulverized it and Curtik flew through the debris, which clunked against the tiles of the vessel.

A loud roar came simultaneously with a warning alarm, indicating a hole in the cabin and depressurization. Oxygen sucked out rapidly. A mask dropped towards Poole's face. She managed to get it over her head.

"Racine!" Zora yelled. "Racine!"

"What's the matter with Racine?" Poole called out. "Has she passed out?"

No one answered her. Poole tried to connect with Racine's implant via her interface, but got no signal. She saw blood spreading on the side of Racine's helmet and she thought she saw red droplets speeding past her up the aisle.

The LTV hurtled earthward, plummeting like a stone.

Lendra, Poole saw, had seated her mask over her mouth and nose.

Down the LTV dropped, the G force increasing.

Quark, his mask also seated over his face, struggled with the free mask next to him—the one designated for Devereaux—pulling on the hose that tethered it to the oxygen tank. Somehow it had kinked and couldn't reach Devereaux, who gasped for breath. Quark ripped off his mask and seated it on Devereaux's face. Then he unbuckled himself and, fighting against the G force that held him to his seat, managed to stand so that he could take a breath through the mask.

The rush of wind intensified until it became a continuous roar. A loud crack echoed as the ship's tiles broke away and the roar became even greater. The viewscreens went black.

Poole gripped the armrests even more tightly. Lendra reached over, placing her free hand over Poole's, and smiled encouragingly. What the hell?

"At least you won't have to kill me now," Poole said.

"I never intended to," Lendra said. "I respect you, Taditha. I like you. I was never going to kill you. I was simply going to find another way to carry out my mission." Lendra wrapped her fingers around Poole's hand and squeezed gently. She smiled. Poole felt her hand relax slightly. She felt something in Lendra's touch: the faint stirrings of calmness: as if the two babies inside them were communicating with each other, reassuring each other.

Curtik cursed repeatedly as the LTV plunged, free falling in a crash dive. "I guess this damn thing isn't as maneuverable as I thought."

Zora yelled, "Our dive is too steep. We're losing structural integrity."

Curtik yelled back: "I can't pull the LTV out without breaking it apart."

So close, Poole thought. So close to home.

Zora took off her mask, unstrapped herself and lurched toward the co-pilot's seat, her body straining against the G-force. She managed to grab an overhead strap with one hand and unbuckle Racine with the other. Pulling Racine's body out of the chair, she ducked as Racine's body sped past Poole toward the rear of the LTV. For long seconds Zora struggled to pull herself into the chair. Finally Curtik released the controls and aided her. But in just that short time, the LTV plunged into a vertical dive. When Zora got herself strapped in, she grabbed the controls to help Curtik pull up the nose.

Another crack sounded, impossibly loud over the rush of wind. Poole imagined another piece of the LTV tearing itself away. She closed her eyes against the pressure. A distant scream sounded in her ears. She wasn't sure of its source. It could have been any of them. Her stomach, rebelling against the forces acting on it, required her to put all her effort into not vomiting. Lendra's hand squeezed tighter.

The LTV lurched again and again as Curtik and Zora pulled on the steering columns. Out the front window, the Australian desert loomed—miles of dry flat sand. Curtik and Zora each had their hands wrapped around the controls, pulling back and twisting to the left, gradually, ever so slowly easing the LTV out of its dive. They're not going to make it in time, Poole thought.

Curtik practically stood in his seat, pulling back on the controls, Zora right with him, straining to level the ship.

Poole told herself to relax. But she couldn't help herself. She tensed as the impact became imminent.

And then they hit the ground. Hard.

They bounced three times before the LTV even slowed enough to be noticeable. One of the wheels apparently gave way, for the LTV lurched down to the left, that wing hitting the ground and breaking away. The LTV flipped just as the stabilizers kicked in and the airbags deployed. Poole felt a burning pain in her shoulders from the restraining straps that held her in place. Quark flew into the ceiling, then bounced toward the back of the cabin. The stabilizers flipped the LTV again, completing its somersault and enabling the LTV to land on its belly, scraping the ground as it trenched forward with a thunderous grating.

Finally the ship shuddered and came to a stop, its floor canted at an angle.

Only a hissing sound intruded into the silence. Poole, gasping, realized she'd been holding her breath. She took off her mask, wincing at the pain in her shoulders, and smelled burning metal and plastic. Quark, on his hands and knees, shook his head, his shaggy black hair flying left and right, pushed himself to his feet and made his way unsteadily forward.

Devereaux, mask still in place, face pale, took deep breaths.

"Are you all right?" Poole asked him.

"I think my collarbone is broken," he said through the mask.

"Don't try to move." Poole's collarbone was likely broken too. Two years under the Moon's low gravity had weakened her bones despite the exercises she'd done to prevent that. And Devereaux, no longer a young man, had been up there a year. Quark and the cadets had the advantage of their Escala natures to keep their bones strong, while the other passengers hadn't been on the Moon nearly as long.

"Did you see that?" Lendra asked.

"What?" Poole said. She looked around, trying to spot what Lendra had seen.

"Rendela. She flew right into those missiles." Lendra's voice carried awe and disbelief. "Their LTV could have gotten through.

372

She could have avoided them. Instead she cut right in front of us, blew herself up."

Lendra, Poole realized, was right. Rendela, from her forward position, could have eluded the missiles.

Up front, Zora stared out the window, perhaps mourning the loss of Rendela or replaying the scene in her mind but more likely using her implant to communicate with someone, while Curtik removed his helmet and turned to face the cabin. His face no longer carried that insouciant grin Poole had grown to loathe. Instead he wore a shocked and grim expression. Poole doubted she'd ever be able to fully forgive him, but at this moment she pitied him.

Now Jeremiah walked forward, pulling himself along with his arms to minimize the weight on his still-healing legs. He reached the front of the LTV and reached out for Curtik, pulling the boy into a hug that Curtik returned. "It's going to be okay," Jeremiah said as he stretched out his right arm and pulled Zora into the embrace as well. The three of them huddled for what seemed a long time.

Then Jeremiah and Curtik patted each other on the back and pulled away, though Jeremiah continued to rest his hand on Zora's shoulder.

Faintly in the distance, sirens sounded, a reassuring cadence announcing the imminent arrival of assistance. Poole felt her heart breaking all over again. She was home. But without Jack Marschenko. Sorrow and self-pity overflowed from within; tears streamed down her cheeks. Great wracking sobs forced her torso up and down, creating twinges of sharp pain centered in her collarbone. She cried not just for those she knew and loved but for all the dead on the Moon and here on Earth. Millions sacrificed for Elias Leach's insane plan to unite the world. Millions sacrificed because of her actions.

Well, no more. She was done following orders. God or the fates or karma had punished her for her wrongdoing by taking away the people she loved. And heaven knew she deserved that punishment because even though she'd told herself she was doing the right thing, she'd known deep down she wasn't.

So, God, Poole thought, whether you're up there or not, I'm going to change my life around. I'm going to be more like Devereaux and Quark and Jeremiah Jones. I'm going to be principled and selfless. I'm going to work for the common good instead of just for myself. I won't ask for anything else for me. You run your universe. I'll run my life in a way that will make me proud of me, no matter what anyone else thinks.

To her surprise, she found she'd actually expected an answer and she immediately realized that it was because of implants and interfaces. Why couldn't God communicate with her that way?

The sirens grew louder, as did the roar of jet-copters.

Quark got to his feet and made his way to the door, where emergency med techs began pounding on it and calling out. He told them to stand back, twisted the latches and put his shoulder against the door. It didn't move. Backing up, he raised his foot and kicked the door, hammering it again and again until it suddenly sprang clear and the med techs were able to rush inside.

The air of Earth flooded the cabin—hot, dry and unprocessed—fresh air that Poole hadn't breathed in two years. She blinked away the tears as she waited for the med techs to assist her.

Chapter Thirty-Three

The air felt cold and thin, as if he were climbing a mountain. The simple effort of chewing an energy bar forced Colonel Truman to take deep breaths. He tightened the blanket around his shoulders as he finished the food, then glanced down at the plastarp that housed the unconscious Russians. It had been sealed on two sides, one of the precious heaters blowing hot air toward the couple to keep them warm, but that left only one heater for the rest of the room. And the Verlorens huddled before that one.

Li Chen and her husband Li Huan had done everything they could for Gregor and Maria, but their bodies were shutting down. Truman had finally dabbed a small dosage of neo-dopamine onto each of their tongues, hoping that might at least keep them in a state of quasi-hibernation, lowering pulse, blood pressure and respiration. He wondered if he ought to concede that they weren't going to make it and take their heater away.

Mottz nudged Truman. "We gotta put the Verlorens in the tarp and seal it up. Those kids ain't gonna survive much longer out here."

Truman nodded as he studied the girls. Kaylee and Kyler sat in their parents' laps, blankets wrapped around them, the heater directly in front of them, and yet their little bodies still shivered. They'd been so brave, rarely crying or whining these past three days.

"And we could use another shot of neo-dopamine," Mottz added.

"Yeah," Mishra said. "Let's get another hit."

"When was the last dosage?" Truman asked.

"Fourteen hours ago," Joffer said.

"Okay," Truman said as he reached for the glass bulb. He noticed Mottz's hands clenching and unclenching, while Joffer bounced on the balls of his feet.

Mottz said, "Hell, we're going to be rescued soon anyway." He glanced over at the kids. "Sorry about the language."

"That's right," Truman said. He wanted the girls to believe that this would be over soon. "The Brazilians and probably the Germans will be the first ones here."

Truman unscrewed the top of the glass bulb, looked at the tiny amount of neo-dopamine remaining, and offered it to Mottz, who dipped a fingertip into the bulb and licked it clean. The other adults followed, each dipping a finger into the gel and sucking on it for a moment. After Roanne and Brian took their share, only a small residue coated the inside of the glass bulb. Truman swabbed it with his little finger and licked it clean. Again he felt a rush of happiness—a pleasure far out of tune with their situation. He knew it wouldn't last, but he savored the moment. For a while, no one spoke.

"Okay," Truman finally said, "time to put the Verlorens in the tarp." He smiled at Kyler and Kaylee. "It'll be just like a big tent. You'll be snug as a bug in a rug—safe and sound—cozy and toasty. Okey dokey?"

Kyler nodded, though her lower lip quivered. Kaylee kept her head pressed tightly into her mother's chest as she sucked her thumb. Brian Verloren ruffled Kyler's hair and struggled to his feet. Truman helped him up.

"It'll be fun," Brian said. "Honey? You ready?"

Roanne looked at Brian, her eyebrows raised, her nostrils flaring. "Let's use the toilet one last time, collect some energy bars and get inside."

Mishra said, "There is one problem with sealing the tarp now, sir."

"What's that?"

"Once we seal the tarp and get the oxygen generator ejecting oxygen into that space, we'll have to wear our spacesuits, and they only provide enough air for ten or maybe twelve hours."

"That's assuming we stay very still," Li Huan said. "If we have to work—sealing up the tarp, moving around—we might only get seven or eight hours."

"There's another possibility," Joffer said. "We might be able to get the door open. There might be breathable air on the other side. We could then move out into the tunnel and wait for a rescue there. The downside, of course, is that we might waste a lot of energy and oxygen in the process, leaving ourselves even less time before we run out of air."

They all looked at Truman, waiting for his decision. Strangely, he felt calm—half-buzzed by the neo-dopamine.

"All right," he said. "Let's suit up and get the Verlorens sealed inside the tarp. Mishra, Li Huan and Li Chen—you lie down and wait while Mottz, Joffer and I try to get the door open. That way you'll be preserving your oxygen as long as possible. If we can't get the door open, you'll at least have the maximum amount of time provided by the suits."

"What about you three?" Mishra said. "If you don't get the door open, or if there's no oxygen behind it . . ."

"We'll be fine," Truman said as he looked at Kyler and Kaylee. "We'll all be fine. You girls go use the toilet and climb into the tarp with your parents. We'll give you a light and the heater. It'll be just like camping. Have you ever gone camping?"

Kyler said, "I camped in a tent with my dad once, but Kaylee was too little."

"Well," Truman said, "this will be Kaylee's chance to camp with you and your folks."

"Are we going to die?" Kyler said. She pointed to the pile of corpses against the wall, covered by blankets. "Like them?"

"No," Truman said. "Absolutely not. Mottz and Joffer and I are going to find a way out."

"Don't leave us out," Mishra said. He gestured toward the Chinese engineers. "You need our expertise. Don't try to stop us from helping."

Li Huan and Li Chen both nodded.

"All for one and one for all," Truman said as he reached for a spacesuit. "It won't be much longer now." He caught Kyler's eye. "I kind of wish there was enough room in the tarp for me to camp with you. I think there might even be marshmallows."

* * *

While Mishra, Li Chen and Li Huan monitored the tarp, resealing the edges as they developed leaks, Mottz and Joffer pounded on the door with heavy rocks. Truman wielded a crowbar, but the door must have been warped just enough to wedge it tightly into the frame. Perhaps if it had opened outward they could have applied enough force to spring it free. But they had no luck.

After an hour, Mishra, Li Chen and Li Huan concocted a winch system that they attached to the door handle. Hoping to maximize the oxygen remaining in his suit, Truman tried to slow his breathing as he helped Joffer reseal a leak in the tarp that wouldn't stay welded tight. Finally Mottz lifted a massive rock and set it atop that spot, which diminished the amount of room available inside the tarp, but ensured a better seal. Hopefully none of the Verlorens were claustrophobic.

Despite the QuikHeal patches, Truman's leg felt weak and rather numb. He supposed the bandages could only do so much. For a moment he wondered if his leg would be so damaged he'd have to retire. He laughed. Yeah, that's my biggest worry—whether they'll force me to retire.

Mishra tapped Truman on the shoulder and gave him a thumbs up, indicating that they were ready to try the winch. God, it would be nice if the comm units in the suits were still functioning. Mottz and Joffer grabbed crowbars while Li Chen took hold of the door handle, turning it so that the latch wouldn't stick in the jamb.

Truman joined Li Huan and Mishra on the cable they had attached to a pulley. Together they pulled as Mottz and Joffer assisted with their crowbars. For a moment the door appeared to move; then the handle flew off and hit Truman's helmet hard, leaving a small star-shaped crack in the faceplate. Truman, Mishra and Li Huan fell in a heap. Truman managed to get back to his feet but he heard a hissing that was louder than the normal sound of oxygen flowing through the regulator. The crack must go all the way through the faceplate. He put his hand to the crack in a futile attempt to stem the flow of air.

Joffer dove past him, searching for something in the toolbox. He came up with a roll of duct tape and a utility knife. He and Mottz used the knife to separate out a layer of tape, their gloved fingers being useless for the task. Mottz brushed Truman's hand aside as Joffer taped the helmet.

Duct tape! Again Truman laughed.

He wondered if he was becoming hysterical or if the neo-dopamine was making him giddy. He stood patiently while Mottz and Joffer applied layer after layer of tape to the crack. Soon Truman could see almost nothing. But at least the hissing had returned to the normal sound of the regulator.

Mottz pointed to the tarp and raised his hands in a question, obviously wondering if they ought to move Truman inside it. But the seal on the tarp was fragile enough. There was no telling how long it would last even if it wasn't tampered with. And there wasn't room for him anyway, so Truman shook his head.

Mottz tapped Truman's helmet and gave him a thumb's up, his eyebrows raised in a question. Truman closed his eyes and listened for a moment. Was there still an ever-so-slight hiss emanating from the crack? He couldn't be certain. He shrugged. Mottz and Joffer went to work with the tape again, sealing off even the tiny area that had allowed Truman to see. He knew they had to because the crack could worsen in any direction, but he didn't like being blinded.

Now he could only wait.

He allowed Mottz and Joffer to lay him down beside the tarp, out of the way. Mottz gently squeezed his shoulder. Then they were gone. How much air had he lost? Did he have hours or only minutes? It was fitting, he supposed, that he should be the first to die. He was their leader, though he'd done little in the way of leading.

When he held his breath he could still hear the flow of air, but he couldn't tell if that was just the regulator or something worse. So instead he focused on slowing his breathing and heartrate. The inside of his suit felt almost like a sensory deprivation chamber—buried alive in nothingness, with only a slight hiss for sound. He wiggled his toes, his fingers. What were Mottz and Joffer planning now? Maybe they'd given up and were conserving their air as well.

The neo-dopamine was wearing off. His leg and back hurt. At the same time he felt a heavy drowsiness coming over him. Was that due to oxygen deprivation? Was this what it was like to suffocate? No. He'd begin to struggle when that happened. Probably.

For some reason his mind drifted to Elias Leach, the son of a bitch who'd created this whole mess. Leach was extremely intelligent and by all accounts well intentioned, and yet he'd proven to be the biggest mass murderer in history.

Devereaux, on the other hand, never forced his will on anyone. Everything about him bespoke a selfless love of others and an ingenuity so far beyond the bounds of genius that Truman could understand his conviction that humans had the potential to become better than they were, for Devereaux had become better than human.

Was he a better man for having known Walt Devereaux? He didn't feel like a better man, although he'd tried to be good. Did it matter anymore, entombed on the Moon? Whatever potential he had, whatever possibilities might have awaited him, were gone now.

Humans were such amazing creatures, so paradoxical. Able to reach the intellectual heights of people like Aristotle, Einstein and Walt Devereaux, yet ever subject to the capricious whims of demanding emotion—the kind of anger and despair that energized terrorists the world over. Perhaps life on Earth would always be that way. Perhaps we would never be able to evolve beyond that paradox.

A beep startled him.

The oxygen tank's warning system. That meant he had less than ten minutes of air remaining. Damn! The suit must still be leaking.

He had to get inside the tarp now.

He reached over and fumbled for it, finally locating the welded seam. He could easily rip it open and force his way inside. Mottz, Joffer and the others might be able to re-seal it. He grabbed the two sides of the seam and prepared to pull it apart.

Then he thought of Devereaux again. And as much as he wanted to live, he realized he couldn't risk sacrificing the others. Even though getting inside the tarp might buy him a few more minutes, it might also kill everyone inside.

Devereaux would say that the greatest power we have is over the self—the ability to transcend our baser desires for the sake of a greater good. We don't have to be greedy or scared or angry if we choose not to be. We can control our impulses and our suffering by ceasing to want more than we have, by celebrating the singular present, without thought to the past or future or even the external. We get to decide how we live. And the greatest expression of our humanity is compassion—not total selflessness, for the existence of self is necessary to the definition of the world around us. We cannot have compassion for others without understanding that they are like us, that we are all the same and yet also different—unique and identical—ultimate paradoxes, striving for the unattainable while accepting our imperfect limitations, refusing to attack ourselves for failing to live up to the standards the best of us set, but always keeping in mind that we can do better by simply making the effort: one thought, one gesture, one prayer at a time.

Truman imagined Mottz and Joffer sitting beside the door, the big Elite Ops trooper's arm over the cadet's shoulder as they waited for the rescue. *Goodbye, friends.* He imagined Mishra lying beside Li Huan and Li Chen, conserving their oxygen as they fought to remain brave. *I wish you courage.* And he saw the Verlorens inside the tarp he had nearly ruined, Kyler and Kaylee playing a game of Name that Animal with their parents as they'd done a dozen times the past few days, Brian and Roanne keeping them calm and distracted. *I wish for you a long and happy future.*

He realized that he was still holding the tarp by the seam and let it go. The air was getting worse inside the suit. He felt a tremor beneath him. Or was that his body reacting to the loss of oxygen? He began to feel heavy—drowsy. And he recalled that one of the features of the suit was that it would disperse an aerosol when the oxygen content reached a critical level. It was designed to offer a painless death in the event of suffocation. That must be what he was experiencing. Would it cause hallucinations or just put him into a deep sleep?

He didn't mind dying. Devereaux had prepared him for this moment. His biggest regret, apart from losing Lendra, was losing the two kids—Kyler and Kaylee. They didn't deserve to die like this. He wished . . .

* * *

He awoke in a brightly lit hospital room. A stranger looked down at him.

"You'll be all right," the man said in heavily accented English.

Truman put out his hand and touched the man. "Where am I?"

"Hospital Santa Lucia," the man said. "My name's Rivera."

"On Earth?"

Rivera smiled. "Yes, Brazil."

"What happened?"

A dark-haired woman walked in the door, and Rivera stepped to the side.

"What's going on?" Truman asked.

The woman said, "My name is Dr. Silvestres. You were clinically dead when they found you. Out of oxygen. Fortunately, our scanners show only minor brain damage—some memory loss, some cognitive processing difficulty. Had they found you a few minutes later they wouldn't have been able to revive you. We've been flushing neo-dopamine out of your system—re-oxygenating your body. I doubt you'll suffer permanent harm." She checked a machine beside Truman's bed. "We hope to cleanse your system completely. You may experience some fatigue."

"I don't care about me. Tell me what happened up there."

Dr. Silvestres smiled. "I'll leave that to your countrymen." She turned to the door and in came Jeremiah Jones in a wheelchair, pushed by Mottz. Beside them walked Lendra. Truman thought she was the most beautiful woman he'd ever seen.

Lendra took the chair by his bed and reached out her hand. When they touched, he felt a tiny electrical shock. She smiled as her thumb caressed the back of his hand. For a moment he just enjoyed the feel of her warm skin against his, the faint, flowery aroma of her perfume, the obvious pleasure she took in his company. Then he remembered Jeremiah, the father of the child growing inside her, and he turned to face Jones.

"You two belong together," Jeremiah said. "Lendra and I talked while we were waiting for you to wake up. We resolved some issues. I hope you'll both be happy."

Truman looked at Lendra again. She pulled his hand to her lips and kissed it. He pulled her hand to his lips and returned the kiss, then said, "But what happened up there?"

Lendra turned to Jeremiah, who looked up at Mottz.

"They found us," Mottz said, "not long after we patched up your helmet. We thought you were dead. Everybody else made it, Colonel— the Verlorens and even the Russians. You did good. They rescued sixty-eight people from LB3. LB2 wasn't too badly damaged. A lot of people stayed behind to try to rebuild the colony from there."

"How long have I been out?"

"A week," Jeremiah said.

"Joffer?"

Mottz said, "He's in jail with Zora, Curtik and the other cadets."

Truman looked at Jeremiah. "We wouldn't have survived without Joffer."

Jeremiah shrugged. "I'm not the one you have to convince. They'll convene a secret tribunal to determine the cadets' future. Devereaux believes—"

"Devereaux's okay?"

"Yes, he's fine."

"He saved me." Truman closed his eyes for a moment. When he opened them, he looked Jeremiah in the eye and said, "I'd like to thank him."

"I'll tell him," Jeremiah said. "Anyway, he believes the cadets' childhood can be restored in part, if they so desire. Their aging can be slowed—their reflexes, strength, endurance: all humanized. He believes they may be spared punishment if they agree to the genetic and nanotech corrections to restore their original makeup. They'll never completely regain what they lost—their bodies are largely adult bodies, after all—but they might be able to salvage some snippet of their childhood. Still, it'll be up to politicians to decide their fate. And there are rumblings among a few in the military that the cadets should remain as they are, with the potential to be super warriors."

"Curtik?"

"He told me he won't revert to his childhood. And if I try to force him, he'll never speak to me again."

"Zora?"

"She won't go back either. She's determined to accept her punishment. I think that's partly because her parents died recently—victims of the Susquehanna Virus."

"And you?" Truman asked.

"I'm retired. They're offering you the same option—a medical discharge with a full pension that should allow you to pursue whatever second career you choose. You don't have to decide now."

Truman felt stunned. He'd devoted so many years to the Army.

"There's one other piece of good news." Jeremiah turned to look up at Mottz, who walked over to the door and gestured to someone outside. A few seconds later, an older black man walked in: short, bald and slender, with a wide smile. It took Truman a couple seconds to recognize him.

"Ned?"

"Hi, Dez." Ned stepped over to the bed. "Officially I'm not here, okay?"

"But how, I mean . . ." Truman couldn't believe this was happening. How could his brother be alive after all this time? Why hadn't he let Truman know he was okay?

"Ah, you still have the gift of gab, I see." Ned put a hand on Truman's shoulder and gently squeezed. "When I saw you on the news,

I wanted to get in touch. I contacted Jeremiah and he made it happen. I'm still officially missing in action so you can't tell anyone about this but I've got a few hours before I have to leave."

"That's my cue," Lendra said as she stood up. "I'll let you two get reacquainted."

Truman released Lendra's hand. He turned to thank Jeremiah, but Mottz must have already wheeled him out.

Ned waved as Lendra departed. "I guess we've got some catching up to do, baby brother."

Truman struggled to keep his eyes open. "I'd like to talk, Ned. But I'm so tired."

"That's okay, Dez. You sleep. We'll talk later. I'll be right here waiting for you."

Chapter Thiry-Four

Devereaux would give his Nobel Prize speech soon.

Curtik planned to march out of the room just before it started. He bounced as he stared at the Blue Ridge Mountains, which Jeremiah called beautiful. To Curtik they just looked like tree-covered mountains—green and brown under a blue and white sky. What makes them beautiful? Curtik glanced at Hannah the Barbarian, doing isometric exercises as she studied the security monitors. He walked outside to the edge of the porch and looked down the winding gravel driveway. He examined the curve about a quarter mile away, where he'd fainted the last time he tried to run. His ankle monitor zapped him with something and out he went. Boom. The previous time he'd run he'd gone toward the mountains and had gotten only slightly further before waking up in bed with a massive headache.

Probably that bitch Hannah had carried him inside. She looked like an Elite Ops trooper—a blond Amazon.

He stepped back inside the house and glared at her until she scowled back. He liked knowing that she hated being here as much as he did.

Curtik wanted to see this world he'd tried to destroy—to see if it matched the one he'd been taught to despise. But apparently he would be stuck here with Jeremiah for a while longer. He turned to the nearest surveillance camera and said, "Just get the damn thing over with. I'm guilty. I admit it. Put me in jail for the rest of my life. Kill me. I don't care."

Jeremiah wheeled himself into the room. For some reason his legs had worsened and he was feeling pain in every joint again too. He'd been in contact with Devereaux often, but apparently even God Himself couldn't find a solution. "You don't want to be saying that," Jeremiah said. "Look around you. You're in a nice house."

"And if I try to leave, I get knocked out and dragged back inside. I gotta spend all my time with you and Hannah Banana over there. They deactivated my implant so I can't keep in touch with anyone from the old days."

"It's just until the hearing."

"Well, what's taking so long? I'm guilty. Everybody knows it."

"You were under a compulsion. You had very little control over your actions."

"I knew what I was doing. I wanted to wipe out humanity."

"But why? You don't know, because you were doing what Eli programmed you to do. No matter how you try to twist it or change it, you were under his control. Now you're free. You don't need to dwell on what happened. They have ways of wiping your memories. You don't have to live with what you—"

"You make it sound so simple. Take a pill and forget the past. You just want your little boy back. But he's dead—forever—and there's nothing you can do about that . . . unless you figure out some way to turn me back into a little kid again."

"I'm not complaining. You're my son and I love you no matter what. I just hate seeing you suffer."

"Who says I'm suffering?"

Curtik turned away and looked out the picture window. This father of his didn't realize that he was happy being Curtik. Should he tell Jeremiah that he liked being the toughest, baddest cadet they'd ever created? No. Jeremiah might be smarter than the average idiot, but he still wouldn't understand.

The mountains rose up in shades of brown and green. Did people find those earthtone colors soothing? He wished he could access his implant to find out. The smells were different though, not like the purified air on the Moon. There was a heaviness to them, as if the greater gravity of Earth lent them more complexity. He wasn't sure he liked that.

What he desired was to be left alone. Even though Jeremiah and Hannah the Barbarian largely let him do as he pleased, he still wanted to be away from here so he could figure out why he felt this way. He found himself conflicted since they'd reached Earth—part of him glad that Jones hadn't died, part of him detesting those warm feelings. He found it difficult to even pretend to be Jeremiah's son. "I'm my own man," he said as he looked out the window, "forged and honed on the Moon, the next generation of human. I'm not part of your world."

"From now on you are," Jeremiah said. "You might as well get used to it."

How much simpler life was when all he wanted to do was kill—when everyone he knew was either target or tool. This whole issue of ethics and morality troubled him. Were people like Jeremiah as good as they seemed to be or were they just better at hiding their darker urges? It didn't matter. Soon they'd either put him down or lock him away—and that might be for the best.

Jeremiah switched on the television and said, "I'm going to watch Devereaux's speech."

"What's he babbling about now?"

"He won a Nobel peace prize."

"Another one?" Curtik pretended ignorance.

Jeremiah nodded. "While he was on the Moon."

"Sounds scintillating," Curtik said.

"You don't have to watch it."

As the man on the dais spoke to the auditorium filled with tuxedo-clad men and long-gowned women, listing Devereaux's many accomplishments, Curtik prepared to leave. He intended to walk out with Devereaux's first words. No doubt they would be platitudes about how wonderful everything and everybody was here on Earth and how, with a little effort, we could all get along. On the other hand, one never knew with God Himself.

Curtik wished he had positioned himself further inside the house. It would have made for a more dramatic exit if he wasn't leaning against the doorway.

Then God Himself spoke:

"We're walking through the fog toward the edge of a cliff," Devereaux said, looking sad, "and if we don't veer away from our course soon, we will fall to our doom. Our future is not without hope. Global peace looks more achievable today than it did even a month ago. These past few weeks, the nations of the world have united to clean up the mess left by a madman who practiced unspeakable evil, unsurpassed genocide."

"Genocide?" Curtik said. "Is that the right word?"

"Shh," Hannah said.

"Never in recent decades," Devereaux said, "have we been this focused, this compassionate. Many nations have contributed to the effort to save not only the people of the Moon but also those here on Earth who were so needlessly attacked by this puppetmaster. Millions died, but millions more are being saved by the actions of all of you who have come together to heal our tragic wounds."

"Tragic wounds," Curtik echoed.

"Yours are on the inside," Jeremiah said.

"They don't hurt."

Devereaux continued: "I wish to especially commend the Brazilians for their expertise and manpower. Because of their leadership, we were able to rescue more than half the lunar colony. And I would like to note those brave souls who did not survive the madness—people like Colonel Dez Truman, who sacrificed himself so that others might live. Can you imagine being in his position? Facing certain death? He did not panic. He did not lash out or risk the lives of others to buy a precious few more minutes, even though—as we now know—he might have been saved had he done so. Instead, he embraced the darkness for the sake of the people he was charged with protecting. I wonder how many of us could be that brave. I wonder if I could be that brave. Could you?"

Devereaux paused for a moment.

"I could," Curtik said.

"Now, maybe," Jeremiah said. "Will you still be that brave when you stand to lose what he lost?"

Hannah said, "Can't you just listen to the man? You might learn something."

"His is the example we must try to follow," Devereaux continued, "rejecting fear and selfishness, thinking beyond the immediate moment, helping others who cannot help themselves, looking to the world around us and asking how we can make this planet a better place. How can we ensure a sustainable home for our children and grandchildren, for our nieces and nephews, for strangers we'll never meet who deserve as good a life as any of us, for the millions who will come after us, generation after generation?

"This world was not put here for me. It wasn't put here for you. It's here for all of us and none of us. We just borrow it for a while. Would you borrow your neighbor's hammer and let it rust? Would you borrow a ladder and fail to return it? That's what we do when we take from this world without repaying our debt.

"I'm not asking us to be perfect. We don't have to do it alone. That's what governments and the rule of law are for—to keep us on the straight path when we might otherwise stray. But we cannot rely only on them. We must act ourselves—taking one step . . . and then another . . . and then another, striving to become better human beings, aware of our selfish selves even as we fight to transcend that egoism to attain an altruism that marks the nobility and strength our species is capable of attaining. With every thought, with every desire, we must consider the world and our fellow creatures within it and how our actions might impact them for good or ill."

"Impact. Pow!"

"Shh," Hannah said again.

"Can we consider the needs of others as much as we do our own? Or will we succumb to the narrow-minded greed that resides at the bottom of our nature? Colonel Truman was able to overcome that desire with his last breath. But can we?"

Devereaux wiped his face with a handkerchief, reached for a glass and took a sip of water.

"Cripes," Curtik said, "all he did was die."

"Some of you may be saying to yourselves, 'What did he do that was so special? He didn't fight back a horde of alien invaders or stop the spread of a terrible virus. He didn't save those people. The Brazilians did. There were other more heroic people who saved many more lives than he did.'"

"He's reading my mind," Curtik muttered.

"Please," Jeremiah said as he held up a finger.

"And to that," Devereaux continued, "I answer, 'Yes, there were.' There were many heroic people on both the Earth and the Moon—some of whom did much more than he did, much more than I did—cadets and Elite Ops troopers and civilians alike. Some of you are still doing more, still giving above and beyond what any of us has a right to ask, while all Colonel Truman did was stop himself from grabbing, clutching, grasping at life no matter who he hurt, knowing that by his one insignificant choice not to act, he might save eleven lives. And so he did.

"And that's what we can do too. We must work together in small ways to improve our chances of success. We must form groups, teams, families of supporters to assist us—people willing to speak the hard truths that will goad us or shame us or motivate us to take the tiny actions that snowball into larger efforts that avalanche into monumental achievements of which we can all be proud. We can cooperate in the fight to regress from our heavy-handed consumerism.

"But we must start now.

"If we fail, we join the dinosaurs. And who will know that we were here? Perhaps some future species will dig us up one day and wonder what brought us to extinction—what tragedy befell us. In time they may discover that it was our failure to adapt, our failure to appropriately plan for the future that caused our demise. We have been short-term thinkers for millennia. But we can no longer afford that luxury. We cannot worry only about today and tomorrow, for the sun will rise next week, next month, next year. Will our descendants be here to greet it?

"Make no mistake. We will fail . . . from time to time. But if we abide by the Golden Rule, if we surrender to the inescapable truth that the needs of the many outweigh the needs of the few, we just may succeed in the end.

"Peace isn't just about the avoidance of war. It's about a total commitment to protect and preserve our communal home from our own baser instincts—from our self-destructive tendencies masquerading as individual rights. We can no longer afford to indulge our narrow political and religious ideologies. We cannot push our conservative or liberal doctrines, nor can we discount the spiritual beliefs of others as misguided or inappropriate. We have to push beyond these self-imposed boundaries to a new world of inclusiveness. We all have a duty to protect our children from ourselves. Too often we think in terms of us and them. We are good and they are evil. We are right and they are wrong. But just as we don't want them telling us how to live our lives, we can't tell them how to live theirs—provided that no one is being harmed."

He looked out at the audience, at the cameras picking up his visage, and again Curtik thought he looked sad.

"This isn't about me. This isn't about the Nobel committee. This isn't just some fancy awards ceremony we get to watch and forget, proceeding with our lives as if none of it happened—none of it mattered. We matter. All of us. And we have to change now. All of us. If we don't, we lose everything. And the efforts of people like Colonel Dez Truman will have been for naught.

"We can't wait for future generations to fix our problems. We can't cede our responsibilities to our children and grandchildren. Our world needs us now. This is our crisis of opportunity. Look around you. See your neighbor struggling and offer a helping hand. Hear the cries of the oppressed and speak out against tyranny. Witness the destruction of our trees and lakes and air, and demand an end to the incremental poisoning of our home."

Devereaux's eyes glistened with moisture and he reached up a handkerchief to wipe them. "Profit at the expense of our future is theft. Comfort at the expense of selflessness is gluttony. Rationalization at the expense of integrity is mendacity. We can do better. We must do better. Dare to make a difference. Dare to be great."

Devereaux ended his speech to great applause, though he wept openly, as if he knew his words hadn't gotten through. For a long moment the camera lingered on him, the tears coming freely as he looked out upon the audience. The image shifted to a commentator and Jeremiah turned off the screen. He sat quietly, staring at nothing.

"I heard you," Curtik said, moved by Devereaux's words despite his best efforts not to be.

"Did you?" Hannah asked. She clenched her jaw as if trying to control her emotions.

"Yes, but I don't wanna change," Curtik said. "I'm a warrior, and I'll always be a warrior. It's all I ever wanted to be."

"It's all you've known," Jeremiah said as he spun around in his wheelchair, tears running down his cheeks as well. "How can you be so certain when you know so little?"

"I'm smarter than you."

Jeremiah nodded. "Perhaps. I'm no genius. But I'm at least smart enough to know there are many things in this world I don't understand."

"How can he feel so strongly about humanity? Are they worth saving?"

"If Devereaux says they're worth saving," Jeremiah said, "they're worth saving. He believes I'm worth saving and I'm one of the bad guys."

"You?"

"I've done—" Jeremiah's voice broke. He took a breath as if to collect himself. "I've done terrible things in my life, Joshua—sorry—Curtik. But he's helping me move past that. And you can too. You don't have to be the person they made you to be. You get to choose. You can be better than you are. We all can."

Curtik felt something welling up inside, a rush of sadness and compassion that threatened to overwhelm him.

He went over to Jeremiah's wheelchair and grasped the handles, then wheeled his father outside so he could look up at the mountains.

A reading group guide:

Eli decides to do something terrible in service to a greater good – uniting the world. Is he evil? If we do bad things to serve a good cause, are we evil? Should we consider the intent behind an action in determining whether it is good?

The cadets are programmed to attack Earth. How much responsibility do they bear for their actions? Science has made great strides in understanding how the brain works. How realistic is it that people can be programmed to think a certain way? Do you think we might some day be forced to believe or desire what others tell us to think or want?

The cadets have been enhanced both mechanically and genetically. Do you think in the future we will use more mechanical or more genetic approaches to enhancing our bodies? And will we still be human? When would such changes make us something other than human?

The virus escapes containment and the cadets break free of their conditioning. Every action has unintended consequences, whether for good or ill. How can we guard against that, or is that even possible?

The moon has one-sixth earth's gravity. How would that affect life? Would plants and animals grow taller? Do you think we might someday establish a permanent base on the moon and if we did, how would that affect those who lived there?

Jeremiah is deceived into believing that a cadet is his son. When he learns the truth, he continues to treat the cadet as family. How has our definition of family changed? Can love and loyalty for family actually be a bad thing because it encourages an "us against them" mentality? Should we still give love and loyalty to family members who do horrible things?

Lendra betrays Jeremiah because she believes what she is doing is in his best interest. Is that just a rationalization or is she sincere? When can we trust our beliefs?

Who is your favorite character and why?

The book leaves a number of questions unanswered. Is that fair? Do you think a book should tie up all the loose ends or leave certain aspects to the reader's imagination?

About the author

Steve McEllistrem has been a writer and editor for more than 20 years. His previous books include *The Devereaux Dilemma, Higher Education Law in America, Students with Disabilities and Special Education Law*, and *Deskbook Encyclopedia of Employment Law*. He is also a producer and host of Write On! Radio, where he has interviewed local, national and international authors for many years. He currently resides in Minnesota.

www.ingramcontent.com/pod-product-compliance
Lightning Source LLC
Chambersburg PA
CBHW020930020726
47495CB00002B/426